THE VILLA OF
MYSTERIES

DAVID
HEWSON

BLACKTHORN

This edition published in Great Britain, the USA and Canada in 2020
by Black Thorn, an imprint of Canongate Books Ltd,
14 High Street, Edinburgh EH1 1TE

Distributed in the USA by Publishers Group West and in Canada by
Publishers Group Canada

Published in Great Britain 2018 by Severn House Publishers Ltd,
Eardley House, 4 Uxbridge Street, London W8 7SY

blackthornbooks.com

1

British Library Cataloguing-in-Publication Data
A catalogue record for this book is available on request from the British
Library

ISBN 978 1 83885 066 1

Printed and bound in Great Britain by Clays Ltd, Elcograf S.p.A.

LUPERCALIA

Bobby and Lianne Dexter were good people. They owned a brand new timber mansion on an acre plot cut into a vast green swathe of pines thirty miles outside Seattle. They put in long hours for Microsoft down the road, Bobby in marketing, Lianne in finance. They hiked every weekend and, once a year, made it to the summit of Mount Rainier. They worked out too, though Bobby still couldn't keep what he called the 'family tummy-pudge' coming through over the belt of his jeans. And that at just thirty-three.

The Dexters were quiet, comfortably wealthy middle-class Americans. Except for two weeks a year, in spring, when they went abroad on vacation. They'd reasoned this through. It was all a question of balance. Work hard for fifty weeks of the year. Party hard for the remaining two. Preferably somewhere the locals didn't know you, where different rules applied. Or maybe didn't apply at all. Which was why, on a chill February day, they were ten miles outside Rome, dead drunk on red wine and grappa, seated in a hired Renault Clio which Bobby was driving much too fast over the potholes of an unmarked lane that ran from a back road behind Fiumicino airport down towards the flat, grey line of the meandering Tiber.

Lianne glanced at her husband, making sure he didn't see the anxiety in her face. Bobby was still fuming. He'd had the metal detector out all morning, hunting around the outskirts of Ostia Antica, the excavated remains of imperial Rome's one-time coastal harbour. Just when he got a couple of beeps out of the thing a pair of fierce-looking archaeology types came out of the site and began screaming at them. Neither of them understood Italian but they got the drift. Either they packed up the metal detector and got out of there pronto or the Dexter annual vacation was likely to end in fisticuffs with a couple of punchy-looking spic students who were only too ready and eager for action.

Bobby and Lianne had retired hurt to a nearby road-side *osteria* where, to add insult to injury, the waiter, an unshaven lout in a grubby sweatshirt, had lectured both on how wrong it was to pronounce the word 'pasta' as 'pahstah', the American way.

Bobby had listened, his white, loose cheeks reddening with fury, then snapped, 'Just gimme a fucking steak then.' And added a litre of *rosso della casa* to the order just for good measure. Lianne said nothing. She knew when it was smart to acquiesce to Bobby's mood. If things got too bad drinkwise they could always dump the car at the airport and take a cab back into town. Not that Italians minded about drunk driving. They did it all the time, it seemed to her. Or at least she assumed they did. Italy was like that. Lax. She and Bobby were just behaving like the locals.

'I cannot believe these people,' Bobby complained as he rolled the Clio over a pile of dried mud that had caked neatly into a solid ridge after the recent winter rain. 'I mean like . . . don't they have enough of this fucking stuff as it is?'

Lianne knew what the problem was. The previous autumn the Jorgensens had returned from vacation in Greece with a gorgeous marble bust the size of a soccer ball. It was of a young man, maybe Alexander the Great they said, with a full head of hair and a pretty, slightly feminine face. They kept it quiet at first, just to get the effect right. Then, out of the blue, Tom Jorgensen had invited them over to their extended Scandinavian-style cabin just down the lane – which had three storeys, mind, and a good acre and a half out back – on the pretext of a social drink. Really it was all about the marble head. Jorgensen let it be known he'd 'found' it by hanging around the edge of some archaeological excavation outside Sparta, waiting till the diggers had gone home and then bribing one of the locals to take him to where the mother lode lay. Tom had talked a good deal about how he smuggled it out of the country as excess baggage. It was all, Lianne suspected, one of Tom's stories. Really he'd just bought it at the store like everyone else. The big, muscular bastard was always spinning a line about something or other. It was why he'd jumped over Bobby's head to get into all the sexy music and TV stuff the company was doing now, meeting rock stars and movie people while Bobby, who was just as bright, maybe brighter even, was still lumbered with the tedious geeks who came over horny about databases.

But Tom's little act had struck home. Two weeks later Bobby announced that their annual vacation the coming spring would be in Italy. He hadn't even asked her opinion. Lianne was quietly hoping for Aruba. All the same, she demurred. It was the best thing to do, and, as it turned out, Rome hadn't been a bad choice. In fact, she was starting to like the place. Then, that morning, it had all turned worse. Some creepy British academic type had given them a history lecture over buffet break-fast in the hotel. About how this was the day of the dead for the ancient Romans, a day when they would sacrifice a goat or a dog and wipe its blood on the foreheads of their kids, just to make sure they remembered their ancestors. The history link pushed Bobby's buttons. Fifteen minutes later he was tracking down a hire company, renting the metal detector.

So now they were in the middle of nowhere, dead drunk, clueless about what to do next. Lianne pined for Aruba and the pain was all the worse because she'd no idea what the place was like. Without letting Bobby see she put a hand on the steering wheel and turned the lurching Clio just far enough away from a boulder coming up at them from the right. The track was getting narrower all the time. There were still mud holes here and there from some recent rain. Maybe they'd get the car stuck and have to walk back to the road for help. She didn't like that idea. She hadn't brought the shoes.

'It's just pure greed, Bobby,' she said. 'What else can you say?'

'I mean . . . what does it matter? If I don't find the shit it stays right there in any case! It's not like you see any fucking Italians digging the crap out of the ground.'

He was wrong there. She'd seen digs all over the place, half of them looking abandoned, maybe because they just didn't have the bodies to do all that digging. All the same it was best to go along with his gut feeling.

6

'They don't need it, Bobby. They got more than they can cope with already. They got it coming out their ears.'

They had too. Her mind was still reeling from all the museums they'd visited these past two days. There was so much *stuff*. And unlike Bobby, she'd read the guide-books. She knew they'd only scratched the surface. The pair of them were spending an entire *week* in Rome and would still come away without seeing everything. It seemed excessive. Bad planning. Poor taste. Bobby was right. If they had any manners they'd share it around a little.

The car headed down into a crater, leapt out the other side, briefly became airborne then slammed onto the ground with a bang. It sounded to her as if something had come loose underneath. She scanned the view ahead. Beyond the funny-looking grass, which seemed more like the kind of plants you got in marshland or bogs than on the beach she was expecting, lay a grey, scummy ribbon of water. The road came to a dead end a little way short of the low bank. Bobby had to get out here, have his fun – or otherwise – and then they needed to take the car back to Avis and scuttle off into the city before anyone noticed the dents and worse she felt sure would be there.

'Don't you worry,' she said. 'You're going to find something here, Bobby. I just know it. You're going to find something and when you do that asshole Tom Jorgensen is going to be as jealous as hell. You—'

He kicked down hard on the brakes, bringing the little car to a sudden halt twenty yards short of the end of the lane. Her husband was now staring into her face with that cold, hard expression she only saw once or twice a year, and hated, more than anything, hated so much that sometimes she wondered whether marrying Bobby Dexter, tubby Bobby, the one all the other girls laughed at behind his back, had really been such a good idea at all.

'What?' Bobby asked in a flat, dead tone that was supposed to be full of meaning.

'I only, only, only—' She stuttered into silence.

He prodded her chest with a stubby finger. She could smell the booze on his breath.

'You really think this is all about Tom Fucking Jorgensen?'

'No!'

'You really think I have researched, booked, paid for this entire fucking vacation, taken you to all these beautiful places, brought you out here to this stinking backwater . . . all because of Tom Fucking Jorgensen and his shitty piece of marble?'

She paused before answering. In three years of marriage Bobby had reduced her to tears only once and that was in Cancun over a sexual demand she regarded as irrational, unnecessary and intrinsically unhygienic. The memory still smarted. She didn't understand why it wouldn't go away.

'I didn't. It just seemed. I don't know—' All the wrong words tumbled out of her mouth.

'Jesus!' Bobby roared. 'Jesus Christ!'

He gunned the accelerator, rammed the Clio into first and let go of the clutch. The little car lurched bravely forward with a gut-wrenching start, veered to one side and impaled itself on a small dried mud mountain which appeared, to Lianne anyway, to contain the stump of a fence post at its heart. They were now pitched up at an awkward, sickening angle. The front right wheel screamed impotently as the mud mountain levered the entire right front end of the Clio into thin air.

Bobby stared at Lianne accusingly. 'Fucking wonderful,' he grunted. 'Oh so fucking wonderful.'

She was crying, trying to choke back the sobs.

'Don't do this to me, Lianne. Not today. You're not in Cancun now. You can't go phone that animal you call a father and get him to come round and threaten to beat my brains to a pulp just 'cos you got a headache or something.'

Telling her old man had been a mistake. She knew that all along. But Bobby had asked for it. He crossed the line in Cancun. She needed to let him know.

'Bobby—' she blubbed.

He stared out of the window at the grey river and the sluggish movement of scum on its surface.

'Yeah?'

'I can smell gas,' she said, suddenly serious, the tears drying almost instantly under the rising presence of fear. 'Can't you?'

'Jesus,' he gasped and punched at her seat belt then stabbed open the passenger door. She smiled at him, glassy-eyed. He'd done it for her. Before he unfastened his own belt.

'Bobby—'

He pushed her out of the door. 'Get out for chrissake. Dumb stupid bitch—'

Bobby Dexter took one last look to make sure she was safe then turned round, flung a few things from the back seat out onto the ground and rolled out of the crazily skewed car himself. He was so drunk he did a quick one eighty and wound up on the cold, hard earth banging his elbows painfully. Bobby got in a good chunk of swearing about that.

He pushed himself upright with a weary hand, picked up his things, then checked she'd got herself well distant from the smell of gas. Lianne watched from the side of the road, a good ten yards from the dying Clio, her hands clasped behind her back looking like a schoolgirl waiting to be told what to do.

He walked over to join his wife.

'You OK?' he asked. He looked a little worried about how far this was going. That was something, she thought.

'Sure.' She'd stopped crying. He looked glad of that. It was something.

There was a sound from the car, a sort of breathy whoosh. They watched as a thin finger of flame flickered out from under the hood and worked its way up the windshield.

'Now that . . .' Bobby said, 'is what I like about rental vehicles. They can do this sort of shit in front of your eyes and you just get to stand back and enjoy the show. Wish I'd hired something bigger now.'

The low scuttering wind caught the flames, rolled them over the roof of the Clio, sent them swirling inside the window, eating up the seats where, just a minute or so before, Bobby and Lianne Dexter had sat arguing. Then, with a sudden roar and a puff of heat and smoke, the Renault was ablaze, devouring itself in a cloud of black smoke and flame.

Lianne clung to her husband's arm watching the spectacle. Bobby was right. This was Avis's problem. This was what they were for. Why they charged the kind of prices they did.

'What are we going to do now, Bobby?' she wondered. Then she looked at him and found, to her relief, Bobby Dexter was smiling, happy once more, for the first time in hours.

He held up one of the things he'd taken from the back seat of the car. The metal detector they'd hired that very morning somewhere near the hotel in Rome.

'What we came here for,' Bobby Dexter said. 'Daddy's going a-hunting.'

She ventured a laugh and wondered if it came out wrong. Maybe it did. Maybe not. It didn't matter anyway. Bobby Dexter wasn't listening. He was working his way down to the river, walking over the odd, boggy ground that felt as if it might give way beneath them at any moment. He had the headphones on, listening. And pretty soon Bobby Dexter was laughing too. Something must have been coming through loud and clear. Lianne walked to join him. They were just twenty yards short of the river now. There wasn't another soul around for miles. Anything they found here now was surely theirs.

'Hear that?'

She took the headphones from him and held one earpiece to her head. It was beeping like crazy, like a kid's game from years ago.

'Fucking Tom Jorgensen,' Bobby spat and she didn't dare look into his eyes when he was talking like this. 'I'll teach that big fat bastard. Get me the gear.'

He was skulking in the little coffee bar around the corner from the Questura when Barbara Martelli walked in, dressed in her immaculate black uniform, helmet in hand, her long, blonde tresses bouncing above her collar with each step.

'Nic,' she said, looking surprised. 'You're back at work?'

'First day,' he replied, glancing at his watch. 'When I decide to turn up.'

'Ah.'

'How are you, Barbara?'

'I'm fine. I'm always fine. And you?'

He drained the macchiato. 'Yeah.'

'In case you forgot, this isn't the café the cops use.'

'So why are you here?'

She laughed. Barbara Martelli was about his height, with the kind of figure that turned every head in the station and a shock of blonde curls that seemed too full to squeeze inside that small black helmet. Her face was wrong for a cop. Too attractive, too ready to break into a smile. She looked as if she ought to be on the TV, announcing the weather or introducing some show. Instead she just floated around Rome on her big bike, handing out tickets with such charm the word was some people simply started speeding the moment they realized she was on their tail.

Back in the old days, before the shooting that put him on his back, fighting demons, Nic Costa wondered sometimes whether she was sweet on him. A couple of the guys egged him on to ask her for a date . . . provided he told everything afterwards. It didn't happen. She was just too perfect. She topped every driving exam, behind the wheel and on the force motorbikes. She was a tidy shot too, a talent that got her into most diplomatic assignments. Barbara Martelli was just a little too perfect to touch.

'Sometimes you have to escape for a while, Nic. Is that what you're doing? If so it's a little early. You have to get back in the ring if you want to hear the bell.'

'I'm having a coffee,' he mumbled.

'How long has it been?'

'Six months.' Six long months of slow recovery from the shooting and the mental damage that followed. Sometimes he wondered if he'd ever make it, whether he wanted to at all.

She looked at him frankly. She was, the more he thought about it, very possibly the most attractive woman inside the Questura. He was amazed he'd never asked her out. Not that he wanted anything to happen. She was just good company to be around, someone who could make you feel special. He didn't really know her at all.

'You do want to come back, don't you? It's not just Falcone pushing you into this?'

'No. I mean. I can't think of anything else. Can you?'

'No.'

'We're all like that, aren't we?' he said. 'Short of a choice.'

He listened to his own voice and found himself disliking what he heard. What was there? Resentment? Self-pity? He was twenty-eight. He'd never talked like that before. He had been changed by what was now known as 'the Denney case', an unresolved mess of entanglements that had cost his partner, Luca Rossi, his life, and almost left Costa dead too. This new Nic Costa no longer ran every time he wanted to clear his head, pounding the pavements around the Campo dei Fiori, arms flailing like a madman. He'd sold his tiny apartment in the Vicolo del Bologna and moved into his late father's old home, the sprawling farmhouse off the Via Appia Antica where he grew up. Costa's physical wounds were, for the most part, healed; the internal ones still ached from time to time.

Nic Costa continued to miss Luca Rossi's taciturn wit and astute insight, wishing he'd learned to appreciate them more during their brief time working together. He knew, too, that he would return to work touched by the cold, sceptical hardness of the world. It had become necessary to embrace what Falcone, who had single-handedly talked him out of a wheelchair and back into the force, would call 'pragmatism'.

Falcone, the cold, single-minded inspector, regarded this transition as inevitable. Maybe he was right. Costa, who with his old self hated cynicism, the defeatism that said sometimes you had to make the best of a bad job because the alternative was to lose the fight completely, was still unsure. He didn't like the idea of trimming his principles to match the awkward, unyielding shape of brute reality. That much of his father – a stubborn, unbending Communist politician who made more enemies from his honesty than most men did through their deceit – remained.

Barbara Martelli downed the tiny coffee. She was thinking. She seemed briefly troubled, he thought, as if there was something she didn't want to say. 'I know what you mean.'

'You do?'

'About the choices.'

Something crossed her face then, some shadow of doubt, of unhappiness, and it struck him that Barbara Martelli's appearance wasn't always an advantage. It could be a burden too. This was how people judged her, on her looks, not the person beneath, who was somehow oddly remote.

'But, Nic. The best thing is just to accept that's how it is and get on with the job. Not . . .' She looked at his coffee cup. It had been empty for a long time and they both knew it. ' . . . not hide away in the corner somewhere. That's not like you. At least, as much as I think I know you.'

He was late already. If she hadn't walked in, he'd still be there, hesitating. And a moment would come, he knew it, when he'd turn round, go back to the farmhouse, maybe open a bottle of good wine, then undo everything he'd achieved these past few months, rebuilding his health, resurrecting what was left of his dignity and self-respect. There was a kind of glory in crashing out that way. If you could only prolong that feeling forever, it would be enough, would see you through an entire lifetime. The trouble was it didn't last. You always woke up. The real world poked its head around the door and said, 'Look.' There was no escape and that was for the simplest of reasons: what he was running from lay inside.

'Do I have to march you into that place or what?' she asked.

'I could call in sick.'

'No!' Her large, green eyes widened with anger.

They were flirting with each other. Not seriously, he realized. This was Barbara's way of getting him moving. She'd use it on anyone she felt needed it.

'This,' she declared, 'is what we do for a living. It's our chosen vocation and there are no halfway houses. You're either in. Or out. So which is it?'

A wild thought ran around his head then popped

out of his mouth without even letting him consider the consequences. 'Do you think we'll ever go out on a date, Barbara? Do you think that's possible?'

A gentle blush rose in her cheeks. Barbara Martelli got asked out a dozen times a day.

'Ask me tomorrow,' she said. 'On one condition.'

He waited, still embarrassed by the sudden intimacy.

She pointed a long, manicured finger in the direction of the station. 'You ask me in there.'

They did everything wrong in Italy. The cappuccinos had insufficient milk. The pasta didn't taste right. The pizzas were too thin. And the booze. Lianne Dexter couldn't work out what was wrong. Ordinarily the effects would be wearing off by now, two hours after lunch. But she felt just as drunk as when they left the *osteria* and it was starting to make her edgy. She and Bobby had finished the single bottle of Pellegrino mineral water from the rucksack he'd snatched from the car before it went up in flames. Now they had nothing to drink, nothing to eat and not a lot of money either. She didn't even want to think about the walk back along the rutted lane towards the main road. How did you flag down an Italian and get him to take you to Avis for a refund on the crappy car they rented you? And what about the stuff Bobby had found? So far a coin, what looked like a very old, very big nail and something the size of a kid's hand, semi-circular, encrusted with crud, which Bobby assured her was definitely an ancient Roman neckband or the like and would come up great once he cleaned off the crap. Which was great except they weren't supposed to be hunting for these things. The Italians would surely know. And maybe the 'necklace' was just a brake lining anyway. Lianne's father was a car mechanic. She knew about these things, a little anyway. It looked awfully like a brake lining to her.

She licked her lips. Her mouth was dreadfully dry. A cheap wine migraine was pumping at her temples. It was now approaching three in the afternoon and the light was fading. They needed to be moving. She didn't want to be stranded all night in this odd wilderness, with its queer smell and the planes from Fiumicino screaming overhead every two minutes or less.

'Bobby,' she whined.

He wasn't satisfied with the haul. Tom Jorgensen still had the marble head and it looked better than any of these things.

He tore off the headphones and barked, 'What?'

'Gonna get dark soon. We gotta go.'

He looked around at the grey sky and sniffed. 'Five more minutes.' Then he popped the headphones back on and wandered over towards the water's edge. It was bog here. Lianne knew that instinctively. It had that odd, acid smell she associated with the cranberry farms in Maine, one of the places they'd trashed on an earlier vacation.

'Peat,' she said, suddenly remembering. Bobby mouthed 'what the fuck now?' at her with the headphones still clamped to his skull. A 747 careered over them so low she felt the earth shake. She had to put her hands over her ears just to try to keep out the bellowing of the plane's engines.

'Nothing,' she whispered to herself in the plane's wake, wishing she was somewhere else. Back home even. The cranberry farms had been nice. Interesting. Run by

17

people who spoke the same language she did and never made her feel out of place. Rome wasn't like that. She felt all the faces in the street were looking at her constantly, waiting for her to say the wrong thing, turn the wrong corner. It was all so *foreign*.

Then there was a new noise, an unexpected one. It was Bobby, whistling. He tore off the headphones and pointed to a patch of damp earth, covered in feeble grass, a few feet in front of him.

'One more thing, sweetheart. Then we're gone. Gimme the spade.'

She did as he asked. Bobby Dexter placed the shovel on the ground then jumped on it with both feet. The thing went straight in like a knife through hot butter. Bobby tumbled off the spade and hit the dirt once more.

'Peat,' she said again, watching Bobby writhe on the ground, cursing. 'It's soft, Bobby. You don't need to try so hard. Look—'

She picked up the trowel they'd brought and squatted down on the ground, next to where his spade had bitten the earth. Lianne had watched an archaeology programme on the Discovery Channel once. She knew how people did these things, though why they bothered, for six, maybe eight hours a day, was quite beyond her.

'You just do it gently,' she said and poked the end of the trowel into the soft earth. The acid reek came up and hit her in the face. It made her think of cranberries: all that sharp red juice mixed up with vodka. 'Look—'

She scraped the surface, trying not to breathe in the smell. And then the trowel stopped dead on something solid. Lianne Dexter gulped involuntarily and wondered whether her throat might seize up. She ran the trowel tentatively through the earth. It encountered the same solid object as far as she could push it.

Bobby lurched over the ground and took the trowel off her. He began working at the soil, a little too roughly she thought.

'What is it?' she asked.

An object was emerging. It was the colour of the peat, a dark, woody brown, and hard to the touch. Bobby scraped some more then the two of them took a deep breath and sat back. What lay before them, emerging gradually from the earth, appeared to be the carved representation of a human arm. A feminine one, probably, with the folds of a simple shift visible through the dirt, reproduced with an uncanny accuracy.

'It looks real,' Lianne said eventually.

'Hello!' Bobby bellowed sarcastically. 'Earth to Planet Lianne. It's a statue. It's supposed to look real.'

'Statues aren't that colour.'

'Lianne—' He was getting exasperated again. His eyes had an angry roll to them. 'This thing's been sitting in the shit for a couple of thousand years or so. What colour do you expect it to come up? Shiny white or something? You think they shrink-wrapped it before putting it there?'

She didn't answer. He had a point.

Bobby scraped some more. A hand emerged at the end of the arm: slender fingers clenched tightly shut around the shaft of something big. The two of them stood back for a moment and stared at the object in the mud. To Lianne the figure now looked very feminine and curiously familiar. Then her head lurched into gear and she realized what the connection was. This odd, dead thing in the ground resembled a cut-down version

DAVID HEWSON

of the Statue of Liberty, trying to raise a big, stone torch, struggling to get it upright in the mud.

'It's not metal, Bobby,' she said with a degree of boldness that worried her a little. 'How come your machine picked it up? You thought of that?'

He glowered at her. 'You amaze me sometimes. I'm sitting here maybe discovering Tutankhamun's fucking tomb or something and all you can do is pick, pick, pick. Get off my back for a moment, will ya? I'm trying to think.'

He scraped down the other side, where the other arm might be. Sure enough it was there, only a few inches beneath the surface of the peat. Maybe the recent rain had washed away some of the crap that had been covering it. Bobby ran the trowel gently across the space in between the arms. The figure's chest emerged. She was wearing what looked like a classical gown, with a V-neck that went low enough to disclose the rising curve of her slight and very lifelike breasts. The surface of the statue, when Bobby pushed away as much dirt as possible, was quite curious. It was the colour of old leather and a little shiny. For one brief moment, as he pushed and prodded with the trowel, Lianne thought it gave a little in places but that must have been the booze.

Bobby shuffled on his knees then pushed aside no more than four inches of soil a couple of feet below the areas he'd already exposed. He'd guessed well. There were the outlines of two ankles, some way apart, perfect, naked this time, no sign of a carved dress or anything.

'It's life-size, Bobby,' Lianne said.

'I know!'

'So what are you going to do?'

20

'Jesus. If only I could see that fat fucker Jorgensen's face right now. You bring the camera?'

She shook her head. 'Forgot it.'

'Typical. Thanks a million.'

'Bobby!'

He looked at his wife. Lianne knew she was close to becoming downright argumentative just then. She didn't care. Something bad was happening here and maybe it was time to take a stand.

'What am I going to do?' he asked. 'What the fuck I like, Lianne. Whatever the fuck I like.'

'It's too big. You can't pack that as excess baggage. Also it's the colour of shit. And it smells. Can't you smell it?'

'It's been in a bog for a million fucking years. You want it to come out smelling of roses?'

She pulled back from the thing and crossed her arms across her chest, mutinous. 'I don't want it smelling like that. And quit swearing at me all the time. It's not nice.'

He cursed under his breath and went back up to the top end, where the head ought to be. Cautiously this time he brushed away at the soil there. She was hoping the head had gone. She was hoping all Bobby would find was the torso and a couple of legs sticking out of the bottom. And wouldn't Tom Jorgensen see the funny side of that?

But there was a head. A beautiful one maybe once someone washed off all the crap. As Bobby Dexter scraped away, whistling again, his wife was beginning to put the pieces together, beginning to understand what they'd found. It was a life-size Roman statue, maybe a couple of thousand years old. Stained like shit from all this time in the peat, maybe, but perfect apart from that.

She understood what Bobby would be thinking too. Who knew what they could do in a lab these days? Maybe get it right back to nice, white marble, like it had been when Julius Caesar or some other dead Italian first ordered it.

And there was the problem. It was just too big. The two of them couldn't even try and get it out of the ground. Five feet or so of stone was bound to weigh a ton. Even if they got someone in to help, there was no way they could ever bring the thing back to the USA.

'Let's just go, Bobby,' Lianne pleaded. 'We can call someone and tell them about it. Maybe they'd give us a reward. Maybe we'd be in the paper. You could stick that under Tom Jorgensen's nose and see how it felt.'

'Fucking reward,' he spat back at her. 'This is Italy, Lianne. They'd steal the thing for themselves and probably lock us up for messing around down here.'

'Then what are you going to do?'
She was defying him now and they both knew it. This was some kind of turning point in their marriage, one at which either life could go in one of two directions: to freedom or to servitude.

He got up and went for the spade, picked it up, felt the weight of the thing in his hands then stared avidly at the queer brown form half buried in the peat.

Lianne looked at him, a cold tangle of dread beginning to form in her stomach.

'Bobby?' she asked, half pleading. '*Bobby?*'

Nic Costa drove the unmarked police Fiat east along the city side of the main riverside drag. Gianni Peroni, the partner assigned to him that morning, was in the passenger seat filling his face with a panino leaking roast pork at the edges. He was a big, muscular man approaching fifty, with an unforgettable face. Somewhere along the line – and Costa just knew he was going to have to ask before long – Peroni's features had walked into a wall or something. His nose was crushed worse than any Costa had seen on a rugby player. His forehead sank low over a couple of bright, smart piggy eyes. A vicious scar ran diagonally across his right cheek. Just to complete the picture Peroni cut his grey hair as short as possible, a crew crop, like a US marine. In a neat dark suit and a crisp white shirt and tie, he looked like a thug dressed up for a wedding. It was station lore that the man had never once raised a fist to a customer in his career. He didn't need to, Costa thought. People took one look at him, gulped and came clean. It was one reason why Peroni was known far and wide as one of the most popular and respected inspectors in the force, the last man Nic Costa expected to be sharing his car with as an equal.

'I don't know how they dare call this *porchetta*?' Peroni grumbled. 'Where I come from . . . it's this little town near Siena. All farmers and stuff, too ordinary to get the tourists. Now there they do *porchetta*, every damn weekend. My uncle Fredo was a farmer. He showed me how. You'd kill the pig, you'd bone it. You'd take out the liver and soak it in grappa and stuff. Then you'd stay up all night roasting the thing. Fredo used to say that was the only night of the week he slept with a pig that didn't snore.'

Peroni watched him, waiting for a reaction. 'OK. Maybe you had to meet his missus to understand that one. Anyway *that* was *porchetta*. All hot and fresh and lots of crackling too. This shit's been sitting in the fridge for days. Want some?'

Costa eyed the pale dry meat. 'Not while I'm driving, thanks. Anyway, I don't eat meat.'

Peroni shrugged then wound down the window and ejected the greasy paper out into the rising temperature of a Roman spring morning. 'Oh yeah, I forgot. Your loss.'

Costa took his eyes off the busy riverside road for a second and looked at Peroni. 'That's littering. You don't do it from my car.'

'You mean, "That's littering, *Sir.*" '

'No,' Costa insisted. 'I mean what I said. You're just another cop. You heard Falcone.'

Peroni's oddly stiff face suddenly became animated. 'Equal rank, equal rank. How can Leo do this to me? Jesus, the stuff he's got away with and no one busts his ass. Leo and I are meant to be buddies, for God's sake. What does friendship mean in this world?'

Costa had made up his mind the moment he knew Peroni was his new partner. He wasn't taking any crap. He wasn't behaving like a subordinate. Maybe that was why Falcone fixed this in the first place. It was a lesson, perhaps a kind of punishment, for both of them.

Gianni Peroni's crime was now well known throughout the Questura, told and retold with a certain awe, a fable about how even the brightest and the best could fall from grace, and for such small temptations too. For years he'd worked his way up through the vice squad, with never a taint of corruption to his name. As inspector he'd busted three of the biggest hooker rings in the city and managed to stem the infiltration of the prostitute trade by the vicious Albanian crooks who'd started to muscle in on territories elsewhere. He never went out of his way to make friends. He never hid the fact that, at heart, he remained a working-class farm boy from Tuscany who didn't feel comfortable mixing with the upper strata of the force. All the same, Peroni's name had been marked out for big things. If he didn't look so weird and scary maybe they'd have happened by now too. Then he blew everything, one night some weeks before, an occasion that rapidly made its way into the hands of a gleeful press.

It was meant to be a sting operation organized by the Direzione Investigativa Anti-Mafia, the civilian force outside police control specifically aimed at halting mob activity. The DIA had set up a fake brothel in Testaccio, manned by real hookers brought in from Bologna. In three weeks it had run up enough clientele to attract the attention of the big-time pimps who would, the DIA knew, soon be round asking for either a cut or the heads of the men creaming off the profits.

Three heavies did turn up one Thursday night. When the DIA pounced they took in the brothel's customers, just out of interest, and went through their wallets before handing them on to the police as a free gift. Gianni Peroni had the misfortune to be in the room of a blonde Czech girl when they walked through the door. No amount of talking on his part was able to extricate him from the mess. Word got back to the Questura. Peroni was first suspended then sent crashing back to earth as a lowly plain clothes detective. And he was supposed to feel lucky. Had it been anyone else, an entire career would have disappeared down the drain.

Demotion and the loss of salary were the least of Peroni's concerns if Questura gossip was anything to go by. He wasn't just admired for being a great cop. He was renowned throughout the building as a family man. His wife and his two teenage kids, one boy, one girl, were well known. Men and women on his squad dined regularly at the Peroni household. When they had problems, Peroni acted like a proxy father, offering advice, trying to keep them on track.

All that had been shattered on a chill January evening. Peroni didn't face prosecution. He'd broken no law. He'd just lost everything. His wife had gone back to Siena with both kids, demanding a swift divorce, shouting his betrayal from the rooftops. In a matter of weeks he'd gone from being an important cop, with a loving family, to a single, middle-aged man, alone, uncertain of his future career. And now Leo Falcone had put him in a car with Nic Costa, whose own position in the police appeared equally as uncertain and directionless. Costa had no clear idea how to handle this. But then, he guessed, neither did Gianni Peroni.

The two small Roman temples that sat beside the Piazza della Bocca della Verità were just beyond the window, a couple of perfect, circular shapes from a different, Arcadian world. It was a pleasant day with enough warmth in it to indicate spring was on the way. Nic Costa wished he could sit next to them for a while, thinking.

Peroni turned to stare at him. 'Shall we have the clearing of the air conversation now?'

Costa looked into that intense, battered face and wondered how long it would take him to get used to sharing a car with someone who looked like a cartoon villain. 'If you want.'

'Let me be candid. It's not so long since you went loony tunes. You did the drink thing too. Me, I just got caught with my pants down with a Czech hooker. For that I have to be the rehab warder. The way I see it is that if I can keep you straight for a month or so, and who knows maybe along the way we deal with a few criminals, I can get myself back in Leo's good books. I can start climbing the ladder to what I do best, which is running a team, not sitting in some stinking squad car playing nursemaid to junior and keeping him away from the bottle. This is important to me, kid. I'll do my best to keep Leo happy. But you have to help me. The sooner you do, the sooner you have me out of your hair and get someone normal. Understand?'

Costa nodded.

'And let me tell you something else. *I hate* the drink thing. I have watched too many men turn into boozed-up pieces of shit in my time. You do that to me and I will feel very cross indeed. You wouldn't like me when I'm cross. No one does.'

'I'll try to remember that. Do I get something in return? A promise you'll stay away from hookers?'

Peroni glared at him and Costa, in spite of himself, couldn't help feeling a little scared. 'Don't push it now. I know Leo's looking out for you. The stupid bastard feels guilty for what happened when you got shot. God knows why. From what I hear you got yourself into that mess.'

Costa refused to rise to the bait. 'No I mean it. I'm curious. Everyone thought they knew you. This stand-up, working-class guy with the perfect family, the perfect life. And now they think they got it wrong all along. And they wonder: was it them, or was it you? Who was doing the lying?'

'Me,' Peroni said immediately. 'But let me tell you.

Everyone's got that little dark spot inside them. Everyone wonders what it would be like to take it out for a walk once in a while. Even you. If you know what's good for you.'

'I thought that's what you didn't want to happen.'

'I was talking about the drink. People who go that way do it for one purpose. To kill something. Maybe it'd be better if they did let the dark side out instead. Just now and again.'

It was a kind of philosophy, Costa thought. Not one he expected from a cop, or the kind of cop Gianni Peroni was supposed to be.

'And you tell me something, kid. I saw you walking into the building today with Barbara Martelli. Isn't she the loveliest thing in the world? What if she just turned round one day, just when you were happily married and thought everything was stretching out neatly in front of you, just when you're feeling a little old too. What if she said: *Nic, I just wished I knew what it was like. Just the once. Where's the harm? Who's to know?*'

'I'm not married.'

'I *know*. I said, what if?' Peroni waited for an answer and realized it wasn't coming. 'You should ask that girl out. She's got something in her eyes when she looks at you. I notice these things.'

Costa laughed. 'Really?'

'Really. And let me tell you one more thing. I knew her old man. He was in vice too until a couple of years ago. One of the meanest, most miserable bastards you ever saw. How he ever spawned a woman like that is beyond me. There. You got a good reason not to date her. You'd have to meet that old sonofabitch.'

'Thanks.'

'You're welcome. You look like the sort of person who appreciates reasons for not doing things. Which is fine by me, until I talk myself out of this seat. Do we understand each other?'

Costa didn't get mad. In a way he felt relieved. At least he knew where he stood.

'Is that out of the way now?' he wondered. 'Can we just settle down to being old cop, young cop, cleaning up the streets of Rome?'

But the big man in the passenger seat was waving at him to be quiet. The radio was squealing their number. Peroni picked up the mike and answered. They listened to the call. Nic Costa gunned the car and headed straight for Piramide and the *autostrada* out to the coast and the airport, casually flicking on the blue light and the siren to get the cars out of the way.

'What a day,' Peroni groaned. 'First I get baby-sitting duties. Now we're the fire brigade. Hard to know which is worse.'

Bobby Dexter's determined expression was one Lianne recognized. It usually meant they were headed for trouble.

'I'll tell you what we're going to do,' he said. 'We're going to take back a head for Tom Jorgensen to look at. One that's a million times better than that piece of Greek shit of his.'

She gaped at him, outraged. 'What?'

Bobby raised the shovel to shoulder height, holding it like an axe, a little breathless already from the anticipation. 'Watch. Watch and learn.'

He brought the metal down hard; where the statue's

neck ought to be. Nothing much happened. Some dirt moved. But Lianne was yelling, louder than she'd ever done before.

'Bobby Dexter,' she screeched. 'What the hell are you doing? This thing's like a piece of art or something. It's history. You're just going to smash it to pieces so you can make out your dick's bigger than Tom Jorgensen's?'

He held the shovel high, swaying slightly. 'What do you know about the size of Jorgensen's dick?'

'It was a figure of speech, moron.'

Bobby Dexter blinked at her. He looked downright ugly. The light was failing now and the world was getting weird. He took one more swipe at the statue's neck and missed, sending up a shower of stinking earth that bounced straight back into his face. A few grains fell into his mouth. He spat out the dirt as if it were poison.

'If you break that statue, we're over, Bobby,' she said, dead serious. 'I mean it. I don't go talking to my father. I get a lawyer. The moment we get back to Seattle.'

He hesitated, staring at her as if wondering whether she really did mean it . . . 'You tell me that when we're back home with the best fucking piece of coffee table statuary in private ownership anywhere in Washington State. You'd be amazed what a nice piece of household ornamentation can do for dinner parties.'

'Bobby—' she yelled.

'Bullshit.' He took a final swing.

This one connected. The sharp side of the spade went deep into the neck. There should have been a sharp, cracking sound that indicated a good clean break, one that went right across the stone in a level line with just enough randomness in it to look convincing. She knew

Bobby well enough to understand what he was thinking. There were probably ideas in his head already.

But everything just went straight out of their heads a moment after the blade hit. Lianne Dexter realized right then that they'd been wrong, terribly wrong, both of them. They saw what they wanted to see. Not what *was*. Maybe there was a reason behind that. Because what *was* turned out to be the last thing they wanted to encounter anywhere on this planet, least of all on their own down a little lane, next to a stinking grey river in a country where their language skills extended only to ordering pizza, beer and wine.

The blade didn't strike hard stone. It met flesh, a kind of flesh anyway. Something that looked like leather, tanned, tough, but supple. The side of the spade cut straight through just where the neck met the shoulders, severing something that resembled a real human tendon, spattering both of them with a mixture of foul-smelling wet mud that seemed to have something distinctly organic, almost alive, inside it.

Lianne's face was covered with the peat gore that had spat back at them when he attacked the thing. She was spitting bits of it out of her mouth, sobbing, dry-retching as she did so.

She stopped for a moment and watched Bobby bend down to look closely at the thing, just a hint of reverence in his face.

On the ground in front of them, partly severed from the body by the spade, was the head of a young girl, sixteen, seventeen, no more, dressed in a classical gown, holding some large, ceremonial wand in her left hand. The force of the blow had removed most of the solid cake of peat that had sat on her features. What they saw now was her face which, beneath the crud, seemed beautiful. She had a high forehead and prominent cheek-bones. There wasn't a wrinkle in sight on her flawless leather skin. Her eyes were closed. Her lips were partly open as if she were uttering a final, dying sigh. She had perfect teeth which were just closed together with a hint of pearly whiteness showing through the brown stain of the earth. Her long hair was tied back behind her neck and matted into solid strands. Her expression was one of utmost peace. She looked, Lianne Dexter thought, happy, which was, she knew, ridiculous in the circum-stances.

And just in case they were in any doubt about the nature of this object before them there was the matter of the neck. When Bobby had come down hard with the shovel he'd done what he hoped: split through into the interior. Bobby and Lianne Dexter were now looking at the inside of another human being's throat and it was black and complicated and messy, with bones and sinews and passages that looked vaguely familiar from some distant school lesson in anatomy.

'Holy shit,' Bobby muttered and started shivering.

A 747 swooped low over them. They felt the heat of its breath. They inhaled the chemical stink of its fearsome engines. When the roar of its gross presence diminished Bobby Dexter became aware of another noise. It was his wife, screaming.

'No,' he pleaded. 'Not now, Lianne. I'm trying to think for chrissake.'

Then he gave up altogether. Two men, one short, one tall, were walking towards them, staring intently. Some way behind them there was something else: a red fire engine struggling down the lane trying to reach the charred and smoking remains of the Clio.

The men were waving badges. They didn't look sympathetic.

The older cop was a bull-necked gorilla with a disfigured, scowling face and piercing, aggressive eyes that looked as if they could see everything. The younger, shorter one was staring at the thing in the ground, the shit-coloured cadaver with the head all to one side where Bobby had lopped it with the shovel.

'This day just gets stranger,' Gianni Peroni murmured. 'Pinch me. Tell me I'm dreaming.'

'You're not dreaming,' Nic Costa replied. He couldn't stop looking at the object half-hidden in the mud. Not for the weeping woman who looked as if she'd thrown up and was now hunched in a ball down by the edge of the river. Or the man, who held a shovel uncertainly in his hands, his body swaying rhythmically.

A man who, for no reason at all, suddenly pointed the spade at both of them and, with a slow, effortful slur to his voice, said, 'Listen. Don't fuck with me. Don't even think about it. I'm an American citizen.'

THE IDES OF MARCH

'How long has she been lying there? Answer me that.'

Teresa Lupo stood next to the brown cadaver that lay at a stiff, awkward angle on the shiny steel table in the morgue. The pathologist looked even more proprietorial than usual about the corpse in her care, and immensely pleased with herself too. It was two weeks now since Nic Costa and Gianni Peroni had encountered the body and the screaming American couple by the muddy banks of the Tiber, just a couple of kilometres from the sea at Ostia. Bobby and Lianne Dexter were back home in Washington State, talking to lawyers about their divorce and who should have custody of the cats, still feeling lucky to have escaped Europe without facing a single charge (which proved, Lianne thought, exactly what kind of people they were over there anyway). Costa and Peroni had, in the mean time, become, if not quite a team, partners of a kind, able to get through the day with a sense of shared duty and the promise that soon their artificial relationship would be over.

The body had made international headlines for a few days. Somehow a photo had been smuggled to the media, showing the serene, frozen face that had emerged from the chemical-smelling peat. It was a genuine mystery. No one knew how old the body was. No one knew whether the girl had died of natural causes or was the victim of some obscure crime. There was wild speculation in some of the Italian tabloids, stories which talked about ancient cults that had killed followers who had somehow failed the entry ceremony.

Nic Costa hadn't taken any notice. It was pointless to speculate until Teresa Lupo had passed judgement. Now she had made up her mind. They had been summoned to the morgue for ten that morning. At noon Teresa planned to give a press conference outlining her findings. The very fact she'd arranged this herself without asking advance permission from Leo Falcone spoke volumes. It meant she was confident there was no criminal investigation on the way. He and Peroni had simply been invited along out of politeness. They found the specimen; they deserved to hear its secrets revealed. Costa wished Teresa had left them out of it. He was starting to get the feel for police business again, starting to like the idea he could be good at it. If this really was a closed case, he'd rather be somewhere else, dealing with a live one.

The three of them – Falcone, Peroni and Costa – sat on a cold, hard bench watching her make a few last-minute, fussy observations of the corpse. Costa understood what this was: a dry run for the press conference which would be part of her re-entry into police life. Teresa Lupo had briefly quit her job after the Denney case, vowing never to return. She had been close to Luca Rossi and felt the pain of his death as much as anyone in the station. More, perhaps, than Nic Costa. More certainly than Falcone who, while quietly racked by guilt over the loss of his man, was too obsessed by the job to be distracted for long.

Grief chased her from the tight, close embrace of the force. Grief brought her back to the fold. She was like the rest of them: hooked, incapable of staying away. She loved getting to know her customers, trying to understand their lives and what had brought them to her slab. Unravelling these mysteries fulfilled her and now she was starting to show it, Costa thought. She was carrying a little less weight. The ponytail had gone, replaced by a businesswoman's crop, black hair short and sculpted carefully to hide the outline of her heavy neck. She had a large, animated face and slightly bulbous blue eyes that darted around constantly. There was something a touch obsessive inside the woman, something that quickly chased away most men who tried to get close to her. Maybe that was what made her the pathologist the cops always wanted on their side, however fierce her temper, however sharp her tongue . . .

'Ten years. Twenty max,' Peroni suggested. 'But what do I know? I'm just a busted vice cop. You got to bear the responsibility for any screw-ups I make, Leo. I'm used to dealing with people I know are guilty from the outset. All this detection stuff . . . it's not my thing.'

Falcone put a hand to his ear. 'Excuse me?'

'Sir,' Peroni said meekly. 'You got to bear the responsibility, Sir.'

Falcone sat there in a grey suit that looked as if it were new that morning, letting his fingers run through his angular, sharp-pointed silver beard, staring at the body, thinking. He'd returned from a holiday somewhere hot only the day before. A deep walnut tan stained his face and his bald scalp. It was almost the colour of the corpse on the slab. The inspector seemed miles away. Maybe his head was still on the beach, or wherever he went for enjoyment. Maybe he'd been through the force disposition. There was a flu epidemic gripping the city. People were calling in sick from everywhere. The Questura had so many empty desks that morning it looked like Christmas Day.

Teresa was grinning. Peroni had said exactly what she wanted to hear. 'That's a good and sensible suggestion, even for a busted vice cop. Your basis for it being . . . ?'

He waved his hand at the table. 'Look at her. She's a touch messed up but she don't stink too bad. Nothing going mouldy. I'm sure you people have seen worse. Smelled much worse too probably.'

She nodded. 'The smell's from the treatment. She's been lying in a shower ever since we got her here. Fifteen per cent polyethylene glycol in distilled water. I've been doing a lot of research on this girl. Reading books. Talking to people. I'm in touch with some academics in England by e-mail who know exactly how to handle a body in this condition. After ten weeks or so maybe we'll need to get her freeze-dried to finish the job properly.'

'Don't we get to bury her in the end?' Costa wondered. 'Isn't that what you're supposed to do with dead people?'

She screwed up her big pale face in amazement. 'Are you kidding me? Do you think the university would allow it?'

'Since when did she belong to them?' he asked. 'However old she is, she was a human being. If this isn't going to become a crime investigation, what's the problem? When does a corpse turn into a specimen? Who decides?'

'I do,' Falcone said, coming out of the daydream abruptly. Costa peered at him. There was something odd going on. Falcone wasn't as cool, as self-composed as normal. He looked glum, which was unusual. It was rare that anyone was able to discern much sign of human emotion in him at all. Costa wondered who Falcone had been on holiday with. The dour inspector's marriage had ended years ago. There were rumours of occasional attachments since then but that could just be station gossip. When Leo Falcone was in the Questura nothing else seemed to exist except the force. When he was gone, he was out of it completely, never mixing with his colleagues, never wanting to be invited round for dinner. Maybe the inspector, who always seemed so calm, so in control when it came to other people's lives, had no hold whatsoever on his own. Maybe he went on holiday by himself, sitting on some sunny beach somewhere reading a book like a hermit, turning browner and browner, meaner and meaner.

'Hear me out,' Teresa pleaded. 'It'll all become clear, I promise. A couple of decades? Nice guess. But I have to tell you it's out. By a touch under two thousand years.'

Peroni snorted. 'Someone's been hitting the wacky baccy around here, Leo. Excuse me. *Sir*. How else can you come up with that kind of shit?'

'Wait for it, wait for it,' she demanded, waving a finger at him. 'I can't be precise, not yet, but I hope to give you something pretty accurate very soon. This body's been in peat all that time. From the moment you put a corpse in that kind of bog it starts getting preserved. Sort of a mixture between mummification and tanning, and completely unpredictable too. Plus, there's no end

41

of industrial effluent getting poured into the river out there and God knows what that does. I got parts of her almost as hard as wood, other areas soft, almost pliable. Haven't even contemplated a conventional autopsy – for reasons that will shortly become obvious – so God knows what kind of state she's in internally. But I have a date. Peat plays havoc with normal radiocarbon dating techniques. I won't get technical on you. Let's just say the acid in the water depletes just about anything we can use for a radiocarbon test. There are things we can try, like getting some cholesterol out of her, since that's virtually immune to long-term soaking. But right now I'm working with some organic material from the dirt beneath her fingernails. And that's somewhere between 50 AD and 230 AD.'

They just stared at her.

'Is that really possible?' Falcone asked eventually.

She went over to the desk and picked up a large brown envelope next to the computer. 'You bet. None of this is new. The archaeologists have a term for it. "Peat bodies". They've been there for centuries but no one noticed until companies started digging up the bogs for the gardening business. The area behind Fiumicino was never big enough to work commercially. Mind you, there's been a lot of rain this winter. Maybe that took off some of the surface soil and made it easier to find.'

She crossed the room and passed them a set of colour photographs. They were of corpses, brown corpses, some contorted, half shrunken, half mummified, a little more exaggerated than the one now on the slab but recognizably similar all the same.

'See this one,' she said, pointing at the first picture. It was the head of a man, apparently turned to leather.

The features were almost perfectly preserved. He had a calm, composed face. His eyes were closed as if in sleep. He wore some kind of rough leather cap, the stitching still visible on the crude seams. 'Tollund, Denmark. Found in 1950. Don't be fooled by the expression. He had a rope around his neck. Executed for some reason. Some good radiocarbon material there. Puts his death somewhere over two thousand years ago. And this—'

The next picture was of a full corpse: a man, reclining on what looked like rock. He was more shrivelled this time, with his neck turned at an awkward angle and a head of matted red hair.

'Grauballe, also in Denmark, not far away, though he's even older, third century BC. This one had his throat cut ear to ear. They found traces of the ergot fungus – the magic mushroom – in his gut. It's not easy to re-create what went on but there's a common theme. These people died violently, maybe as part of some ritual. Drugs tended to be involved. Here—'

She began scattering pictures over their laps, corpse after mummified corpse, many crouched in that tortured, agonized position any cop who'd visited a modern murder scene already knew too well. 'Yde Girl, in Holland, stabbed and strangled. She was maybe sixteen. Lindow Man, England. Beaten, strangled then dumped in the bog. Daetgen Man, Germany. Beaten, stabbed and beheaded. Borremose Woman, found in Denmark, face caved in, probably by a hammer or a pickaxe. These were all people in primitive, pagan agrarian societies. Maybe they did something wrong. Maybe there was some kind of sacrificial rite. Peat bogs often had a kind of spiritual significance for these tribes. Perhaps these were offerings to the bog god or someone. I don't know.'

Falcone put down the photos. He seemed remarkably uninterested in them. 'I don't care what happened in Denmark a couple of millennia ago. What happened here? How, specifically, did she die?'

She didn't like that. Teresa Lupo had been expecting a little more credit for what she'd found out, Costa thought. She deserved it too.

'Listen,' she answered sharply. 'We have limited resources. Like Nic said, when do we have a body and when do we have a specimen? I can make that judgement for myself, thanks. This is a very old corpse. I'm a criminal pathologist, not a historian. There are people who can perform a full autopsy on this girl and the rest. It's not a job for us.'

'How did she die?' Falcone repeated.

She looked at the frozen, leathery face. Teresa Lupo always felt some sympathy for her customers. Even when they'd expired a couple of thousand years ago.

'Like the rest. Badly. Is that what you wanted to know?'

'Usually, it's the first thing we need to know,' Falcone said.

'Usually,' she agreed. Then she gestured at the cadaver on the shining table. 'Does this look usual to you?'

There were times when Emilio Neri thought himself a fool for hanging on to the house in the Via Giulia. He'd taken on the property thirty years before, in return for an unpaid debt from some dumb banker who'd got in over his head gambling. Neri, then a rising *capo* in the Rome mobs, reluctantly became the owner. He'd rather have driven the yo-yo into the countryside somewhere and put his eyes out before dropping him in a ditch. But this all happened at a time when his actions were circumscribed by others. It would be a further ten years before Neri became don in his own right, giving him the sway to order executions directly, and take a cut of every transaction running through the family's books. By then the banker was back in business and never made the mistake of getting into his debt again, much to Neri's disappointment.

In the 1970s the Via Giulia was still pretty much a local area for everyday Romans, not the chic street for rich foreigners and antique dealers it was to become. Created in the sixteenth century by Bramante for Pope Julius II, it ran parallel to the river, set some way below the level of the busy waterside road, and was originally intended to be a grand entrance to the Vatican, by the bridge to the Castel Sant'Angelo. The market of the Campo dei Fiori was no more than a two-minute walk away. Trastevere was maybe a minute more, crossing over the medieval footbridge of the Ponte Sisto. On a fine summer evening Neri used to make that walk regularly, pausing in the middle of the bridge to look along the river towards the vast, sunlit dome of St Peter's. He was never much interested in views but this one pleased him somehow. Perhaps that was why he held on to the house, although by now he could afford just about any property in Rome, and was beginning to acquire a portfolio that would include homes in New York, Tuscany, Colombia and two country estates in his native Sicily.

The walk to Trastevere took him out of himself for a

while. The restaurants were good too, which was something Neri could never resist. Until he was fifty he'd been relatively fit, a big, powerful, muscular man who could impose his will by force and brute physical violence if need be. Then the food and the wine took hold. Now he was sixty-five and carrying way too much weight. He looked at himself in the mirror sometimes and wondered whether there was anything to be done. Then he remembered who he was and knew it didn't matter. He had all the money a man could want. He had a beautiful young wife who did anything he pleased, and was smart enough to look the other way if he felt like the occasional distraction. Maybe he was fat. Maybe he wheezed now and again, and had halitosis so bad he popped mints into his large, grey-lipped mouth the way some of his underlings sucked on cigarettes. Who cared? He was Emilio Neri, a don to be feared in Rome and beyond. He had influence. He had hard cash pouring into his offshore accounts, from prostitution, drug trafficking, money laundering, arms and any number of semi-legitimate investments. He didn't care what he looked like, what he smelt like. That was their problems.

In all this pampered life there was just one minor sore and, to Neri's occasional annoyance, it lived downstairs, one floor above the six servants he employed needlessly, just to fill up the space and dust things before they ever got dusty. While he and Adele occupied the top two storeys of the house – and had sole use of the vast terrace, with its palm trees and fountains – his only son, Mickey, had, after three fraught years pissing off Neri's friends in the States, come home to stay. It was a temporary arrangement. Neri wanted to keep an eye on the boy just to make sure he didn't start messing up with dope again. Once he'd found some kind of even keel, Neri would cut him loose. Maybe find him an apartment somewhere else in the city, or move him on to Sicily where there were relatives who could keep him in check. Neri did this partly out of self-interest – Mickey had grown up inside the organization. He could cause some harm if he started blabbing to the wrong people. But there was a degree of paternal loyalty there too. Mickey was an asshole. Maybe he inherited this from his mother, an over-tanned American bit-part actress Neri had met through a crooked producer he knew when he was pumping hot money into a Fellini movie. The marriage had lasted five years, after which Neri knew he either had to divorce the bitch or kill her. She now basked in the permasun of Florida and doubtless bore a close physical resemblance to an iguana, a creature, Neri thought, which could probably out-think her in its sleep.

Mickey never wanted to be near mamma. Mickey wanted to hang around his old man. He thought he was a don in the making and never missed an opportunity to throw his weight around. He had problems with women too, just couldn't leave them alone, whether they were married or not. His one saving grace was that he worshipped his father. Everyone else, Adele included, did Neri's bidding out of fear. Mickey went along with everything his old man decreed for a simpler reason. Most kids idolized their fathers until they were seven or eight, and then started to see them for what they were. The scales had never fallen from Mickey's eyes. There was some undying adulation stuck fast in his genes and Emilio Neri found it strangely touching. It led him to do crazy things, such as letting the kid wander around the house whenever he felt like it, even though he and

Adele, who, at thirty-three, was just one year older, loathed the sight of one another. It led him to overlook the problems that came when Mickey got a little too close to the drugs and the booze, problems that were, on occasion, expensive to fix.

Sometimes Emilio wondered who was indulging whom. Since Mickey moved in, he'd begun to wonder that a lot.

It was now mid-morning and the two of them had been bitching at each other, on and off, since breakfast. Adele half reclined on the sofa, still in her mauve silk pyjamas, face in a fashion house catalogue. Emilio thought she looked gorgeous but he knew it was a matter of taste. She was sipping a *spremuta* of blood-red orange juice which was almost the colour of her expensively cut hair. She sent out one of the servants to buy these things by the kilo from the market then watched as Nadia, the sullen cook she'd picked herself, squeezed them in the kitchen. Adele almost lived off the stuff. It drove Mickey crazy. Maybe it was why she was so skinny, he said. He bugged his old man about that constantly. Why marry some redhead with the figure of a pencil when you could have just about any woman in Rome?

'I still can have just about any woman in Rome,' Emilio told him.

'Yeah. But why?'

'Because I don't want the same picture over the fireplace everyone else has. Leave it at that.'

'I don't get it.'

Emilio had thrown a big arm around the kid. Mickey inherited the physique of his mother. He was lean, muscular, good-looking too. It was a shame he always chose clothes too young for him, though. And that he'd dyed his shoulder-length hair an overpowering, unnatural blonde colour. 'You don't have to. Just don't snap at each other all the time. Not when I'm around anyway.'

'Sorry,' he'd replied, instantly deferential.

The old man never said as much but sometimes he didn't get it either. Adele was unlike any woman he'd ever slept with: cool, adventurous, always willing, whatever he wanted. Young as she was, she actually taught him a few new tricks. Maybe that clinched it. He knew for sure it wasn't her personality, which he didn't really understand beyond her basic need for money and security. She was an expensive pet, if he were honest with himself, a living ornament to add some beauty to his life.

'So,' Neri declared, looking in turn at the two of them. 'What does my family plan to do today?'

'Are we going out?' she asked. 'We could have lunch somewhere.'

'Why bother?' Mickey said, smirking. 'I could send someone down the Campo. Buy you a couple of lettuce leaves. They'd last all week.'

'Hey!' the old man bellowed. 'Cut it out! And quit sending servants out to buy stuff you can get yourself. I don't pay them to get you cigarettes.'

Mickey went back to the sports car magazine he was reading and said nothing. Neri knew what the kid was thinking: *so what do you pay them for?* Neri never liked the idea of servants in the house. Adele said their position demanded it. He was the boss. He was supposed to own people. It grated somehow. Emilio Neri grew up in a traditional Roman working-class family, fighting his way out of the Testaccio slums. He still felt embarrassed by these minions downstairs. A couple were made men, there for security. He had no problem with that. But a house was for family, not strangers.

'I got work to do,' Emilio said. 'People to see. I won't be back until this afternoon.'

'Then I'll go shopping,' she answered, with just a hint of hurt disappointment in her voice.

Mickey was shaking his blonde head in disbelief. Adele did a lot of shopping.

'You!'

'Yeah.' Mickey closed the magazine.

'Go see that louse Cozzi. Squeeze his grapes and ask for some accounts. The creep's screwing us somehow. I just know it. We should be taking more in one week than he hands over in a month.'

'What do you want me to do if I see something?'

'If you see something?' Neri walked over and ruffled Mickey's wayward hair. 'Don't play the tough guy. Leave those decisions to me.'

'But—'

'You heard.'

Neri looked at the pair of them. Adele was acting as if the kid didn't even exist. 'I wish you two could work up the energy to be civilized to each other once in a while. It would make my life a whole lot easier.' He watched. They didn't even exchange glances.

'Families,' Neri moaned, then phoned downstairs, telling them to get the Mercedes ready. He keyed in the security code that unlocked the big metal door. It felt like a prison sometimes, hiding behind the bodyguards, riding around in a car that had been discreetly filled with bullet-proof panelling. But that was the way of the world these days.

'Bye,' Emilio Neri grunted, and was gone, without even looking back.

Mickey waited a while, pretending to read the magazine. Finally he put it down and looked across at her. She'd finished the orange juice. She was lying back on the sofa in her perfect silk pyjamas, eyes closed, glossy red hair splayed out on the white leather. Pretending she was asleep. She wasn't really. They both knew that.

'Maybe he's right,' he said.

She opened her eyes and turned her head lazily, just enough to meet his gaze. She had very bright eyes, vivid green, never still. Not smart eyes, he thought. Just sufficiently expressionless to hide the odd lie.

'About what?'

'About us getting along a little better.'

She became alert, alarmed perhaps. She looked at the door. There was a hard cast in her face: *fear*.

Mickey got up, stretched his arms and yawned. He was wearing a thin tee-shirt and tight designer jeans. She watched him, worried. They heard the sound of the big main door to the street slamming shut three floors below, and then, directly after, the growl of the departing Mercedes.

Adele Neri got up from the sofa, went to the door and threw the bolt, walked across to her stepson, put a hand on his fly and ran the zip down, clutching at what was inside.

'You need to shop for new pyjamas,' Mickey said.

'What?'

He took hold of the neckline of her top and tugged hard with both hands, tearing at the silk. The fabric ripped wide open. Her meagre white breasts came under his fingers. He bent down, sucking at them briefly, then jerked down the pants, helping her shrug out of the things, running his palms everywhere, letting his tongue work briefly into her small, tight navel, then slide lower into the thatch of brown hair.

Mickey got up, cupped his hands around her thin, tight buttocks, gripped her thighs, lifting her into the air, pushing backwards until her shoulders were up against the door. The green eyes looked into his. Maybe there was an expression there. Need. Maybe not.

'Never much wanted to bang a skinny chick until you came along,' he mumbled. 'Now I don't want to bang nothing else.'

She was doing things with her hands, things that were sneaky and gentle and rough and unsubtle at the same time. He was hardening in her fingers. His jeans were round his ankles now. She hitched up her legs and straddled his waist, holding on tight, guiding him.

'If he ever finds out, Mickey—'

'We're dead,' he said, and felt his body meeting hers in all the right places.

Mickey Neri pushed himself forward, stabbing into her. It was the best feeling he'd ever known. She was squealing. She was going crazy, chewing on his neck, whispering filthy words into his ear, pulling his long hair. He pushed harder. He was in deep, as deep as it got.

'Worth it,' he panted, knowing already he'd have to work hard to prolong the pleasure. Maybe she knew some tricks there too. 'Worth every second.'

'OK,' Teresa Lupo said briskly. 'I spent many nights sweating over this but I'll try to compress it as much as I can. Look—'

They did as she wanted, and got up to stand over the cadaver. She seemed quite young, Costa thought, halfway between girl and woman. Perhaps seventeen, if that. Her face was disconcerting, still alive somehow and undoubtedly beautiful. Her features seemed Saxon or maybe Scandinavian. They had the precise, symmetrical perfection he associated with fair-haired northerners. Someone had washed part of her matted hair. It was now a kind of muddy blonde, tinted by the redness of the peat. The smell was pungent close up too.

'You will recall,' Teresa said, pointing at the cavity around the cadaver's throat, 'that our thoughtful American friend tried to remove her head believing it to be that of a statue. This wound was caused by the sharp end of his shovel. I'm amazed you people let the bastard go without doing a single thing to him, by the way, but that's your decision not mine.'

'Here, here,' Peroni agreed.

'We went through this, Gianni,' Costa said. 'What were we supposed to charge them with?'

'Drunk driving?' Peroni suggested.

'Couldn't hold them in the country until trial.'

The older man scowled. 'How about disrespect? Yeah, I know. It's not a crime. Maybe it ought to be.'

Teresa smiled at Peroni and said, 'I agree.' Then she took a pointer and indicated an area on the girl's neck, just above the deep gash made by Bobby Dexter's spade. 'You can still see what happened originally though. That shovel wasn't the first time someone struck a blow here. The girl's throat was cut. From behind too. From the wound you can see whoever did it worked from side to side. It doesn't work like that if they come in from the

53

front. Then you just get a slash from the centre out. Here—'

There were more pictures on the desk. Careful blow-ups of the neck. 'There's the slice the bozo made. There's hardly any earth on the tissue. But here—'

They looked closely at the photos. Close up the second, older wound, clearly tinted by the brown, acid water over the years, was unmistakable.

'That didn't happen two weeks ago. That happened not long before she got put into the bog. That killed her.'

Falcone nodded at the pictures. 'Good work,' he said. 'That was all I wanted to know.'

'There's more,' she added, trying not to look too eager.

Falcone laughed. She found it disconcerting that she amused him. 'Don't tell me, doctor. You've solved the case. You have a motive. You know when. You know who did it.'

'That last part's beyond even me. The rest . . . be patient.'

The inspector smiled, amused, and waved her to go on.

There was a book on the desk. She picked it up, and held it up for them to see. It was entitled *Dionysus and the Villa of Mysteries*. The cover photograph was of an ancient painting: a woman in a dishevelled dress, holding her hand over her face in terror of some half-seen night creature with staring, demonic eyes which leered at her from the edges of the image. The shapes had been damaged over the years. The creature was largely unrecognizable. But they could see what was depicted here. It was some kind of ceremony, one in which the woman was, perhaps, assaulted. Or even sacrificed.

'This was written by a professor at the university here,' she said. 'I got put onto it by an academic at Yale who'd done some work on a bog body found in Germany, close to a Roman town.'

'This is relevant?' Falcone asked.

'I think so. Most of these deaths weren't accidental. There was some kind of ritual going on. The guy who wrote this is trying to work out what that might be.'

'Something to do with Dionysus?' Costa asked. 'I don't get it. That's Pompeii. We went there on a field trip when I was at school.'

'So did we,' Peroni added. 'First time I ever got drunk.'

'Jesus,' she said. 'What a pair you two make. Yes, Nic. The Villa of Mysteries is at Pompeii and, according to this guy, who is, I am reliably informed, the world's living expert on the Dionysian mysteries, it is important. But it wasn't the only one. Pompeii was the provinces. Suburbia if you like. It was small time compared to what went on elsewhere. In Rome in particular. Ask yourself. Who's got the biggest churches? Us or them?'

Falcone sighed. 'Point taken. And this book says what exactly?'

She waved the cover at them. Costa glanced at the terrified woman there. It seemed such a modern image. 'Dionysus was a cult imported from Greece. You probably know him better as Bacchus.'

'Booze?' Peroni wondered. 'You mean this is the result of a drunken orgy or something?'

She grimaced. 'You watch too many bad movies. Dionysus was about much more than drink. This was a secret cult, banned as a pagan one even before Christianity because of what went on. Not easy to stamp out either. There were Dionysian rituals going on in Sicily and Greece until a few centuries ago. Maybe they're still happening and we just don't know about them.'

Falcone stared pointedly at his watch. 'My jurisdiction ends at Rome.'

'OK, OK,' she conceded. 'Rome.'

Teresa Lupo opened the book at a page marked with a yellow sticky note. 'Here are some pictures, from a place in Ostia. Still suburbia, but around the time this girl was put in the bog this was Rome's harbour town and a sight bigger than Pompeii. Lots of rich people. Lots of substantial villas on the edge of town, including this one . . .'

She pointed at an outline on the map then turned the page. There was a series of photographs of an old, churchlike building, then some interior shots of wall paintings. One of the scenes was the image from the front of the book. The rest was a frieze of dancing figures, human and mythical, dancing, coupling.

'Pompeii has a much fuller set of wall paintings. What they seem to show – at least the book claims – is the initiation ceremony for the cult. Not that anyone much understands them these days. The point is that they were all over the place. At Ostia. In Rome too. Probably with the big one hidden somewhere not far from the centre. The holy of holies.'

'What he calls the Palace of Mysteries?' Costa asked.

'Exactly,' she said, nodding. 'Which is probably where this poor kid died. I took a good look at the dirt beneath her fingernails. It's not estuarial. It didn't come from Ostia. It could be from anywhere in central Rome.'

Peroni looked lost. 'You mean these were temples or something? And they kept them hidden?'

'Not quite. More like fun palaces in the dark they could use when the time came.'

Peroni put his finger on the page and traced over the paintings. 'Use to kill people?'

Teresa shrugged. 'I dunno. You read this book and sometimes you think the guy is sure of what he's saying, sometimes he's making it up. What he thinks is that there could be bad consequences if the initiation went wrong. There was some kind of mysterious act which had to be performed with a representative of the god. Sexual, probably. Everyone got doped up to the nines so I imagine most of the time they didn't have a problem getting their way with these kids. But if the initiate backed off . . .' She didn't need to say the rest.

'She a virgin?' Peroni asked.

'I told you. I put off performing a full autopsy until I could get some idea of the date. Now we know I can pass it on to the archaeology people at the university. They can try to find out. From what I've seen it's going to be impossible to tell. Sorry. Do you need to know?'

'Maybe not,' he admitted. 'Look. Like I said, I'm no detective. But it seems to me there's not a lot of meat here. Could be it's all coincidence. Also – and I hate to point this out – that dating stuff just dates the dirt beneath her fingernails. Don't date her.'

'I know, I know,' she said firmly. 'Stay with it. I'm building a case here. You see what's in her hand?'

The girl was holding some kind of wand or standard about a metre long, clutched to her side, the head disappearing under her arm. At the base was a protuberance of some kind, round and knobbly.

'This is exactly what the book describes, and that isn't conjecture. It's based on historical sources. I took samples. It's made from several bound stems of fennel. At the top there's a pine cone, wound into the staff. The thing's called a "thyrsus". It's standard issue for Dionysian rituals. Look—'

She turned the pages of the book. There was a picture of a female figure, half dressed, holding the same kind of object, waving it in the face of a satyr, half man, half goat, leering at her.

'It's used for protection. And purification.'

'Have you dated that?' Falcone asked.

'Radiocarbon costs,' she snapped. 'You want me to spend time and money on this instead of something fresh off the street?'

Falcone nodded at the book. 'Just asking. You've worked very hard, doctor. Congratulations.'

He still didn't seem that interested.

'There's one thing left,' she said quickly, as if she thought they might leave the room any moment.

'That is?'

'They found it with a metal detector, remember. How? There's nothing metallic on her body. No necklace. No rings. No armlet.'

She wanted them to come up with an answer. It didn't happen. Teresa Lupo went back to the desk and returned with an X-ray of the head. She placed it on the cadaver's stomach. 'See?'

It was a straight-on image of the girl's skull. There was a bright object there, quite small, in the lower third.

'A coin beneath the tongue,' she said. 'To pay Charon, the ferryman who took the dead across the Styx to the Underworld. Without it you never got there. I

58

didn't need any book to tell me that. I loved mythology when I was a kid.'

To Nic Costa's surprise, Falcone was abruptly animated by this discovery.

'You've got it? The coin?'

'Not yet,' she said. 'I was waiting for you.'

'Please—'

'Hey! I have other work you know.'

They did know that. They also knew how much she liked to be right, and seen to be proved so.

She looked at the face, the half open mouth, the perfect stained teeth. Then she examined the X-ray again, wondering where to start.

Teresa Lupo picked up a scalpel and, with one careful, clean movement, made an incision in the girl's left cheek, level with her lower lip. She put the scalpel down then picked up a small pair of shiny steel forceps.

'They dated coins in those days. If this one's anywhere in the range I outlined I expect you gentlemen to buy me dinner, one by one, in a restaurant of my choosing.'

'It's a deal,' Falcone replied immediately.

'Ooh!' Teresa squealed with a fake girlish glee as she exercised the forceps, making sure they would do the job. 'Dinner with cops! Aren't I the lucky one? What will we talk about? Football? Sex? Experimental philosophy?'

The forceps entered the slice in the cheek. She turned the instrument deftly, probing, feeling, pushing. Then the arms clamped on something.

'Pass me one of those silver trays,' she said to Costa. 'This is going to cost you guys plenty.'

Slowly, she retrieved the forceps from the girl's mouth and placed an item in the dish. Then she poured some fluid into the pan and cleaned the thing gently with a tiny brush.

The object was a small coin which came up quite shiny. It was silver on the edges with a bronze centre, though both colours looked as if they were slowly transforming to copper through the stain of the peat. It was also familiar.

Teresa Lupo pulled over a large magnifying glass on a swan neck stand. The four of them crowded around the lens, peering at the thing. She turned it over. Twice. Just to make sure.

Peroni stood next to her, shaking his head. 'My boy used to collect coins until someone told him it was uncool,' he said. 'I helped him sort out his collection. Bought him one of those, mint condition. Dated the first year they issued it, 1982. Five hundred lire. You know something? It was the world's first bi-metallic coin. No one had made one that was silver on the outside and bronze in the centre before. One other thing. If you look at the obverse, above the picture of the Quirinale, you'll see the value written in Braille. That was unique too.'

No one was really listening. Peroni bristled. 'Hey. Stupid old cop is sharing information here. Are you taking notes or am I speaking for my own benefit?'

'Shit,' Teresa Lupo whispered, glaring at the coin. '*Shit*.'

'You mean the body's been in the peat for not much more than twenty years?' Costa asked.

'Not even that,' Falcone said.

They all turned to look at him. The inspector had returned to his briefcase and now had a folder in his hands. He opened it and took out a photograph. It was a portrait of a girl in her teens. She had long fair hair down to her shoulders. She was smiling for the camera.

He placed the photograph on the cadaver's chest, over the X-ray of the skull. The features were identical.

'You knew?' She couldn't believe this, couldn't contain her amazement and anger. Peroni was chuckling, his shoulders rising and falling as if they were plugged into the mains.

Falcone was bent over, examining something on the girl's left shoulder. A mark. A tattoo maybe.

'Just guessing to begin with. You have to remember, doctor. I didn't get back from holiday till yesterday. I hardly had the time to dig this . . .' he waved the case folder, ' . . . out of the vaults.'

'You *knew?*' she repeated.

He bent down and looked at the mark on the girl's skin. Costa did the same. It was a tattoo, circular, about the size of the coin: a howling, insane face with huge lips and long dreadlocks.

'It's supposed to be a mask from an imperial Roman comedy,' Falcone said. 'Dionysus was the god of theatre too. This was used by the Dionysian cults. You deserve that dinner, doctor. I'll honour the bet. You were almost there. Just a couple of millennia out.'

Teresa Lupo pointed a stubby index finger at the inspector's chest. 'You *knew?* Eat your fucking dinner on your own.'

'So be it,' he answered. They watched him. Falcone couldn't take his eyes off the tattoo. There was something going on inside the inspector's head, something he didn't seem much inclined to share.

'You'll cancel the press conference,' he said.

61

'You bet,' she grumbled mutely. 'But what should I say?'

'Make an excuse. Say you've got a headache. Tell them we don't have the people, what with this flu thing and all. It's the truth anyway.' He picked up the photograph from the dead girl's chest and put it back in the envelope. Costa couldn't help but notice Falcone hadn't even let them see a name.

'Sir?' Costa asked, puzzled.

'Mr Costa?' Falcone's sparkling eyes gave nothing away. 'It's so nice to have you back with us.'

'What do you want us to do?'

'Catch a few crooks I imagine. Go help out down the Campo. There's a lot of pickpockets there at the moment.'

'I meant about this.'

Falcone took a final look at the corpse. 'About this . . . nothing. The poor kid's been lying in the mud for sixteen years. A day or two won't make much difference.'

He rounded on all three of them. 'And let me make one thing clear. I don't want you breathing a word of what we have here to anyone. Not in this building. Not outside. I'll call you when I need you.'

They watched him walk purposefully out of the room. Teresa Lupo stared at the body, her big, pale face a picture of misery and disappointment.

'I had it all worked out,' she moaned. 'I knew exactly what happened. I talked to these academics and people. Jesus . . .'

'You heard him,' Costa said. 'You did well. He meant it.'

Teresa was running her fingers over the dead girl's mahogany skin. She didn't need Nic Costa's sympathy.

She was over her disappointment already. It had been displaced by something new, something potentially more interesting.

The cadaver on her dissecting table was no longer a historical artefact. It was a murder victim. It required her attention.

Costa looked at the silver scalpel in her hand then looked at Peroni.

'The Campo it is,' he said and the older man nodded back in agreement.

'I guess there really is no rush,' Peroni said in the car. 'I just wish Leo would talk to us some more. I hate getting left in the dark.'

Costa shrugged. He knew Falcone well enough not to let this bug him. 'In his own time. It's always like that.'

'I know. He'd be a disaster in vice. You got to take people with you all the way there.' Peroni must have watched Falcone work his way up the ranks. Their relationship was hard to fathom, half amiable, half suspicious. That was hardly unusual. Falcone was a smart, sound cop, one who trod a fine line sometimes when he felt a case merited it. He'd won plenty of respect for his talents. He was straight, unbending on occasion. But he didn't give a damn about popularity. Sometimes, Costa thought, Falcone actually liked the antipathy and near-hatred he generated. It made tough decisions easier to take.

Peroni lit a cigarette and blew the smoke out of the window. 'You asked Barbara Martelli out yet?'

Where did that one come from, Costa wondered. 'Haven't found the right occasion.'

Peroni stared at him with a face that said: *are you kidding me?*

'I'm not ready. OK?'

'At least that's honest. How long's it been since you went with a woman? You don't mind my asking. We have these conversations in vice all the time.'

'I guess in vice you measure it in hours,' Costa answered without thinking and immediately wished he could bite back his words. Peroni's face fell. He looked hurt.

'I'm sorry, Gianni. I didn't mean that. It just slipped out.'

'At least we're on first-name terms now. I guess that means we can say what we want to each other.'

'I didn't—'

'It's OK,' Peroni interrupted. 'Don't apologize. You have every right to tell me when I'm acting like a jerk.'

Peroni was more complicated than he liked to appear. That much Costa had come to understand. Some part of him wanted to talk about what had happened too, even if he felt he ought to make a play of avoiding the subject.

'Why did you do it, Gianni? I mean you got a family. Then you go with a hooker.'

'Oh come on! It happens every day. You think it's just single men get horny from time to time?'

'No. I just wouldn't have thought it of you.'

Peroni let out a deep sigh. 'Remember what I told you once? Everyone's got that dark spot.'

'Not everyone lets it out.'

The big, ugly head shook slowly. 'Wrong. One way

or another they do. Whether they know it or not. Why did I do it? Won't a simple answer do? The girl was damn beautiful. Slim and young and blonde. And young. Or did I mention that? Maybe she made me feel alive again. When you've been married twenty years you forget what that's like. Yeah, before you say it, so does your wife. Blame me twice over.'

Costa said nothing, worried he might cross the line and destroy the delicate bonds the two of them had managed to build over the last few weeks.

Peroni's damaged face wrinkled some more in puzzlement at his silence. 'Oh. I get it. You're thinking, "Who does this hideous bastard think he is? Casanova?" '

'You don't look like the great Latin Lover. That's all. If you don't mind me saying so.'

'Really?'

'Really.' Costa knew what was going on here. He wondered if he dared ask.

'Are you calling me ugly? That happens from time to time, Nic. I have to tell you I don't like it.'

'No . . .' Costa stuttered. He took a good look at that battered face. 'I was just wondering.'

'What?'

'What the hell happened?'

Gianni Peroni burst out laughing. 'You kill me. You really do. In all the time I've worked here you are the first person who's come out and asked that question direct. Can you believe that?'

'Yes,' Costa said hesitantly. 'I mean, it's a personal question. And most people wouldn't like the idea that you could take it the wrong way.'

He waved a huge friendly hand in Costa's face. 'What

the hell do you mean a personal question? You guys have to look at this ugly mug every day you come to work. I got to live with it. This . . .' he pointed a fat index finger at his face, ' . . . is just a fact of life.'

Costa felt he'd made progress of a kind anyway. 'So . . . ?'

Peroni chuckled again and shook his head. 'Unbelievable. Just between the two of us, OK? This goes no further? No one knows this. Most of the guys out there think I look like this through getting into a fight with a hood or something. They wonder what the other guy looks like too. I'm happy with things that way.'

Costa nodded his agreement.

'A cop did this to me,' Peroni said. 'I was twelve years old. He was the village cop. I was the village bastard. I mean that literally. My mamma worked for the couple who owned the lone bar in town and got knocked up after the fair some time. She always was a little naïve. So I spend twelve years being the village bastard, getting the village bastard treatment all those years. Spat on. Beaten up. Laughed at in school. Then one day the moronic kid in the same class who was my principal tormentor went just a touch too far. Said something about my mamma. And I kicked the living shit out of him. First time I ever did that. You want the truth? It's the *only* time I ever did that. Don't need to now. I just look at people and go, *Boo* . . .'

Costa thought about it. 'I can believe that.'

'Good. The stupid thing was, I forgot the moron I was beating up was the village cop's kid. So Daddy comes along, and Daddy's been drinking. One thing leads to another. He gets done with the strap and he's still not happy. So he goes and gets these metal things he carries, just for protection you understand, and he puts them on his fists.'

Peroni watched the cars go by out of the window. 'I woke up in hospital two days later, face like a pumpkin, Mamma by my side. I couldn't see a thing. The first thing she says is, don't even think of telling anyone. He's the village cop. Second thing she says is, don't look in the mirror for a while.'

Costa sighed. 'You could have told someone.'

Peroni gave him a frank look. 'You're a city kid, aren't you?'

'I guess so.'

'It shows. Anyway, a couple of weeks later I come out of hospital and I notice things are different. People look at me and suddenly their eyes are on their shoes. A couple cross the road when they see me walking down the street. You know the worst thing of all? I was helping my uncle Fredo sell those pigs at weekends then. I went back to it. What else could you do? After a while he comes to me, tears in his eyes, and fires me. No one buys food from someone with a face like this. That was the worst thing of all at the time. I didn't want to do anything else when I grew up except raise those pigs and sell them every weekend. Those guys . . . they all look *so* happy. But—'

He folded his arms, leaned back in the passenger seat, and glanced at Costa to make sure this point went in. 'That was not to be. I became a cop instead. What else do you do? Partly to spite that old bastard who beat me up. But mainly, if you want to know, to even things up a little. I've never laid a finger on anyone in this job.

Never would, not unless there was a very good reason and in more than twenty years I never found one. It's a question of balance.'

Costa didn't know how to respond. 'I'm sorry, Gianni.'

'Why? I got over it years ago. You, on the other hand, have spent the last six months going loopy inside a bottle of booze. I'm sorry for you, kid.'

Maybe he deserved that. 'Fine. We're even now.'

Peroni was peering at him with those sharp, all-seeing eyes. 'I will say this once, Nic. I am starting to like you. A part of me says that I will miss this time we're spending together. Not that I wish to prolong it you understand. But let me offer some sincere advice. Stop trying to fool yourself you're something special. You're not. There are millions of people out there trying to cope with fucked-up lives. We're just two in the crowd. And after that little lecture . . .' he said, stretching up in his seat as Costa parked the car in a tiny space off the road by the ghetto, ' . . . let me make a request.'

Peroni looked into his face, hopefully. 'Cover for me. I got something important to do. I'll meet you back here at two.'

Costa didn't know what to say. Bunking off for a couple of hours wasn't unknown. He just didn't think Peroni was the kind of cop to do it.

'Anything I should know about?' he asked.

'Just personal. It's my daughter's birthday tomorrow. I wanted to send her something that might make her think her father is not quite the jerk she's come to believe. You can cope with the Campo on your own. Just don't pick on any big bastards, OK?'

Leo Falcone was reading the file on his desk, trying to focus on the case. He didn't want to rush anything. Going public too quickly only alerted those he would wish to interview, though given how leaky the Questura had proved of late they probably knew by now anyway. The pause would also give him time to turn his mind back towards work after a solitary two weeks spent at a luxury beachside hotel in Sri Lanka. He had met no one of interest, and had scarcely sought the company of others. It was an unsatisfactory, tedious respite from routine that left him mildly disturbed. He was glad to be back at his desk and with a challenging case to tackle.

Even so, a rare note of self-doubt lurked at the back of his mind. Falcone had, to his surprise, been aware of his own loneliness during the long, drab holiday. It was now five years since his divorce. There had been women in that time, attractive, interesting women. Yet none had stimulated him sufficiently to take the relationship beyond the routine round of meals, the cinema, and the physical necessity of the bedroom. He'd come to realize the previous night – when, completely out of character, he'd consumed an entire bottle of a wonderful, deeply perfumed and expensive Brunello – that there had been only two real lovers in his life: his English wife Mary, who was now back in London, pursuing a legal career; and the woman who was the reason Mary left, Rachele D'Amato.

Here, in the light of day, obscured only slightly by the remains of a hangover, lay a curious coincidence. In Sri Lanka he had thought consciously about these two women for the first time in several years. When he returned to Italy, it was to find them ready to re-enter his life. Mary had written to invite him to her marriage, to another rich English lawyer, at a country house in Kent. He would find an excuse and decline. She would, he thought, expect this. The invitation came out of politeness, nothing more. His infidelity had wounded her deeply, and her abrupt departure, without the slightest attempt at reconciliation, hurt him more than he realized at the time. Or perhaps the pain came from Rachele D'Amato, who had abandoned him with the same degree of certainty Mary had shown, and rather less grace, the moment he became free.

He'd never forgiven himself for allowing these events to happen. He never forgave them either. And now Mary was getting married, while Rachele was a successful lawyer turned investigator, steadily working her way up the ranks of the DIA, an organization which, thanks to the case Teresa Lupo had placed before him, Falcone knew he must soon approach.

His feelings about the DIA went beyond the recent sting that had wrecked Gianni Peroni's career, an exercise that was more about public relations than the defeat of organized crime. They stretched back years. There was scarcely a cop in the Questura who didn't hear those three initials and feel a small sense of dread. He realized, the moment the dead girl's identity became plain, that there could be no avoiding them. Strictly speaking he should have acted already, as soon as he realized the kind of people he would have to interview.

Falcone stared at the pages and pages of reports and tried to remember what the case was like when it was fresh. Sixteen years before he'd just been a plain detective. The inspector in charge was Filippo Mosca, an old-fashioned Rome cop who walked both sides of the track and, like many a man of his generation, made little effort to hide his friendship with people who were best avoided.

Eleanor Jamieson was reported missing on 19 March, a full two days after her American stepfather last saw her. She had just turned sixteen and had been living in Vergil Wallis's rented villa on the Aventine hill since arriving from New York the previous Christmas. The girl was English. Her mother had left Wallis a year before, after a marriage that lasted just six months. Falcone never could find out why. Nor would he. The woman killed herself in New York ten days after the disappearance of her daughter.

It was, Falcone recalled, a maddening case. Wallis was a curious man: educated, almost scholarly, yet black and originally from the ghetto. He was in his mid-forties then, vague about his business and his antecedents, a reluctant witness, unforthcoming about the girl's movements, what friends she had made in the city, any motive she might have to run away. The man had no good reason to explain why it took two days to report her absence, simply pleading that meetings had called him out of Rome. He had even seemed reluctant to hand over the few photographs he possessed, which revealed a young, naïve-looking girl, very pretty, with shoulder-length blonde hair and a ready smile. And, on her shoulder, fully revealed in a picture taken a day before she vanished, the curious tattoo, for which Wallis had no explanation. It had fascinated Falcone from the moment he saw it. There was a craze for tattoos at the time. All the rock stars and the hotshots in the movie world were doing it. But they didn't have anything like this etched into their skin. The ancient hieroglyph looked wrong on the girl, more like a branding mark than some badge of fashion.

It seemed out of character too, as much as any of them could judge. According to Wallis, Eleanor had bummed around Italy for a while then spent two weeks on an intensive Italian course at a language school near the Campo. She was an intelligent girl, with good exam grades. There was talk of her going to study at an art college in Florence later that year. She had few acquaintances beyond the school and, if Wallis was to be believed, no boyfriend, current or ex. Nothing they could turn up explained why she should suddenly disappear. She had, her stepfather said, simply set out for school on her scooter around nine on the morning of 17 March and never arrived.

It only took a couple of days for Mosca's team to acquire the sickening sense of powerlessness that comes with abduction cases. No one had seen Eleanor on her way into the city. A re-creation of her supposed last movements on TV failed to elicit a single reliable response from the public. It was as if she had existed one moment and then been abruptly removed from the face of the earth.

All along Falcone wanted to scream foul. Because something stank to high heaven and pretty soon he had an inkling what it was. Mosca had taken him to one side on the third morning and told him, in confidence, what he'd heard the previous night from a friend in the Foreign Ministry. Vergil Wallis was not, as he claimed, a straight-forward businessman from LA who loved Rome so much he was thinking of buying a second home in the city. He was a high-up figure in the West Coast mob, a black fixer who'd risen through the ranks to live in

Italy half the year for his own crooked reasons. Interpol had been following Wallis for years and steadfastly failing to bring him to justice on a wide range of counts, from racketeering to murder. Nor had the carabinieri, who had been assigned to Wallis's case, fared much better.

This was shortly before the creation of the DIA. Then, as now, the civilian state police maintained an uneasy rivalry with the carabinieri, who were part of the military. The lines of responsibility were, at best, blurred and on occasion deliberately murky. Privately Falcone was in agreement with the growing number of critics calling for a single, unified state police force. It was a logical, inevitable solution. But this was judged a heresy by those in charge of both organizations, and one that could cost a man his job. He was careful never to make his views known. They were, in any case, irrelevant. Soon the DIA came along, adding another layer of complexity to the business of chasing the swelling tide of crime that seemed to grow stronger with every passing year.

And Vergil Wallis was still free. So much for progress.

Mosca quietly closed the case of Eleanor Jamieson, marking it unworthy of further investigation without new evidence. Wallis's relationship with the Italian mobsters was far from easy. Some stories, garnered at great expense and with no small risk to those who supplied them, placed him in the role of criminal diplomat, a go-between trying to ensure the interests of his own particular buddies meshed with those of the Sicilians. It made sense to Falcone. The West Coast mob that Wallis represented was only loosely connected to the Italian organizations in the USA. There was plenty of room for misunderstandings. The bosses had learned long ago that pacts and partnerships, even with those they hated, put

DAVID HEWSON

more dollars in their bank accounts than ruthless competition and turf wars. Money was what mattered these days. No one went to the barricades over honour any more. These were practical times in which cash was king.

Falcone had been present at three different interviews with Wallis and still couldn't work out what to make of the man. The American was thoughtful and articulate, quite unlike any crook Falcone had ever met. He was well read. He knew more about ancient Roman history than some Italians. The word was that he'd been groomed for the role of diplomat for years, put through law college after rising through the black ranks in Watts. It wasn't hard to see him smoothing out the rough edges of a relationship which must always have hovered on the brink of disaster.

There was, however, one fundamental problem. If the street gossip was right, he had been given as his prime contact Emilio Neri, a brutal thug who had worked his way from the public housing slums of Testaccio to the pinnacle of the Rome mob through the vicious and heartless disposal of anyone who stood in his way. Neri now sat on the boards of opera houses in Italy and America. He lived in an elegant house in the Via Giulia, behind an army of servants and bodyguards. It was a place Falcone knew only too well from his many futile visits there. The old crook had a carefully cultivated outward appearance of elegance, a mask of deceit worn for the public. It only fooled those who were too stupid or too scared to realize the truth. Almost from the moment Falcone had joined the force he had followed Neri's career, and with good reason. The man habitually bribed any cop who would take his money, simply to put him on side. Falcone himself had turned down a thinly disguised offer of money from one of Neri's hoods in the middle of an investigation into a protection racket involving some of the smaller shops off the Corso, an assignment Filippo Mosca had closed down just when it was making progress. Three cops who were known to be on Neri's payroll had been jailed for corruption in the past decade. Not one named him as the source of the largesse found in their bank accounts. They preferred prison to the consequences of his fury.

What set Neri apart from his fellow hoods was the obsessive system of personal control he wielded over his own family. Most bosses of his stature had long since ceased to dirty their hands with the day-to-day business of running a crime organization. Neri never stepped back from the front line. It was in his blood from the old days in Testaccio. He liked it too much. Word had it he still enforced his rule in person from time to time, with the same harsh violence he'd employed as a young hood. Maybe he got one of his junior thugs to hold the poor bastard down while Neri went about his work. Falcone had looked into the old crook's dead, grey eyes often enough to understand the pleasure it would give him.

He read the last page of the report and, knowing the volatile and untrustworthy Neri as he did, understood every word. It said that Wallis and Neri had, initially, proved the best of friends. Their families had dined with each other. Six weeks before Eleanor Jamieson died, she and Wallis had spent some time on holiday with the Neri family on one of their vast estates in Sicily. Some undisclosed form of business had been done. The Americans were happy. So were the mob.

Then, around the time of the girl's disappearance, a coldness had entered the relationship. There had been reports that, while in Sicily, Wallis had gone over Neri's head to talk to some of the senior bosses there, something Neri would soon learn about. There was rumour of a drug deal that had gone wrong, leaving the Americans out of pocket and angry. Neri never could resist taking people to the limit. He skimmed every last dollar that went through his hands, even after his 'legitimate' cut.

Some huge row took place between the two men. One informer even said they came to blows. After that, they were both in trouble with their bosses. Neri was told bluntly he was losing the job of linkman with the Americans. Wallis got a dressing-down too, though he continued to live in Rome for half of the year, with precious little to do except save face. It was an uneasy truce. One of Wallis's lieutenants was murdered two months later, his throat cut in a car close to a Testaccio brothel. Not long after, a cop on Neri's payroll was found dead in what had been made to look like suicide. Falcone wondered, was there a link here? Would the semi-mummified body of a sixteen-year-old girl raise these old ghosts from their graves? And if it did, how different would the world be now, with the DIA peering inquisitively over his shoulder every step of the way?

Leo Falcone looked at his watch. It was just after twelve. He thought of all the careful protocols which surrounded cases involving known mobsters. Then he took out his diary and placed the call.

'Yes?'

Rachele D'Amato's cool, distanced voice still had the power to move him. Falcone wondered briefly whether he was phoning her for the sake of the job or for more personal reasons. Both, he thought. Both were legitimate too.

'I wondered whether you'd be there. Everyone else I call right now seems to be at home, sick in bed.'

She paused. 'I don't get to bed as much as I used to, Leo. Sick or not.'

There was a deliberate, slow certainty to her voice. Falcone understood what she was saying, or thought he did. No one else had filled her life after the affair ended. He knew that already. He'd checked from time to time.

'I was wondering if you had time for lunch,' he said. 'It's been too long.'

'Lunch!' She sounded pleased. 'What a surprise. When?'

'Today. The wine bar we used to go to. I was there the other evening. They have a new white from Tuscany. You should try it.'

'I don't take wine at lunchtimes. That's for cops. Besides, I have an appointment. I have to run. We've got people sick everywhere too.'

'Tonight then. After work.'

'Work stops for you in the evenings these days, Leo?' she sighed. 'What happened?'

'Nothing,' he said. 'I just thought . . .'

He felt tongue-tied, embarrassed. She'd always said it was the work that drove them apart after Mary left. It wasn't. It was him. His possessiveness. His passion for her, which was never quite returned.

'Don't apologize,' she said wryly. 'It doesn't stop for me either. Not any more.'

'I'm sorry.'

'There's no need,' she said, and there was a new note

in her voice. A serious, professional one. 'You have a body. Is it Wallis's girl?'

'Yes,' he sighed, inwardly livid, wondering immediately who had talked.

'Don't sound so cross, Leo. I have a job to do too.'

The corpse had been lying in the morgue for two weeks. Anyone could have seen the tattoo and put two and two together. It would be impossible to find out who had blabbed.

'Of course. You're very good these days, Rachele.'

'Thank you.'

He wondered why fate had made him fall in love with two lawyers. Why not women who were a little less curious? A little more forgiving?

'Then we'll meet,' she announced. 'I'll call you. I have to go now.'

She didn't even ask if it was convenient for him. Rachele never changed.

'Leo?'

He knew what she'd say. 'Yes.'

'This is professional. Nothing more. You do understand that?'

Leo Falcone understood, though it didn't stop him hoping.

Costa crossed the busy road and headed for the Campo dei Fiori, reminding himself he used to live here and there were memories, important ones, pieces of his personality stamped on the place. He missed the Campo from time to time. He was an innocent when he lived here, young and unbruised by the world. There'd been fleeting relationships, brief flings which Gianni Peroni probably wouldn't count as love affairs at all. There was the place too. The cobbled *piazza* was grubby at the best of times. The market attracted too many tourists. The prices were higher than elsewhere. Nevertheless, it was a genuine part of Rome, a living, human community that had never been dislodged from its natural home. As always, he got a small rush of pleasure when he walked along the Via dei Giubbonari and came out onto the square. The stalls were still doing good business, selling spring greens, chicory, calabrese and cavolo nero alongside vibrant oranges from Sicily, stored over the cold months and now fit for little more than juice. The mushroom stand was piled high with all kinds of funghi, fresh chiodini, dried porcini. The handful of fishmongers tucked into one corner had scallops and giant prawns, turbot and sacks of fresh mussels. He worked his way through, picking up an etto of wild rocket and the same of agretti for later. Then he added a chunk of parmesan from the lone alimentari van.

'We got good prosciutto, Mr Policeman,' the woman said, recognizing him. 'Here . . .'

She held out a pink strand, waving it in front of his face. If he ate meat, Nic Costa thought he'd be hard pressed to find much better in Rome. 'I'll pass.'

'Vegetarianism is an unnatural fad,' the woman declared. 'You come back here one day when you've got time and we'll go through this in some detail. You worry me.'

'Please,' Costa said. 'I have enough people worrying about me just now.'

'Means there's something wrong.'

He took the prosciutto anyway. When she was out of sight he gave it to the scruffy young boy belonging to the Kosovan who was always begging in the square, playing an ancient violin badly. Then he handed the father a ten-euro note. It was a ritual he'd forgotten somewhere along the line too: twice a day, every day, as his late father had always told him. Being back in the Campo reminded him why it was necessary. He'd been spending too much time on his own, closeted inside the farmhouse on the outskirts of the city, thinking. Sometimes you had to get out and let life happen to you.

He'd just pushed his way through the crowd at Il Forno and was taking a bite of pizzetta bianca, salty and straight from the oven, when he saw what was happening. Leo Falcone was right. The Campo attracted tourists, and with the tourists came trouble. Pickpockets. Conmen. Worse sometimes. The police always had people on duty there, in uniform and out. The carabinieri liked the place too, parking their bright shiny Alfas in the most awkward of places and then lounging on the bonnets, eyeing the crowds through expensive sunglasses, trying to look cool in their dark, well-pressed uniforms.

Costa made a point of avoiding the carabinieri as much as possible. There was enough rivalry inside the Questura itself without extending it to these soldiers masquerading as cops. The demarcation lines were dimly drawn between this branch of the army and the civilian police. They could arrest the same people he did, and in the same places. Most of the time it was simply a matter of who got there first. There was an old joke: the good-looking ones joined the carabinieri for the uniform and the women, the smart and the ugly ones went into the state police because that was all they could get. It wasn't all exaggeration either.

A couple of carabinieri were in the Campo now, standing stiffly upright by their vehicle as a slender blonde woman harangued them in mangled Italian, wagging her finger in their faces, holding a large, portrait-size photograph in her left hand.

'Don't get involved,' Costa said to himself, and wandered over towards them in any case. The woman was livid. She knew a few good Italian swear words too. Costa took a bite of his bread and eavesdropped on what was going on.

Then he looked at the photo in the woman's hand and something cold ran down his back, made him shiver so hard the pizzetta dropped straight from his fingers.

This was crazy. He knew it. The face in the photo reminded him of the picture Leo Falcone had thrown onto the strange corpse on Teresa Lupo's dissecting table that morning. He thought of what he had seen there: an old image of a blonde-haired girl looking distinctly like the face he saw now, still at the beginning of her adult life, thinking there was nothing in the future but love and joy.

And it ain't necessarily so, an old, old song sang at the back of his head.

The carabinieri were the pick of the crop. Prize assholes, more interested in keeping their Ray-Bans clean than working out what seemed to have happened in front of their very noses. He thought he recognized one. But maybe not. They all looked the same. These two sounded the same as well, with their middle-class nasal voices.

They were sneering at the woman in front of them, exuding boredom.

'Are you listening to me?' she yelled.

'Do we have a choice?' one of them, the older one, Costa guessed, replied. He couldn't have been more than thirty.

'This,' she said, pointing at the photograph, 'is my daughter. She just got abducted. You idiots watched it and yawned.'

The younger uniform shot Costa a warning glance that said: *don't even think about getting involved*. Nic Costa didn't move.

The talkative one leaned back on the Alfa, shuffled his serge-clad backside further up the shiny bonnet, took out a packet of gum and threw a stick past his perfect teeth.

She stood in front of them, hands on her hips, full of fury. Costa glanced at the photo she was holding. They could have been sisters, but ten or fifteen years apart. The woman was a touch heavier. Her hair was a shade darker, more fair than her daughter's bright, almost artificial, blonde, practical cut.

He walked over, watched her trying to get her breath back, then, struggling to remember his English, asked, 'Can I help?'

'No,' the senior uniform said immediately. 'You can just walk away and mind your own business.'

She looked up at Costa, relieved to be talking English at last. 'You can get me a real policeman. That would be helping.'

He pulled out the badge. 'I am a real policeman. Nic Costa.'

'Oh fuck,' the uniform with the working mouth muttered behind him.

He got up off the car and stood upright in front of Costa. He was a lot taller. 'Her teenage daughter ran off with a boyfriend on a motorbike here. She thinks that counts as abduction. We think that sounds like some young kid looking for fun.' The Ray-Bans cast the woman a dead, black look. 'We think that's understandable. If you people playing amateur hour think otherwise, please yourself. Take her as a present from me. But just take her. I beg you.'

Costa managed to grasp her arm lightly at the elbow as it moved towards the man. Otherwise, he thought, the moron in the dark uniform would have been in for a shock.

'You saw this?' he asked them.

The younger one found his voice. 'Yeah, we saw it. Hard to miss it. You'd think the kid wanted the whole world to watch. You have any idea what you see if you hang around the Campo day and night? Caught a couple hard at it a few days ago. In broad daylight. And she wants us to start jumping up and down just because her daughter's got on the back of some guy's bike.'

The woman shook her head, as if somehow angry with herself, then stared in the direction of the Corso, the way the bike had gone, Costa guessed.

'It's not like her,' she said. 'I can't believe this is happening. I can't believe you people won't even listen.'

She closed her eyes. Costa wondered if she were about to cry. He looked at his watch. Peroni would be back at the car in forty minutes. There was time.

'Let me buy you a coffee,' he said.

She hesitated then put the photo back in the envelope.

There was a stack of others there, Costa saw, and he wondered again: was he really letting his imagination run away with him? The girl looked so like the teenager in Falcone's picture.

'You really are the same as these people?' she asked.

'No,' he replied, and made sure they heard every word. 'I'm a civilian. It's complicated. Even for us sometimes.'

She dropped the envelope into her bag and slung it over her shoulder. 'Then I'll take that coffee.'

'Nice job,' Costa said and patted the senior uniform on his serge arm. 'I love to see the carabinieri do public relations. Makes our life so much easier.'

Then, ignoring the torrent of curses directed at his back, he took her arm and led her away from them. She was pleased to go. When her face lost its taut anxiety she looked different. She'd dressed down, in jeans and an old, bleached denim jacket. But it didn't fit somehow. It was almost a disguise. There was something alluring, almost elegant underneath, something he couldn't quite put his finger on.

Costa led her round the corner, to a tiny café in an alcove behind the square. There were pots of creamed coffee on the counter, with people ladling spoonfuls into their cups to beef up the caffeine. She leaned on the counter, looking as if she came into the place every day.

'My name's Miranda Julius,' she said. 'And this is crazy. Maybe *I'm* crazy. You'll regret ever asking me here.'

Costa listened as she told her story, slowly, methodically, with the kind of care and attention he wished he heard more often.

'What's the matter?' she asked when the story was finished.

'Nothing.'

She stared into his face with a frank curiosity. 'I don't think so.'

He thought about what she'd said. Maybe the girl really had just run away with a boyfriend her mother had never even met. Maybe it was all as innocent as that. Her misgivings were based on intuition, not fact. She just felt something was wrong. He could understand why the assholes from the carabinieri just wanted to send her on her way.

'You said she came back yesterday with a tattoo.'

'Stupid, stupid. Just another reason for an argument. It wasn't supposed to be like this. It wasn't why we came to Italy.' She shook her head and it annoyed him he couldn't stop watching her. Close up she was older than he first thought. There were stress lines at the corner of her bright, intelligent blue eyes. But they just added character to a face that, when she was young, must have been too perfectly pretty for its own good. She looked like a model who'd later taken up manual labour or something just to make life more interesting, just to get a few scars.

'What was it like?'

'The tattoo? Ridiculous. What do you expect from a sixteen-year-old? She had it done a couple of days ago apparently. It was only yesterday she plucked up the courage to tell me, when the scars had healed. She said it was his idea. Whoever *he* is. But she liked it, naturally. Do you want to see?'

'What?'

She reached into her bag and withdrew the folder of

photos. 'I took a picture, just for the record. I had the film developed this morning which is why I have all this stuff with me. Taking pictures is what I do, by the way. Call it an obsession.'

She sorted through a set of photos then threw one on the table. It was a close-up of the girl's shoulder. There was the dark black ink of a tattoo at the top of her arm, and the howling face.

'You know what that is?' he asked.

'She told me. A theatre mask or something. If it was the Grateful Dead I might have understood. She wasn't that pleased when I said I wanted a shot of it for the record.'

She stared into his eyes with a sudden, determined frankness. 'I wasn't taking no for an answer. A tattoo. Jesus, if I'd done that when I was her age.' She hesitated. 'Mr Costa?'

'Nic.'

'What's wrong?'

'I don't know. I need to call some people. Give me a minute.'

She was starting to look scared.

'It's probably nothing,' he said, and heard how lame the words sounded.

Miranda Julius rented an apartment on the top floor of the Teatro di Marcello, the sprawling, fortress-like complex in the shadow of the Capitol Hill. She'd taken the place over the internet, she said, because the owner offered a good deal for the couple of months they needed, and it came with history. Though much changed over the centuries, the theatre was begun by Julius

Caesar, finished by his adoptive son Augustus and used variously as a fortress and a private palace before it was converted into private accommodations. The apartment looked out towards the river and Tiber Island. The steady drone of traffic was audible through the thick, double-glazed windows. Nic Costa had walked past this building countless times and never seen inside. Now he was there he didn't envy anyone who owned such a fancy address. It was too noisy, too detached from the city. It was in Rome, but not a part of it.

He was worried, too, that he'd over-reacted. He'd called in Falcone without discussing the matter with Peroni, which was probably a mistake. His partner had turned up only to find events shaping around him. Costa had risked Falcone's wrath even further by inviting Teresa Lupo along to join them. It seemed important. Teresa had read the book she kept quoting at them in the morgue. If he was right, she was the only one with immediate access to the research and insight they needed. Now the four of them sat listening to Miranda Julius, each wondering whether this could be coincidence.

Miranda Julius and her daughter Suzi had arrived in Rome one week before from London. She was a news photographer based there but working on assignment anywhere the agency sent her. Suzi lived with her grand-mother, and had for most of her life. She was studying art at a local college. Her mother had taken her out of class for two months on a kind of 'get-to-know-you' holiday in Rome. Suzi had enrolled at the language school in the Piazza della Cancelleria for Italian lessons – the same school that the dead Eleanor Jamieson had attended. The two of them had begun a round of the

Rome galleries in their spare time. After a few days Suzi had made a friend. Not at the school, but somewhere nearby. A boy, she said, and one who was reluctant, at the time, to meet her mother, for reasons Miranda could only guess.

'How old is she?' Falcone asked.

'She was sixteen in December.'

'And you?' Falcone persisted.

Teresa risked glaring at him. Falcone was always direct with women, direct to the point of bullying.

'I'm thirty-three, inspector,' Miranda said immediately. 'Yes, I'm sure you're doing your arithmetic already. I was at school when I got pregnant. The father was a jerk. He was gone before she was born.' She had an upper-class English accent which sat uneasily with her crumpled, laid-back appearance. There was money somewhere. The apartment must have cost her plenty.

'Is this relevant?' she asked. 'I don't mind answering these questions but I would like to know why.'

'When you have a missing teenager anything could be relevant,' Costa said.

She turned away from Falcone and stared out of the big windows, out at the traffic roar. 'If she is missing. Perhaps I am overreacting. She could walk right in that door any moment and then how am I going to feel?' She watched them. This was a show of false confidence, Costa thought. There was fear in her face although he couldn't help wondering how responsible he was for placing it there. 'Will you please tell me why you're suddenly taking this so seriously?'

Falcone ignored the question. 'The tattoo. Tell us about that.'

The point of the question was lost on her. 'What's

there to tell? I noticed she'd been wearing long sleeves all the time. Then yesterday she just comes out and announces it. *He* told her to get one. He even suggested what it should be like, took her down some stupid tattoo parlour he knew. Paid for the thing, would you believe.'

'Does he have a name?' Costa wondered. 'Did she say where he lived?'

She shook her head. 'Apparently she wasn't ready for him to meet me. Not just yet.'

'Why? Did she give a reason?'

'She's still a kid. Young even for her years. She's still at the stage where a parent's embarrassing. What was I supposed to do? It wasn't as if she was spending the night with him or anything. And that's what's really strange. Look, I'm never going to win mother of the year contest. Most of the time Suzi's been growing up I've been in some shit part of the world photographing dead people. But I know my daughter. We can talk to each other. She wasn't sleeping with this boy. Not yet. It was as if they were waiting for something. In fact . . .'

She hesitated, wondering whether this was going too far, ' . . . she's never slept with anyone. She's a virgin. Her decision. Perhaps she looked at me and realized where it could get you.'

'Waiting for what?' Falcone asked.

'If I knew that I'd tell you,' she snapped. 'But I'm sure of one thing. When. It happens in two days' time. March the 17th. I heard her talking on the phone. Making arrangements to meet him. She sounded excited. Not that she'd talk to me about it, of course.'

Costa thought about the date. There were too many coincidences. 'Can we take a look in her room?'

'Feel free. It's the tidy one at the end.'

Falcone nodded at Costa. Teresa got up and followed him without being asked. The two of them wandered down the corridor, listening to Falcone's persistent drone continue to wear at Miranda Julius behind them. Costa couldn't help glancing into what he assumed was Miranda Julius's bedroom. It wasn't the tidy one. There were clothes scattered everywhere, a couple of professional-looking cameras, and a notebook computer, open, ready for work.

'Jesus,' Teresa groaned, when they were out of earshot. 'That man has the manners of a warthog. Can you believe he ever got married? What are we looking for, Nic? Why am I here for God's sake? It's a missing kid, isn't it?'

'I'm sorry. I thought you might like the opportunity to do a little cop work.'

She came to a halt, giving him a filthy look. 'I've got a corpse half finished back in the morgue. One that looks two thousand years old but only went in the ground sixteen years ago. I've got scientific problems with names you couldn't even pronounce. And you think I might "like the opportunity"?'

He opened the door to the girl's room. 'You want to look or don't you?'

'Lemme in.' She barged through and stared at the contents. Then she carefully closed the door behind her, not wanting to hear Falcone's voice, needing the privacy herself too. 'This is a teenager's room? Hell, my place is worse than this. Come to that . . .' She was thinking on her feet. Costa always liked to watch this. ' . . . how come the mother looks like that? Like the kid's sister? She's just a year younger than me, for God's sake, and if you walked her through the Questura every last jack-ass in there would be clutching at his groin making those heavy breathing noises you like so much.'

'They'd do that for you if they thought you wouldn't hit them.'

She glared at him. 'You couldn't stop staring at her. I couldn't help noticing that.'

He ignored the remark and went over to the table by the girl's single bed. There was a portfolio of photographs, black and white, printed in large format. He flicked through them: images from every war that had made the headlines in the last decade, Afghanistan, Palestine, Rwanda, places in Africa he couldn't begin to identify. Teresa came to join him.

'Is that what she meant?' she asked. 'When she said she went around photographing dead people?'

'She's a war photographer apparently.'

Corpses lay still on the ground, broken, bloody. Lost children, their eyes like saucers, stared back at them from the prints. 'Makes my job look kind of normal,' Teresa said. 'What drives you to that kind of work? Particularly when you've got a kid waiting at home?'

'I don't know.' Were the photos in the daughter's room because Suzi liked them? Or because she kept asking herself that question too? There was something complicated going on here, he thought.

'If I had a mother who took photos like that I'd maybe think of running away myself,' Teresa said carefully. 'You understand what I'm saying?'

He'd done plenty of missing kid inquiries. He knew what they felt like. And it wasn't like this. 'Of course I do. Half the time the kids aren't running towards something; they're running from it. Do you really think that's what's happening here? They're on holiday, Teresa. I've dealt with more runaways than I can remember. I don't recall one of them ever being a foreign tourist.'

'Point taken,' she said quietly. 'All the same—'

There was a pile of family snaps on the bedside table. Miranda Julius did take them all the time. Most were of the girl, looking lovely, happy. A few were taken by someone else, a stranger perhaps, or a waiter. There they were outside the Villa Borghese, on the Spanish Steps, eating pizza, laughing. Nic Costa looked at them and felt a pang of guilt. If he was right, Suzi Julius could be in big trouble right now, trouble that would bring her mother pain and possibly grief, whatever the outcome. Pictures spoke, they told stories. These two were close. They loved each other.

Teresa was staring at them too. 'Nice photographs,' she said simply. 'Nice to know she doesn't just snap dead people.'

For a moment he wondered: was there a small, bitter note inside Teresa Lupo's voice, whispering: *Look on with envy, because you'll never know this, you'll never feel the joy or the pain?*

'Can you imagine the feeling of responsibility?' she asked. 'What it must be like? Knowing someone else depends on you that much?'

He thought of his own dead father. He did know it, but only from the point of view of the dependant.

'You can see it on her face,' she continued. 'Whatever happened, whether there was a row or not, she's just sitting in there asking herself, "Is there something I could have done?"'

'It's always like that,' he said by way of an explanation. 'You're a pathologist. It's just that you don't see it.'

She toyed with one of the best photos: the two of

them laughing in a pale winter sun on the Ponte Sisto. 'Just because it's always like that doesn't make it any easier.'

'No.' He wondered if the resemblance was just his memory playing tricks. It was hard to compare this living, breathing kid with the mahogany corpse on the silver table. 'Does she really look like the dead girl? Or is that my imagination? Could the resemblance have sparked something? Made whoever was responsible sixteen years ago suddenly get the itch again?'

Teresa shrugged. 'Pushing it a bit, isn't it? She's blonde, pretty and young, if that's what you mean. From the pictures I'd say she's a bit on the thin side for most Italians. The mother's more our size. I wish. Nic, there are skinny blonde kids in Rome all the time. Why would it take sixteen years for him to run across one again? Face it. She's probably just one more runaway kid.'

He looked at the scattering of disjointed facts that faced them. 'I don't think so. It feels wrong. What the hell does it all mean? What does it say in that book you read? What exactly happens? Where do they get their victims from?'

'They're not victims, Nic,' she insisted. 'If you think that you're misreading everything. What happened to them was a privilege, even if it didn't feel like it at the time.'

'Unless it went wrong,' he reminded her.

'Unless it went wrong. But that can't have happened often. These girls were gifts. Some of them were slaves handed over by their owners. Some were daughters led there by their own fathers. They went through the ritual. They came out changed. Acolytes of the god, remember. That must have meant something.'

'But what?' he muttered. 'I still think this feels wrong.'

'Don't ask me. I'm a pathologist. Not an archaeologist. Or a cop. Or a psychic for that matter. Listen to yourself. *It feels wrong.* Are you really going to go back out there and tell Falcone that?'

Yet he felt sure she had seen some kind of link too. He could recognize it in her face, the bright spark of intelligence mixed with the dread of what that new information could mean.

'You're the only person I have right now who's researched all this. Please—'

She sat down and sighed. 'Don't do this to me, Nic. Don't take what I say as gospel. I don't like being imprecise. I'm trained for the opposite.'

'Just point me somewhere. I'll check it out. I promise. Tell me more about this ritual.'

'All I know is what I read. The ceremony was about the initiation of chosen girls into adulthood. On one particular day: 17 March. Sounds familiar? This was party time. There'd be men there, for sure. Priests, hangers-on, hoping they could get in on the fun. They drank, they danced, they swallowed every ancient Roman narcotic they could find. Then they did tricks to each other that would make a bunch of Hell's Angels walk out of the room feeling things were going a little too far. But this was about the girls. It was about giving them something they could use in adulthood. An advantage, maybe. Or some kind of membership of a club they could use later on.'

Costa stared at her, expecting more. 'Look,' she said. 'The man who wrote the thing said himself it's all guesswork. No one really knows what happened. All they know is that it got out of hand sometimes. It got bad enough for the Romans to ban it after a while. Long before the Christians came along with peace and love. It was all too much for them. They just carted off the organizers, put them to death somewhere, then relaunched the thing as some toned-down happy-clappy ceremony called the Liberalia. The same kind of stunt they pulled off to wind up with Christmas, if you recall. What preceded it? Who knows?'

He tried to make sense of this. 'So maybe two thousand years later someone's playing the same tricks? Using the same rituals?'

'We don't know that. All you've got is a tattoo. A date—'

'And a dead body.'

She tried to look hopeful. 'Which has no connection whatsoever with this girl. Be honest with yourself. The mother's probably right. The kid'll walk back in with a certain smile on her face thinking, "Thank Christ I got that out of the way". Jesus, a virgin at sixteen. What kind of lives do these people lead?'

He wasn't listening. He was doing the cop thing – opening drawers, looking into the contents, only with a touch more respect than most of them had. Nic Costa didn't up-end the things and turn the stuff out onto the floor. He just sifted carefully, as if he felt he were intruding.

'Do you realize,' she said out of nowhere, 'that if I meet someone now and we have a kid, when that kid is Suzi Julius's age I will be turned fifty? My God, who's the virgin here?'

Costa opened the bottom drawer, slid his hand beneath a neatly folded nightdress and stared up at her.

'What?' she said.

He took out a couple of items: obscure things, hidden, wrong.

One was the stalk of some plant, dried. A pine cone was attached to the thinner end, clinging clumsily to the stump, held there with tape. It looked like a schoolkid's craft project.

'She was working out how to make it,' Teresa said glumly.

'The name again?' he asked.

'Thyrsus.' She took it from him and sniffed the stem, her face deadly serious all of a sudden. 'That's fennel. Just like the one from the peat.'

'And this?' It was a plastic bag, full of seeds. Costa smelled the contents. 'It's not dope.'

'Not ordinary dope.'

She looked inside the bag, deeply miserable.

'Teresa?'

'I found something similar in the dead girl's pockets. I'm waiting for the full lab report. From my limited culinary expertise I'd say it's a mixture of herb seeds. Cumin. Coriander. Fennel again. Something hallucinogenic too maybe. Something fungal. Magic mushroom in all probability.'

He waited, wondering how she knew.

'According to the book it was part of the ritual. A small gift from the god. A thank you for what he was about to get in return.'

'Which was?'

She was silent.

'Guess,' he said. 'Give me some female intuition.'

'If you got it right? Paradise. You lost your virginity, probably to some temple creep wearing that spooky mask from the tattoo just to look the part. This was about ecstasy. Physical ecstasy. Mental, spiritual—'

She screwed up her eyes, thinking, remembering. 'The book said that, in public, 17 March was the day Roman boys attained their manhood. In private the women achieved some special kind of status too. At least the ones who were hanging round the cult.'

'And if you got it wrong? If you said no . . . ?'

'Then I guess you met one very angry god.' She hesitated. 'You really believe this poor kid's a part of all this? And she thinks she's just playing some game?'

He looked at the home-made wand and the little bag of seeds. 'It's a possibility, surely? We can't ignore it.'

'There's not enough here to push any of Falcone's buttons.'

She was right. These were just coincidental wisps of smoke in some distant, hazy mirrors. There was nothing to suggest an answer to the biggest question of all: why her? Why an English kid who'd only been in Rome a week?

They returned to the living room. Miranda Julius was red-faced and puffy-eyed. Falcone must have been working her hard. She looked at them as they came in and read their faces instantly.

'What is it?' she asked.

Costa showed her the thyrsus and the packet of seeds. 'Have you seen these before? Do you know what they are?'

She looked at them and shook her head. 'I've no idea. Where did you find them?'

'In her bedroom,' Costa replied.

'What *are* they?' She could be crying again soon.

'It could be coincidence,' Costa said.

'It could be anything,' Falcone interjected. 'We'll log your daughter's disappearance, Mrs Julius. We'll circulate her description. Usually these cases end with the child coming home. Usually they'll call. Probably today.'

'Look,' Teresa interjected, 'there's time. There are a lot of loose ends to work on here. If . . .'

Falcone stood up, glowering at her. She knew when to shut up.

'Doctor,' he grunted. 'Here's the deal. I don't go around cutting up bodies. You don't go around interrogating potential witnesses.'

Costa thought, for one moment, she might hit him and wondered what would happen after that. Instead Teresa went over to Miranda Julius, sat next to her on the sofa and put an arm around her shoulders.

Falcone led Costa and Peroni away from the women.

'This is serious,' Costa said. 'I know it looks odd but—'

'Don't tell me my job,' Falcone said curtly. 'We've got one clear-cut case of murder and one missing teenager to add to the scores we get every week. There's nothing that links them. Nothing you can count on. Be honest, Nic. If there were . . .'

Costa looked at Falcone. He wished the inspector wouldn't play his cards so close to his chest so often. It was coincidence. But that didn't mean they should reject it.

'We could hand out her picture to the media,' Costa suggested.

'And say what?' Falcone asked. 'This is a girl who hasn't been seen by her mother since this morning? Do you want us to look like fools?'

'I don't care what we look like.'

Peroni patted Costa on the back. 'Think about it, Nic. What's there to go on?'

'Circulate the girl's picture internally,' Falcone ordered, walking for the door, watching Teresa Lupo glower at him from the sofa, her arms still round the mother. 'Make sure it gets seen all round. And pull out whatever CCTV footage we've got of the Campo. We can look at that later. You could be right, Nic. I just don't feel ready to jump straight in at the moment. Beside, we've got an appointment.' He scowled at Costa. 'And note that word "we". Keep your friend from the morgue out of this. She's got other work to do.'

These days when Emilio Neri went out on his rounds he left most of the muscle work to Bruno Bucci, a muscular thirty-year-old hood from Turin. Bucci had been on the payroll since he was a teenager running dope dealers around Termini Station. Neri liked him, as an employee and as a man. He was taciturn, loyal and dogged. He knew when to talk and when to shut up. He never came back until the job was done, whatever it took. If Neri felt like slapping someone around person-ally, Bucci didn't mind holding the yo-yo still, making sure he didn't get any stupid ideas just because the individual rearranging his face was pushing sixty-six and wheezing and croaking like a set of malodorous old bellows.

Sometimes Neri wondered why Mickey hadn't turned out this way. If that had happened, he'd feel a whole lot easier about what would become of his empire when he was too old to stay in the driving seat. Which could be sooner rather than later the way he was starting to feel.

It wasn't a question of age. Neri felt sure he could carry on for a good decade more without handing over the reins. Something else, boredom maybe, or a sense of being out of place, bothered him. The big house, the servants, even Adele lounging around like a pampered plaything . . . all these accoutrements of wealth and power now seemed unreal, almost improper, silky bars for a prison that threatened to drown him in luxury.

He ought to be thinking about the transition. He knew that. The problem was Mickey's character. The kid did as he was told, mostly, but he was always chasing something on the side too, pursuing private scams that he liked to keep to himself. Neri had found himself forced to clean up this kind of mess – dope, women, money – too often. Mickey never lied when confronted like that. Neri just had to know to ask the right questions. He could put up with that when Mickey was twenty. Now it was getting tedious. Maybe there was some kind of a trade-off he could work. Bucci got to run the business, Mickey could sit back and take his cut from the proceeds.

Neri thought about this from Bucci's point of view. He knew what any decent working-class hood with ambition would do in that position. Wait till the old man was out of the way then take the lot, leaving the spoilt brat to drive a cab or wake up dead one morning more likely. Maybe that was the way of the world, Neri reasoned. He'd have done the same. Families were imperfect entities. Nothing said they had to last forever.

They spent the morning chasing up debts around the city, Neri fuming all the time about the way Mickey and Adele squabbled in his presence, wondering whether he ought to punish them both. He couldn't get them out of his head and he couldn't figure out why. His mind wasn't as quick as it used to be. Was there something going on that he should have seen? Some new scheme of Mickey's? He sat back in the rear seat of the armoured Mercedes and closed his eyes, wishing to hell he didn't have to worry about those two constantly. The bitch ran up a small fortune on credit cards. He footed every penny of the gigantic bills that fell through the door each month. Mickey was no better. The kid seemed consumed with a desire to own anything that possessed an internal combustion engine. He'd been through four sports cars in as many months, dabbled with a plethora of two-wheeled vehicles and was only cut short from buying a four-seat Piper Comanche when the owner of the flying school discreetly rang Neri on his mobile to warn him of the deal his son was trying to nail down. Then there were the women. All shapes, all sizes. All colours, all backgrounds. The only thing they had in common was the money they consumed with a vengeance, and none of that was Mickey's.

In his own way, Neri loved them both. Or, more accurately he thought, enjoyed owning them, having them dependent upon him in every way. In return they were supposed to stick to the rules, and one of those was never to display their antipathy towards each other in his presence. But they just couldn't bring themselves to do that one small thing and the resentment he felt was growing by the minute, making it impossible for Neri to concentrate on the work in front of him. On one occasion he broke off from watching Bucci beat the shit out of some cheating Termini pimp to call Mickey and find out what the louse was doing to earn his keep. All he got was the recorded message from the mobile.

Later he'd got Bucci to pin down Toni Lucarelli, a Trastevere bar-keeper who was siphoning off the dough Neri
was due in order to pay for some piece of Algerian skirt
on the other side of town. Neri punched Lucarelli a few
times in the face, not hard, because his heart wasn't in
it. Lucarelli was a nice guy. He just wanted more fun
than his wallet allowed.

Then the stupid bar-keeper spoiled everything by
breaking down and blubbing instead of taking it like a
man. Neri wanted to let the big guy from Turin loose
on the jerk, crying like a baby there in the storeroom of
his crummy little bar. But he couldn't get the picture
of Adele out of his head: cold, heartless Adele, who knew
more tricks than a woman of her age ought to, looking
down on his son like he was nothing, so cold it was
deliberate, as if she were laughing about something. He
told Bucci to rough up Lucarelli just a little then called
her and didn't get through there either. It was a great
day. Life would be so simple if he didn't have to go
around like this, with a bodyguard dogging his footsteps
all the time. You couldn't be the boss and expect not to
have enemies. All the same, sometimes it made life hell.

Neri didn't beat up anyone else after that. He just let
them look at Bucci and ask themselves how it would
feel. At lunchtime, when he'd had what was supposed
to be his pleasure, he called in to see an old friend on
the staff at the Vatican. They talked about a different
side to Neri's business: offshore funds and tax havens,
covert bank transfers and double taxation schemes. Then
they ate lunch in a small *trattoria* around the corner,
one run by a man Neri had once employed, so he never
ever paid the bill. The man from the Vatican skulked off
back to work after a single plate of spaghetti carbonara,

worrying he'd been seen. Neri hung on for some lamb with chicory and then *zabaglione* and still he couldn't get Mickey and Adele out of his mind.

Then came the phone call about what was happening in the Questura. He tried to cast his mind back sixteen years. He made some notes on the little pad he kept inside his jacket pocket: names, events, people to call. Everything went into the book. He needed it all the time these days. His memory wasn't what it was.

'To hell with it,' he grunted, staring at the empty plates in front of him. 'It's history. I am too old and too rich to let this shit get me down.'

When he came out into the side street close to the Piazza del Risorgimento Bruno Bucci was sitting on the wall next to the black Mercedes looking odd. Neri finally worked out what it was. There was emotion on his large, featureless face. He was pissed off.

Neri walked over and sat next to him on the brickwork. It was a nice day. Spring was working its way into the world. There was some blue sky, a touch of heat. Pretty girls walked by in dresses that had some colour. Some of them had long, brown legs. They got fake tans these days, he guessed, or maybe their boyfriends took them to the Caribbean for some sun and plenty of bedroom stuff. There'd been a time when Emilio Neri felt sufficiently free of the shackles of labour to do the same himself.

'Car's fucked,' Bucci said. 'Won't start.'

Neri shook his head and stared at the big, black hunk of metal. 'All that money. And what does it get you? Why do I bother with this?'

'I phoned the garage. They said two hours. Tomorrow I'm going to go round. Explain a few things in person.'

Neri looked into Bucci's brown eyes. Most of the time they appeared dead but that was just an act. Bucci was a smart guy. He didn't miss a trick.

'You do that,' he said, patting one of his big knees. 'Tell you what. Life's too short for this crap. Take the afternoon off. We're done. It's spring. Go back and see that pimp. Tell him he should give you a little something extra, keep us sweet.'

Bucci twisted inside his tight grey suit. 'That's nice, boss. But I don't need that kind of thing. Not now. Not that I don't appreciate the offer.'

Neri looked at him and thought again of Mickey. 'You're some guy, Bruno. I like the fact you're working for me.'

'Me too. Let me find a cab. I'll bring it round here. Go back with you.'

'No!' Neri laughed. 'I meant what I said. It's spring. Wake up a little. Feel alive. I'm done chasing debts for the day. Bores me stupid sometimes. You go enjoy yourself. Take some chick out this evening. On me.'

'That's kind of you,' Bucci answered. His brown eyes were dead again. 'But I'm not supposed to leave you on your own.'

Neri's face fell into a scowl. 'What're you talking about? You make me sound like some old cripple or something? You think I can't look after myself?'

Bucci was worried. 'No, boss. It's just . . . you always said . . .'

'Fuck what I always said! I'm saying something different now. Who the hell's gonna try something on me here anyway? Also, the way I intend to go home—' Neri grinned. 'A man's gotta feel free sometimes, Bruno. You understand that?'

'How're you getting home?'

'A unique form of transport. I'm going to catch a bus from round that corner. I want to look in the eyes of a few strangers, try to see what makes them tick. Haven't done that in years. It's a mistake. You get isolated. You forget how to read people.'

'A bus?' Bucci repeated.

'Yeah. Why not?'

Neri hesitated. He hated throwing his personal problems onto other people. 'You mind if I ask you something?'

'No.'

'That stupid kid of mine, Mickey. And Adele. What do you think I should do about them, huh? They're driving me crazy.'

Bruno Bucci shuffled uncomfortably on the wall. Neri watched him, wondering at the discomfort a few simple words could cause, not quite sure he could believe the slight flush that was creeping up the cheeks of the man from Turin.

'Cat got your tongue? Did I ask the wrong question or something?'

'I'd like to help, boss,' Bucci said eventually. 'You know that. If there's ever anything I can do . . . you've just got to ask.'

'That *you* can do!' Neri laughed, still struggling to work out Bucci's reaction. 'What are you talking about, Bruno? I was asking your opinion. This is my problem. A son I love. A wife I love. And the two of them can't stand the sight of each other. You think I'm going to ask *you* to fix it. Jesus—'

'I don't have an opinion.'

105

He slapped Bucci's shoulder. 'Yeah. Right. You northern guys. You think you've got the answers to everything. Just don't want to say it, that's all.'

'Got me there,' Bruno Bucci replied, brown eyes staring into Neri's face with no visible emotion in them at all.

'Here.' Neri flashed him some big notes. 'You're right. It's my business. I never should have put you in that position. You go have fun. Whatever. I don't care. "You've just got to ask . . ." You guys kill me sometimes.'

Bruno Bucci pushed himself up and came off the wall, counting the notes.

'Thanks,' he said.

Neri watched his broad back disappear down the street. 'Humility,' he said to himself. 'That is what the world is lacking today.'

Then he walked round the corner into the square, wondering how long it was since he sat on a bus, trying to remember what it felt like to be young, trying to separate several conflicting strands of thought in his head.

The benign mood didn't last. There was a queue. There were foreigners, pushing and shoving and asking stupid questions. It took ten minutes for him to work his way inside the doors. By the time Emilio Neri was on the 64 his mind was back where he had left it an hour before, stuck inside a foul mood, thinking about his stupid family.

There were no seats either. Not until a man not far short of his own age, smartly dressed, constantly smiling, stood up and offered his own.

Neri looked into the stranger's face, wondering why

he'd been stupid enough to refuse Bucci's offer of a cab and climb on board this thing in the first place. 'Because you're an old fool,' he thought to himself. 'And maybe they're starting to know it.'

The man couldn't stop smiling. It was beyond Neri why anyone would smile on a stinking, overcrowded bus. He couldn't wait for the thing to lurch across the bridge and into the Via Arenula so he could waddle home along the Via Giulia.

'Use the seat yourself,' Neri growled. 'I don't need it. What makes you think I do?'

'Nothing,' the man said, still smiling. He looked like a confidence trickster or some two-bit actor in the Fellini films 'I just thought—'

'You thought wrong,' Neri snarled.

And so he clung to the strap, wishing all the way that he'd fallen into the seat and taken the weight off his sweating feet. There was some black teenager in it now, headphones clamped to his skull, a hissing noise emerging from them.

He got off at the Via Arenula, in a big jostling crowd. He had to wait almost five minutes to cross the busy road. When he got home he was out of breath and stank of sweat, Mickey and Adele's fighting still in his head, jostling for attention with the call from inside the Questura.

The house was empty. He wanted them there. When the phone rang he knew an ancient corpse really was rising, in a way he'd have to anticipate, couldn't hope to avoid.

*

Twenty minutes after leaving the Teatro di Marcello Nic Costa and Gianni Peroni followed Falcone's car into a narrow private lane off the Janiculum hill, the sprawling piece of parkland that rose up from behind Trastevere and overlooked the river.

Peroni downed the remains of his second *porchetta* panino of the day, brushed the crumbs off his jacket into the floorpan of the Fiat and said, 'You know, I like the way you drive, Nic. It's careful without being over-cautious, sensitive to circumstances and a little rash if required. When I'm restored to my true position I will offer you a job, my boy. You can drive me anywhere. Most of the guys I have spend their time bouncing off other vehicles which is a little unsettling for a sensitive man like me.'

Then he unwrapped a chocolate bar and took a single bite before sticking it in his pocket, half-eaten.

'You're going to put on weight eating like that,' Costa observed. 'It's not natural.'

'Been the same weight for fifteen years. I burn it up inside, what with my nervous tension and all. You just see the exterior me. Calm, unflustered, ever-vigilant, ugly as a horse's ass, just what I want you to see. But inside I'm a tortured cauldron of torn emotions. I've got traumas that can burn off any amount of carbohydrate and cholesterol I throw at it. You watch. You seen so much as an extra gram on me since we started this relationship?'

'No.'

'Also, you should be aware that meat – even the shit they sell under that name in Rome – and bread, they're the best antidote there is against this flu thing. Forget all that crap about fruit and vegetables. You ever seen a chimpanzee? Fucking things never stop sneezing. Or doing the other thing. Sometimes simultaneously.'

Costa thought about this. 'I've never seen a chimpanzee sneeze.'

'You need to develop your powers of observation. Now do you want me to come in and hold hands with you for this or can I just stay in the car and nap awhile? What with mummified bodies and Roman history lessons this has been a tiring day for a nocturnal animal like me.'

Peroni took the cigarette packet out, saw Costa's face and thought better of it. 'OK. OK. One concession a day is all you get. About the English kid, Nic. Falcone's doing all he can in the circumstances. Putting the picture around. Getting the CCTV. I mean, I'm no detective but what this mother says seems so *vague*.'

'Things often are. Isn't it that way in vice?'

He shook his head. 'Not really. We're law enforcement, not detection. We just try to keep a lid on everything, make sure no one truly innocent gets hurt and the dope stays out of the equation as much as possible. I'm not like you. I'm a kind of social worker if you want the honest truth. You got to remember. If it comes down to violence and worse it all comes out of our hands anyway. We're just licensed informers who hand on some gossip you people can use. A popular job, you'll agree.'

'And when you want some information?'

'I ask,' Peroni replied. 'Straight out front. I'm a good asker. No messing. It's the only way. So let me say this again? What's the problem? You want to spend a little more time around the mother? A man should always consider his sex life but I told you. Ask Barbara out. She's a nice girl.'

'Meaning?' Peroni could be too direct for his own good. Too observant too.

'Meaning I saw the way you looked at the English woman. Don't get me wrong. She's great-looking in a kind of second-hand way. Older than you, though that's not necessarily a bad thing. Not my type. Too much of something – booze maybe, and bad dreams – been through her head.'

'I just think there's more to it,' Costa replied. Peroni hadn't heard as much as he had. Or maybe he was uncharacteristically slow off the mark.

The older man put his hand on Costa's arm. 'Nic. You heard Falcone. He said you could be right. But think this through. You just got back on the job. There are people in the Questura who happen to believe Falcone's crazy to give you a second chance at all. You're *on probation*. Just like me.'

'And you think that if I push this I can ruin your chances along with my own?'

'If you want to look at it that way, yeah,' Peroni conceded. 'That's a part of it. But mainly I'm thinking about you. Honest. I got to know you a little these last couple of weeks. Sometimes you take things on yourself. Someone else's problem becomes yours.'

'Thanks for the compliment.'

'It's a back-handed one. The flip side is that's a great way to get screwed. Or screw yourself.'

'I won't screw up, Gianni. Forget about me. What about the missing girl? What if these two are connected? All that stuff about the rituals—'

Peroni sighed and shook his head. 'A piece of vege-table and some seeds? Look, they don't call her crazy Teresa for nothing. I love her as much as anyone, but you got to admit this is stretching things. Even if she has it half right about the corpse there's no way it can have anything to do with the Julius girl. They're sixteen years apart. They have absolutely nothing in common except the looks. What are you saying? Someone's still doing all this mumbo-jumbo? How come we heard nothing all this time? You think Rome hasn't seen a pretty teenage blonde since the girl in the peat?'

It was a good question. He'd thought about it too. 'Maybe it went all right before. Maybe someone only gets killed if there's a foul-up. If the girl suddenly doesn't want to play ball. I don't know.'

Peroni nodded. 'So all the Julius girl has to do is let this creep have his way with her? Then she gets free?'

More than that, Costa thought. He recalled what Teresa had said about the book. The girl gets *rewarded*. She gets a taste of paradise. She becomes an initiate, part of the club. And the next time round she sees the ritual from the inside. She watches someone else *become*.

'Maybe,' he said.

'Doesn't seem a big deal. Women have been getting on that way since we all crawled out of the slime.'

Gianni Peroni came from a different generation. Costa reminded himself to keep that in mind. 'In this century it's a big deal.'

Peroni gave him a sharp look. 'Sorry. Just the dinosaur in me talking. Let's forget it, huh? My advice is: we just keep our heads down and do as we're told. That is the way of progress in the modern police force.'

There was the rumble of a sports car. A black Alfa Romeo coupé drove up and parked close to Falcone's vehicle. Costa watched as an elegant woman in a serious dark jacket and tight skirt, cut to just above the knee, climbed out and, very gingerly, embraced Falcone, kissing him lightly on the cheek.

Peroni closed his eyes. 'Oh shit. There goes my nap. There really is no God after all. Or if there is he's a bastard. Behold, one more reason to listen to what the dinosaur's saying. Know who that is?'

Costa shook his head.

'The ice maiden from the DIA. Rachele D'Amato. Big number there these days too. Does things like setting up stings in brothels and you wouldn't tell anyone in vice first if you did that, would you? Listen. Never, ever do you mess with her, understand? Not until you make inspector class and even then I'd wear gloves. She's the woman Falcone was porking way back until his wife found out. What the hell is she doing here? Come to that, what the hell are *we* doing here? I am living in darkness with you people.'

Falcone and the woman were talking animatedly outside the gates. It was a professional conversation, from the woman's side anyway.

'Anything else I need to know about her?'

'Oh yes,' Peroni added. 'She hates cops. At least . . . let me be more precise. She has a thing about us. Maybe it comes from her experience with Falcone. We're all assholes. Crooked assholes too in all probability. Before stiffing me she took down two men from narcotics last year for receiving backhanders.'

'More fool them,' Costa scowled. He hated bent cops. He couldn't work out why anyone had any sympathy for them in the Questura.

'Oh, I forgot,' Peroni groaned. 'You're the one with a conscience. Let me tell you something, kid. These were good guys. They put a lot of people in jail who deserved to be there. Until you've worked that beat yourself I suggest you don't pre-judge people. In that line of work it's sometimes hard to be black and white, because if you are, no one talks to you at all.'

Costa stared at his partner. He wished he could understand Peroni better. Sometimes the man said things that disturbed him.

'Whatever,' Peroni continued. 'The bitch has balls, I'll say that for her. Word was someone put out a contract on her a year back. When she found out she drove round to his house, walked in on him and his old woman over breakfast and . . . reached an understanding.'

The DIA people did walk a dangerous line. Costa knew one who'd been badly injured in a bomb blast in Sicily. They weren't just cops in the force either. Some lawyers were in there too. Somehow that seemed to make them easier targets in the eyes of the mob.

'Is she still on the list?'

'She's alive, isn't she?'

Peroni climbed out of the car and walked to the gates, Costa dogging his footsteps. Rachele D'Amato was slim, in her thirties, a type Costa recognized: businesslike, serious, but not above turning on the attraction to get her way. She had plenty to work with. She was just a touch taller than Nic Costa, with the kind of figure other women hated to see. The suit emphasized her slender waist. Her jacket hung open to reveal a tight, cream silk shirt, cut revealingly low. She had a hard, beautiful face, with a phoney smile accented by deep-red lipstick, and immaculate, long brown hair, pulled back from her forehead and tied behind. Costa could imagine Falcone with her. They'd make a convincing couple. He just wondered how much mutual trust they'd ever manage to share.

'Not that I'm complaining but why's a civilian here?' Peroni wondered.

Rachele D'Amato turned and smiled. 'Oh. Let me remember the name. It's *Detective* Peroni. Right?'

'Yeah,' he grinned. 'And there was me thinking you wouldn't recognize me with my clothes on. You know, I don't recall you looking at my face for one moment that memorable evening. Ah well. Meet the DIA lady, Nic. Rachele D'Amato. She's just so cute, isn't she? Why don't we get them that pretty in the police?'

Costa smiled and said nothing.

'So,' Peroni continued. 'You just passing or something? No need to answer. Nice that you should stop by and say hello. This, by the way, is what we call police work. You're currently looking at the only three cops in Rome with clear nasal passages, though I cannot guarantee how long that will stay true for my veggie-eating partner here. Best you run along in case something nasty happens.'

Falcone gave him a filthy look then pressed the button on the videophone. 'Miss D'Amato is here because I asked for her help.'

Peroni wasn't about to give up. 'You mean this is a brothel too? Jeez. They show up in the strangest places these days. Oh, oh. Icy stare time. I got it wrong. This guy's some kind of hood? No! Don't recall any of them living in this part of town. Place looks like it ought to belong to some playboy or something.'

It was a shrewd observation. The main house lay a good hundred metres beyond the big secure gates. It resembled a reproduction imperial villa, a single-storey palace built around an open patio. An avenue of classical statues lined the pathway up to the house. At the end there was what looked like a fishpond and a fountain.

Rachele D'Amato looked Costa up and down while Peroni stood there, grinning. 'I don't know you. Leo made you his partner. You must have done something very bad.'

'Nic Costa,' he replied, and held out his hand. 'I like challenges.'

'Me too, kid,' Peroni growled.

'Well that's the formalities done,' she said. 'I'm here because you can't do this without me. Sorry, but that's the way it is these days. Wallis has antecedents. He doesn't worry me now but he's got a past. And he knows people who do worry me. Is that enough?'

Costa watched as a face filled the videophone screen: a middle-aged black man, handsome, speaking perfect Italian.

'Police,' Falcone said, holding up his card. 'We need to talk.'

'What do you want?' the man asked.

'It's about your stepdaughter, Mr Wallis. We've found a body. We need identification. Now please.'

Costa watched the head on the screen. Falcone's words gave the man pain.

'Come in,' Vergil Wallis murmured, and the lock on the gates began to buzz.

Silvio Di Capua had learned a lot in the three years since he became Teresa Lupo's deputy pathologist in the morgue. She'd taught him tricks of the autopsy trade they never told you in medical school. She'd shown him any number of smart-ass quips to make when cops fainted or threw up. She'd ingratiated him into the Questura too, introduced him to people so that he became her eyes and ears, the source of most of the hot gossip running through the station. Above all, though, Teresa had revealed to Di Capua – a good Catholic boy brought up by monks, a man who, at the age of twenty-seven, had still never been out with a member of the opposite sex – the unbridled joys of language when freed from the restraints of custom, taste and dignity.

Until she came along he'd been of the opinion that Italian was the structured, civilized tongue he knew from books and newspapers and conversation with fellow students in the monastery school. Teresa Lupo dispelled this myth within a matter of weeks, filling his head with all manner of slang and colloquialisms so colourful and bizarre that, for the naïve and awestruck Silvio Di Capua, it was as if he had entered some new and glorious world.

Even three years on he found listening to her in full, florid flow a thrilling experience, one that revealed arcane, hidden dimensions of profundity to a language transformed from that of his childhood. He swore like a trooper now too, not always appropriately and, he knew, without her masterful timing. On occasion he muffed his words, which had led to some awkward situations and, once, almost got him beaten up by a uniformed gorilla who misinterpreted a friendly jibe as some obscure hint at unnatural private practices.

Sometimes he wondered if he were in love with his boss. In his imagination this occurred in a wholesome, chaste and ethereal way, one that precluded physical sex, something Silvio Di Capua found as baffling and undesirable now as it was when first described to him in all its squalor fifteen years before in the school dormitory.

Nor would he dwell long on these thoughts. Di Capua accepted his failings. He was marginally shorter than Teresa. His thick black hair had begun to fall out when he was eighteen. Now it formed a priestly fringe around his bald skull, which, out of laziness, he allowed to grow lank and long. His voice was a scratchy falsetto that some found deeply annoying. He was chubby running to fat. His face was so blandly amorphous he had to reintroduce himself to people all the time. And he looked a good ten years younger than his true age. Silvio Di Capua's life was an incidental happening in the passing of human history and he knew it. Nevertheless, that didn't stop his admiring Teresa Lupo to the point of adoration, more with every new day of this warm spring.

There was, also, the matter of the nickname which had been inflicted on him the previous year by a garrulous traffic cop and stuck with a dogged and annoying persistence. No one dared call Teresa Lupo 'Crazy Teresa' to her face. Silvio Di Capua's standing within the morgue was less sure. He just had to learn to answer to it. On occasion even Teresa used the damn thing.

He'd just pushed the body from the bog back into what the morgue drones now called the shower when the thug from plain clothes appeared at the door. There was a dead junkie fresh on the slab awaiting Di Capua's attention. Teresa had done a little work on the corpse – the usual overdose pre-check, this time on a grubby hirsute man who'd been stripped for the examination – then passed it over to him with a few brief instructions before grabbing her coat and leaving. He was head down into the PC, logging some records, lost in thought.

'Hey, Monkboy,' the cop barked. 'Why don't you go to Google and type in "a life"? But before you do, tell me where Crazy Teresa is. Falcone says he wants that autopsy on his desk soonish and I, for one, don't wish to disappoint him.'

Di Capua looked up from the screen and scowled at the moron. '*Doctor* Lupo is away from her desk.'

The detective was messing with some of the specimen trays, picking up scalpels, touching stuff he was supposed to leave alone. He sniffed over the corpse and then, gingerly, with the end of a pair of forceps, flicked the dead man's grey, flaccid penis.

'Listen, sonny. Don't get snappy with me. It's bad enough dealing with her. What's with that woman? It's like the red flag's flying every day of the month. Don't tell me you got the same problem?'

Di Capua got up and walked in between the jerk and the cadaver, pushing the cop out of the way. 'You should never go near junkies unless you've had the right injections,' he said. 'There's a theory doing the rounds now that you can catch Aids just from the smell. Did you know that?'

The cop took one step back. 'You're kidding me.'

'Not at all. The early symptoms are very like this flu that's doing the rounds. Sore throat. Mucus.' He paused. 'And a nose so itchy you just can't stop scratching it.'

The cop sniffed then started dabbing at his face with a grubby handkerchief. Di Capua pointed at the sign that hung on the wall above the dissecting table. 'I don't suppose you happen to read Latin?'

The cop stared at the words. *Hic locus est ubi mors gaudet succurrere vitae*. 'Sure. It says, "You don't have to be crazy to work here but it helps." '

'Not quite. "This is the place where death rejoices to teach those who live." '

'What kind of crazy shit is that?'

Di Capua looked down at the corpse. The bloodless Y-incision Teresa had made earlier, from the shoulders to mid-chest then down to the pubic region, sat on the dead man's flesh as dark, narrow lines. The same feature ran across the scalp, which was now loose, ready to be reflected back to enable entry to the skull. Ordinarily, if they had the staff, he'd expect some assistance, But Teresa was gone and, what with the flu epidemic, there was no one else around. Except the cop.

'Pathologist shit,' he replied, and with a firm, sure hand took out the vibrating saw, turned back the loose scalp and began carefully to carve open the skull vault from the front.

The cop turned white then belched.

'Don't throw up in a morgue, please,' Di Capua cautioned him. 'It's bad luck.'

'*Shit*,' the man gasped, watching goggle-eyed the path the small electric saw was taking.

'The preliminary report's over there,' Di Capua said, nodding towards Teresa's desk and the folder that sat next to the PC. 'Note that word "preliminary". It's just a scant first look. And next time, for your information, the name is Silvio. Or Doctor Di Capua. You got that?'

'Yeah,' the cop answered with a burp.

He watched the idiot vacate the room, clutching the report with one hand and his mouth with the other.

'What *is* all the fuss?' Di Capua wondered out loud. 'It's just a body, for chrissake.'

There were bigger things to worry about. Teresa, for one thing. Where she'd gone, feeling so mad he didn't even dare question her wisdom. Why she was poking her nose into police work. Again. And, most of all, why she never noticed the way he felt.

'Do you know what month this is?' Vergil Wallis asked. 'The month of Mars. Do you know what that means?'

They sat in the main room of the fortified villa on the Janiculum hill. The place was odd: half oriental, half classical Roman. There were statues from imperial times, copies maybe, next to delicate porcelain vases covered in Japanese designs: chrysanthemums and country scenes sparsely populated with stick figures. A slight, pretty, oriental girl in a long, white smock served tea. Wallis scarcely noticed her presence.

In a brief conversation as they walked to the villa Rachele D'Amato had told them the man was long gone from the mob and now spent most of his time in Italy or Japan, source of his twin obsessions. In retirement he was a history freak: imperial Rome and the Edo Period. Wallis looked about fifty, a good ten years younger than his true age. He was tall, fit and strong. His dark hair was cropped short. He possessed an alert, fine-featured face dominated by large, intelligent eyes which were constantly active. Without the benefit of D'Amato's briefing, Costa would have said he had the dignified bearing of an intellectual or an artist. There was just one outward sign of his past that she'd warned him about. Before coming to Rome as an emissary for his bosses, Wallis had lived in Tokyo for several years, liaising with the *Sumiyoshi-gumi*, one of the three big Japanese yakuza families. Somewhere along the way the little finger of his left hand had gone missing in some kind of brotherhood ritual with the Japanese mob. Unlike most ex-yakuza

gangsters, he didn't try to disguise the loss with a pros-
thetic. Maybe Wallis seemed to think himself above that
kind of trick. Or past it, if they were to believe Rachele
D'Amato. It occurred to Costa, too, that this act was in
itself a ritual, one of belonging, in this case brotherhood.
If Teresa Lupo was right something similar had claimed
the life of his stepdaughter.

'War,' Costa said. 'Mars is the god of war.'

Wallis beckoned to the girl for more green tea. 'Right.
But he was much more than that. Indulge me. This is
how I amuse myself these days, for half the year anyway,
when I'm here.' His Italian was near perfect. If Nic
Costa closed his eyes he could have convinced himself
he was in the presence of a native. Wallis's soft, intelligent
tones sounded like those of a university professor. 'Mars
was the father of Romulus and Remus. In a sense he was
the very father of Rome. They worshipped him more for
that than his warlike aspect. The month of Mars was
about the health of the state, which for Romans meant
the health of the world. It was about rebirth and renewal
through the exercise of power and force.'

'And sacrifice?' Costa asked.

Wallis looked around him, considering his answer.
'Maybe. Who knows what you would have seen in the
spot two thousand years ago?' He scanned their baffled
faces. 'You don't know? Really. I thought the DIA knew
everything. I built this villa from scratch ten years ago,
on the site of an old temple. It filled my time. I have
plenty to fill. Some of the pieces you see here came
out of the ground. You won't tell the Soprintendenza
Archeological will you? I've left them to the city in my
will. It won't harm anyone if they spend a little time
with me, surely? You've got plenty else besides.'

'We're not here about statues,' Rachele D'Amato said.

Wallis stared at her and there was a note of icy disdain in his dark eyes. 'Listen to the Roman talking. You grow up in a place like this and walk around with your eyes closed. Still, people change. It was easier to handle the planning people a decade ago than it would be now. They were more . . . pliable. I would never have done this today, of course. They're different. So am I.' He waited. 'Signora. You're from the DIA. We've met before, of course. Twice is it? Three times?'

'Twice I believe.'

'Quite. I was generous with my time then. I don't feel that way any more. This doesn't require your presence. You know as well as anyone that I retired not long after my stepdaughter disappeared. You've no cause to be here now. I can understand why, in the present circumstances, the police have to call. But I've got nothing to say to you.'

Peroni caught Costa's eye, winked and held up a sly thumb.

'I know all this—' she said, taken aback by his frankness.

He interrupted her. 'Then why are you here?'

'Because of who you were.'

'Were,' he repeated. 'I try to take this lightly but you must understand. These are recollections of a double loss for me.'

'A double loss?' she asked.

'My wife died in New York not long after Eleanor disappeared.'

The memory broke her confidence. 'I forgot,' D'Amato stuttered. 'I apologize.'

'You forgot?' He seemed more perplexed than offended. 'A detail like that?'

She was struggling to come up with something to
keep this conversation alive.

'What happened?' Costa asked, trying to help.

'Ask her,' he nodded. 'Like I said. They're supposed
to know everything.'

'I don't recall,' she murmured.

'No?' There was a brief hint of ironic victory on
Wallis's handsome face. It gave Nic Costa pause for
thought: something dark still lurked inside this man.
'Read the files. My wife and I separated a year before
this happened. I rented an apartment for her on the
fiftieth floor of a block near the Rockefeller Center.
Shortly after Eleanor went missing she stepped off the
balcony.'

The three men looked at each other. Costa knew what
each of them was thinking: it was impossible to work
out precisely how Wallis felt about this event.

'I'm sorry. Nevertheless,' D'Amato persisted, 'the
protocols demand that the DIA are present if the police
interview someone with your kind of record.'

Wallis smiled wanly. 'What record? No one's ever
prosecuted me for a thing. I've never confessed to any
crime. Perhaps I have never *committed* any crime.'

'Then I apologize but it's how it must be.'

Wallis shrugged. 'The Italian love of bureaucracy is
one of the few things about this country I fail to understand. I don't wish to offend, Signora, but I will repeat
myself: you are out of line. I don't see how I can refuse
to speak to the police in these circumstances. You are
different.' He pointed to the double doors that led

outside to the patio. 'This is nothing personal. You must go. If you don't, I talk to no one. Please . . .'

'I . . .' she stuttered, looking at Falcone for support. The inspector shrugged his shoulders. Peroni uttered a low chuckle.

'This is wholly improper,' she hissed, rising from her seat. 'We . . .' she glared at Falcone, ' . . . will talk outside.'

Wallis smiled and watched her walk brusquely out of the door. 'There's a Japanese saying. "Yesterday's enemy is today's friend." Not always. A shame. She's a charming woman.'

'First time I heard her called that,' Peroni grumbled.

Wallis looked at him, just a hint of reproach in his eyes. 'You think you've found my stepdaughter. Are you sure?'

'We're sure,' Falcone said.

'So why the hell has it taken this long for you to tell me? It's two weeks since that body turned up.'

Falcone was off his guard. 'You knew we had a body?'

'Give me credit,' Wallis said pleasantly. 'Eleanor may not have been mine but I loved her anyway. She was a great kid. Bright, charming, interested. I loved her mother too, not that it was easy. I blame myself for most of that. But Eleanor . . .'

His eyes sparkled when he spoke of her. 'She took every good point her mother possessed and just made it bigger. Even at sixteen she was full of life, involved in everything. History. Language.' He waved his hands around the room. 'Let me tell you something I never told that woman from the DIA. Together Eleanor and her mother gave me . . . this.'

'How?' Costa wondered.

Some long-hidden pain flickered in his eyes. 'Because they made me realize it existed. They had the education. They opened the eyes of some kid from the ghetto who'd only dreamed about things up till then. The guys back home put me through a law degree. I got a taste for Latin through that. But until Eleanor and her mom came along I just didn't get it. The irony is that, if she were alive today, I wouldn't be what I am. It was her disappearance made me consider what I was. Her loss reshaped my life. It was a bum deal for her. I wish it had never happened.'

He looked at Falcone. 'Of course I knew there was a body. A parent who loses a child, even a stepparent, looks at the newspapers differently. We think: is this the end? Do we now *know*? Because that becomes the source of the pain. Not the loss itself. Not the images in your head about how she might have died. It's the absence of knowledge, the doubt that nags away at you, day and night.'

Wallis made a gesture with his hands. He had no more to say.

'You could have called us,' Costa said.

'Every time a girl's body is found in Italy? Do you have any idea how often I'd be on the phone? Do you know how soon people would start labelling me a crank?'

He was right. Nic Costa had seen enough missing person cases to know what happened when the investigation dwindled to nothing: no body, no leads, no clue as to how someone had disappeared. There was all too often an awkward juncture at which the grieving parents became a burden, one which ought to be supported by the counselling services rather than the police, since they were the only ones who, in truth, could help.

'You're sure?' Wallis asked again. 'You're absolutely sure?'

'Yes,' Falcone said.

'Yet the papers said something about the body being old?'

Falcone frowned. 'It was a mistake on the part of the pathologist. She'd been laid in peat. It made it hard to carry out the normal tests. Also, I was on holiday. There was no one around from the original investigation who could put two and two together.'

'Everyone makes mistakes,' Wallis said. 'What can you possibly want of me in these circumstances?'

'I need you to come to the Questura for formal identification.'

Wallis shook his head and almost smiled. 'What's the point in identifying a sixteen-year-old corpse? Besides, you said you knew it was her already.'

'It's not what you think,' Costa intervened.

'No. I know that. They printed a picture of her in the papers. I saw it at the time and thought . . . maybe. But what you've got isn't my stepdaughter. It's a corpse. I'll make arrangements with an undertaker for the burial. I'll see her then, when we're both ready.'

'No,' Falcone said firmly. 'That isn't possible. This is a case of murder, Signor Wallis. The body won't be released until I allow it. If we bring someone to court . . .'

They all heard the uncertainty in Falcone's voice.

Wallis stared at him. 'If —'

'I need you to think back to that time again. We

have to reopen the case. We have records but perhaps something else has occurred to you.'

'Nothing's occurred to me,' Wallis replied immediately. 'Nothing at all. I told you everything I knew back then. Now I remember less, and maybe that's for the best.'

'If you think about it,' Costa suggested.

'There's nothing to think about.'

'The girl was murdered,' Costa said. 'Brutally. Perhaps in some kind of ritual.'

Wallis blinked. 'Ritual?'

'An ancient Roman ritual. Dionysian perhaps,' Costa continued hopefully. 'There's a place in Pompeii. The Villa of Mysteries. A professor at the university wrote a book about how they might be interpreted. Have you read it?'

His cropped head turned sideways. Something in this idea intrigued Vergil Wallis. 'I read history not conjecture. I don't know anything about any Dionysian rituals.'

Costa glanced at Falcone. The villa was full of imperial Roman artefacts. It had been built on the site of an ancient temple. For all he knew, Wallis spent six months of the year pursuing only his private, historical interests. It was inconceivable that he was entirely ignorant of the subject.

'Signor Wallis,' Falcone said quietly. 'This may be coincidence, but another girl is missing. She ran away today with someone. It's possible, I put it no more strongly than that, that someone acted out these rituals when your stepdaughter was killed. It's possible the same person is re-enacting them now. Do you have any idea whether Eleanor was mixed up in some kind of cult?'

Wallis's passive face creased in surprise. 'What? Are

you guys kidding me? She was too smart to mess around with that kind of crap. Besides, I'd have noticed something, wouldn't I?'

'And you didn't?' Costa asked. 'The day she went missing was just like every other?'

Wallis scowled. 'I told you all this sixteen years ago. The day she went missing she climbed onto her scooter and rode off for the language school. I watched her go and you know something? I *was* worried. A kid like that riding a scooter through the middle of Rome. I was worried someone might knock her over. Shows how smart I was, huh?'

Falcone handed over one of the photos from Miranda Julius's apartment: Suzi, smiling happily outside in the Campo. The man's reaction was extraordinary. He seemed more shocked by this than anything else they had said or done. Wallis's face creased with the same pain Costa had seen on the videophone at the gate. He closed his eyes and was silent for almost a minute.

Then he looked at them all, one by one, peering into their faces. 'What is this shit? You think you can pull some kind of stunt on me?' Wallis shook his head, unable to go on.

'This is no stunt,' Costa said carefully. 'That's the girl who has just gone missing. She met someone. Someone who persuaded her to have the tattoo on her shoulder, the same one that Eleanor had. Someone who talked to her about these rituals, and told her something would happen. On 17 March, the same day Eleanor went missing. Do you know her?'

Wallis listened attentively. He took a final look at the photograph then handed it back to Falcone. 'No. I'm sorry. I shouldn't have lost my cool like that. The girl reminded me of Eleanor. Her hair . . . blonde like that. It's just the same, that's all. I suppose that's what you wanted.'

Falcone avoided the man's fierce gaze. 'I want the truth. That's why we're here. Nothing else.'

'This is the past for me. You must have some ideas.' Wallis seemed to be pleading for a way out.

'Nothing,' Falcone admitted bitterly. 'A corpse. A few coincidences.' He stared at Wallis. 'And you.'

'I'm no use to you, Inspector. I'm no use to anyone. Just an old man trying to find a little dignity out here on my own. My stepdaughter's long dead. I knew she had to be, years ago. You never really believe they just disappear like that, go marry, raise kids or something, and never call. Let me mourn her. This missing girl now . . . If there was anything I could do I would, I promise.'

Falcone was beginning to flounder. 'I need you to come to the station. I need you to identify the body. Go over the statements you made—'

'Statements I made sixteen years ago! There's nothing I can add to them now.'

'Sometimes, Sir,' Costa interjected, 'you remember more when you see things from a greater perspective. Small details that meant nothing to you then become important.'

'No,' Wallis said firmly. 'I had enough of this crap back then. Listen. Am I under suspicion or something? Do I need to consult a lawyer?'

'If that's what you want,' Falcone replied. 'You're not under suspicion as far as I'm concerned.'

'Then there's nothing you can do to force me to come with you. Don't forget, gentlemen. Way back when I did a law degree. Put through college by guys who needed legal people bad. Maybe this was American law but I still got the attitude if I want it. Don't pull any funny business. I won't allow it. This meeting is at an end. I'll appoint an undertaker to talk to you about the body. When you're ready for me, I'll bury the child.'

Wallis clapped his hands. The girl in the white smock came into the room, bending her head, awaiting her orders.

'The gentlemen have finished their business here, Akiko. You'll show them out, please.'

She bowed and looked pointedly at the door.

' "Here's the deal. I don't go around cutting up bodies. You don't go around interrogating potential witnesses." Who does Falcone think he is? If it wasn't for me he wouldn't even know half of what he does now. Gratitude, I know, is unreasonable. Just a little respect now and then wouldn't go amiss.'

Teresa Lupo was at the wheel of her cherry-red Seat Leon doing 160 km/h on the *autostrada* that led to the coast past Fiumicino airport. Her remarks were addressed to the grubby orange Garfield toy that dangled from the mirror, flaked with grey tobacco ash, like a polyester puppet caught up in the aftermath of Pompeii. The cat was her constant companion on the many solitary journeys she made. It was a good listener.

Falcone's remarks had stung her all the way back to the office. They burned in her head as she finished the preliminary report on the body from the bog, based on just a few exploratory procedures. They didn't, she hoped, cloud her judgement. On the face of things there was nothing more to be said about the corpse than they already knew. The girl had died because someone had cut her throat. The knife wound was, she now accepted, rather clean and tidy, more so, in all probability, than one might have expected in Roman times. Then there was the collection of grain and seeds which she'd sent off to a horticultural expert in Florence for analysis. These were the plain facts and, though a fuller autopsy would take place in the morning, Teresa Lupo knew from instinct there was precious little else to be extracted from the body. All the scraps of information that helped them in normal cases – fabric threads, paint, human hairs, traces of blood and, most of all, DNA – were either never there in the first place or got washed away by the brown acid waters that had worked on the poor kid's corpse.

What continued to bug her was the way Falcone was so cool about the cornerstone of her original theory. Maybe the girl had died only sixteen years before, not the couple of millennia she originally thought. Nevertheless, the idea she first came up with – that all this was somehow hooked into the obscure rites and rituals of Dionysus – still stood. When she held Miranda Julius's taut, nervous body in the apartment in the Teatro di Marcello she knew that Nic Costa was right. That part of the mystery – who had disappeared with Suzi and why? – still deserved an explanation. Maybe it was more important. Suzi was, as far as anyone knew, still alive.

Falcone was taking a cop's eye view of affairs. He could be right. He usually was. Still, she couldn't shake off the idea that there was an intellectual argument that needed resolving too. Come tomorrow, when Suzi Julius would surely still be missing, Falcone could, if he felt like it, throw people on the street looking high and low for her. He could give her picture to the TV channels and the newspapers and hope someone would recognize it. These actions were, she felt, good and proper. They just weren't happening soon enough. Falcone had missed a bigger question. With Eleanor Jamieson someone had acted out a ritual that was a couple of thousand years old. Why? What kind of people would behave that way? What motivated them? And – this seemed to her a very big question indeed – where did they get their ideas from? Was there an instruction manual, handed down from generation to generation? If so, by whom?

Teresa Lupo couldn't shake the picture of Miranda Julius from her head. She had no idea what it was like to be a mother. Instinct told her she never would. All the same she'd felt some extraordinary emotion burning inside the woman on the sofa in that plush, impersonal apartment, a place that already felt as if it belonged to one person alone. Maybe Miranda was a lousy parent. Maybe the kid was just wilful, playing some kind of game. It wouldn't be the first time they'd launched a missing person inquiry on the basis of what was nothing more than a childish prank. But none of that mattered. They were still under a duty to act as if this were the most serious possible crime imaginable, and keep on acting that way until Suzi Julius walked safely back into her mother's arms.

Or not.

This, she told herself, was why she was driving like a crazy woman, racing down the *autostrada* out to the coast and Ostia. This was why she was bending the rules so much they might fracture in a million different directions, any one of which could seriously damage her career. They needed to know more about the side of things that Falcone seemed least interested in: what happened with those ancient rituals, and why someone seemed to think they deserved resurrection.

There was, she knew, only one man to talk to. Professor Randolph Kirk of the University of Rome ought to hold the answers. His book refused to leave her imagination. It wasn't just that it was the single academic work on the subject she could find. It was also part academic, part speculation. Kirk almost sounded as if he knew every last answer to every last question and didn't want to let on. Maybe there was a sequel in there somewhere. Maybe she'd offer to proofread the manuscript when she got to the dig where, as she'd ascertained in a couple of phone calls, Randolph Kirk was working this very day.

She turned off the motorway and pulled into a side lane to check the map. This really wasn't very far from where the girl's body was found – two, maybe three kilometres. A random thought surfaced. She pushed it away. Five minutes later she found the place. It was on the edge of the established archaeological site of Ostia Antica, not far from the station on the slow line back to Rome. There was a wire fence around the property and modern walls to protect the dig. She kept her finger pressed on the bell at the gate, wondering if it was making a noise anywhere. Peering through the fence the only accommodation she could see appeared to be a couple of portable office buildings parked at the back.

After a while a lone figure came out. He was a balding man in his fifties with a scraggy grey and black beard, thick glasses, and absent-minded eyes. Randolph Kirk was about her height and running to seed a little. His cheeks were florid behind the beard. His nose looked like a rosy-red pincushion. Booze maybe. He walked with a funny, rolling gait, like someone who had hip problems. Instead of the safari suit she'd expected he wore very baggy, very cheap jeans and a faded-green windcheater. She couldn't help but be disappointed. She had been imagining an Indiana Jones kind of figure, unkempt but romantic. Maybe digging up old houses didn't attract that type.

Then he sneezed, an astonishing sneeze, a two-lungs-full sneeze, with a big hooting follow-through loud enough to wake the dead and decidedly liquid too. Automatically she closed her eyes, aware that the air around her was, for a good few seconds, misty with fluid. When she opened them Randolph Kirk was digging into that big, red bulbous nose as hard as he could with the scruffiest hankie she'd ever seen, one covered in dark curlicues that looked like alien hieroglyphics.

'Professor Kirk?' she asked, smiling as hard as she could and wishing she could stop the little refrain 'Booger Bill, Booger Bill' running round her head like a schoolyard chant.

'Yes?' He looked around. He was on his own, she guessed. Was a lone woman that frightening?

'Teresa Lupo. I called. About the book.'

She'd laid the praise on thick over the phone. People who wrote books always liked that.

'Oh, excuse me,' he gasped, attacking the padlock with some keys. 'I'm being so rude. Come in, please. You're most welcome.'

He spoke with that clipped, precise accent the edu-cated English always used in Italy. The kind you got from Cambridge and Oxford academics who thought a touch of local slang and vernacular was beneath them.

He broke off for one more cataclysmic sneeze. 'Blasted cold. Hate these things.'

She circumnavigated him at a suitable distance. They walked past the excavated remains of an old villa, covered in scaffolding and tarpaulins, and on towards the bigger of the two portable blocks. There, Kirk led her to his office, which was a mess. Papers everywhere. Bits of rock. Photographs of paintings. And one small window that hardly let in any light. He slumped into an old leather chair that looked as if it had come out of the ark. She perched on a flimsy cane stool opposite that was, she guessed, meant for students. He offered her a warm can of Coke. She declined.

'You liked the book?'

'I loved it, Professor. It opened my eyes. You know I always thought that period of history was so interesting. You just lit up so many new corners for me.'

'My,' he sighed then popped a couple of pills in his mouth and washed them down with the Coke. 'Too kind. And you know I never did make any money out of it at all. Damned publisher paid me a pittance for the manuscript, printed a few copies then hid them in a garage on Romney Marsh somewhere. It's a miracle you found it.'

'Miracles happen.'

'They do,' he said smiling, toasting her with a can.

She looked outside. The place was deserted.

'Not digging today?'

'The rest of the team are on a field trip in Germany for a week. I just came in to do some paperwork.' He waved a hand at the pile of documents on his desk.

'Are you sure you should be at work? What with the flu and all?'

'It's needed,' he said then added, with no small measure of pomposity, 'I am a head of department you know.'

'Of course,' she said ruefully, unable to take her eyes off the hankie which was burrowing away again.

'Would you like to see it?'

'What?'

'Our Villa of Mysteries? What else? Normally we don't let people in without an appointment. And then we're pretty choosy. You wouldn't believe the amount of theft that goes on around here. Only a couple of weeks ago we had two Americans hunting around outside the gates with a metal detector, would you believe? Had to send a couple of lads to chase them off.'

'Quite. Later, perhaps.'

He seemed disappointed by her reaction. She should have looked more enthusiastic. 'It's not as famous as the one at Pompeii, of course. But that doesn't make it less interesting.'

'Is it as big?'

'Oh yes. Bigger probably, once we finish digging.'

'As big as they get? Temples like this?'

He looked briefly uncomfortable, as if this was a question he hadn't expected. 'Temple's not the right word. These places were more a private religious establishment. Temples tend to be more public.'

'Of course.' She thought about the dirt beneath the dead girl's nails. It couldn't have come from Ostia. It was Roman, no doubt about it. 'I just wondered . . . if you find something so fascinating in the suburbs. What would a place like this be like in Rome?'

He sniffed. 'Vast. Astonishing. It's out there some-where I imagine. Waiting to be found. As I said in the book, it is the Palace of Mysteries. The wellhead of the cult. The place every acolyte wished to visit, perhaps, before they died. Not that anyone will give me the money to look for it, of course.' He stared sourly at the papers in front of him. 'Even if I had the time.'

He was a curious mix of arrogance and self-pity. He liked to tantalize, too. Perhaps that was all his book amounted to, a kind of historical tease. 'I would love to see around Professor,' she said. 'The thing is I have some important questions I need to ask you first.'

He suddenly looked worried, off-guard. 'You do?'

She folded her arms, placed her elbows on the desk and peered frankly into his beady eyes. Randolph Kirk didn't look well and it wasn't just the cold. He seemed tired, as if he hadn't been sleeping much lately. Nervous too. 'I've got to be honest with you. When I said I was a fellow academic who needed a little advice I wasn't being entirely frank.'

'You weren't?' he said quietly.

She pulled out her ID card. 'Professor, strictly speaking this is not official business. Actually no one back at the Questura even knows I'm here so there's no need to get worried or think this is a police thing in any way. I won't waste your time with the reasons.'

You wouldn't even believe them, she thought. You wouldn't credit how stupid cops can be when it comes to using academic, intellectual resources.

'The point is this. I'm a pathologist attached to the state police. I've got a corpse on my slab right now that, for the life of me, looks as if it came from one of the selfsame rituals you described so accurately in your book.

The corpse those same Americans who came here found. The papers wrote all about it.'

'They did?' he bleated. Randolph Kirk didn't look as if he read papers much or watched TV.

'She's got a tattoo on the shoulder. A mask. Screaming. She's clutching a thyrsus. Fennel with a pine cone on the end. There's grain in one of her pockets. Just the kind of thing you wrote about. The body was found not far from here. In peat, which preserved it and threw out conventional dating techniques, which confused me . . . us for a while.'

He shuffled in the old leather seat, making it swivel and squeak and squeal. 'Oh.'

She was starting to find him annoying. 'All that is just as you described in the book. She was sixteen, too. The right age. What's different is this. Her throat was cut. From behind. One move, sharp knife.'

Teresa Lupo made the gesture, arcing her arm as if she were wielding the blade. Kirk's florid cheeks went a shade paler and the hankie performed a double dance across his face.

'And it can't be what I thought. She's not a peat body from a couple of thousand years old, maybe sacrificed here and then buried in the bog. We know who she is. Or at least we think we do. And she died just sixteen years ago. They even put a coin in her mouth. A tip for the ferryman. Can you beat that?'

'No,' he whispered. 'I can't.'

'I just need to understand more about what motivated these people. What exactly did they hope to gain? Knowledge?'

He shook his head. 'Not knowledge.'

'What then? Some kind of personal advantage? Or was it just like joining a club or something?'

He thought about those ideas. 'A club,' he said. 'That's an interesting idea.'

Teresa was beginning to get exasperated. 'I was hoping, because you knew so much about all these rituals, you could maybe help me. You see there's another girl. She went missing today and somehow . . .' she struggled for the right words to describe this odd situation, ' . . . it all looks similar. It all looks as if something could happen the day after tomorrow, 17 March.'

'17 March?' He had another habit, too, when he wasn't poking at his adenoids. He kept moving his glasses up and down his red, pock-marked nose with the forefinger of his right hand. Thinking, she guessed.

'You're a police officer?'

'No,' she corrected him. 'I'm a pathologist working with the police.'

'You didn't tell them you were coming here. Why?'

'Because—' It was an odd question. The alarm bell that was beginning to sound somewhere at the back of her head was just plain stupid. It had to be. 'Can you help me, Professor?'

The glasses were going up and down his nose. He didn't look the physical type. He didn't look anything much at all.

'You must excuse me,' Professor Randolph Kirk said, suddenly getting out of his chair. 'I have a digestive problem. I really have to go.'

He paused at the door and looked back at her. 'One moment please. I may be a little while.'

Thirty minutes later, feeling more and more stupid, she got up and tried the handle. Randolph Kirk had locked it. She walked quickly to the window and took a good look at the frame. The ancient clasp for the latch had rusted long ago. It must have been years since anyone opened the thing.

'Shit,' she groaned. 'Shit, shit, shit and double shit.'

There was just the trace of a signal on her mobile phone. She wondered who to call, what to say. Falcone was going to go ballistic. As if that were the biggest of her worries.

'Don't sweat, girl. He's an academic. He's got a nose like a pineapple and flu bugs doing the Macarena in his veins. Unless he comes through that door wielding a pickaxe I've got no problem at all.'

All the same she looked around the room for something to use as a weapon. There was a small, short hammer on a filing cabinet, nothing more.

'Nic,' she murmured, starting to dial. 'Come save me, Nic. Oh crap—'

The number rang once and then went dead. There was a sound outside. It was a motorbike. A powerful one, judging by the low rumble of the engine.

She stopped dialling and listened hard. This could be important.

After a couple of seconds, Teresa Lupo couldn't hear a thing. Some unseen force, the pumping of her own blood in her ears maybe, was drowning out the sounds beyond the door and she felt she ought to be grateful. She was familiar with death, not with dying. Just then she was an outsider, overhearing some important dumb show happening in the shadows. Even when she was a real medical doctor and people died in hospital it was, somehow, appropriate. Nothing ever really came out of the blue, violently, as it did for so many of the customers on her shining silver table. But she knew nothing of what it was like to witness such an act.

And here it was, happening unseen just a few metres away, beyond the flimsy door of Professor Randolph Kirk's office. Over the beating of her heart, she could hear the drama being enacted, like a scene from a radio play leaking out from a neighbouring window. The voices, two, both high, one rising, one falling in grim fear.

Then the scream and the report of a gun, so loud it blocked out everything.

Her breathing stopped for a moment. Something had happened then. A void had opened in her head, a blank page of expectation, and into it walked some dark, shrouded certainty that a human being, Professor Randolph Kirk to be precise, had, at that instant, ceased to be. A living person was gone from the earth and the scariest thing of all was that Teresa Lupo, in her imagination felt as if something, his spirit perhaps, his departing shade, had stepped through her own body leaving a single word imprinted in her mind: *run.*

She couldn't think straight. She could hardly catch her breath. There were footsteps and she found herself frozen, looking at the door, hearing someone rattle a set of unfamiliar keys at the lock, searching for the right one.

'Turn that damned thing off,' Falcone barked. 'I want to think.'

They were in Falcone's office watching the clips of CCTV from the Campo when Costa's phone rang. It sounded once before he hit the power button. The mood wasn't good. Rachele D'Amato was nursing a tender ego and uninterested in pursuing any link with Suzi Julius. Falcone had scowled at a skimpy preliminary report on the Jamieson girl from Teresa Lupo. The video seemed predictable at first but it bothered Costa all the same.

The bike rider wore a shiny helmet with an opaque visor and a full-length leather black suit, just like a street punk out to do some bag-snatching. The girl had 'tourist' written all over her. Here she was, dashing through the dwindling crowd in the Campo, dressed in tee-shirt and black jeans, a small canvas bag over her shoulder, right in front of the two uniformed carabinieri men who stood by their car yawning, uninterested. Costa couldn't believe their lack of attention. Suzi seemed to be running from something, or so it seemed to him. It should have rung an alarm bell somewhere.

The rider's wrist flicked on the throttle. There was something odd going on with the girl. He couldn't work out whether she was laughing or crying. Then another figure came into view, sprinting: Miranda Julius fighting her way through the tangle of shoppers, yelling at her departing daughter's back.

Costa wondered whether he was reading this all the wrong way. Sometimes cops took too much upon themselves. They walked into domestic situations that were best left alone. They interpreted events mistakenly and wound up with egg on their faces. Suzi reached the big, powerful bike, kissed the side of the helmet quickly, then hopped on the back, wrapping her arms around the rider's waist. The machine bucked once as it went into gear. Then the two of them were off, bobbing and weaving through the crowds.

As the bike negotiated the corner of the square the

girl turned round, one hand still clinging to the rider's waist, looking for someone. Miranda halted then looked back at the carabinieri. She was panting, out of breath. Suzi brought her fingers to her lips and blew a farewell kiss across the Campo before the bike disappeared, out into the Corso.

Just a teenager running away with her boyfriend? Maybe, Costa thought. This was meant to look like some simple, domestic drama, almost enacted deliberately for public consumption. Maybe for the girl it was. But there was something wrong here. The bike didn't have a number plate. Even street hoods didn't favour black like that, with opaque visors. Nor did they like such big, powerful bikes. Little scooters were cheaper, more man-oeuvrable. It was all too much of a giveaway.

'I don't like it,' he said when the clip came to an end. 'Why does the bike have no plate?'

Rachele D'Amato wriggled on her seat. 'Can we focus on the task in hand, please? I'm not here to chase run-away teenagers.'

'It could be linked,' Falcone said. 'Costa's right. There's something strange going on there.'

He got up and threw open the door of the office. The staff room was horribly depleted, no more than ten men at the desks, close to half the normal manning level thanks to the flu. Falcone looked at the officer nearest to the door.

'Bianchi. Who's hottest on this CCTV stuff around here?'

The man thought about this for a moment. 'You mean of the people who're in? Me. Ricci's the real expert but he's home sneezing his eyeballs out. I can call him, though. Get some tips. What do you want?'

'Get some footage in from the cameras in the Corso. Find out where that bike went afterwards.'

Bianchi hesitated. 'Er, that's some job, sir. You get no more than a hundred metres or so coverage from each camera. I've been through this before. All you can manage is about a kilometre a day, no more. If he's gone any distance we're talking a week, if we're lucky.'

Falcone scowled and scanned the office again. 'Give it a day. Maybe he didn't go far.'

'Sure,' Bianchi said.

'And get a couple of pictures out to the media. Keep it low key enough not to start a panic. Just say she's a missing girl and we're looking for information. Say there's no reason for concern just now but we'd like to hear from her, or someone who's seen her, all the same.'

'It's done, boss,' Bianchi said and picked up the phone.

Then Falcone went back to his desk, closing the door behind him and looked at D'Amato. 'So tell me something about Wallis I don't know.'

Her eyes widened. 'Are you serious? The position as I understand it is he won't talk to me at all. And when it comes to having a meaningful conversation, he won't talk to you either.'

'I don't think he's his own man in this,' Costa said. 'Not completely. It's as if he's looking behind him all the time. Why's that?'

She cast him a cold glance. She knew the answer. She wanted to make them work for it.

'Well?' Falcone demanded.

She swore quietly under her breath. 'Wallis fell out big time with the hood he was supposed to befriend. Emilio Neri.'

'We know that,' Falcone declared impatiently.

'Perhaps,' she snapped. 'But do you understand the implications? Both sides, the Americans and the Sicilians, had to come in and keep those two apart. Big people don't like that. Wallis's punishment was retirement. The punishment sticks. My guess is that if they think he's messing around again with things he shouldn't, even talking too freely to us, he's in big trouble.'

'And this Neri guy?' Peroni asked. 'I remember him from my beat. What was his punishment?'

'A slap on the wrist,' she said. 'Neri was on his home turf. He was bound to come out on top. Besides . . . Neri's a different kind of animal. Wallis is educated. He's got limits. He was in this for business reasons, not some personal vendetta. Neri would rob his grandmother's grave if he felt like it and go home to boast.'

None of this helped them understand what had happened to Wallis's stepdaughter, Costa thought. Or where Suzi Julius might be now.

'What if Neri was involved with the death of the girl?' he wondered. 'Maybe that was the way he punished Wallis?'

'Neri's a thug,' Falcone said. 'If he wanted to kill someone, he'd kill Wallis himself.'

He nodded at D'Amato. 'You're wrong if you think Neri doesn't have a code, by the way. Men like him still have some rules. They need them to maintain their position with their troops. Killing a teenage girl to punish another hood . . . It doesn't look proper. It would damage his standing. Besides, he'd have to let it be known he'd done it, otherwise why bother? If he'd taken responsibility we'd have heard.'

'There's still plenty of reasons to talk to him,' she suggested. 'No harm done.'

'I get it! I get it!' Peroni said, a little too loudly. 'That means, of course, the DIA still have to tag along because we got the mob in the loop. And if it's just a plain murder inquiry it's nothing to do with you.'

She shot him a savage glance. 'I'm trying to help! Will you people kindly stop treating me like I'm the enemy?'

Peroni looked out of the window and whistled.

'And the girl?' Costa wondered. 'Suzi Julius? Where does she fit in?'

Falcone looked at the image frozen on the TV screen, of the Campo, with Miranda Julius static, staring at the route the bike had taken from the square. 'I wish to hell I knew. Let's hope she's just another runaway kid. I don't see how we can treat this as anything else but a missing teenager inquiry until I see something that says different. If there's any indication this is something more – and I mean *any* – I want to know about it instantly. Until then . . .' he made sure Costa looked at him, ' . . . let's get our priorities straight. We have a murder case on our hands and that's what we focus on. It's the only thing we know for sure right now.'

'Suzi Julius is still alive—' He couldn't get the picture of the mother's face out of his head, all the pain there, and the fearful anticipation.

'I know that,' Falcone said firmly. 'We're doing all we can, Nic.'

'And we're in too?' D'Amato asked. 'You know the rules, Leo. This involves organized crime. Like it or not, the people you're talking about here have been up to their necks in it for years. Neri, for one, still is.'

'Yeah, yeah. You're in.' Falcone looked at his watch then looked at her. 'Provided it's share and share alike. Understood?'

She smiled. 'How could it be otherwise?'

Falcone rose from his chair and the three of them got ready to follow him. 'Let's talk to the harpy in the morgue about that body. This report is skimpy and she knows it.'

Costa punched his phone back on as they left the room. He didn't like losing the call. He didn't want to be out of touch with anything for a moment.

It came alive halfway down the corridor, ringing straight away. Teresa Lupo's voice was so loud it almost hurt his ear.

There was a single, snatched message then the line went dead.

Stupid things come naturally in some circumstances.

You think about throwing an ancient PC monitor through the jammed window of a dead academic's portable office, knowing all along the frame is too small for you to squeeze through even if you succeed.

You sit in a fake Roman villa on the Janiculum hill and try to remember what it was like in the days when you had to scheme to stay alive.

And, in the case of Emilio Neri, whose phone had burned long and hot that afternoon, you storm around your rich man's palace in the Via Giulia, amazed at the way the past can resurrect itself out of nowhere, cursing your errant son and your profligate wife, wondering where the hell they were when you needed to yell at them.

Fear and fury share the same ill-defined borders. Watching the door handle twist just an arm's length away from her, Teresa Lupo felt both mad and scared as she tried to force some sense and reason into her head. Then blunt instinct took over. She stood to one side, by the hinges, gripping the puny hammer with both hands, waiting.

It took no more than a moment. The lock turned, the door began to open, slowly. She held her breath, wondering what he was expecting: a figure cowering in the corner. That had to be it.

'I don't cower,' she whispered to herself, and waited until he'd pushed it to forty-five degrees, enough, she guessed, to get his body positioned in the potential vice between the door edge and the frame.

She had a pathologist's muscles. She was carrying some excess weight too. She snatched some air into her lungs, stepped back briefly, then lunged with her shoulder into the centre of the plywood slab. It closed on the rider's body. She bounced harder. Someone screamed: high-pitched, pained. Teresa Lupo darted round the edge of the door and saw him: a black figure in leather, face invisible behind the dark visor of the helmet. He was crouching, clutching his chest. Maybe she'd broken a couple of ribs. She hoped so. A long black pistol lay on the grubby office floor where he'd dropped it. She stabbed at the thing with her foot, was dismayed to see it slide only a metre or so away from him. Then she threw aside the hammer, grabbed the creep by the back of the helmet and yanked hard.

The biker fell into the room. He wasn't a big guy. If she'd gone to self-defence lessons as she'd always intended, Teresa Lupo reckoned she could have taken him on there and then. Beaten him up a touch. Tied him to a chair. Waved a magic wand over the gun just in case. Been Linda Hamilton out of *Terminator 2*, all muscles and vengeance. Or something. Her head was running away with itself. Dangerous. She kicked him hard out of the way, struggled through the door, was glad to see the dim light of a clear early evening sky drifting through the bigger windows here.

The old cheap wood slammed shut behind her. She turned the key in the lock then snatched the bunch and threw them across the room, gasping, short of breath, trying to think about what to do next.

You look.

Professor Randolph Kirk lay on the floor in a bloody bundle, face uppermost, dead eyes staring at the ceiling. There was a ragged black hole in his forehead leaking gore. Automatically, she began to think of the autopsy. All the incisions, all the organs she'd have to examine, just so that she could come up with the obvious conclusion: *this man died because someone pumped a piece of metal into his brain. I see no sign of improvement in his condition. The likelihood is that this is a permanent affliction.*

With shaking fingers, Teresa Lupo dragged the phone out of her jacket pocket again, stabbing Nic Costa's number on the keys, struggling to get it right, praying, praying.

His voice crackled in the earpiece, surprised, and sounding very young.

'Nic, Nic!' she yelled. 'I'm in deep shit. Help me.'

There was silence on the line. She wondered whether that was really his breathing she could hear or just some digital static blowing in with the chemicals from the Mediterranean a kilometre away to the west.

'Just outside Ostia Antica,' she screeched. 'The place I told you about. Please—'

Then there was a sound behind her, a sound so loud it just had to go down the phone and convince Nic Costa this was indeed serious. A sound that reminded Teresa Lupo she really was stupid in these matters.

He still had the gun.

'Idiot,' she hissed at herself, and dashed out of the door, the blasts of the pistol, emptying its load into the lock, ringing behind her.

Three police Alfas sped past Piramide, sirens blaring, blue lights flashing. Falcone sat in the front vehicle, with Peroni driving down the middle of the road, pushing everything to one side. Costa held onto the dashboard, trying to make sense of things.

'Stupid bitch,' Falcone murmured. They'd talked to Monkboy who'd come clean about Teresa's destination once they scared him witless. 'Who does she think she is?'

'We should've talked to the man ourselves,' Costa volunteered.

Falcone leaned forward from the back seat and prodded his shoulder. 'It was on my list for tomorrow, smart-ass. We take things one step at a time.' The inspector leaned back in his seat and stared at the lines of grey suburban houses flashing past the window. A red, poisoned sun was setting through the smog in the distance. The city looked grim and dead. 'And we don't go anywhere on our own. In case you two hadn't noticed we're dealing with big boys here. I don't want any risks. I hate funerals.'

Rachele D'Amato was in the car behind. Falcone had organized it that way.

'At the risk of repeating myself,' Peroni ventured, 'do we really need the woman from the DIA along?'

'Who knows?' Falcone replied. 'Until we get there.'

'This is some university professor she went to see, right?' Peroni wondered. 'What's a man like that got to do with the Mafia?'

Falcone said nothing. Peroni braked hard to avoid a street-cleaning truck, then wound down the window and began yelling obscenities into the smoggy evening air.

She came back at five thirty, laden down with shopping bags bearing the names of all the best designer labels. She looked perfect. Adele always did. Her red hair was newly trimmed and a little less red somehow, with a blonde tint shining from beneath. Not a strand was out of place. She wore a trouser suit in crumpled white silk and a grey mink jacket. Neri couldn't work out whether they were new or not. She bought so many clothes he guessed she must throw half out each week just to make room for more.

He watched her go to the open kitchen and make herself a *spremuta*, topping up the juice with black Stolichnaya. 'Where the hell have you been? I tried getting you on the phone.'

'Battery went flat.'

'Then charge the fucking thing next time you go out. If there is a next time. Maybe I'm introducing a curfew around here.'

She walked over and kissed him on the cheek, taking care to let her loose hand idly stroke the front of his trousers. 'Bad day, sweetheart?'

'The worst. And where are my family when I need them?'

She blinked at him. She had long, very fine black eyelashes. He wondered how much they cost, how much of them was real.

'You need me?' Her hand went down again. He pushed it away.

'Don't have time for that shit.'

'What else do I do for you?' she asked plainly. 'What else is there?'

'You're supposed to be a wife. You're supposed to be here. Giving me some support. Instead I just got a couple of my own men and them stupid servants who piss around doing nothing downstairs.'

'Support? What kind of support do you want?'

He wished she'd just let this go. Normally she did. Lately, though, she'd been different. It began soon after Mickey had come to live with them. The kid was bad news, like a piece of grit getting inside an oyster, always rubbing away, making things worse, and no pearl at the end. Neri couldn't help wondering what scams he was running on the side too, and keeping it quiet whenever he got asked. The stupid clothes and the dyed blonde hair were beginning to bug him. And the way he and Adele just kept going at each other. A thought floated across his mind. Sometimes, Neri knew, you saw what you wanted to see, what you were supposed to see. You never saw the truth.

'Never mind. Was Mickey out with you? He should've been back here hours ago.'

'Out with me?' She looked at him as if he were crazy. 'Don't you think I see enough of him lounging around in here? He's your son. Not mine. You work out where he is, who he's fucking now.'

Neri couldn't believe his ears. She just didn't talk like this. He raised the back of his hand. 'Watch your mouth.'

Adele waved a long skinny finger in his face. 'Don't hit me, Emilio. Don't even think of going down that road.'

He balled his fingers into a fist, made as if to swipe her with it then stopped. There was too much going on to let distractions like this worm their way into his head. He could deal with Adele later. And Mickey if need be.

'Where is he?' Neri repeated.

'I haven't seen him since this morning. He went out before midday. Maybe he's out screwing some dumb hooker in his car. It's what he likes to do, isn't it?'

They'd argued about this before. Two months ago the police found Mickey shafting some cheap African whore in Neri's own vintage Alfa Spyder down a back street off the Via Veneto. The stupid kid didn't even know the law, which gave the cops the right to impound the car. It had taken all the powers of persuasion Neri possessed, and a substantial bribe, to get the thing back. Another expense. The cost of parenthood. Had Mickey learned? Probably not. The kid just didn't care.

'Listen,' Neri said, taking Adele by her slender, bony shoulders, shaking her just a little. 'Listen carefully.'

She pulled free, but she looked a little worried all the same. Maybe, Neri thought, she sensed the atmosphere was changing somehow, was wondering how it might affect her.

'In case you haven't noticed, this is not a good time

for me,' Neri said. 'That means it's not a good time for you either, if you could just get it into your scrawny fucking head. There are bad things happening I don't need at my age. Some of it of my own making maybe. Some of it because of other people who ought to know better. I just want you to understand.'

'Bad?' she asked, looking puzzled by his sudden frankness. 'How bad, Emilio?'

There was a noise outside: a couple of cars drawing up. They went to the window. It had started to rain now. Thin lines of drizzle came down silvery black through the night, drenching the steady traffic on the Lungotevere.

Neri watched her eyeballing the men who got out of the cars. She was no fool. She knew their type. Normally he didn't even allow them into the house.

'Why are they here?'

'You ever been in a war?' he asked, hating the word as he said it. Wars weren't supposed to happen. They cost money. They could get you into big trouble with people who thought those days were past.

'Of course not.'

'Start learning,' he murmured, as much to himself as her. 'These are what we call troops.'

'Four wheels good, two wheels bad,' Teresa Lupo chanted to herself as the Seat lurched along the rough, potholed lane leading from the dig, topping a hundred and twenty as it tackled the bumps. She'd just made it to the car in time to see him stumble out of the portable office, still with the helmet and black visor in place, looking like some deadly insect hunting its prey.

Bugman was riding a motorbike. She was in a car.

There had to be some advantage there. It was dark now too, with a little greasy rain falling from the sky. *Four wheels good . . .*

Except it didn't mean much right then. The bike rider seemed to possess his own special brand of gravity. The Leon breasted the hard shoulder of the main road, leapt briefly into the air, and turned, tyres screeching, towards the airport.

When she managed to get control of the car once more, seeing with some relief the lights of the main terminal a couple of kilometres off in the distance, she plucked up sufficient courage to glance in the mirror. He'd made up ground. He must be riding the Honda from hell. It seemed to stick to the greasy road in a way the Seat couldn't. They'd been a good three hundred metres apart when she approached the end of the track. Now half the gap she'd enjoyed had disappeared. The thing moved like crap off a hot shovel.

'Holy fuck,' she whispered idly and stared at the mobile phone on the seat. She didn't even dare try to call again. She needed both hands on the wheel. She needed her mind set on survival, nothing else.

The car dropped into fourth, she floored the accelerator and roared past a couple of slow-moving trucks, one of which was just lumbering into the outside lane to overtake. The mirror was briefly a mass of metal as the two leviathans leaned into each other for dominance. Then the bike came through between them, squeezing into a gap no more than a metre or so wide, speeding ahead.

'Jesus.' She stared into the mirror. 'What did I do? Where are the cops, for God's sake?'

The terminal didn't seem much closer just then. All

her ideas of safety in its bright lights were starting to disappear. And anyway, her mind told her, Mr Insect Head didn't care about bright lights. She could run in and march straight up to check in at the Alitalia First Class desk and he'd still follow, all the way on his bright and shiny machine, pausing only to pump a couple of bullets into her head before riding out of the doors again, because that's what men on motorbikes did.

Four wheels good . . .

The shape was getting closer all the time now. If he made a couple of flicks with his insect wrist he could draw right up at the driver's window, even tap on the glass.

'To hell with that,' she said, and dragged the wheel hard over to the left, braking all the time.

The bike rider caught on quickly. He wasn't going to plough straight into her side and pop his black frame right over the roof, thrown by the deadly weight of his own momentum. Instead he just put down a strong leather foot, slid the machine along the damp road, in control all the way, staring, staring.

'Point taken,' Teresa murmured, and hit the accelerator once more, straightened the Seat with a vicious lurch, and found herself heading straight for the no entry barrier over a side road in construction just a hundred metres or so ahead.

There were men in white jackets and yellow hard hats working there. She held her hand on the horn, watching them scatter. The Leon went into a long, lazy sideways skid. She found the wheel twitching in her hands like a wild creature with a mind of its own.

Instinctively, she turned into the slide, felt the car come back under her control. Something smashed into the window behind her and exited out of the front windscreen, taking with it her vision of the road ahead. A circle of opaque shattered glass now sat between her and the black emptiness that was the world racing up to greet her. She glanced at the dashboard. It read ninety. She couldn't hear a thing except the car screaming.

'Not a good day,' Teresa Lupo murmured, and was minded, for some reason, to take her hands off the wheel because there was something else demanding her attention.

A figure kept bobbing up at the driver's window: long and black and deadly. Its arm was extended. The insect looked ready to sting.

Knowing it was stupid, and doing this very suddenly, very deliberately, she released her hands, crouched down in the driver's seat, hands over her head, praying for protection, muttering over and over again that odd word they told you on the airplanes, 'Brace, brace, brace . . .'

The Leon bounced once. The universe turned turtle. She was aware, for one brief moment, that things were not as they should be and wondered whether this was the start of the great secret called 'death'. And then another unsettling thought, as the Leon rolled, and bounced through the air, making her feel giddy and sick.

'Not Monkboy,' she murmured. 'Let anybody do it but Monkboy.'

There was the noise of shrieking metal. A sharp pain stabbed at the top of her skull. She felt herself rolled around inside the dying Leon like a bean in a can.

Finally, the world stopped moving.

Teresa Lupo was upside down in the car. Something warm and sticky was dripping down her face: blood. She reached up and felt for the damage. Just a cut above her right temple.

'What fucking awful luck,' she gasped, and suppressed an urge to laugh.

There was a desperate, scrabbling sound at the driver's door which was now pointed at the black night sky. She heard voices and cowered in the front seat, wondering if the insect had bred. All the world seemed hostile at that moment. Logic and plain humanity had disappeared from the planet.

Then cold air blew into her face. Faces peered at her. Men said all the usual things they liked to say about women drivers in these situations.

'Can you move?' someone wearing a yellow hat asked, holding out a hand.

She tried lifting herself. It worked. Just bruises, that was all. And a little cut in the hairline.

He had to be gone, she thought. He wouldn't dare come into this mass of people, all of them extending their arms to her.

Teresa Lupo climbed out of the car, wondering whether she was about to burst into a fit of hysterical giggles. The Leon was on its side in what appeared to be the middle of a building site. A few metres away was a vast hole with concrete round the edges, a chasm cut into the earth big enough to take a train.

'Where's the bike?' she asked.

The man who'd helped her out looked into the dead mouth of the hole and pointed downwards. 'Not good,' he said. 'Boy was he moving.'

'How deep is it?'

'*Very* deep. We're doing some work on the metro.'

'Wow,' she said, and couldn't stop herself beaming, in spite of the bruises and what felt like a cracked rib.

There were sirens in the distance. The lights of police cars. She thought about Falcone and his temper. Then she thought about Randolph Kirk and a lost girl called Suzi Julius, who was the point of all this in the first place.

'We're getting a crane in,' the man said. He hesitated. 'Did you two argue or something? We called a doctor.'

Teresa Lupo nodded, smoothing down her clothes, trying to put on a professional face, wondering how she could even begin to square this with Falcone.

'A doctor?' she asked. 'Thanks, but I'm fine.'

The man gave her an odd look and nodded at the big black chasm in the ground. 'For him . . .'

'Oh?' She walked to the edge of the hole and peered into nothingness. Then Teresa Lupo picked up a big block of smashed concrete and launched it into the air, watching it tumble downwards and yelled, '*Impudent fucking bastard . . .*'

She came back and took the man by the arm. He flinched.

'I can deal with him,' she said with a smile. 'I'm a doctor. I'm with the police too. So go tell the rubber-neckers to run along now. Nothing to see here.'

Police tape ran around the site of Randolph Kirk's excavations. Floodlights stood over his portable office illuminating the bloodstains on the bare floor. Monkboy had been assigned the job of dealing with the body. Teresa Lupo had argued, with some justification, that she should be kept away through a conflict of interest. In truth, she wanted to be with the second team, watching the cranes lower a recovery section down into the big black hole near Fiumicino, waiting for them to come back with a corpse, desperate to see it transformed from the dark insect of her imagination into a real and dead human being.

Falcone had deferred to her judgement. He didn't even look mad. Maybe he was saving his fury for a time when she'd feel it more.

Nic Costa watched Monkboy and his men remove the corpse. Falcone stood to one side with Rachele D'Amato, deep in some private conversation, Peroni eyeing them, making grumpy noises all the time.

'She's here for the duration,' Costa said when he could stand no more. 'Best learn to live with it.'

'But why? This guy didn't work for the mob. He was a professor for God's sake.'

'We don't know,' Costa said. 'We know less than we did a couple of hours ago.'

Suzi Julius was somewhere, though, even if her name, and her mysterious disappearance, were now sinking deep into the squad's collective unconscious, despatched there by bigger, more pressing events. Maybe she was nearby. Here, even, dead already because all those well-laid plans for two days hence suddenly seemed imprac-tical. He glanced around the site, at the other office and the low, hulking shape of the old Roman villa.

'I'm going walkabout,' he announced. 'Falcone won't miss me.'

There was nothing of any interest in the other office. The villa looked more promising. It could have been an old church or something: brick walls, loose, crumbly mortar. The darkness hid most of the detail but he guessed the building was that familiar pale honey colour he knew from the spent masonry on the Via Appia Antica where he'd grown up. The place was about forty metres square with an open courtyard at the front full of wrecked stones and, fenced off, a small mosaic, unidentifiable in the dark. The colonnaded entrance was open to the air. He walked in and found himself inside a cold, dank anteroom with two adjoining chambers on either side running back into the heart of the building. They were open too, and empty. The centre of the place must have been a windowless hall. The design was odd. This couldn't be a normal home. It didn't make sense.

There was an old wooden panelled door blocking the way to the interior, with a padlock on a rusty chain keeping it closed. He went back to the car and returned with a big torch and a crowbar. It took a minute to prise the rusty links from the lock. Then the torch made a bright arc into the pitch-black interior, illuminating the shadows on the walls. The place seemed empty: just a bare room. So why was there a padlock on the door? What was it protecting?

He made a careful circumnavigation of the small, windowless space: nothing. Then, just before he gave up, his foot stumbled on something. It was a wooden panel on the floor, built into the ancient brickwork. Modern, by the looks of it. And it had a padlock too, bright and shiny, hooked through a clasp.

Costa worked at it with the crowbar and forced the fastening free. When he removed the panel he exposed a series of narrow, shallow steps leading down into blackness, a subterranean cavern of some kind.

There were lights here too. Wires ran down one side of the steps, with a switch cut into the rough wall at the base of the stairs. A bare bulb, perhaps the first of several, dangled ahead in the darkness. Nic Costa didn't know anything about archaeology but that struck him as odd. Surely they would use portable floods? A string of bulbs seemed like normal lighting, the kind you got in a hall.

Costa checked himself. You were supposed to do these things in twos. It was possible there was someone else around. This could be a perfect place to hide, to stay out of sight until it was all over.

And then drag Suzi somewhere else. Or just leave a body on the mouldy earth.

'No time,' he said to himself. Besides, he was sick of the way they kept giving him that tired look whenever he mentioned the girl.

He took the gun out of its holster, hugged the wall, and walked down into the subterranean cavern, step by step. The temperature immediately seemed to fall a couple of degrees. The place had the dank, fungal smell of something rotten.

There wasn't a sound. At the bottom he flipped the switch on the wall and walked through a doorway so low he had to duck to get through.

The room was brightly lit. This must, he realized, have been restored somewhat. It was impossible that original wall paintings could have remained so bright and vivid for two thousand years. Or maybe they weren't original at all. Maybe someone had painted them there recently for some reason.

Nic Costa looked at them and thought: *here lie night-mares*. And maybe that was what they really were. Some desperate effort to take this poison out of the human mind, to exorcize it by transforming the living demons inside a man's head into images on some ancient, pagan wall.

They ran around the rectangular chamber in a series of frames, each with the same bright red background behind the detail. A figurative mosaic frieze of dolphins and sea monsters capped every scene. Painted columns divided one frame from the next. The pictures were designed, he understood, to be viewed as a series, a set of linked images which told a story. From what he recalled of Teresa's brief lecture that morning, it had to be that of an initiation into the Dionysian mysteries.

To his right, covering the short wall by the door, was what he assumed to be the beginning of the tale. An imposing male figure, the god himself perhaps, reclined lazily on a golden throne, with a horned satyr on each side, both peering into silver water bowls. At his feet lay a young woman, her face covered by a veil, holding a phallic object topped with a pine cone: Teresa's thyrsus. The long wall next to this contained three further frames. A naked child read out loud from a scroll. Three female dancers, hands clasped together, faces ecstatic, turned around an urn. An old crone in a dark robe, crouched on a decaying tree trunk, peered malevolently at a beautiful young woman seated in front of a mirror, toying with her hair.

The main wall opposite the entrance was occupied by a single work. The young woman was entering the presence of the god. Black slaves scourged her with whips. Satyrs played lutes in the background. There was terror on the initiate's face. The god leered hungrily at her from his throne.

Costa turned to face the left wall. Here were more rituals: scourging, drinking, dancing, coupling. The four

frames depicted an orgy but one that sat at the edge of
sanity, like something from the imagination of a Roman
Hieronymus Bosch. In the corners of the images there
were revellers who were unconscious or vomiting. A
pregnant mother suckled a child on one breast and a
goat on the other. Women lay on their backs embracing
horses and lions. Two girls were engaged in a bloody
fight, rolling on the floor, scratching at each other's eyes.

And in the last image an execution: one woman
walked on, blindfolded towards the god. The second
was killed, her throat cut from behind by a grinning
satyr who pressed his groin against her buttocks.

He turned to face the final frame, the counterpart to
the first, set on the other side of the door. The god still
sat on his throne but now he wore a mask, the obscene
screaming mask that was the source of the tattoo he'd
seen on both the dead Eleanor Jamieson and the living
Suzi Julius. They were poor imitations. In the god's face
lay a blind, hungry fury that couldn't be reduced to a
scrawl on flesh.

The initiate was naked, half standing over him, face
forward, as he savaged her from behind, his hand
reaching round to grip her left breast hard between his
fingers. Her face was partially covered with a veil. Her
mouth was wide open in a screaming rictus of agony.
The shape of his massive erection was visible beneath
her open legs. Satyrs and hangers-on watched avidly,
with wild eyes and open, hungry mouths.

Was this the ordeal Wallis's stepdaughter had refused?
Costa wondered. Perhaps in a room very much like this?
And if she hadn't, where would she be now? Anywhere,
he realized. If Teresa was right, this villa was just an
outpost. Somewhere in Rome there stood the Villa of

Mysteries, the heart of the cult, a hidden temple, just like this one, buried beneath the earth.

It didn't add up. One man, surely, would not go to these strange lengths. Randolph Kirk couldn't have been the figure racing a bike across the Campo with Suzi Julius happy on the back. That was someone young, someone she knew.

Costa tried to think practical thoughts. This wasn't an active dig. There was no sign of recent excavation. Yet people did come here regularly. He could see the odd cigarette butt and a few sweet wrappers. The university maintained the site. They would use it for study, surely.

He walked around the corners, using the torch to illuminate the darker parts.

Something bright lurked close to the image of the god and the screaming initiate. He took a plastic envelope out of his pocket, bent down and picked it up. It was an elastic hair-band, bright red, green and yellow, Rastafarian colours, the kind a young girl would use. He searched the rest of the room as best he could. There was nothing else of obvious interest.

Then he walked back up the stairs, back to the portable office. It was getting late now. Falcone looked tired, gloomy. D'Amato stood silent by his side.

'The scene of crime people can take a look at the place once they're done here,' he said after listening to Costa's ideas. 'There's probably nothing left from sixteen years ago, Nic, if that's what you're thinking. Besides, Lupo already said she was probably killed somewhere in the city.'

'I know,' he answered and held up the hair-band. 'But this isn't sixteen years old.'

Rachele D'Amato peered at the plastic bag. 'It's the

kind of thing a child would wear,' she said. 'Did they let children in there on visits?'

He thought of the pictures on the walls. 'I can't imagine they'd allow that.'

Falcone raised a grey eyebrow. 'You think so? These are liberated days. Look, it's late. If you think there's something to chase here go and see the mother. On your own. We're a little short of men. If she recognizes it, try the lab. There must be millions like it. We need to know for sure. Then get some rest. We're all going to be working overtime tomorrow.'

'You can say that again,' she whispered.

Costa saw them exchange a glance. He wondered if something was going on between them and whether that could cloud the man's normally excellent judgement.

Then Falcone took him to one side, peered inquisitively into his face. 'How are you doing? You look dog-tired. You been drinking recently?'

'No,' Costa snapped. 'Are you my boss or my keeper?'

'A little of both. For now anyway.'

Falcone's phone rang. He listened then said, 'Wait for me.'

Costa hesitated, wanting to know the news.

'We'll follow you part of the way,' Falcone said. 'That was the crew at Fiumicino. They're about to bring up the body. It seems Crazy Teresa can't wait to get her hands on it.'

'Can you blame her?' D'Amato wondered.

'Damned right I can,' Falcone murmured, walking away so quickly they had to struggle to keep up.

*

The rain had stopped. The heart of Rome was growing silent. A generous moon now stared down at its own hard reflection in the black shiny waters of the Tiber. The day's warmth had fled, a reminder that winter was relinquishing its grip with a slowly dying reluctance.

Adele Neri lay alone in the bedroom. Her husband was still up, talking long and hard to the bleak, grey men he'd invited into their lives. Their voices crept beneath the closed door, intruding into her most private thoughts. Mickey was nowhere to be seen. Nor had he called. It was unusual, but not unexpected. He'd been crazier than normal recently. Some of it was due to the dope, which he was taking unseen by his father. Some of it was down to the deals on the side, and his terror that his father would find out about them. But most of it came from this sudden and fierce fixation for his stepmother, one she had no intention of discouraging. She liked the way he thought of her, the things she could do to him drove Mickey wild. Adele had some power over Emilio, but it was muted, fixed by boundaries, and always had been. Now it was waning too. Emilio was feeling his age, realizing that change would soon be inevitable.

Mickey was different. He'd do just about anything she asked. Anything. And he was young. He didn't thrash away for a couple of minutes then roll over and go to sleep, grunting, snoring. He gave her something back. Although, when she thought about it, Adele Neri realized those gifts no longer contained the attraction for her they once had. The physical world had limitations. With age came a realization that there were more intangible goals in life: power, control, security. The ability to shape one's own destiny.

Mickey wasn't the only one she held in thrall like this either. When she thought about it, she was amazed she'd got away with her secret lovers for so long. She'd been careful, discreet, and sure to choose those who knew better than to boast. All the same Emilio Neri was a curious and vengeful man. There was a look in his eye just now that she didn't like. He'd find out one day, and then she could only guess at what he'd do. There was, she thought, an inevitability to a life like hers: a period of infatuation, a time of spent satisfaction, then the final leg of the journey, *ennui*, sloth, disaster. Unless you planned. Unless you moved when the moment came. Emilio was getting slow and stupid. It was time, she thought, to think of the succession, before the hourglass ran dry and the empire crumbled to dust.

Nic Costa parked the car outside the looming bulk of the old Roman theatre, walked to the apartment and pressed the doorbell. He was still fighting to clear his head, to make some sense of what was happening. It was like untangling a skein of wool.

'Yes?' Her voice sounded anxious, expectant. He could hear the disappointment, fear perhaps, when he answered.

'It's just a small thing,' he said quickly. 'I have to check. I'm sorry.'

'Don't be,' she murmured and let him in.

Miranda Julius was alone in the living room which was still echoing to the buzz of traffic on the Lungotevere. She was wearing loose white-cotton pyjamas and a red dressing gown. Her fair hair was still damp and dark from the shower. She appeared younger somehow.

Maybe it was her eyes, which seemed wider than he recalled, and shone a bright, intense blue. The pain lent her face a delicate, stressed beauty. He couldn't start to imagine how she felt.

She took one look at him and said, 'There's no news, is there?'

'No. Sorry.'

She sighed. It was what she expected, he thought. 'Do you want a drink? Or is that out of bounds?'

She was clutching a glass of red. He remembered how many times he'd dived into that rich, fragrant lake since his father died, and the struggle required to get out and shake yourself dry. The longing never disappeared.

'Just a small one,' he said and straight away she went into the kitchen and came out with a bottle of Barolo, a good year, an expensive one.

'This all goes tonight. I couldn't sleep. I just keep wondering . . . Didn't *anyone* see her?'

He'd watched women in these situations before. Sometimes they went to pieces. Sometimes they just turned inside themselves. Miranda Julius was different. She seemed determined not to let the agony of her daughter's disappearance defeat her. He hoped this act of defiance would last.

'No,' he answered honestly. 'It's early. This isn't good or bad. It's just how it is. She could still just be another runaway for all we know. You'd be amazed how often that happens.'

She raised her glass. 'Thanks, Nic. Thanks for trying.'

Then she poured his, clumsily. Some of the purple liquid stained his jacket.

'Sorry,' she apologized, dabbing at the fabric with a tissue. 'Had a couple of glasses earlier. It helps.'

'Don't worry.'

He tried the wine. It tasted gorgeous: rich and full of subtle delights.

Costa pulled the plastic envelope out of his pocket. 'This is a very long shot but I have to ask. Do you recognize this? Did Suzi have something like it?'

She stared at the coloured hair-band. 'Yes . . . Yes, I think so. But they're not exactly rare.'

'I know. Is it still here?'

He followed her to the girl's bedroom. They sorted through the piles of clothes and the drawers. Everything was very tidy, he thought. There was a handful of bands in a bedside drawer. None in the same style.

'Where did you find it?' she asked.

'It could be anybody's. I'll get the lab to look. I need something of hers they can check it with. A hairbrush?'

There were two on the dressing table. She nodded. He took the biggest. It was full of stray blonde hair, soft and golden, a couple of shades lighter than her mother's.

The blue eyes shone at him, unyielding. 'Nic . . . *where?*'

'Someone was killed out near the airport this afternoon. A university professor who was working on an excavation. He could have been involved with some kind of cult. There was a villa there. It seems to have been used for some kind of ceremony, perhaps recently. We don't know.'

'Killed?'

'We don't know why. I doubt there's a connection at all. There's no evidence Suzi went there. We'll check the hair-band, of course.'

'Was there—?' She clutched the glass, her shoulders

hunched. 'This ceremony. Had someone else been hurt there too? Before?'

'We don't know that anything's happened to Suzi,' he said firmly.

'But you know something you're not telling me. This ritual. This isn't the first time, is it?'

'Maybe not,' he conceded.

'And someone died then?'

'Sixteen years ago. It's a long time.'

The blue eyes fixed on him. 'Who was she?'

'I can't tell you. In any case it's probably just coincidence.'

He could see she didn't believe him. Miranda Julius walked back into the living room and poured more wine, standing by the table, nervous, uncertain of herself. He followed, watching her. She was shivering. He put down his glass and, very gently, held her by the shoulders. 'I can get someone to come and stay here, Miranda. A policewoman. You don't have to be alone.'

There was an intensity about her at that moment, as if she were grasping for something important. Costa was suddenly aware that he felt attracted to this odd, damaged woman, against all his better judgement.

'You know the thing about kids?' she asked. 'They drive you mad. They keep you sane too. It took years to work out, that was why I stayed away from Suzi. If I lived with her she'd force me to be responsible. She'd make me try to become something I'm not. So I just dumped her, somewhere safe, somewhere invisible, and went wherever I felt like. Places that made sense to me because they were stupid and pointless and perhaps I could forget she even existed.'

'What changed?' he asked.

'You think something changed?'

'You're here. You came with her. From what you've said that wouldn't have happened a while ago.'

She seemed to appreciate this insight. He took away his hands. There were thoughts rising in Nic Costa's head he didn't want there.

'I wanted to do what was right for once,' she said. 'It was almost as if I'd forgotten about her. Forgotten about a part of me—'

She refilled their glasses quickly and gulped at the wine.

'She deserved better than that. So I went out and bought the tickets, booked this place. It was a last-minute thing. It seemed a good idea. Just get up and go somewhere. Together.'

'Why now?'

She didn't seem to want to think about this too much. There was pain there. He wondered why he wanted to know.

'Because I needed someone I guess. There was a gap in my life and, in my own selfish way, I thought perhaps it was time to fill it with family.'

She turned her head to one side, remembering. 'Last year, when I was still working, I was in yet another shitty hole in the Middle East, watching people shoot the crap out of each other. I had a man at the time. A reporter. French guy. He made me laugh. That was all. But it was enough. All I needed. Then one day he climbed into a jeep and—'

She put down the wine glass and came close to him, peering into his eyes, shaking her head. 'It was just a car crash. Can you believe it? All those years, both of us had been walking past bullets, driving over land mines. And then one day he's going down the road and the idiot behind the wheel turns right instead of left. Bang, they're over a cliff. Dead.'

'I'm sorry.'

'Why?' she asked severely. 'You didn't know him. You don't know me.'

Her breath smelled of wine, her body of something else. Expensive perfume.

'And I didn't love him. I liked him. Respected him. Before all this happened I'd promised myself I'd dump him. That ought to make it easier. Instead it makes it worse.'

She reached forward and splayed her fingers across his chest. Costa stepped back, put his hands up and said, 'Miranda. You're upset. Let me get a woman officer in here.'

'Don't want one.' Her voice was slurred but more through tiredness than drink he thought.

'Sorry,' she whispered. 'It's a habit I have when things start to go wrong. Sleeping with strangers. You know something?'

He didn't dare say a word. His head was racing to places he wanted to avoid.

'Sometimes it helps. Sometimes it's the best thing, the kindest thing, you can find.'

Gently, she placed her arms around him, let her damp head fall onto his chest. Nic Costa felt the warmth of her lips brush his neck.

'I don't want to be alone tonight. Please. Just hold me if that's what you want. But don't leave me. Please—'

He pulled himself away, and it was the hardest thing. 'I have to go. I'll call you in the morning. This will work out. I promise.'

There was a hungry, desperate look in her eyes.

'Of course,' she said, and it was impossible for him to read what she was thinking.

It was cold outside, with a little light rain falling gently as a veil in front of the moon. He walked to his car thinking how close he'd been to giving in, whether she was right, and whether it mattered at all.

Teresa Lupo was jerked awake by the bright lights of the crane swinging its burden out of the artificial cavern. The gurney swayed from side to side as if it were teasing her. She yawned and looked at her watch. It was close to midnight. The day seemed endless. Her bruised body hurt like hell. She needed sleep desperately. Yet a man had tried to kill her. This was a new experience. His corpse deserved her attention. For her own sake she needed to peer into his dead eyes and search for some meaning.

Falcone had been on the phone for almost an hour before she nodded off. After the brief factual account she gave of what happened in Randolph Kirk's office he'd hardly spoken to her. If that was as far as the punishment went, she would be lucky. Teresa Lupo had overstepped the mark several times over and she knew it. But if it helped, if it found Suzi Julius, if it began to unravel the riddle of Eleanor Jamieson's death, everything would be worth while. Perhaps everything would be forgiven.

Rachele D'Amato sat in her own car, talking to no one. The morgue crew, short-staffed because they had divided between Kirk's site and the airport, did their work mutely, knowing something was wrong. Here were three arms of the state, Teresa reflected: the police, the morgue and the DIA. And none of them talking to each other much. Private matters, bruised egos and past relationships had intruded into what should have been a professional, impersonal assignment. She was as much to blame as any of them.

'To hell with it,' she whispered to herself. 'If we find out just one more thing about the girl we're better off than we were.'

Falcone walked over with Peroni. D'Amato got out of the car and joined them. All three looked dog-tired. 'We've got a body,' the inspector grunted. 'I presume you want to see.'

'You bet.' She'd spent hours waiting for them to find a safe way of bringing it to the surface. They'd had to bring in extra machinery, longer cables, teams of men in white hats who disappeared into the ground looking grumpy and puzzled by why they were there. It wasn't a crime scene. It was a construction site.

Now the corpse was here, on the ground, strapped to a gurney that shone under the artificial sun of the crane lights, Teresa Lupo didn't feel as keen to see it face to face as she had earlier. The image of the black-headed insect trying to take away her life was one that would stay with her a long time.

'What do you want from me?' she asked as they walked towards the small team gathered by the trolley, on the side away from the pit.

'Identification would be useful,' Falcone said.

'I can take the helmet off. I can go through his pockets. What about the bike?'

'Checked that already,' Peroni replied. 'The number was false but we managed to ID it from the code on the frame. Stolen from Turin three weeks ago. They've been losing a lot of high-powered machines from there recently. They think it's some kind of organized ring.'

'It is,' D'Amato added. 'The Turin mob ship them here all the time. We've got intelligence. Neri's involved in that. He's not the only one. But—'

'Later,' Falcone said.

They stood over the corpse which lay face up on the gurney, limbs awry, pointing at crazy, unnatural angles, like a broken doll. The left arm was almost wrenched from its socket. Bare skin was visible next to bone and torn flesh from the shoulder joint. Teresa Lupo ordered them to turn off the big, bright lights of the crane. They were dazzling her. They had enough illumination of their own with the kit they'd brought along.

'He's smaller than I remember,' she said. Maybe that always happens, she thought. Normally she just saw dead people. She had no idea what they were like breathing, talking, being alive.

Falcone gazed at his watch and sighed.

'Patience,' she murmured and crouched down, wondering how she felt, whether she could draw up the customary amount of respect for the dead that she tried to bring to every autopsy.

The rider was probably gone the moment he hit the wall of the pit, before his shattered body fell to the bottom of the hole with the bike. His neck was broken, crushed down onto his right shoulder. The helmet had withstood the impact – just. A crazed pattern on the crown marked the impact. The black visor was covered in scratches and mud and dust.

'Poor bastard,' she whispered automatically, and scraped away at the fastening straps. Ordinarily she'd tell

Falcone to get lost. Tell him it was too awkward to try to remove the thing here, close to midnight, out in the freezing dead land by Fiumicino. He could wait till they got back to the morgue, with her tools and her easy tricks of the trade. But he didn't want to wait, and neither did she. The man was dead anyway. It wasn't going to be a pretty funeral whatever happened.

Teresa Lupo asked one of the morgue assistants to bring over a medical bag, took out a scalpel, carefully cut open the clasps then, as gently as she could, pulled the helmet back towards the top of the head. There was some initial resistance. She adjusted the position of the skull and found an easier path. The plastic moved under the pressure of her fingers, the wrecked corpse nodded forward, and slowly, with great caution, she tugged the fragmented casing free.

Matted yellow hair, coated in blood, fell beneath her fingers.

Peroni turned his back on them, swearing constantly. No one spoke for a minute.

Beneath the bright portable arc lights lay Barbara Martelli, the traffic cop most men in the Questura had, at some stage, fantasized about. Her blonde locks fell in spent and bloodied curls around a face that wore a pained, final sneer. Her dead eyes were half open. Her teeth, normally so bright and white and perfect betrayed the signs of her cruel death. Behind full, curled lips now turning pale, the gore had risen in her throat, staining them a dark, sticky black.

'For chrissake,' Peroni yelled at no one behind her. '*For chrissake.*'

Teresa Lupo reached down and unzipped the jacket, revealing beneath the torn leather the unmistakable female form. Martelli still wore her uniform shirt. A wet, black stain was seeping through her chest, up towards her throat. She remembered the woman well. She looked so unlike any other female cop. Sometimes she'd watch her walk through the station, knowing every male pair of eyes was following her, and a good many female ones too. She'd wonder how it felt to be that attractive, how much maintenance you needed to do on a body that looked as if it just fell out of bed perfect every morning. She'd been jealous. It all seemed so petty now. Teresa Lupo was at a loss to put together any of these pieces. Why Barbara Martelli of all people should be the hitman – sorry, *hitperson* – deputed to despatch Randolph Kirk to hell. Whether Martelli had decided to extend these deadly privileges to the hapless pathologist locked in the next room from her own initiative, with a little on the spot improvisation. Or whether she was under orders. And whose? It was as if time were running backwards: with every passing minute they knew less and the world got murkier and more illogical.

'If you'd asked I'd have looked the other way,' she said softly to herself. 'I didn't even warm to Booger Bill.'

Then her eye caught something else and she couldn't work out whether the mist was clearing or had just become downright impenetrable.

She was shaken from this reverie by Falcone's hand on her shoulder, his sharp, sour face, with its silver pointed beard, staring into hers.

'Thanks, doctor,' he said.

'It's nothing.'

'No.' The inspector was making a point. She should have seen the signs. 'I meant thank you. Now I have a dead cop too.'

'What?'

Falcone was turning his back on her, starting to walk away. She couldn't believe it. Even Peroni seemed embarrassed.

'Hey!' she yelled.

He turned. She remembered a trick from when she'd briefly played women's rugby, before they threw her off the team for too many fouls.

Teresa Lupo lunged out with her foot at Falcone's falling leg, jerked him off balance, grabbed the arm of his jacket and had him down on the ground in one, letting his own weight do most of the work. Peroni was shaking his head, cursing again, looking at them as if they were beneath contempt. Rachele D'Amato watched this little drama in shocked silence. Teresa didn't want to think about what the morgue team were doing. Holding their heads in their hands in all probability.

'Fuck it,' she mouthed, and dragged Falcone down to the corpse; she let go of him, then pointed to the dead woman's shoulder, half ripped from its socket.

'See that?' she spat at him, forcing his head close up to the torn flesh. '*See that?*'

The inspector was breathless, struggling to regain some dignity.

'Yes,' he said and she believed she heard just a faint tinge of regret, apology even, in his cold reply.

It was small but distinct. Drawn with care into the flesh of Barbara Martelli's ruined limb was an inky black mark. A tattooed face surrounded by a head of snakelike hair, and a grinning mouth with bulbous lips, howling, howling, howling.

'You're welcome,' Teresa Lupo said softly to herself then barked at her men to load the body.

VENERDI

Spring was arriving with vigour. Emilio Neri had ordered the men to put some outside burners on the terrace. With them it was sufficiently warm for his family to eat their first breakfast of the year in the open air, over-looking the Via Giulia. It was eight in the morning. The house felt different. Neri had sent the servants away. He needed the room for his troops. The place was better without them. One of the foot soldiers had gone out to bring pastries and fruit from the Campo. Neri wasn't that keen to make a move himself, not until he'd thought this through. There was another reason for talking on the terrace, out in the open, high above the cobblestones of the Via Giulia. The scumbags in the DIA would stop at nothing to nail him. Sometimes he thought they were bugging the house, recording every word he said. Some-times he wondered if he were getting paranoid in his old age. Either way he would feel more comfortable seated beneath the wan rays of the morning sun, with the growl of traffic from the Lungotevere murmuring away in the distance, overlooked by no one.

Or perhaps that was a distant hope too. They could have cameras trained on him from somewhere, helicopters hovering overhead. This was the way the modern world worked, peering into your private existence, sneaking around, asking stupid questions. And all the while real life just turned to shit and no one ever really noticed.

Adele and Mickey sat side by side opposite him. They seemed even more antagonistic towards one another this morning. The performance – the word seemed appropriate to Neri – just went on and on. His son had arrived home not long before midnight, in a foul, uncommunicative mood. Some date had failed to show maybe. Neri didn't know, and didn't want to know. The happiness or otherwise of the kid's dick was the last thing on his mind.

He had six soldiers downstairs, all equipped for the occasion should it arise. He'd called a few old *compari* from the past too, men who'd taken a back seat when they'd banked enough to keep them happy. He had called each one into his office separately, stared into their eyes looking for signs of disloyalty, finding none. Then he told them to keep the next few days free in case they were required. These were men who had reason to be grateful to him. They all knew some debts never got repaid in full. If there was to be a war, Neri would need every hand he could get. His was a Roman firm. He didn't have the rigid, militaristic structure the Sicilians liked so much. He had no *consigliere* to turn to for advice, to negotiate with the other mobs to keep them sweet. He didn't keep a bunch of *capi* running their soldiers beneath him. Just Bruno Bucci, who was a kind of skipper but never acted much in his own name.

Neri had always liked to do things himself. In the past there'd been time. Now, the more he thought about it, he was exposed by his own obsessive need for absolute control. Nothing could be delegated easily. There were insufficient troops on the ground. Rome hadn't seen an all-out mob war in more than two decades. The game should have moved on from those days. People were supposed to be more *civilized*. They'd been fools, Neri included. Human nature didn't change. It only went underground for a while. Now he had to adapt – and quickly.

Bucci walked up the metal stairs onto the terrace carrying breakfast on a tray: pastries, juice, coffee. Adele watched him place them on the table, nod respectfully to Neri then leave, and said, 'Would anyone care to tell me what's going on here? We've got a gorilla waiting on table. There's people down below who don't match the decorations. Why am I sharing my home with a bunch of zombies wearing black suits before I'm even out of pyjamas?'

Neri was going to have to say something about that. She was wandering around as if nothing had changed. She sat next to Mickey, beneath one of the burners, in a new silk outfit that looked like pure gold. There was nothing on underneath. She didn't bother buttoning the front that well. He couldn't help noticing. He didn't want the men getting a free look too. He guessed people did get ideas around Adele, then wondered again about the way Mickey wouldn't even look at her in his presence.

'You could try dressing a little earlier,' he said and gulped down some coffee, trying to think.

She sat there primly, one hand on the table, and gave Mickey an icy stare. 'You woke me. Coming home late like that. Can't you get hookers who work normal hours?'

Mickey smiled, his dyed blonde head lolling around stupidly. 'What hookers? I got busy. It took me a long time to chase down all those debts. I was working. How about you?'

He was lying there. Neri knew it. Mickey's brain lay behind his zip. Always had done. The kid was up to something, maybe some new private business on the side. Neri could see it in his face. 'So what happened to your phone? We seem to have a lot of phone problems in this family.'

He shrugged. He looked a little odd. There was sweat on his brow. His eyes rolled when he spoke. 'Gone wrong. I'm getting it fixed.'

'Do that,' Neri snarled. 'I got enough on my plate without having to worry about you two.'

The old man wondered how to phrase this. How much to tell them. Adele deserved to know for her own sake. Mickey probably thought it was owed him.

'We need to be careful,' he said. 'Maybe, just maybe, there's trouble.'

'From who? The Sicilians?' she asked immediately, and Neri wondered why the question came from her, not Mickey.

Neri waved an impatient hand at her. 'Nah. Listen to me. We've got nothing to worry about from our own people. We know each other. We go back years. Do you think I've spent half my life crawling around those peasants for no good reason? We're safe there, provided we let them suck a little blood now and then.'

'Who then?' she asked again and Neri couldn't take his eyes off Adele. She was holding a piece of pastry with her delicate, skinny hand and she couldn't stop herself yawning, didn't even try to stifle it or cover her face. This was all so distant from her life.

'We had,' Neri said calmly, 'a little problem way back when the boy was just a teenager. With some Americans.'

Mickey took a deep breath. 'That's over and done with.'

Neri smiled unpleasantly at his son across the table. 'Maybe someone thinks otherwise. Maybe someone thinks we're responsible.'

'Are we?' Adele stared at him with those wide open, guileless eyes. It was, Neri thought, perhaps the worst question anyone should ask in the circumstances.

'People have got short memories,' he said. 'Do you remember what you were doing sixteen years ago?'

'Sure,' she answered. 'Don't you? I was learning how to fuck. It seemed a useful skill to acquire.'

'Yeah, well not everything happens below the waist,' he snapped. Not always, Neri thought. 'What matters is that we take care. This is our town. Until everyone realizes that I want you two to stay here, where I can look after you.'

Adele shot Mickey a theatrical glance of pure distaste. 'You want me stuck here with him? Like a prisoner?'

Neri watched the two of them, thinking. 'Try to see it as therapy. A break from shopping.'

'Sometimes,' Adele murmured, 'I just can't stop laughing around this place.'

Mickey giggled. The kid looked odd. A touch red-faced. Maybe he was back on the dope again, Neri thought. That was all he needed.

'Me neither,' Neri grunted, then got up from the table and waddled downstairs to talk to the men. His family depressed him sometimes.

Adele watched him go. Mickey closed his eyes in delight. It was a beautiful morning. There were a couple of gulls screaming in the sky. A helicopter hovered somewhere overhead, maybe getting a good view of what was going on. Her fingers gripped him tightly, stroking, cajoling, running up and down with a certain, insistent rhythm, as they had throughout his father's tedious lecture. His dick sat upright, begging, in her hand beneath the table.

A finger crept close to the rim. Some insistent flood was moving, racing north. She lifted the tablecloth. Adele's head went down, dipping towards Mickey's groin. He felt her soft red hair fall beneath his hand. Her lips closed on the heat rising from inside him, her tongue performed two perfect circles of pleasure.

Mickey yelped, couldn't help it. When he opened his eyes she was back above the table, dabbing a napkin to one corner of her mouth, the tip of her scarlet tongue just visible.

'Did she do that for you, Mickey?' Adele asked when she was done. 'This slut of yours last night?'

'I told you,' he answered dreamily. 'I was working.'

'I hope that's true.' She was looking at him in an odd way. Adele had changed the last couple of days, he thought. There was something she wanted, something more than just the fucking.

'Did you listen to what he said?' she asked.

'Hard to pay attention to your old man when your stepmother's jerking you off under the table.' It was too. He was making a genuine point there, though it all came out like a wisecrack.

'Maybe I shouldn't do it any more. Maybe I should give this up altogether before he finds out.'

He blinked, unable to countenance the thought.

'Or maybe,' she continued, 'I should tell him you made me. You wouldn't leave me alone. I could just throw myself at his feet and beg for mercy. He'd listen, you know.'

He twitched and with it came the occasional stammer he had from time to time, when he was stressed. 'D-d-don't joke about stuff like that, Adele.'

Her hand gripped his arm. Her slim fingers bit into his flesh. 'We need to get serious, Mickey. You need to listen. He's old. He's out of his depth. He doesn't know what he wants to do. And the Sicilians . . . You know these people?'

'They're friends,' he explained, trying to give the words some conviction.

'They're associates. If they think he's weak or out of line they'll just walk in and hand all this to someone else. And you'll be dead in a car somewhere out in the stinking countryside, while I go back to doing tricks for any rich old jerk who can't get it up any more.'

'What are you saying?' She was starting to scare him. Mickey liked Adele. Maybe this was love even. Weird things happened in spring.

'I'm saying—' She hesitated, thinking. 'We need to be prepared.'

There was a sound beyond the balcony: cars, sirens. They went to the edge and looked down to the narrow street. Mickey took a deep breath then stepped back. He never did like heights. He didn't like what he saw down there either: a fleet of blue vehicles swarming across the cobblestones, blocking the narrow street completely. At their head, close to the church on the Tiber side of the road, a tall, distinguished-looking man had stepped out

189

of an unmarked Alfa. With him was a woman: elegant, well-dressed, young.

'Shit,' he murmured, then pulled back from the edge, head swimming. On the floor below the bell rang repeatedly, insistent.

Costa got into the Questura early and took the hairband and the brush over to forensic. The surly-looking lab assistant in the white coat sniffed at the plastic envelopes.

'What case do I assign them to?'

'Excuse me?'

'We got some new cost management procedures sent down from above. You got to tell me the case so I can lay it against the right budget.'

Costa sighed. 'The missing teenager. Suzi Julius. I need to know if the hair on both of them match. By this afternoon.'

The man's eyebrows rose. He was about forty, short, skinny, with a long bloodless face. He held the plastic bag up to the light on the desk and took a good look at the contents.

'I can tell you right now, detective. They don't match.'

'What?'

'Take a look for yourself. The hair's a different colour.'

Costa snatched the bag off the man and stared at the contents. Maybe the man was right. There was a subtle difference in the hair colour. The sample on the hairband from the villa was darker. Perhaps it did come from someone else. Or maybe it had been stained by the ochre earth on the floor.

'Is a person's hair colour the same everywhere on the head?' he asked.

'Not unless they've done a very, very good dye job.'

'Then do me a favour,' Costa begged. 'Satisfy my curiosity. Check.'

The assistant grunted and made a note. 'This is gonna look good on the weekly audit. We're half down on manning right now 'cos of the stinking flu. I think I'm going down with it myself. Don't expect miracles.'

'So how long?'

'Three days minimum,' the man replied. 'It's the best I can do in the circumstances. Sorry.'

'Jesus . . .' Costa murmured and went back to the office to find Peroni slumped in a chair at his desk, eyes closed, face grey and downcast.

'Morning,' Costa said.

'You left out the word "good". I approve. You got a visitor. The Englishwoman's outside.'

Costa gave him a sharp look.

'Hey,' Peroni protested. 'Don't get grumpy with me. I offered to listen. Seems you're her main man. No Nic Costa, no talkie talkie.'

Costa went out to the reception area. Miranda Julius sat on a bench looking miserable. There were bags beneath her eyes.

He led her through to a reception room, past Teresa Lupo who scuttled along the corridor, head down.

Peroni followed and pulled up a chair at the desk, staring at her. 'What can we do for you, Mrs Julius?' he asked. It was, Costa guessed, a deliberate act, an attempt to make it clear they were a partnership, and she had to deal with both of them.

'Have you heard anything? Anything at all?'

Peroni frowned. 'We'll be in touch the moment we have some information. I promise.'

'So what are you doing?' she demanded. 'What about the hair-band you found? Do you know for sure if it's Suzi's or not?'

The two men looked at each other. 'Tell you what,' Peroni said. 'I'll just go ask about that outside.'

Costa watched him leave. 'It takes time,' he said. 'Everything takes time. You weren't sure about that hair-band yourself. It's probably just something left there by someone else. A school party.'

A school party out to study some Roman porn, he thought. Or a bunch from the university.

She leaned over the table and gripped his arm, peering into his face with that unavoidable intensity he was coming to know. 'Nic. My daughter is missing. I heard on the TV all that speculation about rituals. You found those stupid things of hers in the apartment. What if she's mixed up in this?'

He nodded. 'As of now, there's nothing to link Suzi directly with what happened in Ostia. Why should there be? Do you know either of these people on the news? The university professor? The policewoman?'

'No.'

Miranda Julius had the look he'd seen so often in these cases, a mixture of fear and self-loathing.

'Suzi ran away,' he said. 'Probably with some stupid kid she met when you weren't around. We're circulating her photo everywhere. Someone will see it. Someone will recognize her. That's if she doesn't call you first.'

She looked at her watch. 'I'm sorry. It's just that I feel so . . . helpless.'

'It's understandable. As I said, I can get someone to be with you if that's what you want.'

'No,' she replied immediately. 'There's no need.' She paused. 'I'm sorry. About last night. Embarrassing you like that. It was inexcusable.'

'Forget it.'

'No,' she said firmly. 'I won't forget it. Most men . . . well, I know what most men would have done. I guess . . . thanks.'

He didn't want to prolong this particular line of conversation. 'What are you going to do now?'

'Just walk around the place. Think. Hope. Just sitting in that stupid apartment on my own is driving me crazy. She's got my mobile if she needs it.'

He gave her his card. 'Call me. Any time. For any reason. Even if there's no news. If you just want to talk.'

She put the number in her bag. 'Don't take this the wrong way,' she said hesitantly. 'I didn't mean it last night when I said I had a habit of doing that. Sleeping with strangers. It wasn't strictly true. I don't want you to think . . . it was just automatic.' She glanced directly into his eyes for a moment.

Peroni saved him. He walked back into the room, shaking his head, saying there was no news from forensic, but they were still looking, they were starting to take phone calls from the public.

Then he sat down next to her, took off his jacket and placed it round the back of the chair, looking serious, businesslike. 'We're doing the best we can, Mrs Julius,' Peroni added. 'If there's anything you can think of that's occurred to you since yesterday . . .'

She clutched her arms tightly to her chest and nodded forward, a tense, nervous gesture. Her fair hair bobbed with the momentum of the sudden movement. 'Nothing.' Then she came to life briefly. 'No. I'm sorry. I'm not thinking straight. Last night, after you'd gone, I found one of those throwaway cameras in Suzi's room. I got it developed just now. There's nothing there. It's just . . . stuff. Places. A young man. It's just the usual holiday snapshots, though. No pictures of specific people, not that I can see. But you're welcome to it.'

'That could be incredibly useful,' Peroni said confidently. 'This is exactly the kind of help we need, Miranda.'

Costa looked at his partner and realized he was beginning to like him. A lot. They both knew there was nothing on the photos. Peroni was just helping her feel involved.

She reached into her canvas shoulder bag, took out an envelope of prints and handed them to Costa. He flicked through them: all the usual tourist jaunts. The Spanish Steps. The Trevi Fountain. The Colosseum. Suzi had done the rounds.

'We'll take a close look,' he promised.

They saw her out, watched her leave.

'I hate lying to people,' Peroni said when she was out of earshot. 'We've had three calls, and all them from the usual nutcases. I can't believe no one's seen the kid.'

'That's exactly what happened with the Jamieson girl.'

Peroni looked sceptical. 'Come on, Nic. I know enough about these things to understand this is what happens half the time. Let's not leap to conclusions. That poor woman knows we're doing that anyway and it's just scaring her stupid.'

Costa sighed. Peroni was right.

'The trouble is,' Peroni went on. 'I'm just like

everyone else here. I can't stop thinking about Barbara. It's driving me crazy. What the hell went wrong there? Her old man is an asshole. A crook and a cheat and a bully. Barbara seemed so different. I used to look at her and think: yeah, you can beat off all the crap you get in this world, so long as you try. And I was wrong, wasn't I? She'd got the poison just like the rest of us. Only worse. Why?'

Costa had seen Falcone briefly before he went to forensic. He knew where they were supposed to go next. 'You worked with her old man?'

'I had that privilege,' Peroni replied, suspicious all of a sudden. Then he looked Costa in the eye. 'Oh no. Don't tell me. Falcone wants you and me to go have a little talk with the bastard. Please, for God's sake tell me I'm wrong.'

Costa threw his hands open in exasperation. 'You *know* him, Gianni. It makes sense, doesn't it? The men who went round to talk to him last night came away with less than nothing.'

Peroni picked up his jacket from the chair and stood up, grimacing. 'Why does this have to happen to me? Let me ask you something, Nic. I've got a daughter too. She's just at that age where you start to see something adult beginning to emerge from all the kid stuff. So how'd you spot if they're going down that road? How'd you know they're not sucking some dark part out of you that you can't even see yourself?'

The big ugly face stared at Costa, full of bewilderment and something close to grief. 'If I couldn't spot that in Barbara Martelli, if she could take all of us in so easily, how are you supposed to know?'

Costa was only half listening. There wasn't time to

deal with Peroni's guilt. There was scarcely time to flick through the snaps again, seeing what he saw before, just familiar pieces of stone and crowds of people, tourists mainly. A sea of expressionless faces keeping all their secrets.

'I have no idea,' he said.

She had aches and pains from the car crash. A plaster was attached to part of her scalp where she'd headbutted the dashboard. Still, this should have been a good morning in the Rome city morgue, one full of interest. Two fresh bodies on the slab. A blank cheque to start running whatever tests she liked on the curiously mummified corpse of Eleanor Jamieson. The work had never been this promising, not in the eight years she'd worked there. Nevertheless, Teresa Lupo leaned against the exterior wall that linked her office to the Questura, hunched, deep in thought, puffing on the third cigarette of the day. Events were moving around her. Falcone had left with an entire team. Nic Costa and Peroni had nodded goodbye as they set off a few minutes later. And they were all, she suspected, headed in the wrong direction.

One obsessive thought had filled her head when she took the risk and drove to Ostia: a young girl called Suzi Julius was in big trouble and didn't know it. Somehow this kid had walked into the hands of a lunatic. An intelligent, careful lunatic, true, but a lunatic all the same. At best she might get off with being raped, and probably not in the missionary position either. At worst . . .

Teresa thought of the tanned, leathery body on the

slab and, for the first time in her career, began to wonder whether the job was finally beginning to get to her. Was it possible her fears for Suzi Julius were really just a manifestation of something else, a deep and growing malaise with the innate futility of what she did? She liked her work. Occasionally she came up with something that helped. She was good, better than average, which was why the authorities tolerated her behaviour. But whatever she did, however smart, however prescient, it always occurred after the event. You could comfort yourself with the thought that putting away some murdering creep could – just possibly – have prevented him killing someone else in the future. It still didn't bring back the ones who were already dead. She was, when push came to shove, just a prurient mourner at their funeral, offering tears and sympathy and nothing else. She helped, but it wasn't enough. Not in Teresa Lupo's eyes anyway.

And now she wasn't even doing that. When she'd gone to Ostia there'd been, at the back of her mind, the hope that she would find something to prove the bigger picture, to make it plain that some odd strand of recurring history linked Eleanor Jamieson's death with Suzi Julius's disappearance. It had to be that way. There was no longer any question of it in Teresa's head, even though she was unable to rationalize her certainties. Falcone was a good cop. Give him the evidence, give him the cards to play, and there could be no one better on the case. But she'd seen the look in his eyes when he sat in the apartment in the Teatro di Marcello the previous day. He already had one certain murder, albeit a crime that was sixteen years old. Next to this – and the gangland connections that were common knowledge around the station even before she left for Ostia – the wilful disappearance of a teenage girl seemed, if not unimportant, certainly minor.

The thyrsus, the dates, the curious collection of seeds . . . all the evidence she and Nic Costa had found in Suzi's bedroom carried insufficient weight. Maybe Suzi had been hooked on some Dionysian cult on the internet. There were plenty there. Teresa had checked that morning. Maybe the tattoo on the shoulder was just one of the things kids did. Still, she didn't really believe this for a moment. Falcone probably felt the same way. But without something stronger, something he could work on, he was lost.

Which was, she thought again, why she'd broken all the rules and driven out to see Professor Randolph Kirk, expecting to find Harrison Ford touting answers and bumping, instead, into Booger Bill who could only offer more complications and unfathomable mysteries. It was the worst possible decision in the world, and not just because it could end up getting her fired. With Kirk's death, Falcone got another real crime to get his teeth into, another spur to push Suzi Julius further to the back of his consciousness. When Teresa got chased by the helmeted beetle on a superbike, only to discover later it was an off-duty cop who was trying to whack her, and one whom most of the Questura lusted after daily, everything moved onto a different level altogether. A missing teenager became peripheral.

Teresa had sent Monkboy walkabout gathering gossip in the Questura that morning, before starting the autopsy on Barbara Martelli, a task she did not relish. Monkboy was good at this. The cops half pitied, half ridiculed him, and along the way he picked up all manner of information. He'd yet to report back. She knew, though, what he'd say. No one had seen Suzi Julius. Try as they might, no one had found any reason to believe this was anything more than the usual: a teenager trying to find out what adulthood was all about, not caring how shit-scared her mother might be in the mean time.

She'd taken a quick walk through the station herself too and seen the looks in their faces, understood what they'd have said if she raised the subject. *So there's this gorgeous traffic cop with hair the colour of gold and tits that never quite fit beneath her leather bike suit. One day this angel, this sex goddess with shades and a Ducati, whacks some university professor guy for no apparent reason. After which she tries similarly to off Rome's resident eccentric pathologist only to wind up dead herself down some stinking pit outside Fiumicino. And you're asking about a missing teenager who, when last seen, was smiling, waving a weirdly intense mamma goodbye as boyfriend number one drives her off in search of a suitable source of condoms? Does the word 'priority' have no meaning where you come from? Do you ever stop to wonder how that soubriquet 'crazy' came about?*

They had a point. A cop point. But she'd seen something else on their faces. When they looked at her it was as if they somehow felt she was to blame. If she'd never driven out to Ostia, Barbara Martelli and Randolph Kirk would still be alive, and we'd all be none the wiser about why one would, if a person was to press all the right/wrong buttons, render the other stone dead.

'Yeah, but—' she said out loud, stabbing a finger at an imaginary antagonist standing in front of her, arguing with the thin, fume-filled air of a Roman spring. 'Not knowing doesn't mean there wasn't something bad there all along. We just didn't understand what it was, or why it existed.'

And we don't now, she thought miserably. We know nothing.

'Could've happened anyway,' she mumbled to herself. 'Not my fault. Ignorance isn't bliss.'

The back door to the station opened. Monkboy stumbled out and shambled towards her, head down, not wanting to meet her eyes.

'Silvio,' she said cheerfully. 'My man. My eyes and ears. Tell me, darling. What are they saying about your beloved boss hereabouts? Am I up for Commissioner next? Or should I think of running for President instead?'

He leaned back on the wall next to her, accepted a cigarette, lit it with all the skill and precision of a nine-year-old, took one deep puff then had a coughing fit.

'You don't have to smoke for my sake,' Teresa observed. 'Frankly, Silvio, I'd prefer it if you didn't smoke at all. You don't look like a smoker. These things don't fit your face.'

Obediently, he threw the cigarette on the floor and stamped on it with his foot. 'They're all assholes. All cops. Every last one of them.'

She took his arm, leaned into his shoulder and, just for a second, twiddled girlishly with his lank, long hair. It required her to duck down a little. Silvio was not the tallest of men. 'Tell me something I don't know, dear heart. What about the Julius girl?'

'They've got nothing new.'

'So what *are* they doing?'

'Falcone's gone to see a hood or something. They sent Costa and the weird-looking guy with him to dig up Barbara Martelli's past. Try to work out why she'd want to kill the professor dude.'

'And me. Let's not forget that, Silvio. She tried to kill me too.'

'Yeah.' His eyes darted across the yard.

'And?' She wasn't letting him go just then. There was more to come.

'They're pissed off with you, Teresa. They are *really* pissed off.'

'That makes a change.'

'No.' His round, liquid eyes came to fall on her and for a moment she actually felt guilty for getting him this scared. 'You don't get it. I've never heard them talk like this before. It's as if—'

He didn't want to say any more.

'As if it's my fault?'

He stared at his shoes. 'Yeah.'

She thought of slapping him out of this state, then decided it might not be the best decision in the circumstances.

'But it isn't. Is it? Look at me, Silvio, for God's sake.'

He did. His mournful face wasn't a pretty sight.

'Say, "it's not your fault, Teresa." '

'It's not your fault, Teresa.'

'Good. So what is their . . . theory, if you can call it that.'

'They don't have one. They think there's some mob connection with the mummy girl from way back. They think – and this is something they do not want to face – that Barbara Martelli was getting paid by one side to keep tabs on things. Informing. Running errands.'

She couldn't get that black helmet bobbing at the car window out of her head. 'That was an errand?'

'They don't really know, Teresa. They're still in shock I think.'

'And Randolph Kirk? Where's he supposed to fit in?'

'When you started talking to him someone got worried he might blab about something or other and sent Barbara out to whack him and nip it all in the bud. They didn't want witnesses either so she went after you.'

'The Prof being in the mob too, then. I mean that's how most Mafiosi hide out from the cops these days, isn't it? By holding a chair in classical antiquities at the University of Rome or something?'

'Didn't get that far,' he mumbled. 'Didn't like to ask.'

'And they really think the Julius kid is just coincidence?'

'They don't know what to think. You know what they're like. They're primitive organisms. They don't multi-task. There's only so much they can handle at any one time. Also they got lots of staff off with this virus thing. Hell, so have we.'

She ran a hand through her hair. She hadn't been as careful as normal with it that morning. It was a mess, if she were honest with herself. Just like the old days. 'But, Silvio. Suzi Julius is still alive. At least until tomorrow, if I'm right. Doesn't anyone understand that?'

He muttered something about priorities and how it was unfair to throw all this at him, then looked helpless again. She hated herself for venting her anger on this hapless minion. It was cruel, unjustified. It was the kind of thing cops did.

'Sorry,' she whispered. 'It's not aimed at you. It's aimed at me if you want to know.'

He put his hand on her arm which was, all things considered, a little creepy. 'Let's just go back inside,

Teresa. We've got work to do and you and me are just about the only two people here right now who aren't sneezing up buckets. Let's keep our heads down and get on with things until it all blows over. They're paid to deal with this crap, not us. If we stay quiet, maybe it'll all go away. They'll find what they want and forget about the rest.'

Which was a nice idea, she thought, and one that had not a snowball in hell's chance of becoming reality.

'There's nothing in there you and the rest of the team can't handle,' she said abruptly. 'Let's face it. You don't need to be a genius to know how the beautiful Barbara and the professor died. And the bog girl's there more for the science than the criminology. We might as well admit it. We've got no answers for them. We should be trying to make sure Suzi Julius doesn't go into our in-tray instead.'

He took his hand away. He looked scared. 'That's what they get paid to do. We've got a big workload on. I can't cope on my own.'

'You can cope, Silvio,' she said. 'You can cope better than you know.'

'What if something else happens? What if—'

She took his arm again, smiling. 'Look. Statistics. How many violent deaths do we get in Rome? There's a week's quota lying on the slab right now. Nothing's going to happen today. Trust me. I need a break. I need to think.'

The pale, flabby face blushed off-pink. 'You're going somewhere,' he said accusingly. 'I know you. This is like yesterday all over again. You're going somewhere and it isn't good at all.'

'I just thought I'd—'

'No! *No!* Do *not* tell me because I don't want to hear. Two wrongs don't make a right—'

'I wasn't wrong! Stupid maybe. But two stupids just make you . . . stupid. And most of the jerks in there think that of me anyway. So where's the harm?'

'Please.' His little hands were together now, praying. 'I beg of you, Teresa. For my sake. Don't do this. Whatever it is.'

She kissed him lightly on the cheek and watched the blood make a big rush all the way from his jowls to his eye sockets. 'Nothing's going to happen, Silvio. Listen to your friend, Teresa. Just hold the fort for an hour and then I'll be back. And they're none the wiser.'

He looked wrecked. He looked terrified. 'An hour. Is that an earth hour? Or one of those special hours you have on that planet of yours?'

'Silvio, Silvio,' she sighed. 'Tell me. What could possibly go wrong?'

Beniamino Vercillo was a measured, organized man. He liked to start work early, at seven prompt each weekday morning, seated at his desk in the cellar of a block off the Via dei Serpenti in Monti. The place abutted a busy optician's on the street. It was a fixed-rent single room of just twenty-five square metres, with no windows, just a door to the iron steps leading down from the street. Space enough to house Vercillo and the female secretary who had been servicing him, in more ways than one, these last ten years. After the bus ride from the quiet suburb of Paroli near the Via Veneto he took breakfast – a cappuccino and a cornetto – every morning in the café across the road. Lunch was a piece of pizza rustica from one of the local shops. By six he was back home, work done for the day, ready for the life of a middle-aged Roman bachelor. Vercillo was now fifty-two. He preferred plain dark suits, pressed white shirts, dark ties and old, worn shoes. He was, it seemed to him, the most insignificant man to walk this busy little street that ran from the dull modern thoroughfare of Via Cavour over to the fashion shops in Via Nazionale.

This was, at least, the public image he wished to present, and for good reason. Vercillo was Emilio Neri's book-keeper. In his head lay every last detail of the big hood's Italian investments, legitimate and crooked. Those that could be written down sat stored on the single PC in Vercillo's office, ready to be transcribed for the annual tax forms, accurate down to the last cent. Vercillo was a good accountant. He knew what he could get away with and what would push the tax inspectors too far. Those items that were of a more delicate nature, Vercillo recorded differently. First to a prodigious memory, honed from the mathematical tricks he used to pull to impress the teachers when he was at school. Then written down, using a code Vercillo never revealed to anyone – least of all Emilio Neri – and kept in a safe, hidden in the walls of his subterranean office.

It was a satisfactory situation. Vercillo made the best part of half a million euros a year keeping Neri out of harm's way. And that secret code lent Vercillo some safety from the fat man's wrath should things go wrong. Vercillo knew only too well what fate befell accountants who served their mob bosses badly. Foul up and you might get away with a vicious beating. Steal and you were dead. But do the job well, keep yourself out of sight, and hold a little key in your head that no one else could share . . . then, Vercillo reasoned, everyone could be happy. The authorities stayed at a safe distance. Neri knew that if Vercillo stumbled up the stairs from his office and fell beneath the wheels of the little 117 tourist bus the secrets of his empire would remain secure, unintelligible to the taxman and the DIA even if they found them. For his part, Vercillo maintained a measure of security, a hold over Neri that both men recognized without having to state it. This was convenient. It meant that he rarely had to call Neri except for information, and the big, old hood hardly ever had to trouble him. This was the way it ought to be. He was an accountant. A money man. Not a foot soldier, out looking for trouble. He liked it that way.

Vercillo had given Sonia, the secretary, a day off to go out and see her sick mamma in Orvieto. She'd turned thirty now. She wasn't as much fun as she used to be. Soon he'd have to find a reason to fire her, get someone younger, someone more interesting, to take her place. He hated the thought. Vercillo always tried to steer away from confrontation. It was getting harder and harder these days. Neri's business empire grew and grew, sometimes into areas that gave Vercillo room for concern. When he was a bookish teenager in Rome in the Sixties, during the brief period of economic happiness they called 'Il Boom', Vercillo expected the world to improve on a constant, incremental basis, becoming happier, more prosperous, more peaceful year by year. Instead, the opposite happened. The Red Brigade came, then went, then came back again. There were bombs everywhere, and madness. He'd lost a cousin in Israel to a suicide attack. Vercillo scarcely thought of himself as a Jew these days but the idea that someone could die like that, just walking down the street, going into the wrong café, appalled him. There was a need for more order in people's lives. And some politeness too. Instead, all you got was this constant stream of bodies, foreigners pushing and shoving to get in front of everyone else. It had all gone wrong somewhere over the past forty years and, for the life of him, he couldn't understand how or when.

It was the tourists that got to him most. The English, drunk for every football game. The Japanese, constantly taking pictures, blundering into you on the street, not knowing a word of Italian. And the Americans, who thought they could do any damn thing they liked so long as they had a few dollars in their pockets. Rome would be better off without the lot of them. They intruded upon the native consciousness. They marred the place. Today especially. There was some kind of street theatre festival going on around the Colosseum down the road. They were setting up when he came to work. Commedia dell'Arte characters climbing into costumes. Africans. Orientals. And all the usual fraudsters pretending to be gladiators, trying to screw some cash out of the tourists for pictures.

Beniamino Vercillo looked up from the desk in his dark little pit feeling grumpy, tasting the sour bile of growing disappointment in his mouth, then wondered how much his thoughts were random, how much the product of what he was half seeing out of the corner of his eye.

In front of him, framed in the open doorway, was a figure from some stupid dream. It stood there like a crazy god wearing some kind of theatrical gown: a long red jacket, cheap brown sacking trousers. And a mask, one straight out of a nightmare, all crazy writhing hair, with a black gaping mouth, fixed in a lunatic grin.

The figure took one step forward, theatrically, like an actor making a point. He had to be from one of the street troupes Vercillo saw earlier.

'I don't give to charity,' the little accountant declared firmly.

The figure moved closer with two more of those stupid, histrionic strides. Vercillo's head started to work, remembering something from long ago.

'What is this shit?' Vercillo mumbled automatically. 'What do you want?'

'Neri,' the crazy god said in a calm, clear voice that floated out from behind the mask.

Vercillo shivered, wondering if this was all some hallucination. 'Who?'

The creature opened its jacket; its right hand reached down towards a leather scabbard on its belt. Vercillo watched aghast as it withdrew a short, fat sword that gleamed in the fluorescent lights.

The shining weapon rose, dashed through the air then dug deep into the desk in front of him, severing the phone cord, cutting straight through the sheaf of letters that sat in front of Vercillo.

'Books,' the crazy god said.

'No books here, no books here—'

He was quiet. The point of the blade was at his throat, pricking into his dewlap.

The crazy god shook his head. The blade pressed harder. Vercillo felt a sharp stab of pain, then a line of blood began to trickle down his neck.

'He'll kill me,' he murmured.

'*He'll* kill you?' It was impossible to guess what kind

of face lay behind the mask. A determined one. Vercillo didn't doubt that.

He threw up his hands and pointed to the edge of the desk. The sword went down a fraction. Vercillo hooked a finger into the drawer handle and gently pulled. With the slicing edge never more than a couple of centimetres from his throat, he gingerly drew out a set of keys.

'I need to get up,' he said, his voice cracking a little with the strain.

The mask nodded.

Beniamino Vercillo walked towards the wall of the office furthest away from the street. His hands trembling, the accountant turned the key in the security door of the safe then fumbled his way through the numbers on the lock. After a couple of attempts it swung open. He reached inside and withdrew something. The two of them returned to the table. Vercillo opened the large cardboard document box and stood back.

The crazy god's leather fingers dipped into the file and took out the pile of papers there. He threw them on the desk, not saying a word, anger leaking out invisibly from behind the static grin. These were just numbers. Numbers and numbers. Unintelligible.

Vercillo quivered, frightened, and wished to God he'd taken an office on the ground floor, with a window out onto the street. Not this stupid, cramped cave where anything could go on unseen by the busy world outside.

'Code,' the god said simply, pointing at the lines of letters on the pages in front of them.

He tried to think straight. He tried to imagine the consequences. It was impossible. There was only one consequence which mattered.

'If I tell you—?'

The lunatic head stared at him, no emotion in its features, nothing human there at all.

'If I tell you . . . I can go?'

He could run. Vercillo had some private money in places no one could ever find. He could go somewhere Neri's wrath would never find him. Australia maybe. Or Thailand, where the girls were young, and no one asked any questions. He looked around the drab little office, thought of his drab old clothes. Maybe this was fate doing him a favour. All his life he'd spent in the service of the fat hood, pretending to be something he wasn't. Lying, cheating, telling himself it was OK all along because, whatever Neri did to earn his money, none of the blood sat on his own fingers. He'd lied to himself there. Neri *touched* him. Always. It was one reason he started messing with girls. Neri offered him the chance, introduced him to that world. It was one way of keeping him in line.

The idea of retirement, of putting distance between him and this bleak existence built on nothing more than numbers, was suddenly appealing.

Besides, a stray thought wondered, what's the alternative? You're an accountant. Not a foot soldier.

'You can go,' the crazy god said, and again Vercillo found himself trying to place the accent, trying to imagine the human face behind it: young, undoubtedly, but not rough, not like Neri's henchmen.

Vercillo picked up the phone. The crazy god briefly raised the sword, forgetting, it seemed to Vercillo, that he'd already cut the cord. The omission cheered the little accountant. There was something human behind the mask after all.

'It's OK,' Vercillo explained. 'This is it. Watch.'

He set a page – a stream of unintelligible letters –next to the phone. 'It's simple. The person it refers to is identified by his phone number. Everything that comes after is a number too. What's owed. What the interest rate is. What's been paid.'

It felt stupidly exhilarating. In twenty-five years he'd never had this conversation with anyone.

The crazy god stared at the characters on the table, matching them off with the phone keypad using the point of the sword.

'It's clever,' Vercillo added. 'Just remember to use Q for zero and Z for one.' It was too. It meant you could encrypt the number '2' in any one of three ways – A, B or C – and anyone with a phone could still get the right answer in seconds. People assumed codes were designed to hide words, not numbers. As long as they kept to that idea the code was pretty much impossible to crack. It wouldn't fool the FBI, not in the end. But it could fool a lot of people. It would fool Emilio Neri and in some curious way that was all that mattered.

The crazy god laughed and there was something wrong inside the sound.

'Is that what you want?' Vercillo asked.

The mask didn't say a thing.

'I—' Vercillo wanted praise, or gratitude even. There was nothing. 'Maybe I could give you more.'

'Don't need more,' the crazy god murmured, beginning to move, beginning to lift the short, sharp blade higher.

'You said—' Then Vercillo fell silent. There was no point in talking to a sword. There was no point in anything at all. The world was mad. The world was a mask leering at him, getting bigger, crazier with every diminishing second.

Barbara Martelli had lived with her old man in a first-floor apartment on the Lateran Square. The communal front door faced the site of the first St Peter's built by Constantine. The place had five big rooms, a quiet view over the internal courtyard, and plenty of expensive furnishings with a personal, feminine touch. She must have bought them, Costa thought. Peroni had brought along the file from the previous night's visit which they'd read in the car outside. The old man had said little but the background was interesting. It contained more than either of them had expected. When they walked in Costa thought about some of the older papers, with their vague, unproven allegations, took one look at old man Martelli and knew straight away where the money came from.

He was in his mid-fifties and skeletally thin, hunched in a shiny wheelchair, staring back at them with cold, dead eyes. Still, Costa could imagine what he would have been like in his prime. Not that different from Peroni: fit, strong, dogmatic. He didn't look well now, and it wasn't just grief. Costa knew that kind of sickness, recognized the signs. The patchy hair from the chemotherapy. The dead, desiccated look in the eyes. And Martelli was still smoking like crazy too. The place reeked of stale tobacco.

Martelli stared at Gianni Peroni and shook his head. 'Jesus, talk about bad apples,' he snarled. 'I heard you got busted from vice. Didn't realize they busted you down this far. You enjoying it, huh?'

'Yeah,' Peroni said. 'Does a man good to get kicked in the teeth from time to time. This detective stuff's interesting too. We always used to think we had the short end of the stick in vice, Toni. We didn't. You know why?'

The sick old man just glared at him.

'In vice,' Peroni continued, 'we knew we were dealing with shit all along. The only question was how bad it was, and how much stuck to us along the way.' He waved a hand at Costa. 'These guys don't have that privilege. They try to assume everyone's innocent before they find out otherwise. Trust me. This really cramps your style. Fortunately, I haven't learnt that trick.'

'If you could've kept your pecker in your pants, you wouldn't be needing it,' Martelli retorted.

Peroni grimaced. He really didn't like this man. 'So I keep telling myself. Why are we talking like this, Toni? Me and the boy came round here to offer our condolences. We both knew Barbara. We loved that girl. We're in shock over what happened. So why are we making a fight out of things? You want some answers just the same as we do.'

Martelli started coughing like crazy, a cruel, rasping hack. It must have hurt. When he finished he took two gulps of snatched air then wheezed at them, 'I said everything I had to say last night. Can't you leave a father alone with his thoughts?'

Peroni pulled up a chair next to Martelli, sat down, gave Costa a look that said 'watch this' and lit a cigarette. 'I know, I know. It's that asshole Falcone. He just pushes and pushes.'

Martelli snorted. 'I remember him. He wasn't such

213

hot stuff. How come he made inspector? Don't they have any reliable men left these days?'

'Some,' Peroni replied. 'A few. How're you doing? People still ask after you.'

'Don't give me that shit. I hadn't seen a soul from the Questura in months till last night. Now I can't sleep for the doorbell ringing.'

Peroni shrugged and stared at the walls.

'Is it long since you retired, Signor Martelli?' Costa asked.

'Six years. The moron I was working with complained about my cough. Next thing you know they're doing X-rays, sending me down the hospital. Medical leave. Compulsory retirement.'

'He did you a favour,' Costa said. 'My father died of cancer. The sooner it's caught—'

'A favour.' Martelli's dark eyes stared back at him. 'That's what you call it?'

'Yes.'

'Well, here I am. Still coughing. Still feeling like shit. With my hair falling out and my guts with a mind of their own. Some favour. I could've worked a few more years. I could've done the job. Then what? Maybe they side me with some dumb kid who doesn't know his left hand from his right and gets me walking straight into one of them nice immigrant types we got working the Termini dope run these days. All knives and guns and shit we never had to deal with till they came along. Hell, I wasn't cut out for retirement.'

The man seemed consumed by his own self-pity. They'd come to talk about the death of his daughter. Instead it seemed Toni Martelli only had time to think about himself, how everything that happened affected his own fragile identity. Costa tried to recall Barbara more closely and found it impossible. There was, now he came to think of it, something fleeting about her, a kind of brittle anonymity masquerading as friendliness. Maybe that was all an act too, like the show she put on of being just another cop. There had to be some answers in this over-grand apartment and in the head of her father. He knew that nothing would be prised out into the light of day readily. Toni Martelli had crawled out from underneath some serious corruption allegations scot-free, and went on to take home a full pension. He wasn't the type to offer up the truth for nothing.

'So you and Barbara must have worked together?' Costa asked.

'Depends what you mean by "together". I worked vice and dope mainly. She was traffic. We met in the corridors. We said hello. We didn't talk about what we did if that's what you mean. A good cop leaves things in the office. Maybe you're not old enough to understand that.'

'Were you glad she joined the force?'

He shuffled, uncomfortable. 'Yeah. At the time. Why shouldn't I be?'

'Who gave her the job, Toni?' Peroni asked.

'Don't recall.'

Peroni scratched his crew-cut, thinking. 'One of those bent guys you liked, huh? What was the name of that big goon you were pally with? The one that did time for taking money from Neri a couple of years ago? Filippo Mosca wasn't it?'

'I don't have to take this shit,' Martelli wheezed.

Peroni smiled, leaned over and took hold of his

scrawny knee. 'That's the trouble, Toni. That's the worst thing of all. You do.'

'Where's her mother? Does she know?' Costa wondered.

'Back home in Sicily. Of course she knows.' Martelli's dead eyes glared at him. 'They got TV and papers in Sicily, haven't they? How couldn't she know?'

'You should have called her, Toni,' Peroni said. 'You got to bury these things sometimes.'

A skeletal finger cut through the air in front of Peroni's face. 'Don't fucking tell me what to do. Don't go places you don't belong. That woman walked out on me for no good reason. She can rot in hell for all I care.'

Peroni's face lit up at Martelli's reaction. 'She left right around the time Barbara joined up, didn't she? Any connection there?'

'Just get out of here.'

It wasn't grief that was eating the man up. It was hatred, and fear maybe.

'Is there something we can do?' Costa asked. 'Help make arrangements.'

Martelli's eyes fixed on the carpet. 'Nope.'

'Is there nothing at all you want to tell us?'

He didn't say a word.

Peroni leaned back and closed his eyes. 'This is such a nice apartment. I wish I could afford something like it. You know I could just sit here all day, smoking, thinking. You got anything to eat, Toni? You want me to send the boy out and fetch something in while we wait for you to get your voice back? Couple of beers? Some pizza?'

Martelli shook his head. 'She was thirty-two years old, for God's sake. A grown woman. You think she told me everything? It just makes no sense. She got here around three thirty after she came off duty. A little while later there's a call and next thing I know she's putting on that leather gear of hers, off for a ride. Hell, it was a nice day. I thought maybe she was doing it for fun. Maybe she was going to meet someone. I don't know.'

'She didn't say anything?' Costa asked.

Martelli turned to look at Peroni. 'Where did you get Junior? Is this one of them work experience things the schools do?' The bony finger jabbed at Costa from across the room. 'If she'd said anything I'd have mentioned it. I didn't do the job you think you're doing for more than thirty years without learning to put one foot in front of the other.'

'Of course,' Costa nodded and thought again: *where was the grief?* Was Toni Martelli just holding it all inside? Or was there something that overwhelmed even that? Fear? A sense that his own skin might be at risk now too?

'We could get someone round to talk to you. We could get you counselling.'

'Send round some grappa and a few packs of cigarettes. Counselling? And they wonder why the force has gone to pieces.'

'We could get you protection,' Costa suggested.

'Why would I need that?'

'I don't know. You tell me. Barbara had secrets. That much we do know. Maybe some people think she shared them with you.' Costa leaned forward. 'Maybe she did.'

'Don't try fishing with me, kid,' Martelli snapped. 'Ate up minnows like you for dinner in my time. You ask something sensible or you get the hell out of here. I was planning to watch some football.'

It was as if what had occurred was an everyday event. Or that Martelli refused to allow it to touch him, scared perhaps of the consequences. Costa couldn't begin to understand this strange old man at all.

Peroni looked at his watch then at Costa. They both knew they were getting nowhere.

Costa persisted. 'Tell me, Mr Martelli. Did Barbara have a boyfriend?'

The bleak, old eyes glared at him. 'Nothing special.'

'Any names? Did you ever meet them?'

'No.' He lit a cigarette, took a deep gulp then closed his eyes. 'None of my business. None of yours either.'

Peroni nudged him, smiling. 'It is now. We got to pry into Barbara's bedroom, Toni. We got to do that for her sake as well as ours. Did she always come home at night? Or did she stay with them?'

'You two getting off on this?' Martelli asked.

Costa was unmoved. 'Did she leave any phone numbers where you could contact her when she was out?'

The old man went silent again, staring at them sullenly. He was thinking, though. There was some kind of revelation going on inside his head.

'She didn't go for men,' he said. 'Don't get me wrong. She didn't go for women either. She wasn't interested. Not for a long while now. I . . .'

Just for a moment he looked pained. 'I wish she had fucked off with someone, got married, had kids. Instead of all this shit. All this lonely, lonely shit . . .'

'Why was she lonely?' Peroni asked. 'Barbara of all people? I mean she could have had any man she wanted. Why wouldn't she try a couple out just for size?'

'I dunno,' he grunted, recovering his composure. 'Why ask me? She never told me nothing.'

Nic Costa felt an intense dislike for this desiccated man. Peroni had hit on something too. Barbara never did go out with anyone, though she must have been asked all the time. Was she scared of men? Had something happened that made her incapable of maintaining an everyday relationship?

'I wasn't interested in you,' Costa said. 'Not directly. If it's at all possible, Mr Martelli, try to imagine yourself outside all this for a moment. I was asking about Barbara. We've only got three possibilities here. Either she did this of her own volition, just acting alone, for what reason none of us could begin to guess. Or she did it as a private favour. Or someone from one of the mobs kept her sweet over the years and used her to do jobs in her spare time. And paid her.'

Martelli sucked desperately on the cigarette and blew a cloud across the room. Costa waved away the smoke.

'You're her father,' Costa continued. 'You were a cop. Where'd you put your money?'

The cigarette burned brightly again.

'In fact,' Costa added, 'talking of money, where are Barbara's bank accounts? Where are yours for that matter?'

'They took them,' Martelli snapped. 'Last night. They're clean. Not a hint of anything bad. Do I look like an idiot?'

Costa stood up. 'You don't mind if we search the apartment again, Mr Martelli? In case they missed something?'

The old man turned his miserable gaze on Peroni.

'I've had enough of this shit. You've got no papers that give you the right to do this.'

Peroni shook his head. 'We're not going away empty-handed, Toni. There must be something. Something you remembered after they left last night. Otherwise we go out for the beer and pizza. I promise you.'

'Thanks,' Martelli said with a scowl. 'Tell them this. She was a good daughter. She cared for me. She always knew her family came first. I wish I'd appreciated that more. I wish—'

His voice broke. His eyes filled with tears.

Toni Martelli was crying for himself, Costa thought. None of this was supposed to happen. The company he kept had saved him from prosecution before. He must have thought himself untouchable, and believed, by implication, this sense of immunity applied to his daughter too.

'It would be a terrible thing to live with,' Costa said quietly. 'Knowing the events that led to your own child's death came from you.'

'Get the fuck out of here,' Martelli croaked. 'The pair of you. And don't come back.'

Costa thought of arguing. But there was no point. The old man felt protected. As long as he could stay inside the big empty apartment in the Lateran he could continue to fool himself into believing the world would never intrude upon his private hell. None of this could last, and he knew that as well as they did. It was just one of the reasons why he was steeped in such terror.

They didn't say anything as they left. The two men stumbled outside into the daylight. The morning was growing painfully bright under the strong sun. It hurt the eyes. It made the city harsh and two-dimensional.

'We need to work on this "good cop, bad cop" routine,' Peroni suggested as they walked to the car. 'I got confused about my role in there.'

'Really? What role did you want?'

'Good cop,' Peroni insisted. 'Maybe not with assholes like him. But temperamentally I'm much better at it. Whereas you . . . I think you could out-hardball Falcone if you wanted. Doesn't that worry you a little, Nic?'

'Not often these days.'

Peroni shot him a puzzled glance. 'I wish you wouldn't do this to me. Make me think like a detective. It hurts. It's not what I'm built for.'

'What are you thinking?'

He nodded back at the apartment block. 'Martelli was on the take. That we *know*. So Barbara must have got into it too. Or maybe her job was some kind of reward for something Martelli had done. She just inherited the crooked mantle.'

Peroni stared at his partner, half offended. 'What? Why are you looking at me like that?'

'You're imagining things,' Costa said with a smile. 'This is good. Maybe you could make detective.'

The older man laughed and pointed to the car. 'Hey, what I make next is inspector. And you get to drive for me. This is just a temporary hiatus, a blip in the natural order. Some things never change.'

But they do, Costa thought. The world was different already. Cops were killing people in their spare time, and getting killed in return. Something was loose, and random too, but that didn't make it any less powerful.

Costa got behind the wheel, waited for Peroni to strap himself in, then set off into the traffic struggling round the big, busy square, thinking about Miranda

Julius and her missing daughter, trying to work out if there was a way in which they might be unwitting parts of the shadowy, broader picture which had taken Barbara Martelli down to Ostia on a murderous mission less than twenty-four hours before.

'At least we've found out something,' he said.

'We have?'

'Whoever it was on the motorbike that picked up Suzi Julius yesterday, it wasn't Barbara Martelli. She was on duty. I'll check her movements but there's no way that could have been her in the Campo. She couldn't have changed uniform, changed bike, without someone noticing.'

Peroni nodded. 'That's right. Jesus, I should have seen that myself.'

'You're doing fine, Gianni. You just have to keep looking for the connections. Imagining what they might be.'

'I don't want to imagine,' Peroni objected, scowling. 'I wanna ask and get told. OK? And don't say I ain't a partner.' He started delving into Costa's jacket pocket as the Fiat sped down the hill towards the Colosseum.

'This is over-familiar,' Costa declared.

Peroni took out the envelope of holiday snaps Miranda Julius had given them and waved them in Costa's face. 'I can look, can't I? There's nothing private going on between you two? Not yet anyways?'

'Hah, hah.'

Peroni snorted. 'That's good. Get all the impertinence out of your system now, Nic. You won't be able to come out with all that stuff when I'm your boss. Firm but fair is my rule. I don't take any crap though and—'

He went quiet. Costa drew to a halt at the red light, tucked in behind a tram, watching in despair the way the tourists ignored every traffic signal on the road, risking their lives dodging between the cars.

'What is it?' he asked.

Peroni had four photos fanned out in front of him. Just crowd scenes outside the Trevi Fountain.

'Did you see our late professor friend out at Ostia?'

'No. I was busy looking around the place.'

'In that case you should have watched the TV this morning. They showed a mugshot of him. We've got the same guy. Here.' He pointed at a bland, middle-aged man in the crowd, staring back at the camera, interested.

'And here.' It was another shot at the fountain, probably just a minute or so later. The crowd had changed, but Randolph Kirk was still there, still staring intently.

'And here. And here.'

'Four shots,' Costa said, and didn't know whether to feel pleased or horrified.

'So was the creep stalking her?' Peroni wondered. 'Was he a distant admirer or something, and never took it any further? Or is this just coincidence?'

Costa glanced in the mirror, hit the pedal and pulled out into the oncoming stream of traffic, generating a furious howl of horns.

'I don't know about you,' he said, 'but I'm right out of coincidences.'

'It doesn't rhyme with "vagina". Try again. I have a rule about this. Kindly indulge me.'

Teresa Lupo was struggling for words. She'd expected

some boring university administrator, not this slender, middle-aged Scotswoman dressed in an elegant, black velvet dress, a string of pearls around her pale, flawless neck, and sitting bolt upright behind a gleaming teak desk. A large, imposing brass nameplate stood between them bearing the name Professor Regina Morrison, Director of Administration, followed by a string of academic letters. Teresa wasn't sure she knew how to cope. What was more, she was starting to feel sick. Her head hurt. Her throat was going dry, her eyes itchy.

'Excuse me?'

The woman adjusted a photograph of a small terrier on the desk so that the dog stared directly into Teresa Lupo's eyes with a fierce, unbending gaze. 'Reg-*een*-a Morrison. I'm not responsible for my own name. Sometimes I wonder if perhaps I ought to change it to something more usual. But then I think: *why?* Why bend to an ignorant world? Why not make it bend instead?'

'Reg-*een*-a.'

'There,' the woman beamed. She had a very neat, mannish haircut, her too-black locks clipped close to her scalp. 'That wasn't so hard, was it? Now tell me. You're a police officer?'

'Teresa Lupo. I'm from the police department.'

Regina Morrison leaned forward and put her hands together in the kind of gesture she must have used with recalcitrant students all the time. 'So you're *not* a police officer?'

There was, she thought, no point in trying to fox this woman. 'Not exactly. I'm a pathologist. This is Italy, Professor Morrison. Things get complicated.'

'In the six months I've worked here I must say I've noticed. Still, I imagine I should be grateful anyone's turned up at all. If this were Edinburgh I'd have no end of people trampling through my office asking all manner of stupid questions with half a dozen TV stations stumbling in their wake. It's almost a day now since Randolph was killed. And all I have is you. Should I be grateful? Or offended?'

'Ask me that when the real cops turn up,' Teresa observed wryly. 'My money's on grateful.'

The slender shoulders moved just a little. That seemed to amuse her. 'So why are you here and not them?'

'Because—' she shrugged. 'The woman who killed your man was a cop and that changes things somewhat. The focus shifts, to her, not him. For now anyway. I got a look at the report this morning. It said Kirk was something of a loner. He lived by himself. No relatives in Italy. Not many friends. Cops are just like . . .' she tried to think of a good analogy, ' . . . university administrators. They put their resources in the places where they think they'll get the best return. The woman who killed Professor Kirk is someone they all knew. I guess they think they'll get further, faster, by checking her first before driving round all day trying to track down any barflies Kirk drank with in his spare time.'

'Randolph Kirk drank alone, poor man,' Regina Morrison said with some firmness.

Then she opened a drawer and took out a half bottle of Glenmorangie malt and two small glasses.

'Cheers,' she said, pouring a couple of shots, picking one up and staring directly across the shining desk at her visitor.

'Sorry,' Teresa said. 'I'm on duty. I didn't mean anything by that. It was a figure of speech. If he was a friend of yours—'

'No,' the woman answered, with equal conviction, and downed the whisky in one go. 'He wasn't that either. Not at all. I'm just a mite put out to discover that he, and by implication the rest of us in the academic community . . . we're all somehow less interesting than this murderous colleague of yours.'

Teresa took Kirk's book out of her bag and waved it in the air. 'Not to me you're not. I was hoping he could clear up a few things that were bothering me. While I couldn't claim to have made much personal contact with him during our brief meeting yesterday, I have read his book. And that I find very interesting indeed. That, Professor Morrison, is why I'm here.'

'It was you?' she asked, intrigued. 'The woman who was with him when this happened?'

'Not with him. Locked in his office. He saved my life, I think. Not that he meant to.'

'Don't undersell yourself,' Regina Morrison said with some admiration.

Unconsciously, Teresa stroked the plaster sticking to her scalp. 'I'll try to remember that.'

'But I don't understand why you, of all people, are here. I'd have thought you had plenty of real work to occupy you.'

Regina Morrison had a way of coming to the point with a remarkable directness. It hit home too. When she thought about Monkboy being left to his own devices Teresa Lupo felt far from comfortable.

'I need to tie up some loose ends. You've read Kirk's book?'

'Oh yes,' she answered. 'I'm an administrator now but I'm a classicist at heart. One day I'm going back to teaching. Sooner rather than later if I lose another member of staff this suddenly. I got parachuted in here from Edinburgh last autumn so don't expect me to provide too many searing insights into Randolph Kirk's persona. But I read his book and admired it greatly. When I took the job I hoped he had another one on the cards and perhaps I'd get an early look-in. That was one reason I came.' She thought carefully about what to say next. 'Little did I know.'

'Know what?' Teresa asked impatiently.

'To be honest with you I thought I'd be telling all this to a real police officer.'

She couldn't wait that long, though. Regina Morrison was itching to get on with her tale.

'I'll pass it on. Promise.'

'I'm sure you will,' the woman chuckled. 'The truth is I was about to fire him. It's just one nasty job after another here at the moment. They brought me in from outside for a reason. No one local, and certainly no one Italian, was going to face up to the . . . difficulties that needed cleaning up. I may as well tell you. It's going to come out anyway one day. Maladministration. Fraud. Some exceedingly dubious academic projects. And Randolph Kirk. A wonderful scholar, one of the best of his generation at Cambridge apparently. But a lonely little man with a lonely little man's habits. He couldn't keep his hands to himself. Most academics move on once in a while. That's the way to get more money. Not Randolph. He stayed here for a reason, my dear. He had to. If he'd pulled some of his tricks anywhere else he'd be out of work for life, sued for every penny he owned, and possibly in jail too.'

For a moment, Teresa felt like a cop, standing on the

brink of some important discovery. It was a wonderful sensation. 'Tricks?'

'He molested young women. The younger the better. I don't know the full extent of what went on. Back home we're like the Americans. Girls scream sexual assault if someone says they're wearing a nice dress. Why Sigmund Freud settled in Vienna is beyond me. We're ten times more anal in Edinburgh. Here it's the opposite. Everyone keeps their mouths shut. Maybe they think it goes with the course. All the same, I had enough evidence to terminate him within six weeks of falling into this chair and had your gun-wielding colleague not intervened I would have done it very soon. Trust me.'

Teresa tapped the book. 'Was it connected with what he wrote?'

Regina Morrison smiled back at her across the desk. 'You and I think along the same lines. Remarkable. I read that a couple of years ago. Then when I turned up here and started hearing some stories about the real Randolph I read it again. You needed to meet the man to understand this. He wasn't just writing history. He was laying out the grounds for some kind of personal philosophy of his, one he thought he was copying from those rituals. You know what I think? He played it out. He persuaded some of those gullible girls. He convinced them what they were doing was worth a try somehow. I can't believe they were fooled by all his mumbo-jumbo, mind, but you know what girls are. Perhaps there was something in it for them. Whatever. My guess is he put on one of those masks he was always writing about, pretended he was the great god himself and had his fun. It didn't fool anyone else, of course. The kids knew why they were doing it. To get the right grades or something.

If old Randolph invited along a few visitors – and I suspect he did because he was a man who desperately needed to be told how clever he was every living second of the day – I don't imagine they bought into his fancy myths either. They were just having a little fun for free. I'm guessing there, which is something no academic should do, but I feel it's right anyway. I talked to a couple of ex-students. They're just too scared to tell, to be honest. I wonder why.'

Teresa's pulse was racing. There had to be evidence here. There had to be something Regina Morrison could give her.

'Do you have names? Places?'

The woman on the other side of the desk eyed her suspiciously. 'You could get me into big trouble. You think I haven't put enough noses out of joint around here already? They brought me in to sort things out. That kind of work never makes you popular. Once I'm finished firing then they fire me. That's the way it goes. But I don't want to give them any early excuses.'

'Regina,' she said, taking care to pronounce the name perfectly, 'this isn't an academic exercise. It's not about finding out why Randolph Kirk died. Not directly. There's a girl who's gone missing. Right now. Maybe she's been abducted. Maybe she went willingly, not knowing what she was in for. But I'm sure it's something to do with all this. There was evidence in her apartment. A thyrsus. Some other items. That's why I went to see him in the first place.'

Teresa Lupo looked at her watch. She needed to get back to the morgue. There were so many questions to ask this unusual, intelligent stranger, and so little time.

'But if Randolph's dead—' Regina Morrison wondered.

'Surely she's safe. You don't think he went around abducting these girls. He couldn't do that. Not—'

Regina Morrison hesitated.

'Not what?'

'Not on his own.' The Scotswoman's composure was broken for a second or two. Teresa could see she genuinely was worried. 'Look,' she said, toying with the photo of the dog in front of her. 'I've been sitting here all morning waiting for you people to turn up. Where have you been? Who are you to start shouting urgent now? When I heard what had happened to Randolph last night I came in here late and took a little look around his office. A raid you might say. I thought I'd get in there before you people did. I didn't understand your timekeeping habits then, you understand.'

'You broke into his office?' Teresa gasped, a little in awe.

Regina Morrison tapped her nameplate. 'That's what titles are for. I came up with something too, locked away in a drawer with some teeny little padlock on it. Randolph hadn't a clue, you know. The man was utterly unworldly. You don't seem the squeamish sort, Teresa. Am I right?'

'I'm a pathologist.'

'Sorry. I meant "prudish".'

'Me?'

Regina Morrison opened a drawer and passed over a manila folder. On the cover, written in a sloping, intelligent hand, was scrawled a single word: 'Maenads'. And a picture was glued there too, a print of a familiar ancient theatre mask, howling through an exaggerated mouth. Then she leaned across the desk and said, in a conspiratorial whisper, 'You know who they were, don't you? The Maenads?'

'Remind me,' Teresa hissed, snatching through the pages of typed text and photographs, breathless, head reeling.

'The followers of the god. Call him Dionysus. Call him Bacchus. Either works. The Maenads were his women. He or – by implication – his followers made them initiates through these mysteries of theirs.'

Teresa's fingers were racing through the documents. 'What happened exactly? At these mysteries?'

'Not even Randolph claimed to know that. Not exactly. From what we discussed I think he had a better idea than he put in that book, though. It was a ritual, Teresa. It's important you remember that.'

She paused over a page of incomprehensible text. 'Why?'

'Because rituals are formal. They have a structure. Nothing happens by accident. These girls weren't snatched from the street. Some of them volunteered. Some of them were gifts from their family.'

'What?' It seemed incomprehensible to her. 'Why would any mother or father do that?'

'Because they thought it was right. Why not? Plenty of girls get given to the Church today to become nuns. Is it that different?'

She thought of the book. 'Nuns don't get raped.'

'They're both offerings to their chosen god. The difference lies in the detail. Take out some of the weirder parts – the parts Randolph liked – it's not that different. Gifts or volunteers, they submitted to the ceremony. They became brides of the god. It's just that the Dionysians consummated that marriage, physically, in the shape of some hanger-on like Randolph I imagine.'

'And afterwards?'

'Afterwards they belonged to him. And the men who followed him. They worshipped him. Or them. Once a year he returned to meet his new brides and renew his gift for those who'd gone before. He gave them all that they wanted: ecstasy, frenzy. If Randolph was right, the nasty parts, the violence and the unbridled sexual encounters, occurred after the marriage, not during it. They enjoyed what we would call an orgy. Pure, mindless, dangerous, liberating. Then they went back to their homes and were good mothers for another year. Have you read *The Bacchae* or is Euripides not to your taste?'

'Not recently.'

Regina Morrison reached into the bookshelf behind her and took out a slim, blue leather-backed volume. 'Borrow it if you like. You can interpret the story in a number of ways. The liberal tradition says it's an analogy for the dual nature of humanity, the need to give our wild side an outlet now and then because if we don't it will surface anyway, when we least want it. The natural order breaks down. People get torn limb from limb by crazy women thirsty for blood just because someone broke the rules, unwittingly even.'

She leaned forward over the desk. 'Do you want to know what I think?'

Teresa Lupo wasn't sure she did but, all the same, found herself asking, 'What?'

'It's just about men and power and sex. How they can have it whenever they want, regardless of how a woman feels. And how we're supposed to be grateful however much we hate it because, well, let's face things, the god lives with them, not us, and the only way we get a taste is if we let them put a little bit of him inside us. Are you getting my drift?'

'Oh, I am, I am,' Teresa agreed.

'One doesn't wish to appear the puritan, Teresa. As a Scotswoman I am all too aware of that. There's nothing wrong with – what was it that American woman called it? – the "zipless fuck". Everyone likes some mindless carnality from time to time. Half an hour of pleasure and nothing to think of afterwards. You must have done the same?'

Teresa Lupo looked at the staid, elegant woman opposite her and after a while could still only think of one thing to say. 'Yes.'

'But a quick fuck in the dark's not the same, is it? Old Randolph *planned* all this. It's all just so damnably male.'

'Agreed. We must have dated the same men over the years, Regina, believe me.'

'I don't date men any more,' Regina Morrison said very sweetly. 'Where's the hunt? Where's the challenge? When you know they're panting for it anyway, with whomever or whatever they can find, what's the point? Here. Let me give you my card. My mobile's on there.'

'Right,' she replied, cursing her own stupidity, taking the item from the woman's slim hand in any case.

'It's a question of timing,' Regina Morrison said. 'Everything is.'

Teresa looked again at the file. There were pages and pages. And photographs. Lots of photographs.

'What is?' she asked idly.

'Finding this girl is your idea, isn't it? That's why

you're here on your own. The police don't think there's any connection.'

Teresa stared at her. The woman had been two steps ahead all along. It was disquieting. 'They're not sure.'

'You'd best hope they're right and you're wrong, my dear. Think about the dates.'

'The dates?'

'You read the book. Tomorrow is Liberalia. The day for making new Maenads. And the day the old ones come out to play.'

'Yes. I know that.' She thought of Nic Costa. *'We know that.'*

Regina Morrison smiled at her, bemused. 'You seem somewhat . . . distracted.'

Teresa Lupo took out one photo from the folder and placed it on the desk. Then she stifled a sneeze with a lone finger.

It was an old picture, shot secretly like the rest, in poor interior light using a cheap camera. Home-developed probably, which explained the thin, washed-out colours. That and its age. She could just about make out the images on the walls in the background. They were almost the same as the dancing fauns and leering satyrs in Kirk's book, from the place that seemed to double as his strange, private playground at Ostia. But not quite. This was somewhere different. The paintings looked even older, and more sinister somehow. The place looked larger too. Perhaps he'd found Rome's Villa of Mysteries and kept it for this one particular purpose.

Barbara Martelli was in the centre of the shot. She wore a plain white tee-shirt and jeans. She looked so young, just a teenage kid, so sweet it almost hurt. Teresa Lupo's head hurt trying to reconcile these conflicting

images into some sane, comprehensible whole: innocence on the verge of being spoiled, of entering the
long path that would transform this lovely kid into a
murderous black-helmeted insect. Was the beast in her
already, a cocoon of hate and death just waiting, growing
over the years?

She didn't want to look too closely at the figure next
to Barbara. It was Eleanor Jamieson. That much was
quite clear. But seeing the girl like this – alive, full of
spark and expectation – was almost more than Teresa
Lupo's pained, congested head could bear. She'd come
to think of her as a mummified corpse on a shining
silver table. This image made her something else, a real,
looming presence haunting Teresa's head, and emphasized, almost to breaking point, the enormity of her
death. This was all *before*. The god hadn't visited them
yet. Maybe they never even knew he was on the way.

And one more thing, one crazy, nagging idea that
couldn't be dismissed. Teresa was unable to forget the
pictures of Suzi Julius she'd seen. She and Eleanor were
so alike they could almost have been sisters, smiling
teenage siblings from the same template of classic blonde
beauty. The thyrsus, the tattoo, the seeds . . . all these
coincidences paled next to the physical resemblance they
bore to one another, and it was this, she knew, that had
triggered Suzi's disappearance, this alone that made her
reach the bottom of some long, dark narrow street and
get called into the shadows. Someone who knew what
had happened sixteen years ago found his memory
jogged when he saw this lovely young stranger walking
down the street. The wheel turned. The ritual was in
motion.

'Teresa?' Regina Morrison looked worried. 'Are you OK?'

'I'm fine,' she said softly, then coughed and felt the mucus move painfully inside her temples. 'I need to take these documents.'

Regina Morrison nodded. 'Of course. Sure you're all right? You look as if you could use that drink.'

'No. I'm fine.'

She was lying. Her eyes had started itching again, stinging cruelly.

She looked into Eleanor's face. It had never happened like this before. They were always dead, truly dead, long dead, dead and gone forever, when they fell beneath her knife. A switch had been turned: life went from on to off, with nothing in between and nothing after.

She remembered cowering in Randolph Kirk's scruffy little office, remembered what happened when she heard the shots, how something appeared to pass through her with a sudden resigned rush, like the last gasp of a departing persona.

When she stared at Eleanor Jamieson she felt the same sensation, the same lack of certainty about herself and what she did for a living. Just to pay the bills, to feed the prurient maw of the state. And now Suzi Julius was out there, walking in these same shadows, towards the same destination, with no one in the Questura paying sufficient attention because Teresa Lupo, Crazy Teresa, had taken matters into her own hands, pretended she was something she wasn't and made it all worse.

'Teresa,' Regina Morrison said. 'Here's a tissue. Take it.'

'Thanks,' she said, and put down the page, her hand trembling, her vision awash with tears, gulping at the whisky, gulping at another too when Regina Morrison briskly refilled the glass.

Falcone cast an interested eye at the bunch of men lurking on the first floor of Neri's house. Then the fat old hood hurriedly ushered him and Rachele D'Amato upstairs.

'I didn't realize you had guests,' Falcone said. 'And you answer the door yourself these days. Servants getting too expensive?'

'I don't need any damn servants,' Neri retorted. 'Don't give me any shit, Falcone. I could've turned you back at the door. You got no papers that give you the right to walk into a man's home like this. And her—'

Neri looked right through D'Amato. 'So you two are on speaking terms these days? I heard that ended when the sheets started to get cold.'

'This is business,' she said briskly, then followed Neri into a large living room furnished expensively with a minimum of taste: modern leather sofas and armchairs, reproduction paintings on the plain cream walls, and a big glass table at the centre.

Two people sat on the couch: a slim attractive woman in her thirties, with fiery reddish gold hair and striking, angry features, and a slightly younger man, slim, nervous, with dark, shifty eyes and a bad bleach job.

'I don't have a lawyer on the premises,' Neri said. 'So you can talk in front of my family. That way if you invent stuff I've got witnesses.'

Falcone nodded.

'You didn't introduce us,' the woman said. 'I'm Adele. His wife.'

'Current wife,' Neri added.

'True,' she agreed. 'This is Mickey. My stepson. Say hello to the nice policeman, Mickey. And stop twitching like that. It pisses me off. Quit gawping at the lady too.'

Mickey ceased fiddling with his fingers and muttered, 'Pleasure.'

Neri fell into a large, fat armchair next to them and waved Falcone and D'Amato to the table. 'I'd offer you coffee but fuck it. Why are you here? What am I supposed to have done now?'

'Nothing,' Falcone said. 'Just a social visit.'

Neri's big chest heaved with a dry laugh.

'When we decide you've done something, Emilio, it won't be just the two of us who turn up,' Rachele D'Amato said, amused by the way Mickey was still staring at her. 'We'll have lots and lots of people. And the TV crews, the newspapers too. I just know they're going to hear of it.'

'Not gonna happen,' Neri muttered. 'Never. There's no reason for it.'

She nodded at his son. 'Do we take him in too? Is he part of the family firm now?'

'You tell me. You DIA scum never give up spying on me. What do you think?'

She smiled at Mickey. He blushed a little and stared at his feet.

'I think he doesn't look like you. Maybe he doesn't act like you. I don't know.'

'No,' Neri agreed. 'You don't know. Tell you what. If you want someone to keep your statistics up you can take him now. Take her too if you feel like it, so long as . . .' He took a good look at them when he said this. ' . . . they get to share the same cell. She's got more brains than him though. You might find it harder fitting her up.'

Falcone smiled. 'Happy families. Don't you love to see them?'

'My patience is wearing thin. Get to the point.'

'The point,' Falcone said immediately, 'is that I want to know what you were doing sixteen years ago. I want you to tell me about Vergil Wallis and what happened to his stepdaughter.'

Neri's bleak, reptilian eyes narrowed. 'You're kidding me. You want me to try to remember all that way back? Who're you talking about?'

'Vergil Wallis,' D'Amato repeated. 'He was your contact with the West Coast mob. Don't try to deny it. There are intelligence photos of you two together. We know you had dealings.'

'I'm a sociable man,' Neri protested. 'I meet a lot of people. You expect me to remember every one?'

'You remember this one,' Falcone said. 'He nearly got you on the wrong side of the Sicilians. You screwed him over some deal. Is there still bad feeling between you? Have you spoken recently?'

'*What?*' Neri's feigned outrage was unconvincing. He meant it that way. 'Look, if you want to throw these kinds of questions at me it's best we do it some other time, in the company of a lawyer. Not now.'

D'Amato ran her fingers through her perfect brown hair, just for Mickey's benefit. 'You don't need a lawyer, Emilio. No one's accusing you of anything. We just want to know what you can recall. You did meet this man. We all know that. That's not why we're here. His stepdaughter was murdered. Sixteen years ago. The body turned up recently.'

'You think I don't read the papers? You think I don't hear things?'

'So?' Falcone persisted.

Neri nodded at Mickey. 'You remember some black guy way back then? Rings a bell for me. Not much more.'

'Sure,' Mickey agreed, looking more nervous than ever. 'He and some kid were with us on vacation for a while. They were both history freaks or something. Couldn't stop talking about all that crap. Museums and stuff. Turned me off.'

'And you remember his stepdaughter?' D'Amato asked.

'A little,' Mickey conceded. 'I thought she was his, if you get my meaning. A black guy with a skinny blonde thing around them. What would you think?'

Falcone considered this. 'Are you saying there was some relationship between Wallis and the girl?'

'No,' he replied defensively, looking at his father for guidance. 'I dunno.'

'He was some jumped-up piece of work,' Neri added. 'Who the fuck knew what was going on? I'll say this, though. Met a few like him in my time. They come here, think they can do business, never have to pay nothing in the way of an entrance fee just because of who they are. Yeah, and one more thing. You ever seen a black guy with a blonde in tow he wasn't fucking?'

D'Amato shook her head, unhappy with this idea. 'She was his stepdaughter.'

'Oh right,' Neri sneered. 'That makes a difference. Tell me. If you found some rich Italian guy shacked up with a teenager, smiling at her all the time like he owned her, you'd say that about him, huh? You don't think

240

maybe there are some double standards here? Men like that can't keep their hands still. Can you imagine what it'd be like to get a couple at the same time? Mother and daughter? You go ask him about that. Not me.'

He had a point. Falcone understood that. Maybe Wallis was just a great actor. Maybe this show of grief was just that, a show.

'What about you, Mickey?' D'Amato asked suddenly.

'What about me?' he stuttered.

'Did you like the look of her? Was she your type?'

He glanced nervously, first at Adele, then at his father. 'Nah. Too skinny. Too stuck up. She talked all the history shit he did. What's someone like that gonna do with someone like me?'

Rachele D'Amato smiled. 'So you remember her well?'

'Not much,' he murmured.

Neri waved his big arm, 'Fuck this. Why are we talking about some kid who went missing ages ago? What's this got to do with us?'

They said nothing.

'Right,' Neri continued. 'Now that's out of the way maybe you can go. This place is starting to smell bad. I want some fresh air in here.'

Rachele D'Amato smiled at Mickey. 'What about Barbara Martelli, Mickey? Was she your kind of woman? Not skinny at all. Got a good job as a cop too.'

His eyes went round and round, flitting between his stepmother and Neri. 'Who? Who? Dunno what the hell you're talking about. Who?'

'The woman who was in the papers, dummy,' Neri snarled. 'The cop who got killed yesterday. They say she offed someone. That right? What is it with the police force today? How's a man supposed to trust anyone?'

'I ask the questions,' Falcone said. 'Where were you yesterday, Mickey? Give me your movements, morning to night.'

'He was here with me all day,' Adele Neri insisted. 'All day. And in the evening too.'

'We were all here together,' Neri added. 'Apart from a little lunch outing I had with one of my employees. He can vouch for me. We can vouch for one another. You got any reason to think otherwise?'

Rachele D'Amato took two photographs out of her briefcase: Barbara Martelli in uniform and one of her old man, back in the days when he was on the force. 'Her father was a cop. He was on your payroll.'

'Me?' Neri whined. 'Pay cops? Don't you think I pay enough already what with the taxes round here?'

'When did you last talk to Martelli?' Falcone asked. 'When did you last speak to his daughter?'

'Don't recall ever making their acquaintance. And I'm speaking for us all now. Understand? If you've got something that says otherwise you go show it to a lawyer. Except you don't have anything. Otherwise we wouldn't be talking like this now, would we?'

She put the photos back in her bag. 'Those men downstairs,' she said.

'We were thinking of having a card game later. They're good guys.'

'Make it last,' Falcone ordered. 'Make it last a long time. I don't want to see them on the streets. You got that?'

The big old hood was shaking his head. 'So Romans don't get to walk their own town now? Is that what you're saying? Jesus. Here I am taking this shit. Here I am listening to your dumb threats and all this crap about things you don't know. And that American bastard's just walking round doing what he likes. No one's asking him whether he was screwing that girl. No one's asking him if he's been paying off dumb cops to get what he wants.' He waved a fat hand at them. 'You tell me. Why's that? Are you people just plain stupid or what?'

Falcone stood up. Rachele D'Amato followed suit.

'Nice seeing you again,' Neri barked. 'Don't feel the need to rush back.'

'Do you know what tomorrow is?' Falcone asked.

'Saturday. Do I get a prize?'

'Liberalia.'

Neri screwed up his slack face in an expression of distaste. 'What? This some new European holiday they're pressing on us now? Don't mean a thing to me.'

'It does,' Falcone said. 'It means that if you know what's good for you, you stay right here. You don't get in my way.'

'Wow,' Neri sneered. 'This is what cops do now. Make a few empty threats.'

'It's good advice. I remember you. Years ago, when I was just a detective. I watched you, I *know* you.'

'Yeah? You think so?'

'And the thing is, you've changed. You're older. You look weaker somehow. Let me tell you something. You're not the man you were.'

'Bullshit!' Neri yelled, getting onto his feet, waving his big arms in the air. 'Get the fuck out of here before I throw you down the stairs, cop or no cop.'

Falcone wasn't listening. He had his phone to his ear and was engrossed in the call. There was something in his face that made them all go quiet and wait for what came next.

'I'll be straight there,' Falcone murmured.

'Leo?' D'Amato asked. 'Is something wrong?'

He looked at Emilio Neri. 'Maybe. Does the name Beniamino Vercillo mean anything to you?'

'All these stupid questions—' the old man grumbled.

'Well?'

'Not a damn thing. Why d'you ask?'

'Nothing,' Falcone replied with a shrug. 'He's a stranger. Why worry? Watch the news. Pay some bent cop to tell you first. Who cares? I'll let myself out.'

'Mickey!'

Neri pointed at the two of them. Mickey led Falcone and Rachele D'Amato downstairs, going first so that he got a chance to turn round now and again and get a good look at her long, lithe legs moving out from underneath the short skirt.

The visitors were sitting around a table in the big room on the first floor, reading papers, smoking, playing cards.

'I recognize a few familiar faces,' Falcone said. 'Is this the kind of company you keep, Mickey?'

'Don't know what you mean.' Mickey Neri continued on to the big front door, with its security cameras and multiple electronic locks.

Rachele D'Amato ducked out of the way of the lens and smiled at him. 'You should be smart, Mickey. It's important to be smart in a situation like this.'

'A situation like what?'

'Change,' she said and handed him her card. 'Can't you just feel it in the air? That's my private number. Call if you want to talk. I could keep you out of jail. If things turn bad, I could even keep you alive.'

He glanced upstairs to make sure no one was listening. 'G-g-get out of here,' Mickey Neri mumbled.

The scene of crime men pulled on their white bunny suits then clambered down the iron staircase into the basement office off the Via dei Serpenti. Falcone watched them, mentally trying to work out the manpower disposition inside the Questura. With the officers already inside that brought the total contingent on the murder scene to six. It wasn't enough. The Questura was getting desperately stretched. He'd already got people trying to persuade the sick to rise from their beds. Even with the few who complied, he was still struggling to keep every thread of the investigation – Randolph Kirk, Barbara Martelli, Eleanor Jamieson and, just possibly, the Julius girl – fully staffed. It was the spring holiday season. A quiet time of the year, or so everyone supposed. The gaps were already starting to appear. He wished he had more people to despatch to watch Neri and Wallis, make sure they didn't develop any stupid ideas. He wished, too, he had time to think about Suzi Julius. Falcone shared some of Costa's fears, though he was reluctant to act in the present circumstances until some hard facts emerged to link her directly to the Jamieson case. There was still no evidence to suggest this was anything other than a wayward teenager out for some fun. He couldn't afford to waste the men he had on hypothetical crimes when there were real ones demanding his attention.

Rachele D'Amato's black Alfa pulled up on the pavement and he watched her get out, watched the way she angled her slender legs carefully so that the tight red skirt she was wearing didn't ride up too much. For a brief moment Falcone let other thoughts dominate his mind. She was thirty minutes behind him. She'd had to call in at the DIA office on the way. He really had no idea what was going on there behind closed doors.

'She doesn't need to be here,' he reminded himself, then managed to work up a smile. 'Not at all.'

She walked up, eyeing him. 'Leo?'

'I don't recall issuing an invitation, Rachele. This isn't an open house. You don't get to walk into every investigation we have.'

She nodded at the door. A couple of the bunny suits were coming out again, taking off their helmets to light cigarettes. The path was clear for the rest of them to go in. 'Don't I get to take a look? You really believed Neri then? You think this guy was a complete stranger?'

'According to what we know Beniamino Vercillo was an accountant. We don't have a thing on him. He was just a little man. Lived in Paroli on his own. The safe's open. It's probably robbery or something.'

She eyed the men by the iron staircase, not believing a word. Falcone resented the idea she always seemed one step ahead of him. 'Is that so? I listened on the radio. I gather you have a witness.'

'You shouldn't go near our radios,' he said. 'That's not part of the deal.'

'I'm saving time. For all of us. What happened?'

He sighed. 'A girl in the optician's saw a character in a kind of costume going in. Something theatrical. With a mask. There's a street theatre troupe performing down at the Colosseum so she didn't think too much of it. We checked. They're performing Euripides. *The Bacchae.*

One of their costumes is missing. I've got men interviewing every last one of them. The trouble is they were rehearsing at the time. Either they're all liars or it's someone else who stole the costume. No one saw a soul coming out. It's—'

Everything was going wrong, heading off in different directions. It denied him the time to think, the opportunity to focus on what mattered. 'It's the last damn thing I need right now.'

D'Amato didn't look impressed.

'Are you going to tell me or do I have to guess?' Falcone sighed. 'We really aren't working together on this one, are we? Am I the problem? Do you want to liaise with someone else instead?'

Her hand went to his arm. Slim, delicate fingers. He recalled their touch. 'I'm sorry, Leo. It's not you. It's me. You're right. This is all . . . out of synch somehow. The DIA's no different to you, really. We expect things to happen the way they always did. None of this fits a template.'

'You can say that again. So Vercillo wasn't some boring little accountant?'

She laughed and it reminded him of how she once was: young, carefree. And how much that used to affect him. 'You didn't really think that, did you, Leo?'

'No.' He'd put on a bunny suit himself for a while and been inside. He'd seen what was there. He couldn't get the idea of that damned mask out of his head. 'I just don't like jumping to conclusions.'

'We could never pin anything on him,' she went on. 'Vercillo was smart. He needed to be. He kept books for Neri. Of that I'm pretty sure. Not that you'll ever find a sheet of paper to prove it.'

DAVID HEWSON

A piece of the puzzle fell into place in his head. Falcone thought of the scene inside the dead man's office and knew she was wrong for a change, though he kept the news to himself.

'Why would someone murder Neri's accountant? Has he been taking from the boss?'

She'd considered that already. 'It's hard to imagine. He'd know what the result would be if he got found out. I don't think Neri would send round a man in a mask either. Vercillo would just be there one moment and gone for good the next.'

'Then what?' he wondered.

'We had some intelligence,' she said eventually. 'Early yesterday evening four, maybe five suspicious Americans flew in to Fiumicino. Separate airlines, separate classes for a couple. As if they didn't know each other. It could be Wallis beefing up his army.'

Falcone stroked his pointed beard. He hated the way she seemed to know so much about the mob, how she seemed to understand their movements instinctively. The DIA were supposed to do that. All the same it left him feeling cheated. 'What army? You said he was retired.'

'He is but that doesn't mean he's stupid. You saw the security on that place of his. Vergil Wallis doesn't let his guard slip, any more than Neri does. Men like that have to be careful, retired or not.'

Falcone wondered: could this be Wallis's first act of vengeance? Then there was a bustle down the street. It was Monkboy and the rest of the path team – except Teresa Lupo – arriving, unusually late.

'What took you?' Falcone barked at them. Silvio Di Capua just put his head down and stumbled onto the staircase. He looked scared.

'You're saying these men have been summoned?' Falcone asked her.

'Maybe.'

He thought back to the cool way Wallis had greeted them. 'It could make sense I guess. If he thinks there's a war on the way. He didn't look like a man getting ready for war to me.'

She gave him a sideways glance, as if she thought he were being naïve. 'You should never take these people at face value, Leo. Not even Neri. That was a perform-ance this morning too, though not one I understand. Perhaps Vergil Wallis just feels he has no choice but to get some muscle around him.'

Falcone grimaced and started walking for the door. She raced to keep up with him.

The bunny suits had their helmets off. They were busy, dusting, poking, peering into corners, putting things into envelopes. Falcone glowered at Monkboy trembling over the corpse. Beniamino Vercillo was pinned to his old leather chair by a curving sword through the chest. His body had fallen forward a frac-tion. It was plain to see that the blade had been thrust up through the ribcage, exiting to the right of the spine and impaling itself into the back of the chair.

Vercillo was a thin man. Falcone wondered how much force such a blow would take. Crazy Teresa would know. She always did know this kind of thing. But she wasn't there and Monkboy looked out of his depth, surrounded by a bunch of junior morgue assistants waiting to be told what to do.

'Where is she?' Falcone demanded.

'Who?'

'Who the hell do you think? Your boss?'

'Had to go out,' Silvio Di Capua stuttered. 'She'll be here soon.'

Falcone was astonished she would have the nerve to play these games twice in twenty-four hours. 'Go out where?' he bellowed.

Di Capua shrugged, looking miserable and scared.

'Get her here,' Falcone barked. 'Now. And where the hell are Peroni and Costa? Didn't anyone call them like I asked?'

'On their way,' one of the bunny suits mumbled. 'They went back to the Questura. Didn't know you were out. They got something they said.'

'Jesus,' Falcone cursed. 'It's about time someone got something. What's going on around here?'

Then he stopped. Rachele D'Amato was standing by the late accountant's body, looking at the table, smiling. There were papers everywhere, printouts from computers, pages from a typewriter that seemed to pre-date these. Even a couple written in a careful, childlike hand.

They were just letters, a sea of letters, spilling everywhere. Apart from a single sheet with text on it, scrawled in a different style of writing, using a black felt-tip pen left by the paper. The ink looked fresh. The page depicted a phone keypad and beneath it a selection of numbers copied from the typed page next to it. The relevant section was ringed on the original page. Falcone had realized almost immediately what it was: the key to a code. A date. A phone number. An amount. And then some more codes that were impenetrable, because they probably related to the kind of transaction involved. Maybe, with more work, they could crack them too. This was a rich and generous gift. A deliberate escalation of the odds.

She reached for the papers, elated. He stopped her.

'We haven't gone over those yet,' he cautioned. 'Afterwards, you'll get to see them. I promise.'

'Do you know what this is?'

'I didn't. From what you've said, I think I do now.'

She was ecstatic, triumphant. He wished he could share her elation. 'These go back years. We can put Emilio Neri away for good. We may be able to nail anyone who did business with him. Have you thought of that, Leo?'

'Right now I'm thinking about a murder,' he answered. Then he wondered: was that the direction you were supposed to take in the circumstances? Did this bloody dumb show exist in order to make you miss a larger though more subtle point? He couldn't work up any enthusiasm for the information that lay on the table. However useful it was, something about its provenance troubled him. This wasn't the way the mobs normally went to war, killing underlings, leaving damning information on their enemies for the police. Not without some pay-off anyway.

For a fleeting moment he wished he'd never left that beach in Sri Lanka, never caught the plane home to these complexities. He'd felt old recently. The renewed, chaste presence of Rachele D'Amato did his mental state no good at all. The pressure was something he could take. It was the doubts that bothered him. He wanted certainties in his life, not shadows and ghosts.

'Where the hell is everyone?' he scowled, and felt, for the first time in many a month, the edges of his temper beginning to fray.

*

The moment Teresa Lupo left Regina Morrison's office Monkboy was on the line, screaming for all he was worth, making it dead plain that Falcone was possibly in the foulest mood in history and wanted her on the scene *now*. She drove through the choked streets, thinking about what she had heard, not wondering for a moment how she would explain her absence or the fact that, for the second time in two days, she'd wilfully trodden on cop territory.

Dead people didn't run away. There was nothing she could do for this new corpse that Silvio Di Capua couldn't. All the hard work came later. Falcone would surely realize that. Most of all, *she had a result*. She didn't expect him to be grateful. She didn't expect to get bawled out either. While the rest of them were stumbling around in the dark, grasping at cobwebs, she'd found something concrete: the photograph of Barbara Martelli and Eleanor Jamieson in the private files of Professor Randolph Kirk, a man the lovely Barbara had despatched so efficiently the day before.

'Shithead,' she mouthed, with precious little enthusiasm, at a white van blocking the street. Some Chinese guy was unloading boxes out of the back and, very slowly, running them into a little gift shop. She looked into the window. It was full of the crap cheap Chinese gift shops sold: bright pink pyjamas, plastic back-scratchers, calendars with dragons on them. It all seemed so *irrelevant*.

She opened the window and yelled, 'Hey. Move it.'

The man put down the box he was carrying, turned and said something which sounded very like, 'Fluck you.'

Red mist swirled in front of her eyes. She pulled out her ID card, hoping the state police seal would do the trick, waved it in his direction and screeched, 'No, ass-hole, fluck *you*.'

He hissed something underneath his breath that made her glad she didn't understand Cantonese, then slowly climbed into the van and started to clunk it through the gears.

The riddle still hung in front of her, grey, shapeless. Was her own presence at the site merely a rotten coincidence? Did Barbara decide to off the professor anyway – maybe through some recurring bad dreams – then add the one and only witness to the list? Had Kirk called her to say someone was around asking awkward questions, in such a panic that she decided to shut him up for good? Was that what a Maenad did? Dispose of the god if he lost his sparkle? Or did Kirk phone someone else, someone who knew Barbara Martelli, understood she'd become a Maenad somewhere along the way and just given her the job: *out you go girl, it's whacking time, and don't forget to clear up any prying pathologists who happen to walk into the firing line.*

They'd never know. The first thing the cops had checked was the phone records. She'd asked that morning. They hadn't a clue whom Kirk had called. There was no redial button on Kirk's ancient handset. The phone company didn't log local calls.

She was starting to think like a cop now and it scared her. All these possibilities lay in the dark, limitless recesses of the imagination, a place she was trained to avoid. A place that, if she were honest with herself, had begun to scare her. That was why she started blubbing in front of a complete stranger, why it took her a good fifteen minutes to recover sufficient composure to get on with the day. That and the shitty virus fighting it out with two quick shots of Glenmorangie in her bloodstream. Life would be so much easier if the dead could come back and talk, just for a little while. She'd drive over to the morgue, stare at the mummified cadaver that had once been Eleanor Jamieson, and murmur, *Tell Teresa all about it, sweetie. Get it off your mahogany chest.*

Still, that corpse had spoken to someone. It had said: *not everything dies.* And Suzi Julius, with her fateful blonde looks, had sparked something too. Cause and effect didn't respect mortality.

The white van lumbered off the pavement and rolled down towards the low shape of the Colosseum at the end of the street. Teresa Lupo's new yellow Fiat, provided by the insurance company and already sporting a couple of fresh dents, sat stationary in the road. The horns behind her began to yell.

She wound down the window and yelled back at the creep in the Alfa on her tail. 'Can't you see I am *thinking*, you crapulent piece of pus?'

Then she put the car gently into gear and drove down the Via dei Serpenti, at a measured, steady pace, trying to put her thoughts in order.

When she walked into Beniamino Vercillo's cellar she felt like putting her hands over her ears, like running away from everything and finding some oblivion in a long, cold drink. She'd seen this so many times before, the path team hanging round the corpse, waiting to be told what to do, the scene of crime men in their white bunny suits combing the place for shards of information. And Falcone, this time with the woman from the DIA, standing at the back, watching everything like a hawk, throwing questions at Nic Costa and Peroni, unhappy, uncommunicative.

The tall inspector broke off from barking at his men. 'And where've you been? In case you haven't noticed there's work to be done.'

She held up both hands in deference. 'Sorry,' she answered meekly. 'Don't feel the need to ask how I am. I get people trying to kill me most days.'

Falcone demurred slightly. 'We need you.'

'I'll take that as an apology though a simple sorry would have sufficed. How's it going with the missing girl by the way?'

'What?'

'The girl?'

Falcone scowled at her. 'Leave the live ones to us.'

She looked at the body behind the desk. There'd been so many over the years, it was like being on a factory line. Now something was different. When Teresa Lupo looked at this corpse, the professional, unconscious side of her already assessing what she saw, a low, rebel voice started sounding in her head, getting louder and louder and louder, until it drowned out everything else, the blood, the questions, the tension and the fears.

'I can't do this any more,' she murmured, and wondered who was speaking: her or the rebel voice. And whether they were, perhaps, one and the same.

Monkboy hovered over the body, watching her, waiting for a lead.

The voice got louder. It was her voice.

'Is anybody *listening* here?' she yelled, and even the forensic people dusting down the office furniture became still.

'I can't do this any more,' Teresa Lupo said again, more quietly. 'He's dead. That's all there is to say.

There's a girl out there still breathing and here we are, like undertakers or something, staring at a corpse.'

She felt a hand on her arm. It was Costa.

'Don't try that one,' she murmured. Her hands were shaking. Her head felt as if it might explode. She could hardly open the bag, hardly get her hands around the file Regina Morrison had given her, find the strength to take out the pictures. 'I trained as a doctor. I learned how to distinguish the symptoms from the disease. This is irrelevant. This is a symptom, nothing else. This—'

She scattered several of the photos on the table, over the sheets of numbers, obliterating them. She made sure the most important one, Barbara and Eleanor *before*, was on the top.

'This is the disease.'

Falcone, Costa, Peroni and Rachele D'Amato had to push their way through the men in bunny suits to get a good look. Someone swore softly in amazement. The girls looked even more beautiful now, Teresa thought. And it was so easy to imagine Suzi Julius just walking into the frame, shaking hands with them, not knowing they were both dead, sixteen years apart, but dead is dead, dead is a place where the years don't matter.

'Where did you get these?' Falcone asked, furious.

'Randolph Kirk's office. This morning.'

'What?' he roared.

'Don't rupture something,' she said quietly. 'You didn't look there. You weren't even interested.'

'I didn't have the damn time!'

His long brown nose was sniffing at her. She thought of the drinks Regina Morrison had given her. The bastard never missed a thing.

'Jesus Christ, woman,' he snapped. 'You've been drinking. This is the end. Because of you—'

He didn't finish the sentence. He was too livid.

'Because of me what?' she yelled back. '*What?* Your beautiful traffic cop is dead? Is that what you think?' She stared at the men in the room. 'Is that what you *all* think? May I remind you of one fact? Your beautiful traffic cop was a cold-blooded murderer. Maybe she did it for herself. Maybe she did it because someone told her to. But she killed someone. She'd have killed me too if I'd let her. I didn't cause any of this. It was just there waiting to happen and if it had been somebody else maybe there'd be two victims, more even, lying in the morgue right now, not one. Hell, maybe there are, maybe there have been more over the years. And we wouldn't know. Because Barbara Martelli would still be riding that bike of hers, smiling sweetly all the time to fire up all your wet dreams, because none of you, not one, could possibly believe what she really was. Thanks to me you found out. Sorry—' She said this last very slowly, just to make sure the point went in. 'I apologize. That's the trouble with the truth. Sometimes it hurts.'

'You have damaged this investigation,' Falcone said wearily. 'You have overstepped your position.'

'There's a missing girl out there!'

'We *know* there's a missing girl out there,' Falcone replied, and threw the four photos Peroni had given him onto the table to join the others. 'We *know* she's been abducted. We know, too, that somehow these things are all linked. This is a murder inquiry and an abduction inquiry and I will allot what precious resources I have in my power to try and ensure no one else gets killed.'

'Oh,' she said softly, staring at the pictures. 'I'm

sorry.' She was shaking her head. She looked utterly lost. 'I don't know what's wrong with me. I've got the flu I think. What a pathetic excuse.'

Costa took her arm again and this time she didn't resist. 'Go home,' he said. 'You shouldn't be working anyway. Not after what happened yesterday.'

'What happened yesterday is *why* I'm working. Don't you understand?'

'Teresa,' Silvio Di Capua bleated. 'We need you.'

'You heard the man,' she whispered, knowing the tears were standing in her eyes again, starting to roll, starting to be obvious to them all, like a sign saying, *Look at Crazy Teresa, she really is crazy now.* 'I'm sorry, Silvio. I can't do this . . . shit any more.'

The place stank of blood and the sweat of men. She walked to the door, wanting to be outside, wanting to feel fresh air in her lungs, knowing it wasn't there anyway, that all she'd inhale was the traffic smog of Rome, waiting to poison her from the inside out.

And she was thinking all the time: what was it the crazy god offered Barbara Martelli and Eleanor Jamieson really? Freedom from all this crap? A small dark private place where you were what you were and no one else looked, no one else judged, where duty and routine and the dead, dull round of daily life were all a million miles away because in this new place, just for a moment, you could persuade yourself you had a part of some god inside you too? Could that have been the gift? And if it was, could anyone in the world have turned it down?

Emilio Neri refused to skulk around like a criminal, hiding from everything, a fugitive for no good reason at all. But even without an unwelcome visit from the cops and the DIA he could read the signs, digest the intelligence coming in through the channels he'd created over the years. He had to face decisions, make choices, and for the first time in his life he found that difficult. This was a new, an unprecedented situation. Until he made up his mind how to proceed he felt he had little choice but to hole up in the house, trying not to let Adele and Mickey's endless bickering get on his nerves. It was time to stop pretending he could lead from the front, as he had twenty years before, when he moved from *capo* to boss. Now he had to act his age, directing his troops, being the general, keeping their trust. He was getting too old for the tough stuff. He needed others to do the work.

There were risks too. He wondered what they thought in the ranks. When he was with the men he had them tight in his hand. Now he was in danger of seeming aloof, his grip less sure. Adele and Mickey didn't help either. A man who couldn't control his own family could hardly demand respect from the ranks. He'd asked Bruno Bucci to keep an ear open to listen for any whispered remarks that might be the first indication of revolt. These were hazardous times, and not just from the obvious direction. Whatever he said in private, he had to make sure the Sicilians remained happy. He had to convince the foot soldiers it was in their interests to keep their hats in the ring with him too. Money only went so far. He needed to cement their respect, to continue to be their boss.

Then Bucci came in with more news about Beniamino Vercillo. The cops were trying to keep things quiet but Neri's mob had good sources. They mentioned the oddest part of the case: that the killer had been wearing some kind of ancient theatrical costume. This was, it seemed to Neri, a message, surely. The situation was more serious than he had foreseen. For a while, he was dumbstruck, floundering in his own doubts with no one to turn to. He blamed himself. As soon as he'd known a war could be on the way – as soon as those reports of American hoods coming in through Fiumicino reached him – he should have acted. If conflict was inevitable, the advantage always lay with the party that struck first. The Americans understood that lesson instinctively. Instead, he'd hesitated, and now they'd punished him in the most brutal and unexpected of ways.

Vercillo was a civilian. If they'd wanted to make a hit in order to prove a point, there were plenty of accepted targets they could nail: neighbourhood capi, underlings, street men, pimps. Instead they picked a skinny little accountant. It made no sense. It was *offensive*. Neri had no time for Vercillo personally. He wasn't even a real employee. It had never occurred to Neri to warn the man to stay at home for a while, to keep his head down until the air cleared. However bitter a war got, it just didn't involve people that far down the ladder. This was an unwritten rule, a line you never crossed.

Like killing someone's relative, a wife or a daughter, Neri thought.

Bucci watched him, impassive, stolid, waiting for instructions.

'Boss?' he said finally.

'Give me a chance,' Neri replied with a scowl. 'You got to think your way through these things.'

The big tough hood from Turin was silent after that.

Neri was glad of his presence. He needed a man of substance in his trust.

'How are the boys feeling?' Neri asked.

'About anything in particular?'

'The mood. *Morale.*'

Bucci squirmed a little. Neri recognized the signs. They weren't good. 'They get bored easy, boss. Men do in situations like this. They get hyped up like something's going to happen. When it doesn't they get to feel awkward. Like they're wasting their time.'

'I'm paying them well to waste their time,' Neri grunted.

'Yeah. But you know their kind. It's about more than money. Besides, one of them's cousin to that poor bastard Vercillo. He's got a score to settle.'

'So you're saying what, Bruno?'

Bucci considered his answer carefully. 'I'm saying that maybe it's not a good idea to sit here waiting for the next thing to happen to us. They're good guys but I don't want to push them too far.'

Neri's cold gaze didn't leave Bucci for a second. 'Are they loyal?'

'Sure. As loyal as anyone gets these days. But you got to recognize their self-interest. You got to massage their egos too. These are made men. They don't like thinking they're just doing security work or something. It'd help me no end if we saw a little action. Let these assholes know where they stand.'

'I was thinking the same thing,' Neri lied. Something else was bugging him. How had they known about Vercillo? He was a backroom guy. From the outside he looked straight. How did Wallis find him? Maybe Vercillo was less discreet than Neri expected. Maybe he'd been selling information on the side, and found out how dangerous that game can be. 'You got any information about who's doing this? Names? Addresses?'

'Not yet. The street's not talking much out there at the moment. Hell, if it's some people the American brought in for the job, our people probably don't know them anyway. If you want my honest opinion—' Bucci dried up.

'Well?'

'We're not going to get any more information than we have right now. People are bound to be sitting back on the sidelines, watching. They want to see who comes out on top. No one's going to want to do you any favours, not unless they're in with us deep already. It doesn't make sense.'

Neri said nothing.

'You don't mind me being frank,' Bucci said carefully.

'No,' Neri moaned, 'it's what I need. Jesus, these are people who've been sucking my blood for years!'

'Look, boss. You got plenty of respect with the guys here. Provided they don't get pushed too far. Outside—' He didn't say any more. He didn't have to.

'Respect,' Neri grumbled, his face like thunder. 'Tell the truth. Do they think I'm too old or what?'

Bucci hesitated.

'They don't think that,' the man from Turin said eventually. 'But they think about what comes next. You got to expect it. Anyone would in the same circumstances. Also, there's rumours.'

'Rumours?' Neri wondered.

'The people I got in the cops are being real secret about this. Falcone isn't letting anyone near except those close to him. And the DIA.'

Neri shook his head in disbelief. 'The DIA? What the fuck has this got to do with them?'

'They think they got our books from Vercillo.'

Neri laughed. 'Sure they got our books! Can't do a thing with them. The little guy put a code on them or something. He was good with numbers. That was his thing. He told me. They could work on it for years and they'd never get nowhere.'

'They got the code. The DIA's trying to work it all out now.'

'*What?*' It was impossible to work out what this all meant. Vercillo had been doing the books for almost twenty years. He was a meticulous man. He logged everything. Emilio Neri understood instantly that if the DIA and the cops managed to peer into that black hive of past misdeeds they could throw all manner of shit in his direction: fraud, tax evasion. Worse.

'Are you sure?' Neri asked in desperation.

'I'm sure,' Bucci replied. 'Also they want to nail you over this dead girl. They seem to think they got something there. This dead professor guy left some photos or something. There's this other girl, the one that's missing now. They think she's down to us too.'

Neri was outraged. 'Do I look like the kind that goes around snatching teenagers off the street? Why'd I need to do that?'

'They think . . . it points in our direction,' Bucci said carefully.

Neri understood what he was saying. 'And does it?'

'Not with anyone under me, boss.'

Neri raised an eyebrow, waiting.

'But I don't get to control everyone. Mickey, for

example. He's just a loose cannon. God knows what he gets up to when none of us are around.'

'Such as?'

'We know about the hookers. I think maybe he's back on the dope too. Maybe he's been doing other stuff.' Bucci paused, reluctant to continue. 'I don't know where he is half the time. Do you?'

'No,' Neri grunted.

'And this thing years ago with the dead girl. It was before my time. But they seem to think he was there.'

Neri shook his head. 'I don't want to talk about that.'

'I understand. Look, boss. I don't feel right saying this kind of thing. It's between you and him. It's just that . . . Mickey affects the way the guys are thinking right now.'

'And you?' Neri asked. 'I got this American asshole fitting me up for the cops and the DIA. I got a dumb son who can't keep his dick quiet. What do you think should come next?'

'Whatever you want. This is your organization. You get to say what happens. It's just . . .'

Bucci didn't go on. Neri couldn't work it out.

'Well?' he asked.

'It's Mickey. He don't help. Not with him and Adele.'

'Yeah,' Neri said, waving a hand, 'I know, I know . . . it pisses me off too.'

He looked at Bruno Bucci. The man appeared deeply uncomfortable. He'd seen him less nervous than this when they were about bad business. It didn't add up. Then Neri wondered about this idea that had been nagging him for a day or more. It was crazy. It was the kind of thing old men got into their heads for no reason whatsoever and that made fools of them if they blurted it out into the light of day. Which always happened anyway, even if they knew as much, because it was the kind of idea you couldn't keep inside forever.

Neri put an arm around Bucci's shoulder and said, 'You wouldn't lie to an old man, would you, Bruno? I always thought you were a bad liar. It was one of your limitations.'

'No.' Bucci's eyes never left the floor.

The old man's hand squeezed, hard. 'You've been in the house a lot recently. When I'm not here. Tell me, Bruno. Mickey's fucking her, right? That's what's really going on, huh? All this bad feeling between them. That's just for my benefit? Right?'

Bruno Bucci let out a long sigh and struggled to say something.

'No problem,' Neri said, slapping him on the shoulder. 'It just adds another job to the list. Now sit down. I want to talk.'

Falcone looked up from the scattered piles of photographs on the table in his office.

'Close the door,' he said quietly. 'We don't have much time. I want this Julius girl found. I want that to be the focus of what we do from now on. Understood?'

'Sure,' Costa nodded.

Falcone looked beyond the glass partition, out into the office. He'd managed to fill most of the desks. The men and women out there were busy, following up calls, chasing the couple of possible sightings they'd had. 'I'm stepping up the media on this. We're telling them we think she's in real danger, not that I'm saying why. We've as many people as I can afford on the case. But we

DAVID HEWSON

need to go back over what's gone before. Someone's collecting the mother. When she gets here, you can talk to her, Nic. Just you. Too many people will make her clam up. Tell her what we know so far. Just the broad details. And go over everything with her again, every place she and the girl visited since they arrived here. There's got to be something she remembers that's of use.'

'Details?' Peroni asked. 'We've got details? I'm missing them. What is it we're supposed to think has happened here?'

Falcone didn't look too confident. 'We've got Kirk on her camera. That's enough for me. Kirk has to have been involved in taking her. If that's the case, we have to assume she's where he left her for safe keeping. We *have* to find where that it is. Not Ostia for sure. I've got a team rechecking that now. She's not there.'

The three men looked at each other. No one liked to think of a kidnap victim being left stranded, trapped in some hole, unable to call for help.

Peroni wasn't happy. 'I buy that but some of these things still don't add up. Kirk was just a dirty old man. The mother said Suzi went off willingly. We've got it on CCTV. The boyfriend riding that motorbike wasn't some man in his fifties.'

'I know,' Falcone agreed. 'I've got men looking into Kirk's background. Trying to work out if he had any close friends. Nothing so far.'

'And Neri?' Costa asked. 'Wallis?'

'All we have on them are some rumours from the past,' Peroni suggested. 'Why put a fire under some old feud after all this time? Why start playing these games all over again?'

Costa thought of the mummified body in the morgue next door. 'Perhaps because we found Eleanor Jamieson. Because that reminded someone of . . . the possibilities.'

'Let's stick with the facts,' Falcone said firmly.

'Which are?' Peroni asked.

Falcone stared at the pictures. 'These.'

Neither of them argued. The pictures were all home-developed. A search of Randolph Kirk's house off the Via Merulana had revealed a darkroom in the cellar. A couple seemed innocent: young girls, clothed, smiling with older men. But most looked as if they were taken later, when the party began. When the rules disappeared.

Falcone glanced at Peroni. 'Gianni. This is more your field than ours. What do you make of it?'

He shrugged. 'Pretty obvious, isn't it? We have a phrase for this kind of thing in vice. We call it a fuck-club. Sorry. The language isn't so great where I come from. What happens is you get some guys. You get some willing girls. Young girls in this case. Then you put them together and, without telling anyone, stick a camera up in the corner of the room, probably on a remote operated from somewhere else.'

Falcone turned over one of the prints. On the back, scribbled in pencil, was the date: 17 March, sixteen years before.

Peroni nodded. 'These days they've got remote controls. Even things that let you see through the viewfinder from another room. Back then they didn't have the technology to do this kind of shot too well. They just pressed the remote shutter and got whatever was there at the time. Hence all these heaving butts, all these shots where you can't really see who's doing what to who.

You wouldn't get that nowadays. Now it'd come back on DVD or something.'

'Why is it we just have the year the Jamieson girl went missing?' Falcone wondered. 'Why would he just keep the one set?'

'Search me,' Peroni replied, flipping through the prints. 'Maybe he only took pictures the once. Maybe they still had some value. Or it just happened on that scale once. Who's to know? I'll tell you something though. This is not the work of anyone on our books. These kids look like amateurs. Not hookers. Not that I recognize anyway. And the clientele? This is the fanciest fuck-club I've ever seen. Where is this place? On the Via Veneto? Next door to Harry's Bar or something? Hell, they *do* have some value. I could pick up the phone and do business with these today.'

Costa scanned the men in the photos. It was a little before his time but he still recognized plenty of faces.

'You got TV people,' Peroni went on. 'You got newspaper people. Couple of bankers I dealt with in the past. And politicians too. They're bound to be there. You know what puzzles me? Only one cop. What kind of club is it that has just one cop on board? And him that penpusher Mosca guy too? Can we go talk to him?'

'Dead,' Falcone said. 'Died in prison. Knifed.'

'Shame. He's in almost all of them. Seems he got pretty friendly with Barbara. I guess that tells you everything.'

'It does?' Costa wondered.

'Sure, Nic. Like I said. This is not just some gentleman's evening. *It's a sting*. Why else would they leave the likes of us out? If this was just a plain party for the boys we'd have a few more people there. You agree, Leo?'

Falcone nodded and left it at that.

'So,' Peroni continued, 'it was a sting. When this was over and done with, when these morons had gone back to their wives and moaned about how late the trains were getting these days, they got a phone call. Maybe a photo of their heaving butt. News of an account to settle. Or a favour to be called in some time in the future. And my, what favours? You ever seen a cast list like this, Leo?'

'No.'

Peroni smiled. 'Embarrassing, huh? Couple of these guys are still jerking our chains now, aren't they? Are we going to ask them if they saw the Jamieson girl before she died?'

'All in good time,' Falcone said. He sorted the photos in front of them, and pulled out a single shot: a beaming Filippo Mosca and Barbara naked, locked together on a thin mattress on the stone floor.

'Nice,' Peroni said.

Falcone threw another picture on the table. 'This one's even nicer.'

Peroni swore under his breath. The final shot almost looked posed: Barbara and Eleanor, dressed, standing around holding wine glasses, looking nervous, as if they didn't know what came next but thought it might not be too great. They were wearing some kind of costume: a thin sackcloth shift, the one Eleanor Jamieson had on when she was placed in the peat. Next to them stood Randolph Kirk, Beniamino Vercillo and Toni Martelli, looking at each other expectantly, grinning guiltily.

'Jesus,' Peroni said. 'So Mosca wasn't the only one

playing this game? Can you believe it? That sonofabitch Martelli was pimping his own daughter and getting off too? Look at the expression on those guys' faces. "Aren't we the lucky ones?" Assholes.'

'But they're not,' Costa pointed out, 'lucky I mean. Three of them are dead. Martelli doesn't look as if he'll be around much longer either.'

Peroni picked up the picture. 'Let me take this and ram it down the bastard's throat. He'll start squealing then.'

'Later,' Falcone said. 'Martelli's been out of the picture for years. Like I said. We've got to focus.'

'On what?'

'Where this happened,' Falcone said. 'We've checked out the backgrounds. We know it wasn't Ostia.'

Peroni's eyes lit up. 'Excuse me for pointing this out but Toni Martelli surely *knows* where.'

Falcone glanced at the table. 'Do you want to spend the rest of the day sitting with him in an interview room listening to nothing? I spoke to him a few minutes ago. I offered him a deal. He's not doing a damn thing. You've talked to him. We can't afford the time.'

'A deal?' Peroni looked amazed. 'You offer someone who could do this kind of thing to his own daughter a deal?'

'Yes!' Falcone snapped. 'Do you want to argue with the Julius girl's mother about this? Do you want to tell her it's wrong?'

Peroni stared at the photos. 'And I thought I had a conflict of morality on vice. So what *do* we do?'

Falcone had already made up his mind. 'We let the DIA handle the mob stuff. Watching Wallis. Going through the accounts from Vercillo's office. We let them see what they can turn up on the Vercillo killing too. It's theirs by right anyway and I'm happy to unload whatever I can. And we try for the girl. Gianni—'

He looked desperate, Costa thought. It wasn't like the Falcone they knew.

'What do you want us to do?' Peroni asked.

'Nic can get a room ready for the mother. For God's sake see if she can remember something. There has to be a face, a name, anything. I want you to get a couple of spare men out there and run through everything we have on the Julius girl so far. See if we've missed anything.'

'OK,' Costa said, and headed for the door. The two older men watched him go.

'It's a good idea, letting him talk to her on his own,' Peroni said after he'd gone. 'She's an attractive woman. He's noticed that already. Hell, I noticed that. Not you, Leo? Just eyes for the one, huh?'

'Don't start—' Falcone was staring at the pictures on the desk. 'And don't make assumptions either. I don't live in the past any more than you.'

'No,' Peroni said, sounding unconvinced, watching Falcone pore over the photos. 'You can ask if you like. I'm menial class for the time being. You've got the right to ask anything you want.'

Falcone turned over another set of prints, revealing another set of familiar faces. 'What the hell do I do with these things?'

'This lot . . .' Peroni pushed the last pile of pictures, with Barbara and Eleanor in them, to one side, ' . . . you guard with your life, because they may be all we've got between that Julius kid and the grave.'

'I know that,' Falcone replied testily.

271

'Oh.' Peroni placed his index finger gently on the others. 'You mean these?'

He pulled away his hand and took a good look at them. 'You know, I hate to place your ego in jeopardy, Leo, but it is possible for other men of your rank to come and dip their beak here. You've now got three murders under your belt and an abduction. Maybe there's been some blackmail going on here too. It's a lot for one man. Pass the goods around a little.'

'They're linked,' Falcone insisted. 'I've had this argument upstairs already. If I'd wanted to split these inquiries off into different teams I'd have done that. My view – *their* view too – is that it would be counter-productive. We don't have the time or the resources and we could end up missing some connections too. I know it's stretching things but we really have no option.'

'No option?' Peroni grinned. 'Give me a break. I'm hearing ambition here, Leo. You bored with being inspector? After a commissar's badge? Or is it higher than that?'

'I want this girl found,' Falcone snapped. 'Don't judge everyone by your own standards.'

'So why are you worried about the photos? Just put them in a drawer. Wait and see if they ever become useful.'

'Useful—'

Peroni laughed. 'Leo, Leo. You're not cut out for this, are you? You can go upstairs and hard-ball your way through anything. Except—' He glanced at the photos. 'This kind of stuff. It embarrasses you, doesn't it?'

Falcone sighed. 'We should be playing to our strengths here. You ought to learn from what we're trying to do, which is make some connections. That's why I don't want this split up any more than it is. In return I'm asking for your advice. This must have happened to you plenty. You go in somewhere. You find the wrong people inside. What do you do?'

Peroni thought about it. 'Sorry. I shouldn't have taken a pop at you like that. You're right. I've got a lot to learn from you people. I just wonder what the point is because, believe me, I am not staying in this asylum for long.'

Falcone stared at him frankly. 'You seem very sure of that. If we screw up on this case . . .'

'You mean if *you* screw up. Look, here's my advice. There's no easy answer, Leo. It depends on the circumstances. But I'll tell you one thing you *don't* do.'

He picked up the bigger pile of pictures and flicked through them, shaking his head.

'You don't sleep on it. Either you walk upstairs with these things now or you let it drop forever. Hesitate and you become something they hate. An unknown quantity, with a little time bomb sitting in his desk drawer. If you're going to lay all the rest of this on them you've got to do it this very moment. If not—'

He picked up one of the prints and walked over to the shredder that stood by Falcone's office printer. Then he fed the photo into the plastic jaws and watched as it sprang to life, devoured the picture, tearing it into a million tiny, irretrievable pieces.

'Ambition's an interesting thing,' Peroni said. 'I had it once. I thought nothing could touch me. And look what happened? Tell me, Leo. If you'd been on that DIA bust, if you'd walked in and found me there with my pants down. Nothing going on except the usual. What would you have done? Looked the other way?'

Falcone didn't even give it a moment's thought. 'No. Because there'd have to be something going on. Why else would you be there?'

'She was beautiful.' Peroni looked at him and almost pitied the man. 'You really don't get that, do you? It just couldn't be enough?'

'No. And I still don't believe it was enough for you.'

'You're a bad judge of character. Is that because you don't have the same feelings the rest of us have? Or you're just scared of them? We've all got to let go sometimes. Even you.'

Falcone nodded at the pictures. '*This* is letting go?'

'Probably all it is. Listen, Leo. Unless you've got the stomach for it, don't complicate things. There's something really bad about this whole thing. Why don't we just get that girl out from wherever she is then close the door and let the dead stay dead?'

Falcone stared at the pile of photographs. 'There could be any amount of information in here. They could be invaluable.'

'Hand those over to the people upstairs and they'll smile, say thanks and hate you forever because you just made their lives hell.'

'If I gave them to the DIA—'

'If you gave them to the DIA they'd be all over you, telling you how wonderful you are, and what a credit to the police. Maybe you'd even get the D'Amato woman back in your bed. Then you know what? In six months your career would be dead. You'd be running traffic, cutting up credit cards 'cos you can't afford them any more. And the DIA wouldn't want to know you. Nor would she. No one likes a man who passes the buck, particularly one as dirty as this. You know that already if you're honest with yourself.'

Falcone took one last look at the pictures then turned his back on them. 'Do it,' he ordered.

Peroni laughed, picked them up and pressed them into Falcone's hands.

'No, Sir,' he said, then walked out of the room, closing the door behind him, and paused for a moment, listening. It didn't take long. Soon there was the whir of distant electric teeth.

Rachele D'Amato was walking down the corridor towards him, smiling, looking as if she owned the place.

'You moved in?' Peroni wondered.

She didn't answer, just gave him a cold look that said it all.

Peroni pointed at the door. 'You go easy with our boy in here. Some of us have fond feelings for him even if he doesn't feel that way about himself. We don't like the idea he might get hurt twice.'

'You have absolutely no worries on that front.'

'Yeah. Just joking.' He grinned. 'I know. Really. I *know*. Nothing could bring you two back together, could it?'

'I got a call asking me to come. You people should talk to each other more often.' She pointed towards an open door at the end of the corridor. 'There.'

Vergil Wallis sat stiff-backed, eyes closed, waiting patiently.

When Bucci opened up it was hard to stop him. Neri listened until he'd heard enough then motioned for him to shut up. 'You could have told me, Bruno. You owed me that.'

'I didn't—' Bucci looked scared. He was hunting for the right words. 'I talked with Mickey about it. Once. He said you knew. It was part of the deal.'

Neri's big shoulders heaved in a humourless laugh. 'Part of the deal?'

'Yeah,' Bucci replied coolly. 'Pretty stupid of me, huh? The thing is . . . I don't like the idea of you getting fucked around.' He flashed a cold stare at Neri. 'But it's not easy telling a man his wife's cheating on him. With his son. I don't know how to handle that kind of thing. I guess I knew Mickey was lying. To be honest though, I wondered how grateful you'd be if I came running with the news.'

Now Neri thought about it Bucci had been acting a little odd for the past few weeks. He was a good man, a loyal lieutenant. Neri could understand his point of view too. Mickey's perfidy was outside the box. He couldn't expect a street hood like Bucci to get involved in that kind of family betrayal.

'It's Mickey, you know,' Bucci said suddenly. 'Not her. I'm not saying you shouldn't blame her, but I don't think she wants it. Not really. You don't see Mickey the way the rest of us do. He just doesn't give up. He just goes on and on until you give him what he wants.'

Neri thought about that. 'But she's got other men, right?'

'I don't think so. You want my honest opinion? It's just boredom. Nothing more.'

Boredom. Neri could understand that one all right.

'I'm sorry, boss,' Bucci said softly. 'If you want me

to ship out or something when this is done I'll understand. I don't like letting you down.'

Neri's grey eyes shone with amusement. It was a good show of contrition. 'You let me down? Come on, Bruno. Let's not play games with each other.'

'All the same—'

Neri stared at him and Bucci fell silent. 'All the same nothing. Let me tell you a little secret. I've been getting bored too. Been thinking about that for a while. I got a little house in Colombia. Way away from all the trouble. No one can touch me there.' He nodded upstairs, in the direction of Adele and Mickey. 'And I could leave some excess baggage behind too.'

'Sure,' Bucci nodded.

'Would you run things for me when I'm gone? All straight and honest? This shit with the DIA won't come close to you, I promise. There's just my name in those files. I'd be wanting to give a few people some leaving presents, you understand. Something to remember me by. I owe them that. But you get a clear run. Nothing touches your name.'

Bucci shuffled awkwardly on the chair. 'You want me to act like I'm the boss?'

'No. I want you to *be* the boss. I can't do this forever. Someone's got to take over. I'd rather it was a man of my choosing, not some bastard from outside.'

'I could do it,' Bucci said. 'I don't think Mickey would be too keen.'

'Mickey, Mickey. Leaving this Adele crap to one side . . . what do you think of him? Be honest. Say I could straighten him out. Would it be worth it? Is he ever going to make something?'

'I don't know,' Bucci said carefully. 'I don't feel

qualified to make that judgement. There's things he's been doing I don't understand.'

'What things?'

Bucci rolled open his big hands in a gesture of despair. 'I dunno. Things he don't want any of us to hear about. And I'll tell you this, boss. He's good at that. Keeping stuff quiet.'

Neri wondered about all the crap that had come out into the open these past couple of days. Falcone wasn't going to leave them alone. It was only a matter of time before he came back, maybe with papers, turning the place upside down. 'We're going to have to hole up here for a couple of hours. There'll be cops swarming front and back. You get busy, Bruno. Find out how long we've got before they come calling again. Find out where they got people waiting out there, who needs to be paid to make those guys look the other way for a while. When we can crawl out from under their noses, we go out to play.'

'To play?'

Neri laughed. 'Yeah. If I'm going into retirement I want one last piece of fun first. I got some evening-up to do, all round. When that's done I'm gone. You call someone. Make sure I can get the hell out of here come tomorrow night, some way nice and discreet. The Albanian boys can do something. They owe me favours.'

Bucci blinked. 'Tomorrow night?'

'That too soon for you?' Neri cast an eye around the room. 'I got to tell you, Bruno, I can't wait to be out of this dump.'

Bucci didn't seem too happy.

'What's up?' Neri asked. 'I'm offering you your own empire on a plate.'

'Don't get me wrong. I'm grateful. I'll see you right. But there's . . . stuff I can't control.'

It was obvious what he meant. 'You're still worried about Mickey?'

Bucci shrugged. He was too polite, too respectful to push it. Neri looked at Bruno Bucci and wondered why he never got a son like that. Bucci was the one guy he could rely on. And if he wanted to fuck with Mickey when the time came, what the hell? To his surprise, it wasn't the news about him and Adele that made him feel that way. He just wasn't particularly warm to his own flesh and blood at that moment. They messed up his life. They leeched off him and gave nothing back in return. This wasn't what family was supposed to be about. As he got older, as he felt less need for the physical pleasures that Adele could deliver with her own particular skill, he was, he realized, beginning to feel happier in the company of men. He knew where he stood with them. So long as he kept to his part of the deal – being a good, fair, profitable boss – they would stick by him.

The old man smiled. 'The kid's right. It's time he got tested. Go get him. Tell him to meet me, up on the terrace.'

'The terrace?' Bucci asked.

Neri was already walking towards the stairs. 'You heard,' he said.

There were pictures of Suzi Julius everywhere. Blow-ups from Miranda's original snaps carpeted the whiteboard on the main wall of the operations room. Smaller colour copies were pinned to people's PCs, scattered across desks. Costa walked Miranda Julius through the twenty-strong team, introducing her to a couple of people along the way, making sure she understood how important the case had become to them. Then they went along the corridor to a smaller room where a further group of officers, most of them female, were manning the phones set up to handle any calls that came in from the public appeals. Suzi's picture was on the TV now. More photos would soon be in the papers. They had an anonymous hotline into the station ready for anyone who answered their plea for even a hint of a sighting. The full-scale hunt for Suzi was under way. But like every other case of its kind that Costa had worked on there was, at the onset, a frustrating lack of information. No one had seen her since she was driven out of the Campo dei Fiori the day before. Not a single clue to her movements had appeared in the three hours since Falcone gave the green light to turn the Julius case into an abduction inquiry.

He led her into a small interview room overlooking the courtyard behind the Questura. She sat down immediately and said, 'I know you're looking, Nic. You don't have to prove that to me.'

'I just wanted you to see it for yourself.'

The stress was starting to show. The impression Nic Costa had first had of her – as a model who'd gone into something manual just to prove she was more than she looked – came back to him. She sat on the other side of the table, hunched inside a plain black bomber jacket, snatching anxiously at a cigarette, trying to blow the smoke out of the half open window. Her sharp, intelligent eyes never left him.

'Do you have any idea where she is?'

Costa was careful with his answer. 'It takes time.'

She stared out of the window, squinting at the bright, late afternoon sun. 'I ought to say it again. I'm sorry. About last night. It must have been very embarrassing for you.'

The sudden close contact they shared continued to bother him. He could, he knew, have gone along with her so easily. 'Forget it. I have.'

For a moment an odd look, almost like anger, crossed her face. He wondered if he'd said the right thing.

'Sometimes I drink,' she said. 'Not to blot things out. It's just that events can make more sense that way. Or it appears they do. I don't imagine you understand what I'm talking about.'

He'd never forget the lost days after his father died, when he would sit alone in the old man's wheelchair for hours on end, talking to the bottle, trying to gauge how much of the hurt was physical, from his wounds, how much existed in his head alone. And how easy it would be to drown both in booze.

'I understand. Will you promise me something?'

'I don't like making easy promises,' she answered quickly. 'You disappoint people if it turns out you can't keep them.'

'It's just this. We need you, Miranda. We need you to think about anything we find. Possibly to react to it. I just don't know. But when that moment happens, it's important for all of us, Suzi most of all, that you're not—' He let the sentence drift off into nowhere.

'Drunk?' she wondered. 'Don't worry. That won't happen.'

'It's not a great idea being on your own. Isn't there someone from home who can come? You mentioned your mother.'

'She's on holiday at the moment. In California. I spoke to her this morning. What with the time difference, changing tickets . . . she can't be here until Sunday.' She gave him a sudden intense glance. 'By then . . . We'll know, won't we?'

There was no avoiding an honest answer. 'I think so. All the same . . . I could arrange for a woman officer to be with you.'

'I'll be fine,' she said firmly. 'I don't need to be treated like a victim. Suzi's the victim here. She's the one I want to help. You just do your job and I'll try my best. Any way I can.'

'Good,' he said, then reached for the tape recorder button, dictated the standard header to the interview – date, time, subject, interviewee, officer – and tried to think of the right questions, the ones that would unlock something hidden, something lost inside Miranda Julius's complex, hurting head.

'Is there anything new that's occurred to you?'

'Not really.' She shook her head, as if she hated herself for being like this. 'I keep trying to think of something. There's nothing that stands out I haven't mentioned already.'

'The people you've met here—'

'They're just people. People in shops. People in cafés. People in restaurants. We've talked to them. Of course we have. But nothing stands out. It never went beyond just being polite.'

He placed one of the photos from Suzi's camera on the table. Randolph Kirk was there at the edge of the crowd by the Trevi Fountain, staring directly into the camera with an odd, focused expression.

'Do you recognize him?'

She peered at the picture. 'No. I've never seen him before. Not until I saw the paper this morning. My Italian's not great but I get the message. He was the man killed out at this archaeological place, wasn't he?'

'Yes.'

She came directly to the point. 'You think he had something to do with this other murder too? The girl from sixteen years ago?'

'There's evidence that he used young girls for his own . . . entertainment. With others.'

She swore under her breath. 'So what happens now? Where *is* she, Nic? Just locked up somewhere this monster's left her? Waiting to be found? It could take forever. God—' She closed her eyes for a moment. 'I can't bear to think of her like that. It's just so horrible.'

'We're circulating her picture everywhere. Someone must have seen her.'

'None of this makes sense. Suzi wouldn't just disappear with a man like that. It's preposterous. He's old. Look at him. What could he possibly offer her? You don't think he was on that motorbike, do you?'

'No,' he admitted. 'Maybe he just found her. Someone else did the rest.'

'But why Suzi? Why her?'

'Bad luck,' he said with a shrug. 'Coincidence. These cases are sometimes just that. Kirk seemed to have a fondness for blondes. Maybe she reminded him of someone else.'

She knew immediately what he was talking about. 'The dead girl you found? I saw pictures of her. They do look similar I suppose.'

'It's just a theory. We have two avenues to work on here. We can do all the usual things. Make sure as many people as possible see her picture. Monitor the calls we get from that. And we can work to try to understand what really happened. Why Kirk played these games. Who with, and where.'

'It could be anywhere, couldn't it?' she asked.

'No.' There was an important point here somewhere, he thought. This was a ritual. It didn't take place at the Villa of Mysteries in Ostia. Teresa's careful forensic work had proved that much already. Kirk had to have another location, larger, more important. In the city most probably. Perhaps Suzi was there now, trapped, waiting. But for whom?

'I need you to look at some more pictures,' he said, and reached for the files.

Miranda Julius stared at a standard police ID photo of Barbara Martelli. 'I saw her picture in the papers too,' she said. 'Blonde. She was another one of his women? The police officer?'

'We think so.'

'Was that why she killed him?'

'We've no idea,' he admitted. 'Have you seen her before, Miranda? Please. Think. Is it possible you or Suzi met her somewhere? Anywhere.'

She sighed. 'We've asked the police for directions a few times, I suppose. Maybe we talked to her. I don't know. I don't think I'd remember one way or another.'

'OK. Point taken. How about him?'

He placed a photo of Vergil Wallis on the table.

'No,' she said immediately. 'Is he Italian?'

'American. Have you talked to any Americans since you arrived?'

She couldn't understand the point of the question. 'I don't think so. I think I'd remember someone as distinctive as that. What's the meaning of this, Nic? Why would an American be involved in this kind of thing?'

'Bear with me,' he said. 'We have to keep trying. Do you know this man?'

She looked at a photo of Beniamino Vercillo. 'No.'

'Him?' Emilio Neri's big, ugly face glared up at her from the table.

She shook her head. 'He looks like a crook. He looks . . . horrible. Are these the kind of people you think could have Suzi? She'd never go away with someone like that. She's not stupid.'

Costa shuffled through the pile of pictures. 'That was taken in the Questura, when we were interviewing him about something. He doesn't always look like that. People have different faces for different occasions. You have to try to think beyond what you see sometimes.'

'Thanks for the advice,' she said icily.

'Look.'

This was a new set of pictures, ones they'd bought in from a photographer covering a social evening at the opera. Neri was there in his other guise, as an art-loving businessman, his wife at his side. They were both dressed to the nines, Neri in a dinner suit, Adele wearing a long, tight-fitting silk gown.

'He does look different,' she conceded.

She stared at the picture. 'Is that his wife?'

Costa nodded.

'She looks very young for him. He's that kind of man?'

Costa didn't answer.

'Nic? The kind who likes young girls?'

'She's not as young as she looks. Not Suzi's age

anyway. He likes lots of things. Maybe he was involved in Kirk's games. Maybe it's more complicated than that.'

She peered at the picture again. 'She doesn't look happy. She looks like a possession or something. Some-one he owns.'

'You read a lot into pictures.'

She nodded in agreement. 'You forget. I take pic-tures for a living. It's like trying to tell a story. You want people to see it and get some sense of what's happening. What the people there are like. Otherwise it's just a snapshot. There's no meaning. No drama. No humanity. Just shapes on a sheet of paper. It's the back story that makes it work.'

She flicked through the set of photos from the opera. 'These are quite good. Whoever he is, whoever his wife is, they make interesting subjects. There's a lot going on there between them and I don't think it's nice. I could imagine photographing them myself. I could—'

Miranda Julius stopped at one picture. She separated the photo from the rest and stared at it in silence, thinking.

'You remember something about him?' Costa asked when he couldn't wait any longer.

'No. I don't know him from Adam. But *him*—'

She turned the photo round and stabbed at a figure at the edge of the photo. Younger, dressed in an evening suit, looking bored.

'I *have* seen him somewhere.' She stopped, trying to order her thoughts. 'It was just after we arrived. We were in the Campo, having coffee outside. He was at the next table. I went to the loo. When I came back he'd been pestering Suzi. Asking for her phone number. Trying to chat her up.'

Costa looked at the photo and felt a sharp stab of excitement.

'What happened?'

'Nothing. I think. He wasn't . . . very nice. He was so persistent. His English wasn't that great either. I didn't like him, Nic. I *really* didn't like him now I come to think of it. He was creepy. Just the kind of pushy young jerk I thought we'd be dealing with in Rome all the time.'

'But he could have given Suzi his number?'

'I'm trying to think—'

There was something here. Costa could feel it.

Miranda Julius looked into his face, her eyes wide open, worried. 'Oh my God. I do remember. Suzi was odd afterwards for a while. Almost shifty. We nearly had an argument. It wasn't like her.'

'So he could have passed her something? A phone number? She might have taken it.'

'Possibly. I don't know, Nic. I don't . . . It was days ago.'

'And she wouldn't have told you?'

He didn't like seeing the pain when she answered. 'I suppose not. Kids of that age do stupid things and don't want to admit it. I know I did. She *was* shifty about something. I should have known—'

Her eyes became misty.

' . . . Jesus, what an idiot I am. Thinking a girl of her age would be happy spending an entire holiday with her mother, never seeing anyone else. As if I'm good enough company for her. For Christ's sake. I haven't even been around for most of her life. Why should she want to be with me? How arrogant can you get?'

Then firmly, with absolute conviction, she said, 'I

remember I told her what an utter creep I thought he was. Exactly the sort of Italian man you get warned about. And she looked at me as if I was talking crap. As if I was *old*. Then we just didn't talk about anything for a while. We just let it blow over.'

He was anxiously gathering up the pictures, keen to end this.

'Except it didn't, did it?' she asked.

'This could really help us.'

'How? You know who this man is?'

Costa wondered how much to reveal. He reached over the table and took her arm. 'Miranda,' he said. 'We have rules about how much we can say in the middle of an investigation.'

'To hell with the rules. I'm her mother. I'm the reason she's in this mess.'

His voice rose. 'You're *not* the reason. Suzi's sixteen years old. She's not a child you can care for twenty-four hours a day.'

She was shaking her head. 'You don't know her. You don't know me. Don't make these judgements.'

It wasn't self-pity, he thought. More self-hate. 'I know enough. You're doing everything anyone could in the circumstances. Don't start blaming yourself before—'

The word just slipped out. She stared at the bright dusty window, blinking back sudden tears. 'Before what? Before there's a reason?'

He shook his head. 'I didn't mean that.'

She paused, trying to let the temperature fall a little.

'Who is he?' she asked. 'You can at least tell me that.'

'He's the old man's son. His name is Neri. Mickey Neri.'

Nic Costa got up, thinking about the possibilities,

what Falcone could do when he got the news. Outside the afternoon was dying. It would soon be dark. These operations were never easy at night. They had to move. There was so little time.

She was by his side, a shadow of hope in her face. 'What kind of man is he? Mickey?'

'The best kind,' Costa said smiling. 'For us anyway. Not a university professor. Not some anonymous figure in a suit. Mickey Neri's a crook, from a family of crooks, not a smart one either. We know him. We know where he lives. We know how to get what we want from him. Miranda—'

They just needed the warrants, and her ID of Mickey in the photo would surely put that straight in Falcone's hands. Then they could storm the big house in the Via Giulia, take Mickey in for questioning, and start to tear apart the whole Neri empire along the way.

Costa rested his hands on her shoulders and wished he could make her feel the same rising sense of anticipation he was beginning to recognize within himself. 'We'll find her. I promise.'

She stepped back from him, doubt still in her eyes. 'Promises,' she said.

The day was dying. Emilio Neri stood on the terrace, leaning on the handrail, looking down into the street, breathing in the smog from the Lungotevere. When he was a kid Rome was cleaner. More whole somehow. It had gone wrong, like most of the world, over the years. Back when he was young people would walk around the *centro storico* on a night like this, arm in arm, just looking in the shops, stopping for a drink before supper. Now they rushed everywhere, or tried to if the traffic would let them. They stood around whispering into mobile phones instead of talking to people directly. Rome wasn't the worst place either. When he went to Milan or London it seemed they spent their entire lives locked in solitary conversations with lumps of plastic. At least his native city maintained a stubborn streak of humanity at its heart. He could still walk across the Ponte Sisto and feel a kick of sentiment.

Except there wasn't time. There never would be time. That part of his life was past. Now he had to consolidate the future, and the reputation he'd leave behind.

He turned to see Mickey clamber up the stairs. The kid stood by the pots of anaemic palms that were still suffering from the winter. He was now wearing a different set of stupid clothes, too young for him as usual: flared jeans, a thin black sweater one size too small. He was thirty-two. He ought to stop trying to look like a teenager. He was shivering too.

Neri waved him over. They stood together by the iron balcony. He put an arm around his son's shoulder and looked over the edge. 'You never liked heights, Mickey. Why's that?'

Mickey shot a fleeting glance down at the street and tried to take one step back. His father's huge arm stopped him. 'Dunno.'

'You remember what happened to Wallis's wife? When she couldn't handle it any more – at least I guess that's what happened – she walked straight out of some apartment block in New York, fifty floors up. One minute she's weeping at the window. Next they're scraping her off the street. You wonder what could make someone do that? Guilt maybe? Or just plain stupidity.'

Neri's arm propelled Mickey straight onto the iron railing. Hard. The kid tried to push back but Neri had him trapped.

'You know,' Neri said, 'sometimes just one simple thing clears up so many problems. The cops get a body. They look at that mess down there on the pavement and come up with a story to fit. It can work out for everyone.'

'Pop—' Mickey gasped, struggling in vain to get free.

'Shut up. You want to know why you hate heights? I'll tell you. One day when you were real young you and your mamma were pissing me off no end. It was summer. We were up here on the terrace. I didn't allow no servants in the house in those days. That was all Adele's idea. Adele gets lots of ideas but I guess you know that. So there's you and your mamma, and you no more than three or four and you're shouting and screaming at her 'cos she ain't got the right toy or something. And I'm lying there on the old wicker sofa we used to have before all this fancy stuff got bought. And I'm thinking: fuck this. I work all day. I keep you parasites alive. And all you can do in return is shout and scream and moan.'

Neri squeezed Mickey's shoulder. The old man stared his son straight in the eye. 'You don't remember, do you?'

'N-n-no—' Mickey stuttered.

'Except you do. A part of you does anyway. It's just stuck deep . . .' He took his arm away for a moment and prodded Mickey in the right temple with a finger, ' . . . in there, along with all the other shit you've got.'

'I don't—' Mickey was saying, and then the old man moved. Two big strong hands took Mickey by the scruff of his neck, bounced him painfully against the railing, propelling him half over the edge, balanced over the tiny cobblestones that, from this height, looked like the pattern on a dead butterfly's wing.

Emilio Neri upended Mickey's legs with a brutal jerk of the knee, dangling his son over the street, letting the kid cling to his arm just as he'd done more than a quarter of a century before. The old man felt just as strong as he had back then, more so maybe. And just as in control. His face was up close to Mickey's this time round though and both of them were starting to sweat like pigs.

'You remember now?' the old man demanded.

Tears were starting to fill Mickey's eyes, his feet kept scrambling against nothing, looking for some kind of hold. Neri could smell fresh piss coming from the crotch of the flared jeans. 'Please—' he croaked.

'I heard a story, Mickey. Just a little fairy tale running up and down the stairs, in and out of the bedrooms of this stinking place. I heard you've been fucking Adele behind my back. People have seen you. People have heard you. Plus there's all manner of other stuff you think I don't know about. Don't you see this from my point of view? Don't you see how nice and easy it would be for me to let you go wipe your face on the cobblestones down there and bite down the blame with your broken teeth?'

Mickey made an unintelligible squeak. Nothing more.

'You're not saying anything, son. You're not telling me I got it wrong.'

The kid scrunched his eyes shut then opened them again, blinking as if he hoped this were all some dream. 'You got—'

Neri pushed down with his arm, just for a second. Mickey's head bobbed down on the wrong side of the railing. The kid let out a terrified screech and went quiet: his father was holding him again.

'You mustn't lie to me, Mickey. If I think you're doing that I just let go. What use is a son I can't trust?'

Mickey sobbed and said nothing.

'So tell me,' Neri said calmly. 'Think about what you're going to say. This story about you and Adele. Is it true?'

The kid's head went from side to side.

'Say something,' Neri ordered.

'It's a lie. *It's a lie.*'

Neri gazed into his son's terrified face, thinking. Then heaved him back over the railing. Mickey sent a couple of plant pots tumbling down to the street as he scrambled back to safety. Neri watched them shatter on the cobblestones. Down the road a man in a dark suit jumped at the noise and looked up at the rooftops.

'You should be more careful,' Neri said and offered his son a handkerchief. 'People could get hurt that way.'

Tears were streaming down Mickey's face. His breath was coming in short sobs. He looked at his father and asked, 'Why? Why'd you do that?'

Neri shrugged. 'A father deserves the truth. If you'd told me different you'd be down there now. You do know that, don't you?'

'Yeah,' he whispered, and Emilio Neri had to fight to stop himself laughing. The kid really did think he'd got away with it.

'I've been a bad father,' he said. 'I tried to protect you instead of letting you get tough from all the shit that people like us have to deal with. I hear you want in on the action.'

'Yeah,' Mickey mumbled uncertainly. Even through

the tears he still had the teenage pout. Got that straight from his mother, Neri thought.

'Good. It's time.' Neri opened his jacket and took out a gun. It was a small, black Beretta. Mickey just looked at it, wide-eyed, speechless. Neri pushed it into his hands.

'Take it. The thing won't bite. It's one of mine. I know it works.'

'W-w-what—?' Mickey asked.

'You know the rules. You only go so far in these circles without whacking someone. You never did that, son. You just beat up a few people from time to time. It's not the same, is it? Be honest with me.'

'No,' Mickey moaned.

Neri patted him on the back. 'So look happy. It's whacking time. Nothing complicated. All nice and simple. You walk in, you don't say nothing, you put the gun to his head and you pull the trigger. You can manage that?'

'On my own?'

'That a problem?'

'No,' he stuttered. 'Who?'

Neri looked at his watch. His mind was already elsewhere. 'Just some cop. Sorry. That's the best I can do right now. Next time round I'll try to find you a real human being.'

Vergil Wallis wore a black suit with a crisp white shirt and black tie. He looked ready for a funeral.

'I'd like to see Eleanor's body.'

'You're in mourning,' Falcone replied. 'Who for? Yesterday you seemed to think there wasn't much point.'

D'Amato glowered at him. Maybe it was rude to talk to retired mobsters like this. Falcone wasn't sure he cared any more.

'You took me by surprise yesterday. I wasn't thinking straight. I hope you never know what it's like, Inspector. You spend all those years praying you'll discover the truth. Then, when you do, you wish you'd never wanted it so badly. You wonder if you somehow brought it down on your own head.'

'We don't know the truth,' Falcone observed. 'We're not even halfway there. There aren't many people helping us either.'

Wallis nodded, conceding the point, and said nothing.

'If we agree to let you see the body, we get to talk afterwards,' D'Amato demanded. '*Both* of us.' The impassive black head nodded. 'Not that I think you're in much of a position to bargain. Do you want me to call a lawyer?'

'You don't need a lawyer,' Falcone said. 'Not yet.'

He led the way downstairs, out to the morgue in the adjoining building. There was one assistant on duty, a short, dark man with a ponytail. Falcone had never seen him before and didn't feel too impressed. Silvio Di Capua and the rest of the path crew were still at Vercillo's, trying to pick up the pieces without Teresa Lupo. It wasn't going to be easy. Too few people, too little talent.

The morgue official nodded when he heard the name. 'We've got a place for that one. Teresa says it needs special treatment. She's gone loopy or something? Is that true?'

'Just show us,' Falcone snapped.

The ponytail headed for a corridor, moaning

constantly. 'Jesus are we in trouble now. They're not going to let Monkboy loose on the shop, are they? Don't get me wrong. He's a nice guy. Knows his stuff. But managerially . . . You should see his locker.'

They entered a side room. Eleanor Jamieson's mahogany corpse lay on a surgical table surrounded by a panoply of technical equipment that looked like a life support system arriving too late. Silver tripods sprouted from the floor, transparent plastic tubing wound around them feeding a network of tiny pipes and nozzles. These sprayed a fine mist directly onto the body, giving it a bright, leathery sheen in the harsh light of the room. The place had a chemical stink from whatever solution was being used to preserve the body. It made Falcone's throat ache.

'Don't ask me what to do when the stuff runs out,' the assistant said. 'Teresa fixed all this up. Says some academic in England e-mailed her the recipe. Told her it was the best way to stop the thing shrivelling up like a pair of old shoes.'

'Out,' Falcone barked, and the ponytail disappeared back into the morgue.

Wallis had taken a seat in the corner of the room. His eyes were fixed on the body. Eleanor still wore most of the sackcloth shift. The autopsy proper hadn't even begun. Falcone understood too that she would remain untouched for the foreseeable future. This strange, half-mummified corpse was beyond Silvio Di Capua. They would surely have to call in help from outside or persuade Teresa Lupo to come back to work. He wasn't sure which was more preferable. The woman was a loose cannon. Only her considerable skill had kept her in the job in the first place. But it would be faster, if they were spared more interruptions.

D'Amato took a seat on one side of Wallis. Falcone fell into a chair on the other. The room overlooked the street. The sounds of everyday Roman life drifted in through the tiny window: cars and human voices, stray music and the angry honking of horns. In spite of countless murder inquiries, Falcone never felt entirely comfortable in the morgue. It wasn't the grim presence of the cadaver that bothered him. It was the way death sat so easily, so effortlessly in the midst of life, just behind the curtain, unnoticed except by the few people it immediately affected.

He looked at Rachele D'Amato, nodding at her to start, wishing he could find more answers to all the questions that were bothering him. She'd brought the DIA into the case with a consummate skill. It was made easier by the fact that she and her colleagues seemed to know so much more than the police did. Someone was leaking, too, and she assumed, all along, it was the police. Maybe she was right. Everyone knew the Questura had its share of compromised cops. But it bothered Falcone that no one ever asked any hard questions of the DIA. Did she ever wonder whether the tip-offs could be coming from within her own ranks? If she did, would she let on to a mere cop? This was a one-way relationship. Just like the personal one they'd enjoyed for a while. He was, once again, at a disadvantage, and it bothered him deeply.

'Mr Wallis,' she said. 'We're in the dark on almost everything here. A motive. A precise time. Perhaps even a place. What do you think happened?'

Wallis shook his head. 'Why ask me? You said yourself I was not under suspicion.'

'You must have some idea.'

'Really?' Wallis asked. 'Why does that necessarily follow?'

'Was Emilio Neri involved?' D'Amato asked. 'How well did he know Eleanor?'

'Neri?' He hesitated. 'The name rings a bell. You should put that question to him, surely.'

'You went on vacation together,' she said. 'To Sicily. Please don't play games with us. Neri was there, and his son. Who else?'

Wallis nodded, conceding the point. 'Hell. It was a long time ago. I don't remember.'

Falcone sighed. 'I was hoping you could help us somehow. I told you yesterday. There's another girl missing now, in very similar circumstances. We're certain she's in danger.'

Wallis thought for a moment then said, 'What you say doesn't make sense. You told me at the outset you didn't know the circumstances of Eleanor's death. Now you say this other girl is in the same position. I don't understand. Which is it?'

'This isn't a time for playing games,' Falcone snapped. 'We need your help.'

Wallis's gaze was fixed on the corpse, bright and glossy beneath the artificial shower of stinking fluid. 'I don't know anything about this other girl.'

Very carefully, watching his reaction, D'Amato said, 'What about Eleanor's mother?' He flinched, just a little. 'Your wife. Wouldn't you want some justice for her?'

'Her mother took her own life,' he replied. 'No one did that for her.'

'You feel no sense of regret?' she asked. 'No . . . responsibility?'

'She died because she wanted to.' The words came out with difficulty. D'Amato was touching a nerve here.

'My question wasn't about her. I wondered what you felt.'

The man looked at his watch, his eyes glassy. 'This isn't something I want to discuss.'

Falcone watched Rachele D'Amato's face harden. There was such resolve there. It was good for the job. It was what they needed. Surely she'd changed over the years, though. The woman he remembered, the woman he had, perhaps, once loved, was not this detached from her feelings. 'Did you love them?' she asked. 'Eleanor wasn't yours. Your wife had left you already. Did you love them at that point? When the marriage appeared over?'

Wallis bridled at the question. 'You're a very persistent woman. Let me say this once and for all. They changed me. Before, I was what I was. They saw something in me that I didn't see myself. In return I learned to love them, and resent them too. A man like me isn't made to change. It's not good business. It makes for an uneasy relationship with one's masters.'

Falcone glanced at the body. 'Could your masters have done this?'

There was a sudden burst of anger on his face. 'What kind of people do you think I mix with? She was a child, for heaven's sake. What possible reason—?' He stopped, his voice breaking. 'This is a personal matter. I'm not talking about it any more. It's no business of yours. *I have nothing to tell you.*'

'Where were you this morning?' Falcone asked directly.

'At home,' he said immediately. 'With my house-keeper.'

'And your associates?' D'Amato demanded.

'Associates?'

She pulled out her notepad and read off some names. 'We have a list of them. Men you know. Men with the same kind of background. They arrived in Rome yesterday.'

'Sure!'

They waited.

'Golf!' Wallis declared. 'Do you think everything's bad news around here? We meet once a year in spring. I've booked a round at Castelgandolfo for Sunday, then dinner. Phone them if you like, and check. They can tell you. We've done this for years. Since I first came to Rome. It's an annual event for old men. Old soldiers if you like. Retired soldiers. Do you play golf, Inspector?'

'No.'

'A shame.' He paused to give his words some weight. 'I thought the cops were fond of clubs. You get to meet people that way.'

'Not all of us,' Falcone replied. 'You didn't ask.'

'Ask what?'

'Why I wanted to know where you were this morning.'

Wallis shifted on his chair. He didn't like being caught out. It was, Falcone thought, the most promising sign he'd seen of an opening in the man's guard.

'I assumed you'd tell me,' Wallis said lamely.

'Neri's book-keeper, a man named Vercillo, was murdered.'

He didn't even blink. The sombre, expressionless face stared at him and Falcone appreciated, for the first time, how Wallis must once have been a powerful, imposing presence. 'Inspector, do I look like the kind of person who goes around killing book-keepers? If I engaged in that kind of behaviour, do you honestly think that is where I'd start?'

'No wars,' Falcone warned. 'You hear me. I don't want any of that crap on our streets. If you people want to fight it out for some reason, you do it somewhere else and make sure no one else suffers.'

'War?' Wallis answered, amused. 'Who's talking about war?'

'I'm just saying,' Falcone said and heard how lame he sounded.

'Saying what?' The American took his arm. Falcone could smell something sweet on his breath. 'Nothing but the obvious. You've got to know, Inspector, you of all people. War's the natural state of humanity. It's peace and harmony that are foreign to us, which is why it's so damned hard to create them out of all this shit. Wars aren't part of my world, not any longer. Not here. Not anywhere. Others . . .' He opened his hands in a gesture of regret, ' . . . they may feel differently. That's none of my business.'

'And if they start to make war on you?' D'Amato asked.

He smiled. 'Then I'll expect the police to earn their keep.'

There was, Falcone thought, only one way to tackle the next question. Directly. 'I've already spoken to Emilio Neri. He suggested we ask you about what happened to

Eleanor. He seems to think your relationship was . . . not simply that of a stepfather and daughter.'

Wallis closed his eyes briefly and uttered a low, unintelligible sound.

'He suggests you had a sexual relationship with her. I have to ask, Mr Wallis. Did you?'

'You're going to believe scum like him?' Wallis asked quietly. 'You think a man like that would tell you the truth, even if he knew how?'

'I think he knows more than he's telling me. I think the same about you.'

'I can't help what you think about me.'

Falcone took a photograph out of the folder he'd brought with him: Eleanor and Barbara Martelli, with their little coterie of admirers. They were dressed, Eleanor apparently unaware of what was to happen next.

Wallis stared at it. 'What's this?'

'We think it was taken shortly before Eleanor was killed.'

'Where did you get it?'

'I can't discuss that,' Falcone said. 'This is evidence. Do you know these men? Do you know what kind of . . . event this is?'

'No,' he replied immediately.

'The other woman. Do you know her?'

'No.'

Falcone glanced at Rachele D'Amato. There was too much hard work here. Wallis's response was all wrong. He should have been asking questions.

'Does this photograph mean *anything* to you?' he demanded. 'If we're right, it preceded her death probably by no more than a few hours. One of these men may have killed her. You really know none of them?'

He pointed at one figure. 'I know him. So do you. He was your colleague. Mosca, wasn't it?'

'How did you know him?' D'Amato asked.

He shrugged. 'A social event, if I remember right. Nothing more.'

Falcone held up the photo. 'A social event like this? You understand where Eleanor spent her last few hours? You understand what went on?'

He took out more photos. From later. Barbara and Mosca, rolling on the floor, naked.

'This is not how I spend my time,' Wallis said coldly. 'Nor was it then. *Nor* do I believe Eleanor would have gone to something like this willingly, knowing what was involved. Do you have pictures of her like this, Inspector?'

'No,' Falcone conceded. 'Which is interesting in itself. But you see my problem? The idea that Eleanor just walked out of your house one day and disappeared, was abducted in some random way by a complete stranger. It's not true. This was where she was before she died. In the company of men who moved in circles you knew. Crime. The police. As if she were . . .' He paused, determined this would hit home, ' . . . a gift perhaps.'

Wallis nodded, considering this. 'An interesting idea. But it presupposes that the men to whom she was given had something to offer in return. To whom? Not me. So who could that be?'

'We may have DNA evidence from the autopsy,' Falcone said. 'I can only request this at the moment but it would help us if you were to provide a sample. Our forensics people can do what is necessary now. It won't take a moment. It's just a mouth swab. Or a piece of hair if you'd prefer.'

'DNA?' He didn't flinch. 'You're telling me that's some use after all these years?'

'Possibly. Is that a problem?'

'Tell me what you need.' Wallis was staring at the body. It was, they understood, a final act. He would not return. 'I've seen enough. I don't want to answer any more questions. You'll let me know when I can make the burial arrangements?'

Falcone called the lab assistant over and told him to organize the sample. They watched the two of them leave the room.

'DNA,' she said when Wallis was gone. 'There's an interesting thought. Wallis asked the right question straight away, though. Is it possible? I thought the path-ologist said there'd be nothing useful because of the peat.'

'I've no idea,' he admitted. 'I just wanted to see if he'd refuse.'

'And the fact that he doesn't?'

'It leaves us in the dark. He could have been there. He could be thinking we wouldn't find out anyway. Maybe we just don't have the photo.'

'Without a real sample it doesn't matter, Leo.'

'No. What about the material I gave you from Ver-cillo's office? When will you be in a position to get a warrant to raid Neri? I want to be in there as soon as I can.'

She was putting on the diplomatic smile again, the one that said: *no way*. She was so wrapped up in all this. It consumed her more than he'd appreciated earlier. She wanted to own this case. She wanted it to own her too. There was, he thought, nothing else in her life right then. All the glamorous clothes, all the semi-flirtatious, teasing behaviour . . . these were simply the tools of her current trade.

'That'll take a week at least,' she said firmly. 'I can't risk screwing up a case like this out of haste. We're writhing in regulations when it comes to privacy these days. All that information is about fraud, financial misdeeds, tax evasion. We have to know for sure what we're dealing with before I can go before a judge. It's easier for you. A murder investigation. An abduction. You'll get a warrant. Just ask.'

He grimaced. 'I talked to legal. They won't countenance it on what we have. I need more.'

'I can't help there.'

She was thinking. Perhaps she really was trying to help. 'You know, Leo, your life would be so much easier if you could get some physical evidence out of Eleanor's body. The trouble is you've lost the best pathologist you have. You could call her. This is bigger than your ego.'

He groaned. 'This is *nothing* to do with my ego. That woman is the bane of my life. Also, she's sick.'

'She would crawl out of her death bed to work on this if she thought she could help. If you could convince her of that—'

'Possibly.'

He moved over into Wallis's empty chair and peered into her face. It wasn't a professional look. This was just him now, trying to be what he once was, trying to test the water. 'Do you ever wonder about what-ifs?' he asked. 'What would have happened if you'd turned left at the corner instead of turning right.'

'What's the point?' she asked warily.

'None I imagine. I just do it anyway. For example, what if you'd said yes to me when I invited you out to lunch yesterday? When all we had here was an ancient corpse? Costa would have talked to that woman and called in whoever else happened to be on duty. We'd have walked back here, got in a car, gone to see Wallis feeling entirely different about everything.'

She didn't like this conversation. 'It would have come your way eventually, Leo. It was on my desk anyway.'

'I know. But maybe we'd have had the chance to put things straight between us before all the crap began to happen. I would have liked that.'

She smoothed down her skirt. 'Things are straight, aren't they? Do I need to spell it out?'

'Not really. After you turned me down I made one more call. When you'd gone. Just to see if anyone knew what meeting you were in. There wasn't a meeting, was there? There's someone else.'

Her cheeks flushed. 'You checked on me?'

He shrugged. 'I'm a cop. What do you expect?'

'Jesus,' she hissed, then stabbed him in the chest with a long, slender finger. 'Understand this, Leo. I have a life. It is nothing to do with you. And it never will be. You keep your nose out of my business. You don't even peek through the door when you're passing.'

'I guess he's not a cop, then. Or a lawyer. We'd all know about it.'

'If I were you I'd be focusing on what's in front of you. Not my personal life. Call the Lupo woman. Apologize and try to get her back here. You need her, Leo.'

He nodded. 'I will. I'm sorry. I shouldn't have done it. It was just—'

But she wasn't listening. Nic Costa was walking down the corridor towards them and, from the look on his face, Leo Falcone realized he wouldn't be thinking about Rachele D'Amato for a while.

It was six forty-five. Emilio Neri was wearing a long grey overcoat, feeling content and, with a fat Cohiba smoking between his fingers, reflective. It was cold on the terrace of the house in the Via Giulia but he wanted to watch the last scrap of sunlight die in the smog and haze to the west. This was part of the ritual, an element in the growing rite of passage. Rituals . . . sixteen years before another one had touched him. He'd been dubious at the time, cynical even. The professor from the university was a nut, just a lonely man looking for some easy company. Neri had gone along with the idea because it suited him and he could see some profit from the photographs. He'd never believed what he heard. He was like the others, just along for the ride and whatever it offered him. Older now, touched by time, he wondered if he'd been wrong. He'd never forgotten what Randolph Kirk had told him. How it was a cycle, one that underpinned the whole of life: the hunting, the courtship. Then the marriage, the consummation. And finally the madness, the frenzy that was, perhaps, the real point of it all, because inside that brief bout of insanity lay some arcane secret about human nature, the simple truth that there was a beast beneath the skin, always was, always would be. When the moment came you had to acknowledge its presence then watch it slink, sated, back into the cage. There was, he now understood, no alternative. Randolph Kirk called it ritual. For Emilio Neri it was human nature, plain and simple. If he'd been smarter all those years before perhaps they could have avoided this mess. Perhaps now he would make better choices.

Neri was not a man to dwell on his regrets. Within the coming frenzy lay an opportunity, the chance to rebuild his life, shape it in his own image. He could throw away the pretence that had consumed him for twenty years. He need never waste his time at the opera again, or sit through interminable meetings for charities he didn't understand, fighting to stay awake. The money, the power, and the control they gave him over men outside his normal circles, had all blinded him to what he truly was. Apart from that brief time sixteen years ago the beast had never been free of the cage, and even then its journey was constrained by circumstances. Now it was time to put things straight, let the world remember him as it should, then flee to a comfortable retirement somewhere on the far side of the Atlantic, some place where he'd be untouchable.

Bucci and the three soldiers he'd hand-picked now stood on the far side of the terrace, waiting for orders. Neri didn't know any of them too well. He trusted Bucci's judgement all the same. The man had too much to gain to get this wrong. This was a night the city would remember. This was a time that would go down in the annals of mob history. A moment when a man of the old guard made his stand, pointed out what belonged to him and how he'd decided to bequeath it.

He recalled some of the crap Vergil Wallis used to spout years before. About history and duty and how this was ingrained into the true Roman soul, how these qualities would always come out, whatever the cost or the risk. Maybe the American wasn't that stupid after all. Surveying the city like this, for one last time from the home he knew he could never see again, Emilio Neri felt like a man moved by destiny, shaped by what had gone before him, determined now to leave his mark.

He returned to the four men with him on the terrace. 'You're all straight about this? You know what's got to be done?'

Bucci nodded.

'No doubts?' Neri said. 'No more questions? When we leave here, it's a one-way trip. You don't get to change your minds. None of us do. You wake up tomorrow morning and this is a different world. You wake up the day after and you're talking to Bruno here. He's your boss and he'll be a good man. Plus you know what you get from me in the way of gratitude. You'll be happy guys. Rich guys. You got opportunities. This city's yours. Understand?'

They were sound men. They wouldn't let him down.

'You gotta understand this too,' Neri added. 'No fuck-ups. We got no room for them. Any one of you fucks up it reflects on everyone else. So everyone else gets to pass judgement on you. That clear?'

'They got that, boss,' Bucci said.

'I hope so,' Neri muttered then sucked on the dying cigar and threw the stub over the railings, watching the red light flare as it fell. 'You know when the cops are coming?'

'Soon. Maybe half an hour.'

'And you think we can get out of here clean?'

'Piece of cake,' Bucci said confidently. 'We get your car up front really quickly. Franco here bundles inside. Then he's gone like he's running for his life. Stupid bastards will be after him straight away. We got some more cars out back. We just crawl off through the Campo. They'll never see us.'

Neri stared at him. 'You *know* that? You paid your dues to these bastards?'

'Yeah.'

'See?' Neri said, stabbing a finger at Bucci. 'You got a guy here who knows how to handle himself. You look after me. Then he looks after you. That's how it works. Now you wait for me downstairs. I want to talk to the family. Bruno, you send Mickey up. I want things straight with him.'

They left without saying another word. Neri sat down at the big table. Crumbs from breakfast were still on it. There was a noise at the door then Mickey stumbled in, looking lost, scared.

He got up and walked over to the kid, took him in his arms, kissed him on both cheeks.

'Mickey, Mickey. Son. Why are you looking so fucking miserable? This is what you wanted all along isn't it? To become a made man?'

'Yeah,' he mumbled.

Neri tweaked his cheek. 'You're still mad at me? Over our little falling-out earlier? Mickey. If I hear stuff like that I got to ask. You understand that, don't you?'

Mickey stared at the floor. 'That was asking?'

'Yeah,' Neri laughed. 'So your old man's a bastard. Why d'you think you live in a place like this? Why d'you think you never went short of a damn thing? That little scene is behind us now. I'm giving you the present I should have given you years ago. This is your coming of age, son. You got to go through with it. I blame myself for not letting you get on with it earlier. I've pampered you, Mickey, and that was wrong. A father wants to shield his boy from all the shit you get in the world. Can't blame him for that. But it don't work. Not forever. Every man's got to prove himself some time. Now's your chance.'

He embraced him again, squeezing hard.

'You're not scared, are you?' Neri whispered. 'Tell me. You can be frank with your own father.'

'No.' He looked terrible. He was back on the dope again, Neri guessed. 'It's just—'

'There's nothing wrong with being scared, Mickey. It clears your head sometimes. First time I killed a man I was real terrified. He was some old asshole who was pimping out in Monti. Wouldn't pay his dues. Thought he was bigger than he was. I stood outside that pit of his with a shotgun underneath my coat for ten minutes, wondering if I'd got the guts to go inside. Then you know what?'

'What?' Mickey wondered. His blonde hair looked more stupid than ever. Neri wondered if he'd been piling on the dye that evening, as if it might protect him from something.

'I realized. If I didn't kill him, some fucker would come along and kill me. That's the way it works in this business. Sometimes you don't get choices. You just go out and do your job. And . . .' Neri drew Mickey close, whispered in his ear, ' . . . you want to know something else? It gets easier. The first time, you got doubts, you wonder what it's like when the light goes out in some poor bastard's eyes. You'll be thinking that, won't you?'

'Maybe.'

'No. For sure. You wouldn't be human if you didn't. The point is . . . second time it ain't so bad. Third time out, you're curious. You're watching, wondering what's going on in his head. You're looking into his face and thinking, hey, maybe I'm doing the moron a favour! He gets to know some big secret quicker than me. Huh?'

He grinned and slapped the kid on the shoulder. 'Except there is no big secret. Fourth time out you know that for sure. They're just breathing one moment and gone the next. Which is as it should be. So after that you don't even think about it at all. If it's some scumbag you hate you even get some pleasure out of it too. Trust your old man. It's in your blood, Mickey. Once you get the feel it just comes natural.'

He didn't look convinced. He didn't look as if he were all there. 'Why a cop?'

'Because that's what I need. Does that worry you?'

'No one likes it when a cop gets killed.'

Neri wrinkled his nose, not liking what he was hearing. 'Depends on the cop.' He nodded downstairs. 'You got to make your mark. You're the boss's son. Don't ever forget it. You'll never get to lead them if they think you're on the same level. Understand?'

Mickey nodded. Neri leaned forward and took the gun from his son's jacket. He examined it carefully, checking the magazine, ensuring it was fully loaded.

'Killing someone's the easiest thing in the world, provided you do it right. Just walk up, pop the bastard quick in the head, and it's done. Work on it, Mickey. It's a talent you're going to need. On your way now.'

'And afterwards?'

A shifty look crossed Neri's face. 'Didn't I mention that? Afterwards things get a little hot for all of us around here. Best we don't hang around this place for a while. We're going to be flexible for the next few days. You just keep that phone of yours switched on.'

'What? Where am I supposed to go?'

He was so slow. Sometimes Neri wondered whether he really was the kid's father at all.

He handed the gun back. 'I'll call. Trust your old man. He's got your best interests at heart.'

Mickey shoved the pistol back into his jacket. 'OK,' he murmured listlessly.

'And when you see Adele tell her to come up here. I want to talk to her.'

Neri had been thinking about this side of things. Maybe there was another way of dealing with it. But that would have been indulgent. That could have wider repercussions. He didn't want to complicate matters any more than necessary. 'You know, now I come to think about it, I never should have swallowed that story about you and her. I always did believe the bad stuff about you and that's unfair. I owe you an apology, son. You never did get on with Adele, did you? You and her just rub each other up the wrong way.'

'Never did,' the kid said, not quite able to meet Neri's eyes.

Costa was walking down the corridor to the big conference room for Falcone's briefing when she came round the corner.

'You look terrible,' Teresa Lupo croaked.

He stopped and squinted at her, trying to work out what was going on. 'I do?'

'No. I just wanted to say it first.'

Then she coughed into a fistful of tissues and stared at him with pink, watery eyes.

'Actually,' he said, 'you don't look bad at all. It's amazing what drugs can do.'

'Lying cop bastard—' she mumbled.

'Ah, ah, ah. You're feverish. You have to try to keep the temperature down.'

'I ought to be in bed feeling sorry for myself. But then that asshole Falcone did the worst thing. Unbelievable.' She looked hurt for a moment. 'He apologized. Can you believe that?'

Costa thought about this. 'No. Do you have it on tape?'

'I wish. I doubt I shall hear its like again.'

'I doubt any of us will. So what are you doing?'

'Oh, just came in to fill in an expenses form. Pick up my mail. Scratch my ass. Doesn't seem much for the likes of me to do around here. Or did I get that wrong?'

'Teresa—' he said, and took a step towards her.

'Don't stand too close. Germs. If I start infecting his men he'll just get mad at me again.'

'Are you OK?'

'No,' she shrugged. 'But I'm back to being as bad as I was before. I'm sorry, Nic. I don't know what came over me. It was the thought of that poor kid being out there somewhere, abandoned, all because of me. And with you guys thinking about nothing but the lovely Barbara. Having people try to kill you is somewhat unsettling I find.'

'I'd go along with that.'

'Of course!' She brightened a little. 'Finally, we do have something in common. We could discuss it over dinner. Nightmares we have known.'

'Not till this is over,' he said. 'Which it will be. Soon, I hope.'

She nodded towards the room. Officers were steadily filtering through the door. A lot of them. Most of the Questura's denuded complement by the looks of things.

'You have that look about you, I must say. Is it promising?'

He tried to look confident. 'I think so.'

She sniffed again and didn't look too convinced. 'That's good. So what am I supposed to do if you smart-asses have it all wrapped up? Why is boss man practising his apology routine on me?'

'You could deal with the autopsy queue perhaps. Your deputy looks ready to crack up.'

'Silvio always looks ready to crack up. You have to give these people some room from time to time, Nic. Can't mother them every waking moment of the day.'

'Point taken. How about this? Take a look at Eleanor Jamieson. See if there's any DNA we can use?'

Her pink eyes grew bigger. 'DNA? As I keep pointing out to people around here she's been in a peat swamp for sixteen years. What do you think I am? A miracle worker?'

'Yeah. That's what Falcone wants anyway. And while you're at it, we'd really love to know who Kirk phoned while he had you locked in that office.'

She put a finger to her cheek. 'Oh, let me think now. Can I remember the ring tones? Beep, beep, fucking beep. No you just lost me there.'

'You asked. I answered. Now I've got to go. Bad guys to catch. Missing girls to find.'

She was dabbing at her nose again, looking a little happier for the conversation anyway. 'Have you talked to the university woman since I stormed in there? Regina Morrison?'

He shook his head. 'Not that I'm aware of. Why should we?'

'Regina was Kirk's new boss. Somewhere in those files of hers she must have a list of every archaeological dig he's ever worked on. Him being dead and what, I can't check this out for sure. But where do you think a man like that would hide someone?'

Costa nodded. 'Where did that thought come from?'

'I was putting myself in your shoes. Or at least I was trying to imagine what it was like being a cop.'

Teresa didn't say it this time but he got the message. They should have thought of it themselves. They would have, if there'd been the time and the people to manage the workload.

'Thanks,' he said, and walked down the corridor, the last man to enter the room.

Adele Neri didn't bother to put on a jacket when she went outside. Maybe she hadn't expected to be there long.

'You're shivering. Here.' Neri shrugged off his overcoat, walked behind her, and placed it on her bare, slim shoulders.

'You're thoughtful tonight,' she said. 'What's wrong?'

'That tongue of yours is getting too sharp, Adele. It never used to be like that.'

He sat down at the table, making a point of brushing away the crumbs. She joined him there, in the seat directly opposite, looking uncomfortable, looking as if she were struggling to read his mood.

'We're just at that stage of being married,' she said. 'Where some of the sheen's come off.'

He scowled. It was a lame suggestion. 'Is that right? I don't recall it being like this with anyone else. Not with Mickey's mother. We were working. Then we weren't working. Couldn't keep our hands off each other one moment. Couldn't stand the sight of each other the next. It doesn't feel like that now. Not for me. For you . . . I dunno. You're young. Tell me, Adele. Does the sight of me turn you over? Thinking about how old I am and that?'

There was a flash of edginess in her bright green eyes. 'Don't be ridiculous, darling. Why would you even think such a thing?'

'Why? Because I'm an ugly old man. Fat too. And you. Look at you. You can't walk down the street without some kid giving you the eye.'

'Kids never interest me. You know that.'

'And I did interest you?'

'You *do*.'

'Maybe,' he said with a shrug. 'Maybe it's just the money. I don't know any longer, Adele. The thing is, we got to spend a little time apart. That's a practical matter. All this trouble I've got now. There's no reason to fuck up your life too. It's none of your business.'

She gave him an acid glance. Maybe she thought he was fishing for sympathy. 'I'm your wife. Your problems are my problems. If—'

'No, no, no,' he interrupted. 'You don't need to give me that shit. You don't have to pretend. We don't have time. Let me put it another way. I don't want you involved in what's going down right now. That's for selfish reasons too. It's men's stuff. We got things to do a woman shouldn't have to know about. You'd complicate matters.'

He looked at her from across the table and felt no feelings for her. 'Maybe some people are going to get hurt. If I have you close it might give the wrong impression. As if you're part of it or something. Some of these southern families . . . you'd think the women are running them sometimes. Don't work like that here. I want you separate from me because I don't want to have to wonder what that mouth of yours is saying. Understood?'

She bridled at his suggestion. 'I wouldn't talk out of turn.'

'Who knows what anyone would do once those bastards from the DIA come calling? The cops I can deal with. These others—'

He looked at his watch. 'The point is I'm going now and I don't know when I'll be back. *If* I'll be back. We need some time apart.'

She nodded. Neri was unsure whether she was upset or not. 'Where will you be?'

He gave her a glassy, dead-eyed look and said nothing. 'How will I contact you, Emilio? I'm your wife.'

He stifled a laugh. 'Don't worry. There's money in the bank. You can pay bills. Buy stuff. Do whatever you like. Give me a couple of months. Then I'll be in touch. Maybe we'll have a second honeymoon. Maybe we'll be ready for that by then. If you feel otherwise, I'll call the lawyers. It'd be best to do it friendly if we can.'

'And now?' She looked as if she wanted to scream at him for behaving like this. She just didn't dare. 'What do I do now?'

He waved an arm around the terrace. 'Stay here. You got a beautiful house. You can bring back all those servants you love. I know how much you hate cleaning up yourself. I could never stand the idea of servants myself. I gave you your head on that one. Maybe I was wrong. Who'd want strangers in their own home? But hell, when I'm gone I don't *care* what you do.' He made sure this last point came across clearly. 'I don't care who you see. I don't care how you spend your time.'

She got up and took off his coat, laying it on his lap. 'You'll be needing this,' she said.

'Yeah. Tell me one thing, Adele.'

'What?'

'You ever been unfaithful to me? Not that it matters any more. I don't care right now. I got bigger things to think about.'

'Why would I do that? she asked.

'I dunno. For the sex. For the hell of it. Or maybe—' It occurred to him that neither of these would really move a woman like Adele. 'Because it suited you.'

'Those are little reasons. Too small to get yourself killed for.'

He laughed. 'Yeah. You're right. You're a smart girl. That's what impressed me most about you in the beginning. I never liked stupid women.'

'Thanks,' she muttered.

'Just remember this. Things have got to come out in balance at the end. Some American creep kills one of my men. I do something in return. Someone screws with me. I screw with them. Except I do it better. Bigger. I make it final. I win because that's how the balance is, that's my place. This is serious stuff, Adele. You don't want to go pushing your pretty face into it. Believe me.'

He stood up, walked over to her, kissed her on the cheek. Just one short kiss.

'You just stay here. Watch TV. Make yourself a drink.

And when the cops come, you tell them nothing. Say I went fishing. OK?'

Outside a familiar engine was gunning hard. Tyres were burning along the cobblestones of the Via Giulia. Emilio Neri knew what this meant. The first part of the deception was under way.

'Ciao,' he said, and waddled towards the stairs.

It was a cold, clear night, bright with stars and the silver disc of a waxing moon. The police convoy, a marked car at its head, blue light flashing, siren screaming, cut straight through the evening rush hour. Falcone rode with Costa and Peroni just ahead of the heavily manned riot van that was the last in the line. The radio was hot with chatter and none of it sounded good. The plain-clothes men stationed outside Neri's had reported the sudden departure of his car just fifteen minutes before. One team had detached itself to give chase but lost the vehicle somewhere over the river. The second saw two more vehicles scream away from a rear alley and were left standing in the street, with no chance of pursuit.

'What are we going to do?' Costa wondered. 'Go after him?'

Falcone shook his head. 'Go after what? We only have a number for Neri's own car, and what's the money on him being in that? Let's see who's still in the house. It's the son I want to talk to first. Wherever he is. Jesus, the timing. How the hell did Neri know?'

Costa and Peroni looked at each other. Falcone had ordered a big operation: ten vehicles, half of them marked. The DIA had two other cars along for the ride, with Rachele D'Amato at the head. It wasn't going to be easy keeping something of this size quiet.

They turned into the narrow lane of the Via Giulia, rattling across the cobblestones, and saw the flash of cameras, the lights of the TV men, a full-scale media mob waiting on Neri's doorstep.

Falcone went rigid with fury at the sight of them. He recalled Rachele D'Amato's promise to Neri that morning. One way or another, she said, his fall from grace would be a very public event. He swore under his breath, peered ahead and saw her car, saw her slim figure getting out and slipping through the pack of hacks, towards the house.

'Stop here,' he ordered. 'We don't want that mob on our backs. And I'd rather not have her getting into the place before us.'

Costa pulled into the side of the road, next to a medieval fountain, and all three of them watched, with rising trepidation, the melee happening in the street. Broadcast crew fought with press journalists, jostling to be close to the action. The first marked police car had arrived and men were leaping out. D'Amato and some of her team stood by as a bunch of burly uniformed officers went through the motions of waiting to be let in then, in the space of a couple of seconds, began attacking the expensive polished wood door with sledge-hammers. There wasn't much room. A small van marked with the logo of one of the minor cable channels was parked directly outside, its back end almost up against the building. The hammer men had to squeeze behind it to tackle their target. The vehicle cramped their action, made it impossible to get the swing they needed.

Then one of them climbed onto the bonnet and took

a hefty lunge at the woodwork. The door crumpled. Hands shot through to tackle the locks inside. Rachele D'Amato was over the door first, a couple of DIA men on her heels as the cops stood back, open-mouthed, wondering.

'Shit,' Falcone hissed and started running towards the mob followed closely by Costa and Peroni. When they got there the uniforms were stuck outside the shattered door, looking for direction.

'Next time wait for me,' Falcone barked at them. 'Don't let anyone else in. Don't let anyone out without my permission.'

Falcone in the lead, they went up the stairs. The DIA crew had a good start on them. The first-floor room, where they'd seen Neri's hoods that morning, was empty. The butt of a cigarette still smoked in an ashtray. There was a half-full coffee cup on the low table.

Peroni picked it up. 'Still warm. They really did cut this fine.'

'They knew what they were doing,' Falcone murmured then stopped. The DIA team were clattering downstairs, arguing among each other until a female voice told them to clam up. Rachele D'Amato walked into the room with her team, stood in front of Falcone and his men and folded her arms, furious.

'There's not a soul in the house, Leo. Is the Questura leaking again or what?'

'Don't start,' Falcone snapped back at her. 'Who the hell do you think you are, jumping in ahead of us? And this joke out on the street? You had the nerve to call the media? This is a police investigation. Not yours. The DIA don't even have warrants—'

She reached into her bag and pulled out a sheaf of papers. 'You want to read them?'

He glowered at the documents. 'You said—'

'I changed my mind. The information we got from the accountant's office this morning is like gold dust. We can lock this fat creep away for years, and scores of others too.'

'If you can find him . . . What do you think the media will make of that?'

'Leo!' she screeched. 'I didn't call the media. No one inside the DIA did. This was as secret as we get. Don't look to me.'

Falcone stared at her. 'No. You people are all so clean, aren't you?'

'Leo—?'

Costa was on the phone, talking to the ops room. He finished the call. 'They've found Neri's car. It just had a couple of his hoods in it. They were riding around, no destination in particular, down in Testaccio. It was just a blind.'

'Where the hell are they?' Falcone demanded. 'The son? The wife? He didn't pack for a family holiday. What's he doing?'

'Getting ready for a war maybe,' D'Amato suggested. 'We still have the house. We've got free run of it. We can tear the place apart. It's a gift.'

Peroni gingerly placed a hand on her slender shoulder. 'We appear to have a conflict of interest, lady. We're looking for a missing girl, in case you forgot. Right now we don't care about finding Mr Neri's cooked books. They can wait for another day.'

'We need the son,' Falcone said, then walked over to the long window and gazed down into the street. The hubbub was dying. The media crews were starting to pack their bags. They'd been cheated too. There was a story for them. A failed raid on a city hoodlum. But there was no real action, nothing to splash over the front pages and the newscasts. A bunch of cops hammering down a door in the Via Giulia was second division news. Whoever tipped them off surely knew they would be disappointed, which pointed the finger at Neri himself, though Falcone couldn't begin to fathom the reason.

He looked at Rachele D'Amato. 'You can do what you like here. If you find something that has a material bearing on the Julius case, call me. That isn't a request. If you delay what we're doing by a single second *I'll* be talking to the media about why we've been hampered unnecessarily. We've got to look for Mickey Neri and that girl. We've got to find someone to talk to.'

She wagged a long, elegant finger at him. 'No, no, no, Leo. Don't try and pass that responsibility on to me. We do DIA business, not yours. Leave some men if you want that.'

'*I don't have the damned men,*' Falcone yelled at her, so loud even the cops outside stopped talking for a moment. 'Don't you get it? We've a day to find that girl. Maybe less. We haven't a clue where she might be. We don't even know where to begin looking. But it isn't here. It's not in your damned books. It's wherever Mickey Neri is.'

Maybe, he thought. Leo Falcone didn't know any more. All he understood was that it was important to cling on to the human side of the investigation. You only got results by finding the right people and making them talk.

'Leo? *Leo!*'

Her voice dogged them halfway down the stairs, arguing all the way. Then she turned back to join her team, to get on with the job. *Her* job. Falcone didn't get it. Rachele D'Amato had won what she wanted. Neri was on the run. She had a *carte blanche* to investigate every last aspect of the old crook's empire. What was it to her to repay a little of the debt? Why was this vendetta the DIA had with Neri more important than the life of a teenage girl?

They stormed out of the house, out into the street, pushing past the TV van which was still backed up against the ruined door. The media mob was almost gone now. There were just a handful of cops, in uniform and out, waiting outside, looking uncomfortable, guilty that they'd overheard the argument.

'You can stand down,' Falcone told them. 'This is a DIA deal for the time being. Let's get back to the Questura. See what's happening with the phones.'

The men nodded. They'd caught the atmosphere.

'Stupid, stupid, stupid,' Falcone repeated as they walked to the car.

'They just got their priorities, Leo,' Peroni observed and got a cold, hard glance for his pains. 'Sorry, *Sir*. You can't expect anything else. The kid and me could go back in there and watch for a while.'

'No point,' Falcone said. 'She'll let us know if she finds something. How would it look otherwise? Besides—' He needed to get this clear in his own head too. 'There can't be a damn thing there that's any use to us. Neri had this planned, right down to the last detail. He's making monkeys of us. He'd love it if we stayed in that place, peeking under the carpet, scraping through dust.'

'Yeah,' Peroni agreed. 'I can see that. Sorry, I still find it hard trying to think like you people. It's all so damn *sneaky*.'

Costa's phone rang. He stepped aside so that he could hear the anxious voice on the other end.

'Why did Neri set this up?' Falcone wondered. It was all too small. It just caused the police some embarrassment and Neri had to be above that. The media didn't even hang around once they realized there was no big arrest coming, no sign of the fat old hood being led out in handcuffs, bundled into a car, head down for the cameras. They'd disappeared altogether.

Apart from the van.

'Boss,' Costa said anxiously. 'I think we've got something. An anonymous call just came in. Someone looking just like Suzi. No more than half an hour ago.'

'Where?' Falcone asked, still thinking about what had just happened, trying to make some connections.

'Somewhere along Cerchi. Didn't get an exact position.'

'Quite some road,' Peroni said. 'We could spend all night going up and down there.'

Cerchi ran the length of the Circus Maximus, now an empty, stadium-shaped field behind the Palatine hill, overlooked by the ruins of Augustus's palaces.

Costa remembered what Teresa had said about Regina Morrison. 'Kirk and Mickey could have used old archaeological digs if they wanted to. We can talk to his boss at the university. She should have a list of everywhere he worked.'

'Get her,' Falcone ordered. He reached the car, put his hand on the door, still thinking. 'Chase it, Nic. Let's go there straight away. This place is dead.'

He looked back at the street. They were parked a good fifty metres from Neri's door. There wasn't a TV crew in sight. The van was still there, up at an angle over the pavement.

'See the vehicle at the front door?' Falcone asked. 'Either of you notice someone using it? Any of those TV bastards go near at all?'

'Not me,' Peroni answered, puzzled.

Falcone looked at Costa, his mind full of possibilities.

'Me neither,' Costa replied. 'What do you think—'

He didn't finish the sentence. The earth began to tremble beneath their feet, cobblestones shaking as if hit by an earthquake. Then came a roar so loud it was unreal, a physical wall of audible fury burying itself deep in their heads.

A fierce, fiery tongue leapt out of the rear end of the van. The vehicle rose off the ground as if tugged towards the sky by an invisible force. For a brief moment the world stood still, then a cacophony of furious noise hit them, followed by a vicious, punishing force as hard as a fist.

When it ended Costa was on the cold hard ground, holding his hands to his ears, stunned, panting too. Peroni leaned against the car, mouth open, looking shell-shocked, gasping for air. And Falcone was running, frantically, as fast as he could, back towards Neri's house where a firestorm now raged out of the blackened, torn tangle of wreckage that was the van, flames licking greedily up into the shattered remains of the building.

Costa staggered in his footsteps, Peroni behind him. The air stank of smoke and the chemical smell of spent explosive. Car alarms, triggered by the shock wave of the blast, sounded all around. A man was screaming

327

in the gutter, clutching at his stomach. Two others lay still on the ground. A team of uniformed officers materialized from a riot van around the corner, wondering where to begin.

It was impossible to think. Nic Costa looked at the faces of the men around him, faces locked hard in shock, and found it impossible to recognize any of them. In this sudden burst of insanity the world had become anonymous, simply a receptacle for its victims.

The blast had taken out two floors of the building. As the dust and debris cleared Costa could see, in the dim street lights, entire rooms in Neri's house now laid open to the elements: tables and chairs, a TV set, a kitchen cut in half by the savagery of the explosion. Flames raged in and out of the severed quarters. Somewhere on the second floor a dark figure danced crazily, as if trying to dodge the blaze that engulfed him, until he fell to the floor, rolled right off the edge and into the dust storm milling around the van.

Leo Falcone was fighting at the mountain of rubble which occupied the spot that, moments before, had been Emilio Neri's front door, clawing at the bricks, snatching them out of his way one by one.

There was a broken body in front of him, poised at an impossible angle, a slender arm, bloodied, blackened by the blast, quite still in the smoking debris.

A small, calm voice spoke at the back of Nic Costa's head and it said: *think*.

As the ambulances arrived, as a screaming fire engine bathed in blue light wove through the cars thrown into the road by the bomb, Nic Costa scanned his notes, found the number, then walked into the relative quiet of an antique shop doorway to place the call.

'Miss Morrison,' he said when he heard the clipped female voice answer. 'You don't know me but I'm a friend of Teresa Lupo's, a detective. I really need to talk—'

There was live football on the TV: Roma versus Lazio. The big local derby. Roma were beating the crap out of their neighbours. Again. Toni Martelli could hear people yelling with delight in the neighbouring apartments. He was a Lazio man himself. For him Roma were still the team of the lower classes, the rabble, the people who ran things these days. Not that Martelli had been to a game in years. Now he was out of the force he'd lost all the favours. With Barbara gone, he couldn't even sponge a few off her.

Falcone had been on the phone ealier saying he could probably release the body for cremation within a week. Sooner if Martelli had something to say. Martelli had told him where he could shove his offer. The girl was dead. What else was there to talk about?

Then came another call with news he half expected to hear. And so he locked himself in the over-large apartment, snuggling up to some cigarettes and a bottle of grappa he'd had sent round from the bar on the corner, waiting, watching the game on the TV, war disguised as sport, brute humanity pretending it was something else, something noble and elegant, like a savage trying to dance ballet.

The key started to turn in the door just after ten, rattling around clumsily as someone fumbled trying to get in.

'Cowboys,' Martelli sniffed. 'They don't even have the decency to send a real man.'

He turned off the TV and the light by his side, making the room appear the way he had planned. He now sat in his wheelchair in the dark. It was not easy to see. He'd angled the two big standard lamps in the living room so they shone towards the door at the end of the corridor. The man would have to walk straight into the light, maybe shade his eyes a little. Toni Martelli had thought this through. He half-guessed what the outcome would be but he didn't plan on making it easy.

A figure blundered down the corridor, too scared to hit the lights. Martelli had the remote control the social people had given him. You had to work your advantages when you were a cripple. He waited for the figure in the shadows to get close to the door, then he hit the corridor light. Three big bulbs running the length of the long passageway came on in tandem. Mickey Neri stood there, dressed in black, hands empty, waving stupidly in front of him.

'I got a gun, asshole,' Martelli grunted from the pool of darkness in the corner of the living room. 'I got a big shotgun. You want to see me use it?'

Mickey turned round, ready to run. Martelli pumped the twelve-bore noisily, ramming one of the four remaining cartridges he owned into the chamber.

'Sit down, sonny,' he bawled. 'Let me take a good look at you.'

Mickey Neri moved cautiously into the room and fell into the chair Martelli had nodded towards.

'Mickey,' Martelli sighed. 'Your old man sent you? That right?'

'Yeah.' There was a pathetic snarl beneath the fear. 'We met before?'

'A long time ago. When we were all up to things we hoped were dead and buried. I'm offended you don't remember. I seem to think—' Martelli started coughing, couldn't help it, and the fit went on and on until he fought back the phlegm. When it was over, he said, simply, 'I seem to recall that, when I gave my daughter up for you and your pop, not quite knowing what was on the cards, you were one of those who got to taste the goods.'

'Like you said,' Mickey grumbled, face screwed up, looking as if it were a struggle to remember. 'It was a long time ago. Lots of people got confused memories about what happened then.'

'Not me.'

Mickey nodded. He was staring frankly at Martelli who knew exactly what he was wondering. How sick was this frail old man really? 'Also,' he added, 'I don't recall you pulling out of what you got *Mr* Martelli. I seem to think you had your fun too. All you old guys . . . You just wanted to get into something fresh and young. You were as greedy as the rest of them.'

Martelli waved the barrel then coughed again, not quite so bad this time. 'You kids are all the same. No respect.'

Then he jerked the barrel and fired. The shotgun exploded a metre or so to the right of the terrified Mickey Neri, blowing a huge tear in the dining room table. And Toni Martelli started counting. This was an apartment block. Someone would hear. Someone would call the cops.

'You fucking madman!' Mickey whined. 'You—'

331

'Shut up. We got a deal, your old man and me. Not that he told you, naturally. If you walk out of here alive, then everything's square with you. If you're a piece of meat on the floor by the time the cops come, then I'm just sweet. I killed some creep who was trying to rob my apartment. I got Emilio Neri in my debt. And I took his scummy little kid out too. What d'ya think, Mickey? Is your old man pissed off with you or what? Where's your money going?'

'You believe that?' Mickey yelled, bright eyes bulging, terrified. 'Are you telling the truth? 'Cos if you are we're both dead, mister.'

'I'm dead already, moron.' Martelli coughed. And coughed some more. Then it was as if something had come alive inside him, as if the cancer had got scared by all this noise and violence too. A big, black pain rose up from inside his guts, freezing what little sensation remained in his spine, making his mind go blank with the agony.

'*Eeeeeeeeeeee*—' Toni Martelli screeched, rocking from side to side in the chair, trying to keep hold of the shotgun in his arms, which had a life of its own now, wanted to call time on this craziness and go for a walk somewhere else.

There was morphine somewhere. Barbara kept it safe for him. He'd not needed it since she died. Something seemed to kill the needling agony the sickness inflicted on him from time to time. Now it was back, with a vengeance, clouding his vision, dimming his thoughts.

Martelli couldn't stand it any longer. He let go of the rifle, let it fall on his lap and, with his free hand, started spinning the wheelchair, as hard and as fast as he could, fumbling for where he left the ammunition. Two cartridges made their way into the chamber, and for the life of him he couldn't remember willing them there. Two explosions rocked the room. The first blew out the big window looking onto the courtyard. Through the shattered glass came the sound of the football match, a wild, insane roar, blaring out of the neighbouring sitting rooms, where another noise, the lowing, frightened murmur of people, was growing too.

The second went in the opposite direction, somewhere towards the figure of Mickey Neri, who'd now thrown himself off the chair, trying to find cover.

Martelli's head cleared a little and the pain diminished. The chair stopped going round and round. The stupid screeching noise died in his throat. And at that moment Toni Martelli knew this was the end, one way or another. Neri's offer was meaningless. A bigger, blacker fate was rising up to grip him now, and all the hoodlums in the world couldn't keep it from his throat.

Mickey Neri was writhing around on the floor. Martelli heard his desperate shrieks, wondered how badly he'd hit the kid, and shook his head.

'Listen to the little rabbit,' he croaked. 'What makes him squeal? The pain? Or knowing what's gonna end it? You got no balls, boy?'

'You crazy old fucker,' Mickey whispered from somewhere beyond Martelli's receding vision. 'I could give you something. We could both walk out of this.'

'You got nothing for me,' Martelli said simply. 'No one's got a damn thing I can use any more.' He raised the gun, knowing there was just the one cartridge left and this had to count, because if it didn't Mickey Neri would somehow walk out of this place alive, and that, surely, was a crime.

Then he coughed some more, coughed and coughed, until the sound of his own breathing entered his ears, grew and grew.

Toni Martelli was choking on his own blood, wondering where this had come from, why the doctors never told him it would end this way. The shotgun still lay on his lap but he hadn't the strength to touch it. And Mickey Neri had stopped wriggling around on the ground. He was half out in the open now, looking up, a little hope in his eyes. The little jerk wasn't even hurt.

'What the fuck—' Martelli tried to mumble, but it all came out wrong because his mouth was full of stuff, his head was all over the place.

And the pain . . .

Different this time.

He looked down at the gun. It was covered in blood. His own. It came out of his chest somehow, poured down the front of his shirt.

He wanted to get angry. He wanted to kill someone.

A woman walked into view from the door. A skinny woman with red hair and a face that made him feel fear.

'Who the fu—?' Toni Martelli began to say.

She had a gun in her hand. She held the weapon purposefully, the way you were supposed to.

Mickey Neri crawled to his knees and looked up as if the light of God was shining out of her bright, glittering eyes.

The woman shook her head, disappointed. The red hair moved slowly in the light of the old apartment.

'You do it like this,' she said, then walked up to Toni Martelli, smiled briefly, coldly into his face, and put a bullet into his brain.

*

There was only so much a man could do with his hands. Brick and glass and rubble tore at Peroni's fingertips. The coarse, choking dust filled his mouth, solidified in his eyes. Every time he and Falcone tried to snatch something away from Rachele D'Amato's torn, unconscious body, another piece of debris seemed to fall around them to fill its place. Neri's house was losing its solidity, just like the world itself. The ancient structure was on the point of collapse, a huge hole rent in its belly. There was so little time. Falcone was grappling with an ancient timber beam that had shattered like an over-long, rotten tooth and now lay across her chest. It refused to move and it occurred to Peroni that maybe this was for the best. In the dark it was impossible to see what part of the wrecked building depended on the rest for support. If they shifted the wrong thing, the fragile remnants of wall around them could so easily topple down too.

He put a hand on Falcone's arm. 'Leo,' he gasped, snatching for breath. 'This is crazy. We could bring the whole thing down on her.'

The tall inspector continued to claw at the rubble and brick. Peroni grabbed him roughly by the shoulder. '*Leo!*'

Falcone stopped. He looked lost just then. Peroni had never seen him this way. It was unnerving. They needed Falcone to keep his cool. The shaky department was beginning to pivot around him. There was no one else. 'The rescue people are here. They know what they're doing. This is their job. Let's stick to ours, huh?'

Vehicles were arriving all around, fire trucks with shifting gear, their officers moving quietly among the carnage of the blast, trying to assess how best to proceed, paramedics in vivid yellow jackets, wondering where to start.

'She's breathing,' Falcone murmured. 'I can see it—'

Rachele D'Amato was alive, just. Peroni nodded at a bunch of paramedics placing black plastic sheets over several unmistakable forms. 'She's lucky. We got at least three dead already.'

Peroni knew it could have been even worse. If the riot men around the corner had been standing outside their van instead of sitting inside it. If the media animals had bothered to stick around to see what this was really about. It was too much for his head to handle right then. This was premeditated slaughter on a scale the city had never known, a calculated act of murder.

Two firemen elbowed past, took a good look at Rachele D'Amato, then yelled at Falcone and Peroni to get out of the way.

'We were trying to help,' Peroni shouted back.

'Nice of you,' the lead fireman retorted, dragging some gear behind them, calling for a back-up team to bring some lifting equipment. 'Now give us some room.'

Falcone closed his eyes for a moment, trying to quell the fury. He gripped the man by the shoulder.

'I'm the officer in charge here—' he began to say. Something in the man's eyes made him stop.

'I don't care who the hell you are,' the fireman bellowed back. 'We're here to get these people out, mister. If you stand in my way God help you.'

'OK, OK,' Peroni said softly, putting a hand on Falcone, gently guiding him away.

The firemen weren't even listening. The two of them were on the ground, carefully scraping rubble away from her body, yelling for more gear and paramedics.

Falcone watched them, his face a picture of misery. 'Gianni? You got any cigarettes? I was trying to give up.'

Peroni brushed some of the dust off his sleeves, then did the same for Falcone. The two men were filthy and they'd hardly even noticed. 'When it comes to cigarettes, I'm always prepared. Walk with me. I'm flattered, by the way, to hear you using my first name again. I thought, perhaps, we'd never get back to that.'

Falcone followed him to the far side of the road, putting just enough distance between them and the wreck of Neri's house to be out of the immediate stench of smoke and dust. Three more ambulances tore down the cobblestones and screeched to a halt next to the emergency rescue unit. New teams of paramedics burst out of their brightly lit interiors and started to work the scene. A short line of black cars arrived behind them. Both Falcone and Peroni knew what that meant. The big guys were coming in to pass judgement: men from the security service, the bureaucrats, the hierarchy of the DIA. This was no longer a simple crime investigation. It bordered on terrorism, and that changed the name of the game.

Peroni used his sleeve to wipe some debris off the bonnet of a Renault saloon and they sat down. He lit a cigarette and passed it over. Falcone's slim, tanned hands were shaking. He took a couple of drags at the thing then cursed and threw it to the ground.

'You know how much those things cost?' Peroni asked. 'I'm the only man in the Questura who buys them straight and honest. No black market stuff for this boy.'

'Yeah,' Falcone grunted. 'You and your cock-eyed ideas about honesty. I don't get it. You were the one man in vice I thought we could trust. Then you go and ruin it all over a woman. What for?'

Peroni cast a sideways glance at Falcone. He was a handsome man, in a hard, emotionless way. This inability to address the real seat of his fears – his apparent concern for Rachele D'Amato – was a rare weakness, one that made him briefly more human. 'She was a *beautiful* woman, may I remind you. A hooker, true, but let's not leave out all the salient facts. People make fools of themselves from time to time, Leo. There's a crazy gene in all of us. You convince yourself otherwise. You say to yourself, nah, the job's bigger than this. Or the marriage. Or the kids. You think: I can just push these thoughts back into the dark where they belong. Then one day, just when you're least expecting it, the crazy gene wakes up and you know it's pointless trying to fight. For a while anyway. Because fighting could be even worse. You're just beating up on yourself. But I think you already know that.'

Falcone glanced back at the chaos across the road. 'A bomb, a bomb. What the hell is Neri thinking?'

Peroni's mind had been working along the same lines. 'You think it has to be him? He had enemies. The American for one.'

Falcone stared dolefully at the firemen working to free Rachele D'Amato. 'Why would any of them bomb an empty building? No one's that stupid. Neri knew we were coming. The bastard left us this as a present and—'

Falcone was struggling to tie the ends together in his head. Peroni hated seeing him filled with doubt like this. 'And it doesn't make sense. This is so final. He can't talk his way out of this one. He can't pick up the phone and bribe some politician, some cop to look the other way.'

That was true, Peroni thought. This was the end of Neri's career. There was no other possibility. Or, to be more precise, it was the act which Neri was using to announce the closure of his time in Rome. Something, the papers on the dead accountant's desk, some threat they failed to understand, must have convinced him there could be no turning back. He had to flee, to seek anonymous sanctuary somewhere he hoped the Italian state could no longer reach him.

Peroni thought of the body, the brown, shining body in Teresa Lupo's morgue. Everything led back to that first corpse. Every event that followed stemmed from its discovery, and still they had no idea why, no clue to explain the strange and deadly demons that flew out of the ground once that small patch of peat near Fiumicino was exposed to the light of day.

Falcone turned a sudden, sharp gaze on him, the one that said: *don't lie, don't even think of it*. 'Tell me the truth. Do you think I'm losing it? Is this getting too much for me?'

'What?' Peroni stared at him, almost lost for words. 'Since when did you get to be super-human? This is too much for all of us. This . . .' he waved a hand at the scene across the road, ' . . . is the world gone mad. Not just that bastard Neri.'

There was a sound from the house. The lifting gear around Rachele D'Amato was being cranked into action. The firemen were shouting to each other. Timbers were moving. Walls were starting to shake. And there was more light now. The bright, unforgiving light of the TV cameras, back to see what they were supposed to witness all along.

Falcone stood up and shook the dirt and dust off

himself, getting ready to go back. Peroni was with him instantly, a hand on his arm.

'Leo,' he said. 'There's nothing you can do. And whatever state that woman's in you can't change it. Furthermore, if she does wake up, she'll be livid to find you sitting by the bed like some dumbstruck husband.'

'Really?' Falcone gave him a familiar, cold look. 'You know her well enough to say that?'

'I know she's just as married to the job as you are. And when she does get conscious the first thing she'll ask is what you've done to get the sons of bitches who did this. You offer a bunch of flowers and you'll get it straight back into your face. Now am I right?'

Falcone glanced at him and Peroni wondered if he had read everything the wrong way. 'You think that's what this is about, Gianni? Me and her?'

'I dunno,' he mumbled, and Peroni realized that at that moment he really didn't. There was more going on in Falcone's head than he appreciated.

'She's got another man,' Falcone said flatly. 'She told me so.'

'Gimme a break,' Peroni answered immediately. 'Does she look like a woman with a man in tow? She's just playing with you, Leo. Women are like that.'

'Maybe.'

Falcone was focused on the meeting going on across the road. The men from the black cars were engaged in an impromptu conference near the sight of the blast. He knew, surely, he ought to go and join them. He ought to answer their questions, try to keep them happy.

Peroni looked at the shattered building and sighed. 'For God's sake, Leo. It's times like this people look to you. If you're riddled with self-doubt, how the hell do you expect them to go on? Here—'

He lit another cigarette and offered it. Falcone accepted reluctantly.

'Listen to your friend Gianni, please. Because he's just got a stupid vice cop brain in his skull and this primitive organ doesn't have a clue what's going on here. All these crazy genes bouncing around tonight. Where'd they come from, Leo? What the hell for? Who flipped that switch and why?'

Falcone scratched his chin and said nothing.

'This is good,' Peroni said carefully. 'This is indicative of cerebral activity. Come on. Reel off some options.'

Falcone shook his head miserably and threw the cigarette away.

'You are costing me big time, man,' Peroni groaned. 'OK, let me change the subject. How about this? You can bawl me out. Some time over the past half hour – don't ask when exactly because I can't tell you – Costa went off on his own, chasing this wild goose story about some blonde girl over in Cerchi. He didn't want to. Or rather, he did but he didn't want to let it show. So I told him to get his ass on the road anyway. Who knows? Anyway, it was me giving orders. So bust my ass.'

There was a flicker of interest in Falcone's face. Peroni was glad even that much was there.

'It was just a report of a blonde girl?' Falcone asked. 'Just that she looked like Suzi Julius?'

'Nothing more,' Peroni agreed. 'You seemed to think – this was just before the big bang event took place – it was worthy of attention, I believe.'

'It was. Hell, it *is*.' Falcone wasn't looking across the

street now. His mind was getting back into gear. 'Or maybe—'

'Maybe what?'

The old Falcone was lurking there somewhere. The one who didn't let go. And the men in black across the road were starting to look around them, wondering why no one had seen fit to acknowledge their presence.

'I'm not messing with you now, Leo. Either you pull yourself together or someone at the Questura's going to be sending you back on leave and finding some young smart-ass to warm your seat. Probably for good.'

'Yeah, yeah,' Falcone conceded. 'Maybe it's what Rachele said all along. A war. And somehow the Julius girl—' He waved his hand at the mess across the street, 'All these people, they're just, what do they call it? Collateral damage. Bodies caught in the crossfire. It's a *war*. Neri against Wallis. Or Neri against us, the world, everything. I don't know.'

Peroni didn't feel convinced. 'Don't wars need something to start them?'

'The girl. Wallis's stepdaughter. Neri or maybe his son did something to her. Wallis wants payback. This is Neri getting his revenge in first. Against all of us.'

'You people do live in a complicated universe. How'd you get there?'

'It's not "there". It's not even part way "there".'

'So what do we do? What *are* cops supposed to do in a war?'

Falcone gave him a withering look. 'Do we have men outside Wallis's place?'

'No. The DIA took that one, remember?'

'Yeah,' Falcone nodded, thinking. 'You remember what Wallis said?'

'Every word. But remind me.'

' "War is the natural state of humanity." '

'Bullshit,' Peroni protested. 'Lethargy's the natural state of humanity. Look at this mess! What's natural about that?'

'Nothing,' Falcone said, looking at his watch. 'Everything, if you've got the "crazy gene". We're seeing this all wrong, Gianni. We're trying to rationalize something that's not rational.'

Peroni patted his shoulder. 'Hey! See! You can still sound like the old Leo when you want to. Can we go out and do cop stuff now, please? This isn't a place for the likes of us. You can phone the hospital later. We got work to do. Furthermore—' He pointed to the men across the street, who were starting to look thoroughly pissed off. 'I believe your presence is required.'

Falcone nodded and walked over to talk to them. Peroni sat on the bonnet of the car and lit another cigarette, trying to think his way around what he had just heard. From across the road the inspector's sombre voice rose in the darkness. He was yelling at these anonymous men, arguing his case, refusing to back down, and it was music to Peroni's ears. Falcone really didn't give a damn. It made him unique. It made him invaluable. It was the reason his men followed him everywhere, even though half the time they couldn't stand him.

In the harsh artificial moon of the TV lights across the road a stretcher moved out from the rubble. Rachele D'Amato was headed for an ambulance, a team of men around her, one of them holding a drip. Peroni could just about make out her face. She was unconscious. If he were honest with himself, she looked dead. He thought again about what Falcone had said, and the distinct impression he'd had that it was curiosity, not jealousy, that lay behind his interest. She didn't look like someone with a man in tow. She was, surely, just saying: *back off, Leo*. Nothing more than that. It was a measure of Falcone's awkwardness in these matters that he just couldn't see this.

And now he was watching the stretcher too, still talking to the men in dark suits, his face impassive. Then he murmured one quiet oath and stomped off, to stand by the doors to the ambulance.

Peroni walked over to his side. 'Leo. She's in good hands.'

'I know.'

Falcone's mind was turning somewhere else. Peroni didn't know whether to feel pleased or sorry. 'So what'd they say?'

The cold grey eyes just stared at him.

'OK, OK,' Peroni conceded. 'Stupid question. They said: "go fix this shit". I get the message.'

Falcone scowled at the suits getting back into their cars. 'Never mind what they said. I want the Julius girl. Have you heard from Costa?'

'Not yet.'

'Get him.'

So Peroni called. And called again, getting madder and madder because of so many things: the dead ring at the end of the line, Falcone's cagy diffidence, his own confused state of mind. Then he phoned the control room asking if Nic Costa had checked in.

The woman handler couldn't believe her ears. 'Do you know what's going down in this city tonight, detective? I got bombs. I got people screaming blue murder

344

about some shooting in San Giovanni. And you want me to find out which bar your partner fell into?'

'He don't drink!' Peroni barked down the phone.

Except maybe he did now. Maybe they all ought to. Maybe something made sense if you saw it through a musky mist of red wine.

'Yeah right,' the handler snarled. 'Maybe he's gone to choir practice.'

Then the line went dead and Gianni Peroni still didn't know what to do. He thought about what the handler had said and felt his mind starting to turn again.

'Shit,' Peroni murmured.

'Where the hell is he?' Falcone wondered, taking his eyes off the ambulance screaming away down the narrow road, lights flashing, klaxon screaming.

'I dunno,' he replied. 'But there's trouble in San Giovanni now too. That address ring a bell?'

Cerchi ran beneath the overhanging escarpment of the Palatine hill, all the way from the Tarpean cliff behind the Capitol to the busy modern street of San Gregorio that led to the Colosseum. Nic Costa had parked next to the open space that was once the Circus Maximus, wishing the tip-off had led him somewhere else. At night this was a seedy part of town, a haunt of down-and-outs and drug dealers who lurked in unlit corners, out of sight of the authorities.

He'd been to all five sites which Regina Morrison's records suggested were linked to Randolph Kirk. They were complex places, with multiple entrances, not all of them obvious. It took time but every last one seemed boarded up, abandoned long ago. He'd shown Suzi's photo to some of the stragglers in the area. Most were too scared or too doped up to talk any sense, and the few that had their wits about them were unwilling to help a lone cop. Peroni was right: Cerchi was a big street.

He thought about his partner and the rest of the team who'd been close to the blast outside Neri's house. Costa felt guilty about leaving them, but Peroni was insistent. One more pair of hands would make no difference, and they had a duty to Suzi Julius too. They had, in all truth, neglected her. Miranda knew that just as well as they did. The knowledge lay in her intelligent, all-seeing eyes. And it was a neglect that could be hard to rectify.

So what do you do? Costa wondered.

Go home, a weary inner voice said. *Sleep.*

He walked back towards his car, realizing how dog-tired he was, and how welcoming it would be to fall into the big, empty double bed in the old house off the Appian Way and listen to the comforting rustle of ghostly voices down the corridor. At that moment he remembered how important family, that tight, near-perfect bulwark against the cruelties of the world, was to him.

Even a family torn apart by tragedy.

The thought pricked his conscience. His father's premature death still haunted him. Nic Costa wouldn't wish that pain on anyone. It was now nearly midnight. If they were right, sixteen years before Eleanor Jamieson had been butchered, victim of some obscure ceremony involving . . . who? The family of a Rome hood? A bunch of sleazy hangers-on out for fun and unaware that Neri's cameras were filming their tricks? Suzi Julius could face a similar fate at any time over the next twenty-four hours, for no reason but bad luck, the misfortune of her looks, of turning the wrong corner at the wrong moment. And no one had the slightest idea of where she might be. Neri and his son had disappeared leaving a bloody trail of destruction behind them. Vergil Wallis, this time round anyway, seemed to be out of the loop. They had no real lead, just chaos and anarchy and violence.

He took one last look around him and narrowed his eyes at a pool of half shade along the street. Twenty metres or more away something had moved, dashing into the shadow of the great Palatine cliff. A head of bright blonde hair disappearing into the darkness, with another shape, that of a man, moving close behind. It could just be a pair of lovers. It could just be the break they'd been praying for.

Costa patted his jacket, feeling the Beretta safe in its holster, and walked towards the shadows, listening to the sounds of the night: the chatter of sleepy pigeons, the low rumble of traffic speeding past the grassy stadium, the scuttering of rats among the crumbling rock face that sat beneath the remains of the imperial palaces.

A distant voice, just recognizable as female, pleading, echoed out from the cavern mouth, now more visible in the leaking radiance of a bright yellow light within.

Nic Costa took out his phone and knew what he'd see. He was directly under the lee of the Palatine's rock face. The signal was blocked by the stone. The sensible thing to do would be to walk back out into the street, make contact with Falcone, call in help. But he had to keep the girl within his reach. Besides, this could just be a couple of secretive lovers. He didn't like heroics, but this time, there seemed no alternative. So he crept into the shadows, letting his back fall against the dusty rock wall, edging his way forward towards the light, towards the sound which was the voice of a man now, talking so low Costa couldn't make out the words.

He aimed for the sound and it wasn't easy. The place was a complex of dimly lit chambers, interlinked, set in a chain from the entrance which was, Costa suspected, just one of many, eaten into the hill like giant rat holes. The site should have been on Randolph Kirk's list. Maybe it was and Regina Morrison just hadn't got to hear of it. Or perhaps, if it was Kirk's most private sanctum, his holy of holies, he kept it private for his own good reasons.

Costa passed through four small chambers, each barely lit by a single bulb dangling from a wire in the centre, just like at Ostia. In the shadows he could make out more rooms and corridors, stretching into the gloom. The place was a subterranean labyrinth, an ancient maze cut into the rock. He wished now he'd waited for back-up. He wished he could hear what the man in the darkness was saying.

He tried to picture what lay ahead of him but it was impossible. When he thought he was heading for the sound, he would turn a corner and find himself floundering in an impenetrable darkness. After a while he couldn't work out which way was forward, which back. His legs dragged across the rough stone floor. His head hurt. More than once he tripped, and was aware of the noise he made. The distant voices rolled incomprehensibly around him from every direction.

Then he ducked to stumble through a low opening and found himself dazzled by the intensity of what lay beyond.

Three bulbs dangled from this ceiling, burning like

miniature yellow suns. On the rock walls around him, plastered everywhere, covering each other like an overlapping skin of living images, were colour photographs, all of the same two faces in the same two poses: Suzi Julius, happy and smiling, bright blonde hair waving around her face, and Eleanor Jamieson, this photo slightly faded from the years, still shocking in its similarity. They could have been sisters, he thought, not for the first time. No wonder Kirk saw her and began to remember.

He turned around, feeling giddy, wondering where to look next, where to go, clutching for the gun instinctively, feeling his hand wander to the wrong places.

'Oh, Jesus,' said a frightened, female voice floating out of the darkness. Then the breathy words faded, were replaced by the sound of something sweeping through the air.

Nic Costa felt an agonizing pain crash into the back of his skull. He was aware of falling, still dazzled by the bright intensity of the room. Then darkness.

LIBERALIA

Something stirred at the back of Teresa Lupo's mind, rumbling around the darker corners of her sleep, buzzing, shifting position, now near, now far. She swore, felt her heavy eyelids start to stir, then rolled awake at her desk in the morgue, just in time to see an equally sleepy honey bee lurch through the air then head off back to the open window.

It was morning. A warm spring morning, just after seven. The city was already alive beyond the window, cars and people, sounds so familiar, so normal that it took her a moment to remember this was no ordinary day.

She'd called in help, from the carabinieri and the health department, from anywhere she could think of, old, retired colleagues, med students looking for some experience. For the moment it had been a question of coping rather than discovering, filing material as she thought of it. Then, some time after three, she'd placed her head on the desk and fallen fast asleep. Silvio Di Capua had had similar ideas. He was still curled up in a crumpled, foetal heap on the floor in the corner of the morgue. A couple of admin people, only one of whom she recognized, were busy with paperwork. A bunch of medic types were working at the tables: the little accountant had just reached his place in the queue. Barbara Martelli's father was next.

'Any more signed up for the ride?' she asked the admin men.

'No.'

'Thank God for that.' She wasn't sure she could cope with another damned corpse. She wasn't sure she could cope with the ones she'd got. Her nose felt as if someone had jammed a couple of wads of leaky cotton wool up each nostril. Her throat was like sandpaper. Sweat soaked her hair. Teresa Lupo looked a mess. She knew it and she didn't care.

Then a figure came through the door, Gianni Peroni so fresh and alert it was unnatural.

He walked over and peered into her eyes, curious, a little judgemental perhaps.

'What drugs are you on that make you so bright and chirpy?' she asked. 'And do you have any for me?'

'Let me buy you a coffee. Outside this place. By the way, have you seen Nic?'

'No . . .' The question puzzled her. She'd almost forgotten she belonged to a world beyond those shining tables.

'Come,' he said, and took her weary arm then led her down the corridor, out into the waking morning.

It was the beginning of a beautiful day. She could even hear birdsong. Or perhaps, she thought, her mind had some preternatural acuity after the recent shocks. Her head didn't feel right. It hadn't for a while. Something was different after the sleep, though. She felt exhausted, drained, physically and mentally. But there was a measure of control inside this state too, and that was welcome.

Peroni led her to the café around the corner, ordered two big black coffees, stirred some sugar sludge from the glass on the counter into his cup, then did the same for hers.

'When you work vice,' he said, 'you come to know about getting through the night. You get to like it after a while. The world's more honest then somehow. People don't have to look you in the face when they're lying. You get to know about the value of coffee too. Here . . .'

He held up his cup and, instinctively, she clipped it with hers.

'What do you want?' she asked.

'Tidings of joy. Information. Enlightenment. For one thing, I'd like to know who Professor Randolph Kirk phoned to start all this crap.'

'Nic asked me that too,' she said. 'Tell you what. I'll ask old Randolph when I get back.'

'You do that. Any further gems for me?'

'Stand in the queue. It's a long one. How's Falcone doing? How's that woman of his?'

He made a tilting motion with his hand. 'She's still in intensive. She'll pull through. That woman's made of stone. As for Leo, I dunno. He's not looking lovelorn any more. Maybe that pisses him off too. Who cares? We got work to do. Big work, Teresa, maybe bigger than even we can handle. We need to get somewhere fast. So you see why I'm here? We need all the help we can get.'

She found herself thinking seriously about Gianni Peroni for the first time. He wasn't the arrogant, bent vice creep she first thought. Underneath that curiously ugly exterior he possessed some stiff, unbending spine of integrity that made his disgrace all the more poignant, all the less understandable. Falcone and Nic Costa were lucky to have him around, although she wondered how much the older man appreciated that.

'When are you going back to your old job?'

Peroni winked. It was a comic gesture. She almost found the energy to laugh. 'Between you and me? As soon as this shit is over. I bumped into my old boss in the corridor during the night. They drafted him in too. Nice guy. Understanding guy. He had some warm words for old Gianni. Thank Christ. This detective stuff is not my scene. It brings you into contact with the wrong sort of people.'

She waited a moment to make sure she understood that last statement correctly. 'And vice doesn't?'

'In vice you just meet people who want to mess with your body. These guys are forever hanging around those who just can't wait to mess with your head.' She didn't say anything. 'But then I think you know that already.'

'Possibly,' she conceded. 'So tell me what you want me to do.'

'Me?' Peroni replied. 'Hell, I don't know. None of us has a clue where to begin here. We haven't had a gang war in Rome in living memory. If that's what it is—'

'What else could it be?'

'Search me. But if it is a gang war it's a pretty one-sided affair, don't you think? Somehow from behind his iron gates, with no troops whatsoever except a few golf buddies, the American whacks Neri's accountant and lays out all those documents that mean Neri has to take to his heels. At least I guess that's how he feels. Then the fat man goes ballistic and puts a little leaving present outside his own house for us.'

She knew what he meant. 'It's a funny kind of war.'

'Sort of unbalanced, don't you think? And Wallis. He's just sitting there in that big house of his, twiddling his thumbs, looking as if butter wouldn't melt in his mouth. The DIA's bugging his phones. Bugging him direct too I suspect because they just love playing with those toys of theirs. He's not retaliating. He's not doing a damn thing as far as we can work out.'

Teresa sat up straight. She could talk cop again, and she liked that. She smoothed down the crumpled front of her blue shirt, wondered if it wasn't time to lose a little weight from the old frame. She was big-boned. That was what her mamma always said. But she could get fit if she wanted. She could meet these men at their own game. 'What about Barbara Martelli's old man? You're telling me Wallis didn't do that?'

'Now there,' he said, with a sudden assurance, 'we do know something. Wallis had nothing to do with it. Not unless he's running Neri's family for him. We got a good ID from a man who was seen leaving the building. The guy saw someone go in before Martelli got shot. It was Neri's own son did that one. Dumb bastard left prints too. Makes sense. I guess Neri thought Martelli might tell us what was really going on in that fuck club of theirs. So he sent his boy round. Still doesn't add up to a war. Not in my book.'

'Unless it's over already,' she suggested. 'The American's thrown in the towel.'

Peroni didn't look convinced. 'Maybe. A part of me hopes that's so. The trouble is I can't help thinking that if that is the case we'll never get to the bottom of anything. We never get to understand why poor Barbara whacked the professor and then drove into that big hole chasing you.'

This repetitive refrain was beginning to piss her off. 'Poor Barbara . . . Why's she always "poor Barbara"?'

He seemed surprised by the question. 'Because she's dead, Teresa. And whatever happened, whatever she tried to do to you, it wasn't *her*. It was something else. Something that affected her. Surely you can see that?'

She could, but she didn't want to face it just then. She'd come close to the edge herself at times. There was craziness in the air.

'What about poor Suzi Julius?'

He shrugged and looked abruptly despondent. 'We thought we had a sighting last night. Just before the bangy thing went off. Nic went over there to chase it.' Peroni hesitated, reluctant to go on.

'Well?' she wondered.

'Haven't heard a word from him since. His phone's dead. No sign of him in the street. Never went home.'

It always happened with bad news. A picture of the person involved just flew into her head. Teresa Lupo had, maybe unwittingly, got very close to Costa over the last year. He had qualities she didn't see in abundance around the Questura: persistence, compassion and a dogged sense of justice. And he never caught the cynicism bug either, which, perhaps more than anything, made him stand out from the crowd. 'Oh crap. What the hell can have happened?'

'We have no idea,' Peroni said honestly. 'But I like that young man, Teresa. He is going to be driving me around when I go back to my old job. No one's taking that privilege away from me.'

He flexed those big shoulders and she began to under-

stand something else about Peroni. He wasn't a man to
give up easily.

'You could have told me about Nic earlier.'

'I didn't want to worry you.'

'So what do you want from me?' she asked again.

'Look, I'm not telling you how to do your job. Nor
is this a request from Falcone or anything. To be honest
with you, everyone back there's clutching at straws
anyway. I just want to say this. We're all short on
resources right now. We all have to think about priorities.
You're a good pathologist, you know the rules, you stick
by them, mostly—'

She finished the coffee, looked him in the eye and
said, 'Cut the crap.'

'OK, OK. I just can't help thinking that somewhere
in that workload of yours there's something that can
help us. And it's not going to be in the obvious places,
or the most recent ones. I know you got to do it on all
those poor bastards. I was just hoping you wouldn't kind
of focus on the easy ones first. I mean, Toni Martelli,
the accountant guy. Those people from outside Neri's
house. We *know* how they died. We need forensic, sure,
but I don't think our answer's going to come from
looking at those corpses. Whereas—'

He left it at that, hoping she'd pick up the bait.

'Whereas—?' she wondered.

'Oh God. Do I have to say this? You were right all
along. Whatever prompted this shit began with that kid
we dug out of the bog. If we could work out what the
hell happened to her, and where, then maybe we'd get
some better perspective on what's going on.'

She looked across at the skinny bartender playing with
his ponytail and said, 'After you've washed your hands

you can make me another coffee.' The youth slunk off to the kitchen then returned and started working the espresso machine.

Peroni eyed her, just a hint of admiration in his face. 'You're direct, Teresa. I like that in a woman.'

'This Mickey Neri. He killed Barbara's old man. The Julius woman identified him hanging around her daughter too.'

'Yeah?'

'And if I recall correctly,' she continued, 'this same Mickey Neri met Eleanor Jamieson. I saw the notes. They said Wallis and she took a family holiday in Sicily with the Neris six weeks or so before she died.'

'Stands to reason—'

'Oh yes.' She swallowed half the cup of coffee and felt the caffeine and sugar buzz start to hit the back of her head.

'You want to be careful with that stuff,' he said. 'It can give you nightmares.'

'I don't need coffee for that. Do you?'

Peroni glanced at his watch. 'Well?'

'We haven't touched any of yesterday's,' she said. 'Well hardly anyway. I spent most of last night trying to complete the autopsy on Eleanor Jamieson. I did try to come up and talk to you people about this. Around two thirty. If I recall correctly, you were all too busy.'

His mouth hung open, hungry for information. Quite deliberately she slowly finished the coffee then wiped out the dregs with her index finger and sucked it, making little squeaks of pleasure all the time.

'Please—' he begged.

'I got it wrong, twice over, big time. She wasn't some virgin sacrifice. Or to be more accurate, she may have been a sacrifice but she wasn't a virgin. I was wrong too that you couldn't get any DNA out of a body that's been sitting in all that acid peat for sixteen years. There's one circumstance that allows this.' She looked at him. 'You want to guess?'

'No!'

'If there's a foetus. Even a tiny one. Eleanor Jamieson was pregnant. Six weeks or so I'd say. Probably just at the stage she was starting to notice, starting to wonder whether she dare tell the father.'

Peroni's eyes were shining with hope and outright joy. 'Jesus, you beautiful woman.'

'I said to cut the crap. The point is that she's pregnant six weeks or so after she met Mickey Neri, who's now been hanging around her look-alike, a sixteen-year-old kid who happens to have disappeared.'

It came so suddenly she wished she'd had the time and the strength to react. Gianni Peroni stepped forward, grabbed her face with both hands, then kissed her rapidly on the lips. She sat, transfixed. The pony-tailed waiter was staring at the pair of them.

'Don't ever do that again,' she whispered. Then added, 'Not without asking first.'

'Give me more.'

'I don't *have* any more,' she objected. 'Not until the lab get back on the DNA.' She smiled. 'We've Mickey Neri on file already. He was accused of rape two years ago. Somehow the thing never got to court. It could be waiting on my desk right now.'

'Oh sweet Jesus.'

Gianni Peroni was beaming. 'Don't even think of kissing me again,' she warned. 'Too early in the morning. Just go and find Nic, will you?'

'Yeah,' he agreed, nodding. 'You bet.'

He stopped and stared out into the road. A tall dark figure was walking across the road, towards the Questura. It was Vergil Wallis, leather coat flapping around his shins, striding deliberately like a man with a mission.

'Two miracles in a minute,' Peroni murmured. 'Maybe there is a God.'

Nic Costa woke up on a large, old double bed in an enclosed chamber that stank of damp. A single yellow bulb cast a pool of waxy light into the cold, dusty room. His head hurt. He ran his fingers gingerly over the faint, tender bump on the back of his scalp then sat upright, legs over the side of the bed, trying to think. His jacket lay crumpled on the floor. Costa picked it up. The mobile phone was still in the pocket. He stared at the screen in vain. He was deep inside the rock of the Palatine now. There was no chance of a signal. No sign of his gun either, or a soul anywhere nearby.

He stood up, paused for a moment to let the pain at the back of his head subside, then walked around the room. It looked like the kind of place Randolph Kirk would have used, professionally and for his private pleasure too. There were paintings on the walls, old, rough ones, never retouched over the centuries. He stared at the images that, just like at Ostia, ran around the place in a continuous frieze a good metre deep. It was the same theme that he'd seen in the underground chamber by the coast, an initiation ceremony. A young girl, more puzzled than frightened on this occasion, was being led through a crowd of revellers, only some of them human.

As he walked round the room, following the story, he realized this was different somehow. The rape looked more like seduction here. The girl seemed passive, willing even, with bright, knowing eyes and the hint of pleasure in her face. There was a graphic depiction of her coupling with the god, locked in his powerful arms, eyes closed, mouth just open, ecstatic, but this was no longer the final piece in the saga. It appeared midway through the frieze and was followed by some kind of frenzied orgy, in which the girl took part, voluntarily, watching the fights and the lovemaking, the vicious wrestling bouts and the acts of bloody violence around her with a nonchalant sense of detachment. Then, in the last frame, she was the central figure once more. The girl stood in front of the god who was now tethered to a stake, his arms held both by ropes and the grip of two female acolytes, his body shrinking in fear. Now she held a knife which she plunged into his right eye. Blood soaked his dreadlocks. A silent scream rose from his throat. The girl was laughing like a maniac and Costa found himself thinking of Randolph Kirk, slaughtered in his grimy little office by a Maenad much like this one, greedy for vengeance over some unseen, unexplained crime. Had the 'god' failed her, and Barbara too in some mysterious way? Was she now more important than him? Or was this simply the last part of an intrinsically inexplicable drama, the fury in which every participant, man and woman, human and mythical, visited the extremes of their imagination?

The simple answer – that the god, and by implication Kirk and his associates, were exploiters of young women – didn't fit this story. There was, Costa realized, some form of reward on both parts, and some kind of revenge if, for whatever reason, the bargain wasn't kept.

He forced himself to stop examining the pictures. They had a hypnotic, openly erotic quality that drew him in, made it hard to think of anything else. Costa scanned the corners, his eyes becoming more used to the shade. There was a door, dimly visible in the shadows beyond the bed. He walked towards it and touched the surface: old, tough wood. It was locked but as he rattled the handle he heard a sound from the other side: a surprised gasp, not far away. And female.

He thought of the night before and the bright blonde head disappearing into the maw of the cave, that repeated again and again in the photographs that covered the walls of the central chamber. Costa drew himself close to the crevice and tried to peer through. The wood wasn't a perfect fit. There was light on the other side, the same dim, faint luminescence as in his own chamber.

'Suzi—' he whispered through the crack. Someone moved on the far side. He heard her breathing.

'Suzi,' he said again, more loudly. 'My name is Nic Costa. I'm a police officer. Please look at the door. See if you can let me in. Let me help you.'

The person on the other side didn't make a sound. He tried to put himself in her shoes: trapped, lost in this labyrinth, not knowing what to do, or who to trust.

'I talked to your mother,' he said in a normal, controlled voice. 'She's worried about you. This will all work out. Trust me. Please.'

He thought he heard a choked sob. Maybe she wasn't alone. Maybe Mickey Neri was there, holding a knife to her throat, trying to work out what to do with the pair of them. Costa hadn't thought about his own fate for a moment. Now he did, something puzzled him. Why had Mickey let him live at all? If Neri just wanted him out of the way he'd surely be dead, or somewhere far from the heart of what was going on.

'Suzi—' he said for one last time.

There was a sound on the other side of the door: a bolt being drawn back.

Costa made a conscious effort to think like a cop again. He needed a weapon. He needed to know where they were, how the hell they could find a way out of this damp, stinking place.

The door didn't move. He heard footsteps receding on the other side.

'It's OK,' he said. He took hold of the handle, turned it and pushed gingerly. The old wood creaked open. On the other side was a room much like the one he'd woken in: small, almost circular, with paintings round the wall, a double bed with a single light bulb above it, and opposite, in the shadows, another door.

She stood against it with her back to him, hair shining under the wan light, shoulders hunched, crying he guessed, most likely terrified.

Nic Costa walked over and put his hands on her shoulders, unable to take his eyes off that bright, gleaming head of hair.

'Suzi—'

She turned suddenly and thrust her face into his chest, threw her arms around him, clenching his back hard with her hands.

He held the taut, slim body, his head beginning to spin, trying to work out why this felt wrong.

Her mouth worked its way to his neck. Warm, damp

lips brushed his skin, a tongue flickered against day-old bristle.

Automatically, his hand went to her head, felt the soft hair, pushed her gently away.

'Suzi—' he said, then was quiet.

It was as if two people had merged into one. Or as if they had never been quite separate in the first place.

Tears starting to stain her cheeks, her face framed by this bright shock of too-young hair, Miranda Julius looked up at him, pleading, drawing him ever closer.

'I'm sorry, Nic,' she said. 'I didn't want you here. I'm sorry.'

'Don't be,' he whispered, and found his hands roaming her shoulders, holding her tight to him, his lips close to her shining head, his eyes locked on the figures dancing over the walls.

Beyond the glass of Leo Falcone's office the Questura buzzed furiously. For once the rival forces of the DIA and the carabinieri were making an effort to work in tandem, sharing information, scouring the streets for any sign of Emilio Neri. The old hood had gone to ground, and it was clear he had done it well. For all Falcone knew he could be out of the country already. The networks of informers used by all three organizations had come up with a few nuggets of information. They told him what he already suspected: the blast outside the house in the Via Giulia was Neri's own work, a parting gift deliberately timed for the arrival of the police. There would be no return. From this point on Neri would hide out abroad, doubtless somewhere he believed the Italian extradition laws would never reach him.

Vergil Wallis sat opposite wearing his long leather overcoat, a brown travel bag on his lap, black face impassive as a rock, and said, 'I'm glad you made time for me in the middle of all this.'

'You seemed to think it was important,' Falcone replied.

'It is.' Wallis opened the bag and took out a digital camera, turned on the screen, and passed it over the table.

'What the hell's that?' Falcone asked.

'Got thrown over my wall at three this morning,' Wallis said. 'With this.' He held up a mobile phone. 'Started the dogs barking. I'm surprised those people you've got outside never saw who did it.'

Falcone screwed up his eyes at the picture on the little screen. 'They're not ours. That was the DIA's job.'

He picked up the camera. Peroni came and stood behind him then swore softly under his breath. The picture was of Nic Costa unconscious, lying on a bed in an anonymous room.

'This is my fault,' Peroni groaned.

Falcone pressed a button. The next picture was of Miranda Julius, her hair dyed the same bright blonde they all now associated with her daughter, scowling at the lens, tied to a chair. Then a third. The lighting was slightly different this time. More harsh. It looked as if the picture had been taken in different circumstances. The face was that of a young girl, with the same blonde hair, looking vacantly into the camera. She too was tied to a chair, but somewhere else.

'That's the missing girl?' Wallis asked.

'Suzi Julius,' Peroni confirmed. 'We got the pictures her mother gave us. It's her.'

367

The big black figure folded his coat around him as if it were a second skin. 'There's a message too. Play the last thing you find.'

They did. It was a little video of Mickey Neri staring straight into the lens, looking scared as hell, glancing around him as if someone else was giving the orders. Mickey gulped once then said, in a mock tough voice, 'Vergil, you bring what I want at ten. Use the phone. I'll call you and tell you where to collect at seven. At nine I call and tell you where to deliver. You'll know the way. Don't come with anyone else. Don't fuck with me. Do anything other than this and they're dead.'

'For all we know they're dead already,' Peroni murmured.

'Maybe,' Wallis agreed testily. 'I can't tell you one way or the other. This is none of my business. What am I supposed to be here? Some kind of messenger boy? What's going on, huh? Can you tell me that?'

Falcone scanned through the pictures again. 'Did you get the call at seven?'

'On the dot. Sent me round to some private banker out in Paroli. He was waiting. He'd had a call too. Got this packed. As soon as I saw it I knew I was passing it on to you guys.'

Wallis opened the bag. It was full of brand new banknotes, big denominations, still with the ties around them. 'Half a million euros there.'

'Whose?' Peroni demanded.

'Man said it came from some woman called Miranda Julius. She'd ordered it collected overnight. Little guy was petrified. Can't say I blame him. So why am I expected to act the bagman for this woman's ransom money?'

Peroni glanced at Leo Falcone, checking he wasn't going too far. 'The word is Emilio Neri and his boy have fallen out big time. Over what exactly we don't know. This Julius girl, maybe. That's not Emilio's style. It seems pretty clear Mickey's the one who snatched her in the first place. Now he's got our guy too. And the mother. He could use the money. Maybe he wants to give up the life and open a café or something.'

Wallis glared at both of them. 'I'm sorry to hear that. Really. But I'm still asking the same question. What the hell has it got to do with me?'

'You do remember Mickey?' Falcone asked.

Wallis's dark eyes glittered at them. 'OK. Yeah. I remember him. He was a jerk. Just like his father. That still doesn't explain why he should be putting out a call for me to run errands. I'm not dumb. This little punk wants my hide or something.'

'Your hide?' Peroni asked. 'Mr Wallis. Please. You're big time. This is Mickey Neri we're talking about here. You don't honestly believe he's got the nerve to take on the likes of you, do you?'

Peroni watched the American's face. Pride was such a powerful emotion.

'I don't deal with punks like this,' Wallis said in the end.

'So why are you here?' Falcone wondered.

'Just being a good citizen, that's all. You get one of your guys to take this stuff, go run this errand.'

'Won't work,' Peroni said. 'You heard the man. It's you or nothing.'

'You want my help?' There was a touch of disdain in his expression. 'These women have nothing to do with

369

me. This cop's your problem. You hear what I'm saying? *This is not my business.*'

Falcone held up his hands. 'I agree. Besides we have a policy. We don't give in to ransom demands. Even ones as unusual as this.'

Wallis pulled his coat around him, ready to go. 'Then there's nothing else to discuss. You keep the camera. You keep the money.' But he didn't move. Falcone glanced at Peroni and wondered: were they thinking the same thing? Vergil Wallis wanted to do this run. He liked the idea of giving the cops information, probably because Mickey Neri had virtually signed a confession with that stupid piece of video. But something inside Wallis was nagging him to go through with this idea.

Peroni pushed a piece of paper across the table. 'Mickey Neri—'

'Fuck Mickey Neri,' Wallis interjected.

He put a hand lightly on Vergil Wallis's shoulder and Gianni Peroni was amazed to discover something about himself. He found a certain degree of pleasure in pushing this man around a little. He could, if he tried, start to enjoy it.

'Vergil, Vergil,' he said mildly. 'Calm down now. This is your decision, no one else's.'

Wallis picked up the paper and stared at it, his eye drawn to the fancy stamp of the state lab letterhead sprawled across the top.

'We just want you to be informed. That's all.'

They sat on the bed, Miranda Julius next to him, shivering in his arms, wearing little more than a short tee-shirt, huddled under the old, dull coverlet, staring into his face.

'Where is he?' Costa asked.

'I don't know. My door's locked, like yours. I haven't heard anyone there most of the night.'

She held his wrist, turned it and looked at the watch. It was now just after eight. 'He said he'd be back for me around nine thirty.'

'To do what?'

She shook her head. 'I don't know any more.'

Costa thought about the voice he'd heard the night before. 'It was the man you saw in the picture? Mickey Neri?'

She nodded. 'He phoned me last night, Nic. Said he wanted to talk. Said I had to dye my hair like this so that he'd know me. Not that that makes any sense, of course.' Her face went down, close to his chest. 'I just wasn't thinking.'

He looked at the walls again and knew: this was the place, the scene of the photographs, one room of several in Randolph Kirk's seedy subterranean pleasure palace, each with a bed, each with a history. And in one Eleanor Jamieson had surely died.

She put a hand to his head. 'Are you all right? I heard him hit you. It sounded horrible.'

'I'm fine,' he said, and took her hands, looked hard into her frightened eyes. 'Miranda. We need to work out how to get out of here. I don't know what this guy's up to but it isn't good.'

There were so many threads of possibilities running inside his head. He didn't know which was true, which imagination. Neri on the run, fleeing the evidence left at his accountant's. The bomb outside the old hood's house. How in spite of that he'd pressed Peroni so hard to chase the sighting of Suzi even though his colleagues lay stricken and wounded on the ground around him. Was this a kind of treachery? It seemed the right decision at the time. Just now, though, his head refused to clear sufficiently to understand what had happened afterwards.

She took his hands and looked earnestly into his face. 'Listen to me, Nic. He's desperate somehow. He just wants money.'

'How much?' It wasn't the question he wanted to ask.

'Pretty much everything I have. Not that it matters.' She sighed and looked down at the bed. 'I got the impression that perhaps his plans had changed. To be honest with you I don't care. Suzi's alive. I *saw* her. She was here before he threw me into this dump. I just want her free. I'd give everything I've got for that.'

He tried to remember now: perhaps there were two female voices in the darkness last night, before he was struck down.

'Where is she now?'

'I don't know,' she shrugged. 'This place seems to be full of rooms like this. Perhaps he just likes using them. Perhaps—'

Her face darkened and he knew what she was thinking.

'Perhaps it's not just about the money after all,' she continued. 'I don't care so long as I have her back. I had to make some calls back home to organize the money. Maybe he's keeping her somewhere just to make sure I haven't pulled any tricks. She's collateral. If she's lucky. I'm sorry, Nic. I know I should have called. But—'

Her eyes bore into him, blue, unrepentant. 'I knew

what you'd do. You'd turn this into a cop thing. I couldn't take that risk. And it's just money.'

Costa took the phone out of his jacket and looked at the screen again. It was still dead. He stared around the room trying to think of some way to escape.

'We can't get out, Nic,' she whispered. 'I tried. We're here till he comes back. What kind of place is this?'

Her mouth was so close to his neck he could feel her breath, damp, hot, alive. She was shivering against him.

'A kind of temple, maybe?'

'To what?'

He knew that instinctively. They both did. 'To losing it.'

In spite of everything she was calm now in some way he couldn't quite comprehend. Perhaps it was simply knowing that Suzi was alive.

She shivered violently. His arms went round her. Miranda Julius reached down and took out a small silver pill case from her bag then shook two tiny tablets, sugar-coated and red, into her palm.

'I need these,' she said, shaking. Her eyes closed, her white, perfect neck went back. Costa couldn't stop looking at her, feeling her pain and her need, pinioned to the bed by her agonized beauty.

It happened swiftly. She moved fully into his arms. Her slender hand gripped the hair at the nape of his neck. Her mouth closed on his, soft, wet and enticing. He responded. Their lips joined. Her tongue ran beyond his teeth, her hands beginning to tear at his shirt, firing something red and senseless in his imagination.

He thought he heard her whisper his name, then the tongue returned, probing, hard, insistent, finding the deepness in his throat. There was just the hint of something solid on the tip, something that made him swallow and, in the heat of the moment, scarcely notice the act.

Nic Costa closed his eyes, not thinking, letting her hands do their work, rising when he was bidden, feeling her straddle him, panting, demanding, feeling the heat rise between them, drowning out the doubts in his head.

In the fevered stream of his imagination painted figures watched from the walls, eyes bright, gaping mouths laughing, particles of dead, dry dust coming alive, waiting for the ancient siren song to rise in her throat, waiting for the ecstasy to bind them.

At some point afterwards he closed his eyes and slept. When he woke she was quietly singing a line from an old song, one his father possessed among that ancient pile of vinyl back in the farmhouse off the old Appian Way. He recognized it: Grace Slick fronting Jefferson Airplane, all those years ago. Miranda Julius was softly chanting the same refrain over and over again.

'One pill makes you bigger,' she sang in a low, breathy voice that ran through his head like a dream.

'He's offering me *what*?'

Emilio Neri couldn't believe his ears. Maybe he'd misjudged the kid all along. It was now almost eight thirty. He'd just finished breakfast in the cellar of the safe house on the Aventine hill, after the best solitary night's sleep that he could remember in years. Bruno Bucci made the choice. Neri had forgotten he even owned the place. The radio and TV stations were now blurting out his name as the chief culprit for the previous night's bomb blast. One of the newspapers had even put up a reward for anyone who helped track him down.

None of this worried him. Bucci was a good guy. He'd done his homework. He'd paid the right people, sealed the lips of those who might be tempted to go for the main chance. The Albanian mob reckoned they could spirit Neri out of the country late that afternoon. By midnight he'd be in North Africa. In a couple of days he'd find himself in Capetown, ready for a little holiday, in preparation for the trip across the southern Atlantic to his new home. Once he was beyond his native shores no one could touch him. A long line of money would grease his path all the way, from one understanding state to the next.

But now, as luck would have it, a little temptation had got in the way, and Emilio Neri knew the moment he heard it nothing would induce him to walk away from Mickey's offer.

'Tell me again,' he said. 'Just so I know I'm not dreaming.'

Bucci grimaced, unhappy with the idea from the outset. 'If you forgive him, if you let him and Adele live, you can have Wallis on a plate. He just wants some money, that's all. And some guarantees.'

'Guarantees?' Neri waddled around the room, shaking his head. 'Tell you what. Get him back on the phone. Let me talk to the kid. I'll give him guarantees. Why didn't he call me direct anyway? I'm his father, aren't I?'

Bucci shook his head. 'He won't speak with you, boss. He's pissed off with you. Says you expected Toni Martelli to off him last night. Seems to think that was an insult or something.'

'Yeah,' Neri laughed. 'Maybe it was. But Martelli's dead and he's alive. So where's the insult now? How much does he want?'

'A cut of the action.' Bucci said gloomily. 'Ten per cent of everything going forward.'

Neri slapped Bucci cheerfully around the cheeks. 'Hey, don't look so miserable, Bruno. There's plenty to go round. Be realistic. Nothing's ever fixed in stone now, is it?'

'Whatever you want, boss.' Bruno Bucci said that a lot, Neri thought. It could get annoying.

'Did you know anything about this?' he asked. 'Mickey snatching this girl on the side? Be honest now. I'm not pissed off with you.'

Bucci threw back his big shoulders as if it were some kind of insult. 'No. You'd have been the first to know. He's always up to stuff. Stupid little bastard. Why fuck around with crap like that? What's the point?'

'His dick's the point. Some things never change.'

Bucci sighed and gave Neri a knowing look. 'Stupid—'

'Don't be ungrateful, Bruno. When the word gets around about this nonsense you come out looking good. No one wants a lunatic running things. You get the business. I get retired. And that black bastard Vergil Wallis gets dead, which is a good lesson for anyone who thinks they can fuck with this house in the future. Understand?'

'Sure.' He really didn't look happy. 'Look, boss. We made lots of good plans here. I can get you out of the country, no problem. If we start messing around like this, I don't know—'

Neri smiled. 'You can do it.'

'Why not let me or one of the boys handle Wallis? We can see to him.'

'Yeah,' Neri grinned. 'Mickey and Adele too, huh? You think I'm stupid?'

Bucci was silent. Neri patted him on the shoulder. 'Hey, I'd do the same thing myself. Hell, you *will* do it when I'm out of the way. Let's not fool ourselves otherwise. But I got a score to settle with Vergil Wallis. Got some personal questions I'd like answered too. He whacked that little accountant of mine. He gave all them private papers to the DIA. It's thanks to him I get to retire now. I wanna show him a little gratitude. Understand?'

'I understand. But is it worth the risk?'

'Yes,' Neri snapped. 'It's worth the risk. Besides, with you planning things, there *is* no risk. Am I right?'

Bucci looked at him oddly. There was something going on in his head Neri couldn't see. 'Am I right, Bruno?'

'I never asked you for anything, boss. Let me ask now. Just this one thing. Stick to what we've got. No distractions. Just go and enjoy being retired. I'll look after things.'

Neri would have given up on him then, changed his mind completely. But he was too far down the road and Bucci, he guessed, understood that already. 'I'm still running things right now,' Neri snarled. 'You do the fuck what I say. A man's gotta leave a few memories behind him. They got last night. Now they're gonna get Wallis too. That's my legacy, Bruno. Don't fuck with it.'

Bucci grunted something incomprehensible.

'So when do we wrap this up?' Neri demanded. 'Where?'

'He's gonna call us back.'

Emilio Neri thought about his son. And about Adele.

Maybe this was all her doing. Maybe this was her way of convincing Mickey she could set him up for life. What a pair they'd make. She'd be screwing the chauffeur before Christmas.

'You know there's just one thing I don't understand,' Neri said, more to himself than to Bruno Bucci. 'How the hell has Mickey talked Wallis into walking out into the open like that? After all this time? Is he just getting dumb in his old age or what?'

'Maybe he's thinking of retirement too,' Bucci suggested. 'Maybe he wants to even things out.'

Emilio Neri grinned. 'Oh, he's retiring. That's for sure.'

They clutch each other on the cold, damp bed. His too-bright eyes, the pupils now dilated, dart everywhere, to places he doesn't want to see. She watches, face close to his, her breath on his skin, smiling, thinking.

He looks into her eyes and just at that moment, when she's caught him completely, she says, in a new voice, a low voice that seems as if it should belong to someone else, 'Every good deed needs a witness, Nic. Every crime has to meet with some punishment. Without that—'

He's laughing, can't help himself, can't believe the words coming out of his mouth.

Call the cops, he says. *That's what we're here for.*

She slides her slim, taut body onto his chest. Firm fingers grip him, force his eyes to look into hers. Then she turns his head and he looks once more at the shapes on the walls, writhing, laughing, chattering in some unknown language. He closes his eyes. From somewhere deep inside, somewhere he can't discern, comes a voice, rough and cruel, rumbling up from the guts through a crazy mask's bulbous lips.

It says, *Look you fucker look. You got to in the end.*

No. He knows the word never leaves his throat.

Sounds from beyond the wooden door. People. Events. Real, perhaps. Or memories, shadows of the past seeping into the present.

I think, she says, *there was a girl here once. Years ago, but not so distant we ought to forget. A young girl. Others too. But this girl was special.*

Everyone's special, he murmurs. How?

She was beautiful.

Everyone's beautiful. After a fashion.

The rough voice laughs from behind the hidden mask, a sound filled with scorn.

Hot breath enters his ear, a torrent of words that transform into pictures inside his head. He sees them now, forced into his imagination by what he hears and the pulsing elements roaring through his veins. They both have a stiff schoolgirl stance, backs to him, arms behind, fists clenched. Long blonde hair falls over slim shoulders onto sackcloth robes. A garland of flowers hangs around each too-young neck, a smaller one crowns each shining head. Carnations for love, lilies for death. Their smell fills the room, bright and harsh and cloying, with something else beneath it, a narcotic perfume worming its way into every hidden corner of every head.

One figure turns and he sees Barbara Martelli, now sixteen years younger than the woman he never really knew, long locks down to her waist, smiling face full of warmth, pleased to see someone.

Barbara opens her mouth. No sound emerges. She is a gift. He understands that just by looking at her, the way she stands, the way she beckons, and something in Barbara's face seems to say she's aware of this too.

Her slim arms, tanned, still a little chubby from her youth, reach out, seeking a man's touch and the gift it will bring.

Barbara knows, he thinks. Barbara wants.

Miranda's lips, damp and scorching, move against his ear.

She whispers, whispers, *Look.*

A second figure turns and he feels his heart become stone, feels the air disappear from his lungs.

Eleanor Jamieson stands in front of him, alive and smiling, and Miranda is right. She is more beautiful than any of them, not because of how she looks, but from the simple light that shines from her eyes, the naïve, unworldly light of innocence begging to be dimmed because it burns too brightly for the rest. This is her undoing. Men will see this flame, perhaps women too, and want to suck on its power, steal the life from within it, jealous of its intensity. And she understands none of this. She simply smiles, and beckons.

She doesn't know, fuckhead, the old voice croons. *She doesn't have a clue.*

Eleanor Jamieson opens her perfect mouth and smiles.

Her teeth are the colour of mahogany. Her wide, unseeing eyes are pools of black, as deep and as dead as the fetid Tiber.

In her throat something glitters, silver and gold. A coin to pay the ferryman.

Behind her back something moves in the shadows.

*

Vergil Wallis said nothing for a good five minutes after he read the lab report. At his boss's suggestion, Peroni went out for some coffee and to find out if there was any news. The men who had been combing had found nothing. Mickey Neri seemed remarkably well organized.

He came back, discreetly shook his head behind Wallis's hunched figure at the desk, and placed a cup in front of the American. Wallis had the makings of tears in his eyes. He wiped them away with the back of his hand.

'Sorry,' he said eventually. 'You've got a lot of surprises around here right now.'

'Too many,' Falcone replied. 'You had no idea? You never knew she and Mickey were messing around together?'

This was the moment, Peroni realized. Vergil Wallis could stick to his guns, pretend he had pretty much told them the truth all along and just try to brazen the whole thing out. And if that happened then Nic Costa would be dead, along with the Julius woman and her kid. Everything hung on this old crook's decision.

'No,' Wallis answered dolefully. 'I still can't believe it. You'd never have guessed it from seeing them together. Eleanor was smart. A little naïve. Maybe that was why I indulged her from time to time. But she could have walked into any college she liked. The Neri kid was just an oaf. Worse than his father, if that's possible.'

'Maybe that's what she liked,' Peroni suggested, trying to be reasonable with this man because he understood how essential he was to them. 'I have kids. You get to understand these things. A little anyhow. Sometimes they do the opposite of what you want just because it *is* the opposite of what you want. It doesn't mean you can go blaming yourself for what happens next. That's how people are made.'

Wallis nodded. 'True.'

'So,' Peroni continued. 'Now you know this, how about we stop pretending, huh? We know she didn't go missing just off the cuff. And I got to say, Mr Wallis, you must have realized that all along. So let's cut the crap. We got a little time before your appointment. You tell us. What really happened that day?'

'Really?' There was some bitter amusement in Wallis's face. Peroni didn't like what he was seeing. This man just might help them, but he'd never relinquish control, and never fully divulge anything he didn't think necessary. 'I've no idea. That *is* the truth. I swear to it. If I'd known—'

He didn't finish the sentence.

'You'd have killed him?' Peroni suggested. 'Just for screwing around?'

Wallis nodded. 'The person I was then . . . I would have killed him.'

'And now?'

'Now I live in Rome and read my books,' Vergil Wallis said quietly.

He pulled the overcoat tighter around him. 'A man can drown himself in a few illusions if he likes. Is there anything wrong in that?'

Falcone and Peroni exchanged glances. Then Falcone tried to get things back on track.

'Where did you think Eleanor was going that day?'

'To some kind of party. Neri knew what interested me. Knew what interested her too. They were the same things. When we went on vacation together it was just after Eleanor's birthday. Neri said he wanted to give her a gift. A surprise. Something out of the past. I'd given her Kirk's book as a birthday present. She loved the stupid thing, read it all in a couple of days. So I mentioned this to Neri and said, maybe—'

Wallis paused and sighed. 'The next thing I know Neri's fixed a meeting round at his house. Me and him and the Kirk guy, who's all eyes at the idea he might get paid to throw the party of his dreams. If I'd thought about it maybe the alarm bells would have started ringing. I didn't even know what a Dionysian ceremony was. Maybe that was why the Kirk guy kept looking at me, weird, all the time. I just didn't . . . imagine.'

He hesitated over this last point. 'Eleanor knew, of course. Neri's kid must have set her up for the whole thing.'

'Where was this supposed to happen?' Peroni asked.

'I don't know,' Wallis replied. 'I never asked. I could have gone along if I'd wanted. I didn't.'

'Why not?' Peroni wondered.

Wallis glowered at him. 'Watching some young kids dance around in costume? That's what I thought it was. I'd been in Rome long enough to recognize all the tourist shit they try to sell you. They say it's culture. I thought it was just one more turn around the block. If Eleanor wanted it . . . fine. I'd better things to do with my time.'

Peroni shot Falcone a look that said *unconvinced*. 'Did you drive her there?'

'No. She went off on that little bike of hers. Like I said.'

'You really have no idea where she might have gone?'

'None at all. And that's the truth.'

They waited. Wallis wasn't going to give this up to them easily.

Falcone pressed him. 'It's nine in the morning and she's left for this fancy dress party. Is she wearing the clothes we found her in?'

'She had them in a bag. The Kirk guy sent them along with some other stuff.'

'Then what?' Falcone asked.

Wallis closed his eyes for a moment and Peroni felt his heart skip a beat because this could just be the point where the American thought '*no further*'. 'Then nothing. For hours and hours. And I'm busy. I got people to talk to, calls to make. So I don't think twice about it. Not until the evening and then I think . . . she never said when she'd be back. She went out there and she was so excited she didn't even care about what time it all ended.'

'Then you call Emilio Neri, right?' Peroni could work this through for himself. It was what you did as a father. Not approach the kids direct, even if you could find them. That was wrong. That was *uncool*. You phoned their dads and said, look, man to man . . .

'Eventually, Neri calls me.' Wallis shook his head. 'I never touched dope. Sold plenty. I never thought about it. It wasn't anything that came near me. It never affected anyone I loved, not even back in the old days when I was just some black punk on the street. Dope just existed. It was a utility for us. Like water or electricity.'

'Pretty lucrative utility, Mr Wallis,' Peroni observed. 'Bought you that nice house on the hill.'

'Bought me part of that nice house. Not as much as you think.'

'Does that hurt? Now you realize the kid got burned by dope?'

For a moment Peroni thought Vergil Wallis might take one of those big black fists out of the pocket of his leather overcoat and smack him with it.

'But she wasn't, was she?' Wallis replied calmly. 'Someone cut her throat. Neri said it was dope. He acted like he was furious too. Said he came in on the thing and found the kids had been popping stuff on the side, and even the professor guy never knew it was that bad. He said—'

Vergil Wallis could have been a good actor, Peroni thought. Or maybe he did feel this cut up after all these years.

'There'd been an accident,' Wallis continued. 'Eleanor had overdosed on some bad crack one of the kids – not Mickey – had smuggled into the party. She'd gone into a coma. They'd called a doctor they knew. They'd tried everything. She was dead. Nothing they could do.'

'Then what?'

Wallis stared at his long black hands. He hunched up inside the coat looking as miserable as any man Gianni Peroni had ever seen. 'For an hour or two I went crazy. Went round smashing things. Beating up on anyone I could find. Trying to find someone else to blame.'

'You blame yourself,' Peroni said instantly, and found, against his wishes, some feelings of sympathy rising inside himself. 'That's how it works.'

'That's how it works.'

'But after,' Peroni continued, 'when you stop feeling quite so mad, what do you do? Go to the cops? No. Because you're a crook, Mr Wallis. And crooks don't go to the cops. We'd start asking where that dope came from. We'd start asking all kinds of stuff.'

Wallis nodded and didn't say a word.

Peroni thought about this. 'And those bosses of yours back home wouldn't be none too pleased I guess. All the same, I'd want to see the body. Didn't you want to see the body?'

'Seen a lot of bodies in my time, mister,' Vergil Wallis murmured. 'That's one I didn't want coming back to haunt me at nights. I just told Neri to get on with it. He'd offed the kid he said brought in the dope. Or so he claimed. I just went back into my shell. And I remembered.' The black eyes flashed at both of them. 'I remember well.'

'Dope.' Peroni hated working drugs. Everything got so unpredictable. 'Once you walk into that place it all gets so messy. Who's to say that wasn't what killed her, really? That it wasn't little Mickey out of his head thinking he was the love god come to call? And getting all cut up or something when she says no, and by the by, Mickey, I'm carrying a little present for you?'

Wallis pushed his big fists deeper into the overcoat. 'What is it you want of me? There's nothing I can do to bring her back.'

Peroni bridled at that. 'There are two women and a cop you could help bring back, Mr Wallis.'

'Why me?'

'Mickey Neri says you know the way,' Falcone reminded him. 'Do you?'

'I have no idea what the hell he's talking about. All I can guess is what you can guess. He wants me there for my hide. I'd need a damn good reason to lay it on the line for people I don't even know.'

Falcone glanced at the clock on the wall. It was two minutes to nine. 'You might get to find out who really killed her. Isn't that enough? Isn't that the lure Mickey's really dangling in your face? Also, you get me and half the cops in Rome behind you. We quit chasing bombers, quit chasing street thieves and dope dealers, pimps and murderers, and try to save your lying ass instead. The choice is yours, Mr Wallis. But if I have to pick up any more dead bodies at the end of this, your cosy sweetheart deal with the DIA goes out of the window. I don't see you sitting comfortably in that house of yours on the hill for much longer now. Do you?'

Wallis grimaced. 'Is that a deal you're offering me? Play ball and you stay off my back?'

Peroni was quietly whistling through his teeth, looking livid.

'If that's the way you care to see it,' Falcone replied.

'And you think you're good enough to keep me alive? All the dead bodies I've seen on the news this past couple of days don't give me much in the way of optimism.'

Falcone shrugged. 'Take it or leave it. Either way we're pulling away all those people from your gate. The DIA don't do security. Who do you think's going to guard your back then? Your golf buddies have got to go home some time. Neri's people aren't going away. And they want blood over that accountant, I imagine. Thanks for the gift, by the way.'

Vergil Wallis leaned over the desk and pointed a long black finger in Falcone's direction. 'Listen to me, man. I didn't touch Neri's accountant. I'm retired. OK?'

Then he fell back into his chair and closed his eyes, waiting.

Bang on the minute – Mickey Neri was punctual – the phone rang. The two men watched Vergil Wallis. He waited, just long enough to make them nervous, then picked up the handset.

Wallis hit the button and barked, 'Speak.'

He listened. It didn't last long.

'Well?' Falcone demanded.

Wallis reached inside his coat and pulled out a piece, a silver pistol, nice and shiny, of a kind neither cop recognized. 'You're not thinking of taking this off me now?'

'My,' Peroni observed. 'The things retired people carry around with them these days. Does that get covered by the state pension or what?'

Wallis opened the bag and dropped the gun inside. 'Front steps of San Giovanni. Twenty-five minutes. I want Mr Sweet Talk here to drive. I hear he played boss class once. Don't want any amateurs stepping on my toes.'

Mickey Neri sniffed in the dead air of the caverns and wished he had the courage to walk outside, out into good daylight, away from the mess he was in. That wasn't possible. Adele had made him place the calls. She said they had no choice. They needed money. They needed his father to give them the chance to start again, free of his anger. So they just sat in one of the chambers in this stinking, dark maze, trying not to bitch at one another. Mickey just couldn't work out the geography of the place. Adele walked around as if she knew every last corner, every last twist and turn. It pissed him off. He thought he was going to end up in charge. He was grateful for what she'd done at Toni Martelli's. But he'd have killed the old bastard without her help . . . in the end.

If it worked out now they'd get some money, some

kind of reconciliation, and they would earn the old man's thanks. Mickey knew his father well. Gratitude was one thing that did count with the old man. Emilio had his faults but he had a thing about fairness, a thing that was almost a virtue. If he and Adele could deliver Vergil Wallis's head on a plate, then it was possible – just – that everything else could be forgiven. Or if not forgiven, forgotten. These were, as Adele was swift to point out, changed times. Emilio Neri couldn't go back to being a resident Rome hood, not after felling a bunch of cops with a bomb. His power was failing him. But the cops couldn't touch Mickey with any of this. He could stick around, live off the cream of the estate. With or without Adele in tow – he hadn't decided on that one yet.

It all hinged on Vergil Wallis showing up. Without him, Mickey thought, they were both dead. And that thought didn't leave him any the happier. If he were the big black crook up on the hill, trying to look respectable for all the world, the last thing he'd do would be to run an errand to his worst enemy. It made no sense.

'What if Wallis don't turn up?' he asked.

'He will.'

'Why are you so sure?'

'You don't understand anything, do you?' she snapped. 'These are serious men. Maybe they do end up trying to kill each other. Maybe that would be good for us. But men like this talk, even in the middle of a war. They have to understand how everything lies, if there's some middle ground between them. Wallis wants this settled just as much as Emilio. And also—' She gave him that frank look, the one that went right through him. 'I imagine he wants to know what happened back then. Don't you?'

'Why ask me?' he demanded. 'Never even knew the stuck-up little kid. Never even touched her.'

'No?' She didn't sound convinced.

'No. Anyway, that was years ago. It's time people started thinking about now, not what happened way back.'

She laughed, shook her sleek, perfect hair and gave him the same kind of look his father wore so often. One that said: *don't be so dumb*. 'That's what happens when you get older, Mickey. You don't have so much future ahead of you. It's the past that gets more real.'

'What do you know? You've only got a year or two on me.'

'Guess I grew up more,' she said, watching him reach for his cigarettes. 'Don't light that.'

'Why not?'

'Because if all this goes bad someone's going to be shooting in the dark. Think, for once in your life. It's easier to aim at a smell.'

He swore and threw the pack onto the floor. 'And if it goes well? What then?'

She moved close to him, smiling, and placed a slender hand against his chest, toying with the buttons on his shirt, a gesture he knew was mocking him somehow. 'Then we get to inherit everything. You and me. We can make a couple. Can't we?'

'Yeah.' He could hear the uncertainty in his own voice. He was trying to stay on top of things. It wasn't easy. 'What's the cop doing here now, Adele? And that woman too? What do we do with them?'

She shrugged, playing with his collar. 'You don't have anything to worry about except your old man. Leave the rest of them to me.'

'What? This guy's a cop. If they think I whacked him they'll never leave me alone. I want this shit over when we get out of here. I want to be free of all this crap.'

'Mickey,' she said firmly. 'When I say this isn't your problem, I mean it.'

He tried to laugh but it didn't ring true. 'So you're the boss? You're going to take on Emilio and that Bucci animal all on your own? There's just the two of us. How's that gonna happen?'

She just smiled and it wasn't a smile he recognized. He wasn't sure he really knew this woman any more.

'You don't need to worry about Bruno. I screwed him before I screwed you.'

Mickey Neri suddenly felt dead stupid. 'Really?' He didn't know what to think, except that it offended him. 'That's nice.'

The cold eyes blinked then stared into him. 'Yes. Nice. I did it just the once. That was all it needed. Thanks to that I got a little warning about what was going on in Emilio's sick head when he found out about us last night. Thanks to that I knew enough to get out of the damn house before he blew it to pieces, and to save your pathetic ass. It means we stay alive and Bruno gets to prosper too. That's called diplomacy, Mickey. It's a skill you have to learn. Bruno knows he doesn't have what it takes to run a family. There'd be a war within months and he'd lose. He's a number two. He's smart enough to realize that.'

'That's good,' he said. 'So long as it stays that way he's got nothing to worry about.'

'No.' She was mocking him and he couldn't do a damn thing about it. Not yet anyway.

Some time the previous day Adele had put some blonde stuff on her hair, mixing it over the red. It was more noticeable under the yellow light of the caves. It made her look different. More classy somehow. And younger.

'You coloured your hair,' he said, and reached to stroke it, thinking that maybe there was time to fit something in. Maybe this damp, stinking place in the earth was just the place for it. She could go down on him maybe. They could even stay in this little room and fuck. 'I like it.'

She snatched his hand away. 'I didn't colour it, you moron. This is what it's meant to be like. And don't touch me, Mickey. Not without my say-so.'

He tried to think back over the years. She was right. She did used to be blonde. It just didn't last too long for some reason. 'Why not?'

The green eyes were so hard now, full of something not far from hate. 'You need to learn what "no" means. You might as well start now.'

She hesitated. She looked a little nervous just then and he couldn't work out whether this was good or bad.

'Do you remember what I told you?' she asked. 'Can I rely on you, Mickey?'

'Yeah. Just don't fuck around with me afterwards.'

Her skinny hand came up and touched his cheek. 'No,' she said, smiling.

'Adele?' She was walking out of the room, without another word. '*Adele?*'

She stopped in the shadow of the open door and blew him a kiss.

'You've got to cope with this on your own now, Mickey,' she said. 'I've got other things to do.'

Teresa Lupo went back to her office with Gianni Peroni's words ringing happily in her head. A little praise went a long way. Her thoughts were beginning to clear a little too. The vicious cold virus in her head was in retreat from a bombardment of aspirin, and with its abatement came some clarity. She'd found the change of clothing she kept in the office, showered, and now felt fresh and clean. Her hair was combed and back in the businesslike crop. If she peered in the mirror – which she didn't plan to do – she guessed her eyes wouldn't even be that bloodshot any more. The mood was a touch infectious. Monkboy had recovered some of his composure too when the report from the lab came through. It had confirmed what Teresa, in her heart, already knew. The paternity of the tiny preserved foetus she'd recovered from Eleanor Jamieson's corpse may have been more about morale than closure. No one had any idea where the Neris had fled overnight. But morale mattered. Maybe everyone was still walking in the dark but at least they had a spring in their step.

One thing continued to bug her. She would have saved everyone so much grief if only she'd carried out a conventional autopsy when the body from the bog arrived. This was a lapse in judgement and it bothered her. If she could fail once, she could fail again. How many other oversights lay around her now in this over-crowded haven for the dead? Gianni Peroni's point, brought home with that sudden, unexpected kiss, was a good one. In times like these it was all about priorities, looking closely under a handful of promising stones, not trying to steal a quick glance at everything. She hadn't focused enough. Most of all, she hadn't focused on Professor Randolph Kirk, which was odd given that he represented the sole customer in her career who had fallen into her care, so to speak, within earshot. Everything was about connections. It had been all along. If she could just find the right one it would all fall into place.

Silvio Di Capua wandered in from the corridor. He looked into her smiling face with a frightened devotion that threatened to bring the black clouds of depression straight back.

'Silvio, my man,' she said, her voice still husky from the cold. 'Tell me about the good professor. What news of him?'

'News?' he replied, bemused. 'He got shot. What news do you want?'

'Oh, how he feels about the whole thing. Who he wants to call.'

He did call someone. The memory, which was less than two days old, now seemed shockingly distant. Randolph Kirk called someone and all hell started to break loose straight afterwards. The conventional thinking around this place, she reminded herself, was that Eleanor Jamieson was the Pandora *du jour*. It was her ossified corpse that summoned the four riders from wherever else in the world they'd been, whipping up a little apocalypse for tea.

'Up to a point,' she said to herself.

Monkboy looked a little scared again. 'What?'

'It was Randolph Kirk.' She recalled that disgusting habit he had with his nose. 'Booger Bill. *He* started this crap off. With a little help from me, of course. Bog girl had been out of the ground for two weeks up till then, and nothing whatsoever had happened.'

Silvio Di Capua blinked then performed a polished impersonation of a terrified rabbit. 'Lots of work to do, Teresa. Nice routine stuff. You've already given the boys next door a present to get along with. From what I hear there's plenty more to occupy them besides.'

Her ears pricked up at the scent of gossip. 'Plenty more what?'

He didn't say a word.

She picked up a pair of scissors and snapped them open and shut a couple of times. 'Speak, Silvio, before I am filled with the urge to snip a testicular sac or two.'

He gulped. 'I heard one of the guys talking down the way. He says this mobster's son's straight in the frame now, even without the paternity stuff. Seems he's trying to get himself a little holiday money by holding them to ransom.'

'Them?' She didn't understand. 'He's only got Suzi Julius.'

He swallowed hard. 'Not any more. Seems he's got the mother too.' He hesitated and dropped his voice to a whisper. 'And a cop.'

Something black turned in her head. She advanced on Di Capua still holding the scissors. 'What cop?' she demanded.

'That guy you like,' he said feebly. 'Costa. God knows how. Or where. But they've got a picture of him and the mother tied up somewhere.'

'*Nic?*' she screeched. 'Oh shit. What are we doing—?'

She was looking round the morgue, mentally counting all their options. 'Let's think this through.'

Silvio Di Capua drew himself up to his full height, which was still a good measure below hers, and yelled, '*No!* Don't you get it? I don't want to fucking think this through! It's not why we're here!'

She'd never made him this mad before. Perhaps that was a failing on her part. This newly assertive Silvio Di Capua seemed a little more human somehow.

'And for God's sake, Teresa, stop saying "we".' He calmed down a little now. 'They are cops. We are pathologists. Different jobs. Different buildings. Why don't you get that?'

'Because Nic Costa's my friend.'

'Good for you. He's their friend too, isn't he? Don't they get the chance to be heroes sometimes? While we settle down to a nice routine of cut and stitch and let things run their natural course?'

'Natural course?' Her voice was a touch too loud. She was aware of this but it didn't help somehow. 'Have you been following the events of the last couple of days, Silvio? What the fuck is natural about any of this? Also—'

'*No, no, no . . .*' His head was down, bald scalp shining under the harsh morgue lights, long hair, even more lank than normal, unwashed for days, revolving around his podgy little shoulders.

Monkboy's miserable face rose to greet hers. 'Promise me, Teresa. Promise me you won't go anywhere this time. Promise me you won't set foot outside this place. Falcone's handling this kidnapping crap himself. It involves ransoms and money and surveillance and all those things we know nothing about. Let's stick to what we do for a living, huh? Just for a change. You shouldn't be involved in these things. If you'd been here more we wouldn't be in this shit in the first place.'

'You sound like one of them,' she said.

His flabby cheeks sagged as if they'd been slapped. 'Maybe. But it's true.'

'I know that. It's just—' How did she explain this? There was something irredeemably personal about what had happened two days before. It wasn't just her own near-death. The memory of Randolph Kirk, Booger Bill, nagged at her. He'd died in her presence, his rustling shade had somehow whistled past her, too busy to say goodbye.

After he called someone.

Booger Bill. Mister No-Friends, whose personal habits surely precluded closeness of any kind, except when wearing a mask and dealing with doped-up juveniles.

She looked at Monkboy. 'Didn't you find *anything* useful in Kirk's pockets? An address book or something? A note with some numbers on it?'

'No,' he said sulkily. 'And before you ask – yes, I looked.'

She bunched up her sizeable arms, folded them on her chest and began to walk. 'Everyone's got to write things down from time to time,' she said, moving briskly across the morgue, towards the storage drawers, Monkboy in her wake, whining every inch of the way.

Teresa Lupo found the one with Kirk's name on it and pulled the handle, listening to the familiar sliding noise, steeling her nose for the inevitable rush of chemical odour that always followed.

'What are you doing?' Monkboy moaned. 'We've finished with him. We got a whole load of others standing in line.'

'Well tell them they can wait.'

Randolph Kirk looked pretty much like any other dead person post-autopsy. Stiff, pale and somewhat messed around. Monkboy never was any good with a needle and thread.

She took a long, professional look at the cadaver in front of them, and picked up each dead wrist in turn. 'Has he been washed?'

'Sure!' Monkboy answered. 'And I gave him a manicure and dental floss too. What do *you* think?'

'Just wondered.'

'Wondered what?'

She was starting to get annoyed with him now and didn't mind if it showed. 'Wondered, as it happened, whether he'd got around to scribbling something on his hands or his wrists. Something like a phone number. Disorganized people do that kind of thing. Or am I not supposed to know that? Doesn't it fit the fucking job description?'

'Yes,' he answered mutely. 'Sorry.'

She went back to the desk, retrieved her notes from the previous day and called Regina Morrison, heard the surprise at the end of the line.

'You have the time to call me?' said the dry Edinburgh voice. 'I'm amazed. Things can't be as busy as the newspapers say.'

'Oh but they are,' she snapped. 'Busier, actually. Now can you tell me please, Regina? Did Randolph Kirk keep some kind of personal address book at the college? Did you pick that up on your rounds?'

There was a pause on the end of the line. Teresa had remembered enough to pronounce the woman's name correctly. That wasn't enough, though. She wanted some deference, and right then there just wasn't the time. 'No. So this isn't a social call?'

'What about a pocket diary? Did you see him use something like that? One of those electronic organizers perhaps?'

A long sigh made its way out of the earpiece. 'Clearly you didn't spend enough time in Randolph's company to gain a true picture of the man. That was the most messed-up, technologically challenged disaster of a human being I ever met. I wouldn't trust him in the company of a toaster.'

'Damn. So you're saying he just kept it all in his head?'

'All what? He didn't know anyone.'

But he did. He had to. He made a call and then the crap hit the fan. Except it couldn't be like that. The crap had to be on its way already. All she'd done was accelerate it a touch, speed up the machine a little. Nevertheless, *he made a call*.

She slammed down the phone, aware that Regina Morrison was, to her astonishment, uttering noises that sounded very like an offer of dinner.

'What is wrong with these people?' she wondered out loud.

She walked back over and stared at the corpse of Randolph Kirk, wishing she could wake him up for one minute and ask a few simple questions.

Her head was back in Kirk's office now, watching him work at his nose with that disgusting piece of cloth.

'Booger Bill, Booger Bill,' she whispered to herself, aware that Monkboy looked ready to call in the men from the funny farm at any moment. 'Never in my life have I seen a handkerchief in that condition, not even in the middle of a flu epidemic. Not even—'

Monkboy watched her, petrified. 'You're not leaving this room,' he warned. 'I will lock that door, I will swaddle you in bandages I swear—'

'Oh my God,' she gasped, then foxed him altogether. She was smiling, beatifically.

'Please—' he whined.

'His clothes, Silvio. I want them. Now.'

They are dressed, moving, through the door, out into the cold and the caves, his legs as heavy as lead, detached from his control. She has to help him round this baffling labyrinth of tunnels, stumbling in and out of the yellow pools of light cast by the random bulbs that hang from the ceiling.

Stay in the shadows, he says. *Until I tell you.*

They enter another room and she holds him, keeping them both close to the wall, in the darkness. It's a large chamber, one he remembers, well lit in the centre. He notices now that there is a table at its centre, dusty, with rickety chairs, maybe as many as twelve. An ancient wand – his head searches for the name Teresa Lupo gave it, thyrsus – lies at one end, in front of a chair that is high-backed and grander than the rest. A theatrical mask, with the familiar gaping mouth and dreadlocks, sits next to it, black-eyed, a dead totem, waiting to be reanimated.

The walls are what he recollects best from the night before. Picture upon picture, blonde on blonde, the same shining colour as Miranda's hair now. Suzi Julius and Eleanor Jamieson, young and innocent, laughing for the camera, thinking they'd live forever. They haunt the room like ghostly, incandescent twins, their glittering eyes following everything.

Miranda Julius darts into the light and picks up the thyrsus, waves it in the air. Specks of dust dance in the yellow light. The smell of ancient fennel, faintly sweet, reaches his nostrils.

She replaces the wand, returns and looks at him. There are voices, distant ones. This curling, twisting tangle of caverns could encompass scores of chambers. He tries to think for both of them.

Her hand is on his arm. Her eyes are bright orbs alight in his face.

There is a dark alcove set back from the table. He pulls her further into the shadows and the effort makes his head hurt, his breath comes in snatched pants.

He takes her face in his hands. His head's starting to clear now. He can hear his own voice and it's real.

'Miranda. The best thing we can do is find a way out of here. Find some help and come back for Suzi.'

There's such fear in her face. She embraces him, her hands reach behind his back for something unseen, her head moves to the back of his neck, lips bite hard on the skin there. She's moving, pressing herself now to his lips. She lunges forward, kisses him, thrusts herself into his mouth, probing, probing, feeling the softness. And this time he is certain. A tiny object rides the tip of her long, strong tongue until it reaches the back of his throat. He gags, begins to fall and a voice somewhere in his head sings, *one pill makes you bigger*.

He opens his eyes and sees her lips moving to the words as she holds him, blocking his mouth with his fingers until he swallows.

*

401

Silvio Di Capua looked at the object on the table, shivered then let out a long, pained groan. It was Randolph Kirk's handkerchief, a piece of once-white pristine fabric now crumpled into a compact ball held tightly together by a random collection of solidified green and grey gloops.

'Don't turn squeamish on me, Silvio,' she said. 'Scalpel?'

'Oh come on,' he complained. 'You want me to find you a surgical mask too?'

Teresa Lupo gave him the extra cold look, the one she saved for special occasions. 'Wouldn't be a bad idea, would it?'

He grumbled and passed her the instrument. 'This is insane. This is the most insane thing I have seen in these recent insane times.'

'Booger Bill wrote those numbers down somewhere,' she insisted. 'It wasn't on the back of his hand. It wasn't on the cuffs of his shirt. And there was more stuff on this damn hankie than mere snotballs. It was only my natural reticence that stopped me remembering this before.'

She could swear he stamped his little feet on the tiles at that. 'Teresa! There's something creepy about this need of yours to please. Even if you're right we shouldn't be doing this. We should be handing it over to forensic.'

'This is human snot, Silvio. *Our* territory.'

'Excuse my pointing this out but we are not looking for snot. Snot we have by the bucket. We are looking for some phone number this weird, dead bastard has thoughtfully written down, hopefully in indelible ink, in between the snot. Which, all things taken into consideration, is both a very strange thing to do and indubitably a job for forensic.'

She found a point of entry and began to ease the fabric, holding down one end with the gloved fingers of her left hand. 'If you'd met Professor Randolph Kirk in the flesh you wouldn't be saying that. You'd think it the most normal thing in the world, as normal as—'

An entire corner of the fabric fell over under the pressure of the blunt side of the blade.

'I did surgery once, Silvio,' she said proudly.

'On a hankie?'

'Adaptability, my man. We live in modern times. Adaptability is everything. Behold . . .'

There were numbers there. Six of them, written in a tiny, cramped hand, mostly so old the ink was blurring into the fabric. One she recognized straight away. It was Regina Morrison's. This really was his address book. She hated to think what the rest were. A dry cleaners? Did Randolph Kirk even grace such an establishment?

But one was more promising. The ink was fresh, the strokes of his spidery hand unblemished. This number had never gone through the wash like the others. Maybe, she thought, written just a day or two before he died.

'Gimme that report,' she ordered.

He clutched the thing to his chest. 'This is not right. Not right at all. We should just pass this information on to the people who need it and let them decide what it's worth. It isn't our job—'

The ferocity of her gaze stopped him dead.

'Silvio, if you tell me one more time what my job is I will, I swear, fire you and fire you good. In case you hadn't noticed, those lovely policemen out there are busy chasing all the big things they like to think of as their prey. People who plant bombs. People who kill and kidnap other people. Were I to walk into their midst bearing a hankie, albeit one of more than minor interest, I would be inviting their ridicule. Who knows? They might even invent a name for me. What do you think? Crazy Teresa? How does that sound, huh?'

He swallowed noisily and said nothing.

'Gimme.'

He passed it over. She scanned the numbers that came with the report Monkboy had purloined from the Questura that same morning, counting off the names.

'Neri's home. Neri's mobile. Mickey's mobile. That office they keep down near the station, Barbara Martelli . . . *shit!*'

'Probably his aromatherapist.'

'Shut up!'

'Teresa! Give it to the cops. They just type it into their computer and up pops a name.'

'You are so naïve,' she hissed. 'So very, very naïve.'

Then her eyes fell on the pad of paper next to his list. Her own notes from the past couple of days, starting from the morning, just forty-eight hours before, when she'd planned to unveil to the world Rome's newest archaeological asset, a two-millennia-old bog body.

'Different lifetime,' she whispered. 'Different—'

She stared at the paper, unable to believe what she saw.

'Teresa?'

There was no mistake. It was impossible but it had to be true, and what it meant for everything was quite beyond her. She needed to see Falcone, immediately, needed to pass the whole damn thing straight over to him, retire to a quiet corner bar somewhere and drown her wildest thoughts in drink.

'Where's the darling inspector?' she asked. 'I am filled with an urgent desire to speak with him.'

'Went out fifteen minutes ago, mob-handed and ready for action. Got tons of people with him. Busy man.'

'Hmm.' Her mind was racing. Nic Costa was out there somewhere, wrapped up deep in all this shit. There was no time for niceties. 'Do you still come to work on that little motorbike, Silvio?'

'Sure but what the fu—' His pale cheeks flared with a sudden rush of blood. '*Oh no, no, no, no, no . . .*'

She gripped him by the collar of his white medical jacket and jerked so hard that his face was just a couple of inches away from hers.

'Gimme the keys now. I've got to talk to Falcone.'

He pulled himself back, folded his podgy arms to give himself a little dignity and displayed as much hurt as his featureless face could manage. 'You want to take my motorbike and catch up with Falcone to talk to him? That's it, isn't it?'

'Yes, Silvio,' she said calmly. 'That's it.'

'OK,' he said very slowly. 'Here's the deal. Do you know what this is?'

She looked at what he was holding and realized he had a point.

'This,' said Silvio Di Capua, 'is what we earthlings call a phone.'

The tunnel ran beneath the Quirinale Palace, cut straight through rock, four hundred metres, built originally for tram cars, now choked by traffic trying to short-cut the hill above. Big tourist coaches were double parked on the Piazza di Spagna side to dump their contents for the short walk to the Trevi Fountain. Construction lorries working on the endless repairs in the Via Nazionale habitually blocked the opposite end. It was, in theory, the easiest way from the Questura to most points east. Falcone had dictated this was the route to take, Peroni with Wallis in front, the cover cars following some discreet distance behind.

Peroni didn't feel at home. He slunk behind the wheel wishing someone else had picked the short straw. This was so far from vice, so distant from the world he knew, he felt like an interloper, just waiting to make some stupid mistake.

They drove straight into the tunnel and hit the jam a third from the end. He banged on the wheel then looked in the mirror. Falcone and the back-up cars were nowhere to be seen. Maybe they'd made it in before the traffic fouled up. Maybe not.

Wallis, mute and expressionless in the passenger seat, took the phone out of his pocket and stared at the little screen. 'Not much use in here.' He tapped the mike wired behind the lapel of his leather coat. 'This isn't either.'

Peroni eyed the man in the adjoining seat and wished he could shake off the idea that something, somewhere was deeply wrong. 'So, Vergil,' he said amicably. 'Here's an opportunity for the both of us. Get this off your chest, man. You can tell me what's really going down here and nobody but the two of us gets to know.'

Wallis peered at him imperiously. 'You're a very suspicious human being. I'm doing you a big favour. A measure of trust wouldn't go amiss.'

Peroni shot him a filthy look. 'Trust. Excuse me, *Mr* Wallis but I don't buy this retirement story. I didn't when that poor bitch Rachele D'Amato spun it for me. I didn't when I met you. Leopards don't change their spots. Crooks don't do the cops favours. Come on. I got a friend involved in this. Level with me.'

Wallis took a deep breath and looked up at the grimy roof of the tunnel. The air in the car was disgusting, just a thin stream of oxygen fighting to get through the clouds of carbon monoxide getting pumped out by the jam around them.

'You know what's up there?'

'Changing the subject? Understandable I guess. Yeah. Mr President in his pretty palace. Don't you just love him? I used to work guard duty at the Quirinale when I wore short pants.'

Wallis gave him a condescending glance. 'Interesting. I meant historically.'

'Oh. Excuse me. I'm Italian. What the hell would I know about history?'

'That's where the Sabines lived. You remember the story? It had rape in it. Gives the thing some modern currency.'

Peroni did remember that story vaguely. It was important. Romulus or Remus, one or the other, stole some women and had to get their act together to clean up afterwards. And out of that mess – out of rape and murder – came Rome. 'They lived up there? I thought they came from miles away. I thought they were like foreigners or something.'

'Up there,' Wallis replied, pointing again. 'But that's an interesting reaction, you know. Maybe we like to deal with bad memories that way. By thinking that the only

407

people who got affected were from some place else, a long way away. It makes everything so much easier.'

'You can say that again.' There was a gap in the traffic out in the daylight ahead. They'd be gone soon. 'You know, I kind of admire you for knowing so much about history and stuff. When you grow up on top of it you tend not to notice things. I still don't understand why, though.'

'Why?' Vergil Wallis shook his head and actually laughed. It was a pleasant sound. It even made Gianni Peroni feel a little less jumpy. 'Because it's Rome. It's where we all came from, in a way. It's about how good things can be. And how bad if we choose to make them that way.'

'Really?' Peroni got ready to kick the car into gear.

'Really.'

'You know,' Wallis said in that low, calm drawl of his. 'I enjoy talking to you. I think that, in different circumstances, we could maybe have a mutually enlightening conversation.'

'Point taken, point taken.' The idiot up ahead was slow to get moving. Peroni fell angrily on the horn. 'All the same, Vergil. I still think you're a lying sonofabitch.'

'That's your privilege. Tell me. Whatever happens now you've got Neri and the kid anyway, haven't you? You know the old man planted that bomb. Now I gave you that camera, you got Mickey too. They're finished whatever.'

'True.' Peroni found his attention split. Between the gap opening up in the traffic ahead and the sudden loop in Wallis's conversation.

'So what if the two of us cut a deal? You just give me a spare thirty minutes dealing with this asshole in my own way. After that I call and you get to come in and do what you want.'

Peroni looked at him and knew at that moment he wasn't driving this black hood anywhere except back to meet Falcone. Something was getting played here he didn't understand.

Wallis put a large, firm hand on his arm. 'Peroni,' he said. 'I got your number, man. I know what happened a couple of months ago.'

'You do?'

Peroni thought about that and wished he'd had more time to go through the details back in the Questura. Nic had gone missing some time before midnight. Vergil Wallis had picked up half a million euros less than eight hours later. What kind of 'private banker' did Miranda Julius use? Who on earth had that kind of money lying around ready to be bundled up in a bag at a moment's notice?

'I heard you got busted down from on high,' Wallis said. 'Why'd you think I picked you for this job? It says two things to me. You're a man who's open to ideas. Plus you could use the cash.'

Peroni noted the growing gap in the traffic ahead and wondered how quickly he could make a U-turn. 'You disappoint me, Vergil. You are a very, very bad judge of character. Best we turn around right now and go through this whole thing again with Inspector Falcone, only in a little more detail and leaving out the lying parts.'

There was enough room, if only the idiot in front would pull forward enough to let him make the turn.

'An honest cop,' Wallis said, nodding his imposing black head. 'Who'd have thought it? I admire that, though. And it's because I do I'm not gonna hit you as hard as I might otherwise.'

Peroni wasn't sure he heard that last one right. He took his foot off the pedal, screwed up his face and said, 'What?'

When he opened his eyes a big black fist was coming towards him, fast, so fast he could do nothing but watch and wait as it crashed straight into his right eye.

It got a little fuzzy after that. Huge hands moved around him. The belt got unbuckled. Vergil Wallis's collar mike got torn off and thrown onto the floor. A big foot came across and kicked open the driver's door. Then a pair of arms came beneath his body and hurled him out of the car.

He fell on the filthy road with a crack, took one breath of the stinking air and started to cough.

The unmarked police car was doing a U-turn into the tunnel, now facing a clear run back into the city, headed anywhere but San Giovanni. And – Gianni Peroni would remember this for a long time he told himself – he'd be damned if the grinning black figure behind the wheel wasn't waving goodbye.

She whispers and, through the chemical fire that rages in his head, he sees.

The thyrsus sits in the same place, now green and vivid, coloured ribbons round its shaft, beneath the bulbous priapic head. The lights are brighter. Men, middle-aged, stiff in their movements, conspiratorial in their shared glances, move beneath them. There are glasses in their hands, brimming with purple wine. A couple smoke, long, hand-made roll-ups that send blue-grey smoke rolling up to the rocky ceiling. They talk among one another: Emilio Neri, the little accountant Vercillo, Randolph Kirk and Toni Martelli, others who are just faces half hidden in the shadows.

Mickey lurks behind them, miserable, uncomfortable, unsure of where he belongs.

They talk and talk and now Nic Costa understands why. These men, powerful men, influential men, are nervous. This is something new for them. An experiment, a break with convention. They look at Randolph Kirk and their eyes say everything: *make this work or else*.

Randolph Kirk knows this. He's more nervous than the rest, almost twitching with anticipation. He speaks but his words are inaudible. He claps his hands and, though they make no sound, the men stop talking and look. A line of young figures gathers at the door. Girls in sackcloth shifts, flowers in their hair, young, young. Some giggle. Some smoke. Their eyes are bright yet hazy. They are, like Randolph Kirk, afraid.

The mood pivots on a breath, a gesture, anything that might break the spell.

One of the initiates, Barbara, young yet knowing, walks forward, expectant, animated. Her hand falls on the mask. Her fingers stroke its ugly features, caress the vile, bulbous nose.

Watch, the chemical screams, a god inside him, so strong it is impossible to fight.

The golden girl lifts the dead, ugly face, looks at each of them in turn and smiles.

They left the house on the Aventine hill just after nine. Bruno Bucci drove. Neri huddled down in the rear with one man either side. Then the Mercedes snaked down the back roads, taking the narrowest it could find, before it emerged in Cerchi, just where the call had dictated.

Not that Emilio Neri needed directions. He'd never forget this place. Too many memories lay behind the scarred earth.

The car pulled onto the pavement. They got out and stood in the shadow of the escarpment that ran into the Tarpeian Rock. The sun was coming up on another fine spring day. If there'd been a little less traffic Neri could have taken a deep breath and believed he would miss Rome.

Bucci looked at him, nodded at the black hole of the cave, behind the broken gate with its ancient city archaeology department notice saying, 'Keep Out'.

'Yeah, yeah,' Neri said and ducked into the darkness. 'I'll handle this on my own. Just make sure he's carrying nothing when he shows, huh?'

'What about Mickey?' Bucci said.

'Mickey?' Neri laughed. 'What about him? He's just a stupid kid. I can handle my own son.'

Neri thought about Bucci again and briefly wondered about his own judgement. 'You think I'm being dumb, don't you?'

Bucci didn't say a thing.

'OK. Don't answer. I got to say, Bruno. I'm being more than fair to you here.'

'Sure. I'd still like to come in with you.'

Was this sentiment? Or just some self-serving show of concern? Neri couldn't decide. Maybe Bucci was right. He could handle Mickey, no problem. But if his son had others in tow . . .

'You heard of anyone going over to Mickey?' he asked.

Bucci laughed out straight. 'Are you kidding? Who'd be fool enough for that?'

Neri nodded at the shadowy mouth of the cave. 'So it's just him in there. And maybe Adele. Do you honestly believe I cannot cope with my own son and a two-timing wife I can slap down with one hand?'

Bucci shuffled on his big feet, uncomfortable.

Neri took that as a yes. 'Just make sure Wallis goes in on his own and he's not carrying anything,' he said. 'I don't share out this pleasure with anyone. Besides. I've been thinking. There's some questions I want to ask, and they're all family. I don't want anyone else listening.'

'Think of me as back-up.'

Neri tapped him on the chest with a single finger, quite hard. 'I was putting men down before you were born, Bruno. Don't get presumptuous. You got the rope and the tape like I asked?'

Bucci nodded and handed them over.

Emilio Neri patted his jacket, felt the butt of the gun there. Then he walked into the darkness, surprised how cold it was, surprised too by how little illumination the bulbs gave.

His memory must have been playing tricks. In the old days everything seemed much brighter.

Leo Falcone watched Peroni dabbing his head next to him in the back seat.

'That's one big black eye on the way,' he said. 'Do you have any idea where Wallis might have gone? Did he say anything?'

'Yeah. First he asked if Neri and his kid were safely in the net anyway, even without this. Then he tried to bribe me to look the other way so he could get a spare thirty minutes with the fat man. I was explaining the problems this posed for my fragile sense of public duty when he whacked me in the face. Said he wasn't hitting me so hard because he admired me. I'm glad I wasn't on the hate list. If he punched like that when he's a fan—'

The radio barked at them. Wallis had dumped the police car in a side road near the Trevi Fountain and disappeared into the tourist masses. Falcone swore and then issued the standard call. Tall black men in flapping leather overcoats weren't that common in Rome. Someone ought to see him.

'Maybe he'll take a cab,' Peroni suggested. 'That guy is as cool as they come. You know what I think? He intended to make that drop all along. And on his own. He just came to us to make sure we got that camera with Mickey on it. Make sure the Neris wind up in the shit whatever.'

Falcone picked up the mike and ordered every man he had to cruise around Cerchi. He told his own driver to get there too. It was the last place Costa had been seen. If they got lucky . . .

It was hard thinking straight. Then his phone went and it got even harder.

'Not now,' he said instantly.

'Yes now,' she yelled at him and Falcone wondered for a moment why he and Teresa Lupo so seldom had a conversation at normal volume. 'Listen to me. I've just been through Kirk's belongings again. I've found some phone numbers. One in particular. The most recent. Maybe the one he called before he died.'

'Maybe?' Falcone roared. 'What the hell use to me is "maybe".'

'He called Miranda Julius,' she said simply. 'At least that's the number on his snotty little handkerchief, as bright and clear as day. She gave me the number when we were in that apartment of hers. Doesn't that sound more than a little interesting? Some time before he died, Randolph Kirk called the mother of the kid we're supposed to think he snatched in the first place.'

Falcone shook his head trying to clear some space for thought then ordered the car to pull into the side of the road. 'What?'

'Her mobile number was there on Kirk's person. There is no mistake about this. And given how disorganized that particular man was I can only think it was there for a very recent reason. You tell me.'

Leo Falcone leaned back into the soft seats of the Alfa saloon and stared out of the window, out at the tourist crowds mingling near the mouth of the tunnel, making their way at a snail's pace to the little square and its overblown fountain. Miranda Julius had given them a picture of Randolph Kirk near the Trevi, staring myopically at her daughter. Or so it appeared.

'Meet me at her apartment,' he said, making a particular effort to keep the volume down. 'I'll send a car.'

'Hey,' said the surprised voice on the other end of the line. 'I'm just a pathologist. I don't want to tread—'

'Be there,' he yelled and cut the call.

Mickey Neri stood with Adele in the shadows, watching his father walk into the big, brightly lit chamber. The old man was grinning at the pictures on the walls, happy as could be, as if they brought back good memories, which was, Mickey knew, ridiculous. Something else must have been making the old man feel this way.

The shadows in this stupid place had such substance. They were places you could hide and feel you didn't really exist as you watched what went on in the light. Mickey Neri knew he would be happy to stay in shadows like this, all the way to one of the several exits she'd talked about, and out into the bright new day. Then Adele gave him a short, damp kiss on the cheek, whispered 'Ciao' and propelled him out into the yellow light.

Neri opened his arms in a welcoming, paternal gesture. 'Son, son—'

Mickey didn't move. Neri took two steps towards him. 'Mickey . . . Why the long face? Are we going to argue about this forever?'

He stood his ground, fearing the presence of the old man.

'I gave you a test, Mickey. What do you do? Not just kill that talkative bastard Martelli but come up with a present for me too? So you've been screwing Adele. What the fuck? If it's gonna happen best it's kept in the family. I don't care. Screwing around's such a little thing for a man of my age.'

He looked around the chamber. 'Jesus, we had some times in here. Where is Adele exactly?'

'Dunno,' Mickey mumbled. 'She said she'd leave us two alone. Catch up with you later.'

The old man gave him a cold smile. 'Yeah. I guess that will happen some time. Except I won't be in Italy much longer so maybe she knows I won't be fixing social appointments for a while. It's always the same with that woman. Adele's in it for herself. Forget that and things just might get dangerous.'

Mickey wanted to kick and scream and yell at the fat, grinning figure in front of him. Neri was behaving as if what happened the previous night was just one of those things. 'Fuck her! You nearly got me killed! Like you wanted it or something.'

Neri took one more step towards him, opened his arms wider, embraced his son, overwhelmed him with his strong, commanding presence. Mickey couldn't remember when they'd last touched like this but he knew that had been a bad time too.

'Don't make so much noise,' the old man whispered. 'You could wake the dead screaming like that.'

'You—'

The big arms enfolded him, buried him in Neri's bulk. 'I've been a lousy father. I know. You've every reason to feel mad at me.'

'Yeah—'

'Quiet,' Neri said. 'I'm talking. I brought you up bad, Mickey. I left you with that bitch of a mother for too long. When you weren't with her I didn't spend the time with you I should.'

'Yeah right—'

'Ssshhh.' Neri put a fat forefinger to his son's lips. 'Listen.'

Mickey pouted and the kid could have been ten years old again. Emilio Neri wanted to laugh out loud.

'There are so many things I never taught you. When it's time for a little honesty for one. People like us need to know that. Sometimes it's the most important thing of all.'

He looked at the photos on the walls, holding on tight to Mickey, turning his head to see. 'She was a good-looking girl, his stepdaughter. Anything you want

417

to tell your old man about her now, huh? And this other one too. All these games on the side. Jesus—'

Mickey's head shook from side to side. 'No. I got nothing to tell you.'

'You think that's what Vergil Wallis is coming all this way to hear? He's not falling for this ransom shit, Mickey. He don't give a damn who you've been messing with now or what you wind up doing with them. He's coming to find out why we lied to him all those years ago. He's looking for answers. When I think about it I got to be honest with myself. Maybe he deserves some.'

His rank, old man's mouth came close to Mickey Neri's face. 'You gonna tell him, son?'

'I didn't do nothing!'

'Mickey, Mickey.' Neri was smiling all the while, loving this. 'You were banging her in Sicily. I may have been a lousy father but I knew that. You banged her so well she was carrying some little bastard for you by the time we came back here. You told me so yourself once I beat it out of you. Remember?'

Mickey didn't look his father in the eye. He'd thought this was all dead and would stay that way.

Neri kept staring at her photo. 'That kid. Lovely as an angel but she was so damn stupid. Stupid as you in a different way. I mean I know why you wouldn't bother with a rubber. I wonder if you use them now with those African whores of yours. But her . . . I guess she just didn't know any better. Tell me now. In Sicily. It was the first time for her, wasn't it?'

'Yeah,' Mickey mumbled.

'So it makes sense. When she told you there was something on the way that made you real worried I guess. I mean Vergil . . . he's not a man to cross now.'

'I told you years ago. I didn't k . . . k . . . k . . .'

It was just like when he was a kid. Even down to the stammer.

'You didn't k . . . k . . . k . . . ?'

'K . . . kill her.'

The old man withdrew his arms and looked sternly at his son. 'Maybe not. But you know something? After all these years I'm not even sure it matters.'

Emilio Neri put his hand gently to the back of his son's head and stroked his soft hair, wishing it wasn't that stupid blonde colour. There were tears in Mickey's eyes.

'Don't cry, son,' Neri said, then brought his head down hard on the table, slamming it onto the old wood, ignoring his screams.

He pulled out the tape and wound it first round his mouth then his eyes. He bound Mickey's wrists, kicked his feet from under him so he landed roughly in the nearest chair and tied him tightly to the back, circling the rope around his chest.

'Plenty of time for crying later.'

Emilio Neri looked at his handiwork.

'*Hear that, Adele?*' he roared into the darkness. 'Just so much time for that later. You listening?'

Two times merge now, and in each he's leading the way, looking, staying close to the walls, in the shadows, Miranda behind, whispering, whispering. Nothing stands between her words and the images in his head. There is a light in one of the side chambers. They steal to the door, peer inside. Something flashes at the back of his imagination. The pictures he saw in Leo Falcone's office

rise again in his muddled head, real this time, rolling past
his eyes. A fat, white naked shape rolls around on the bed
lunging at something only dimly seen beneath him. The
air reeks of dope. A spent needle sits by the table. On the
floor lies the girl's sackcloth shift and the garlands of
flowers, discarded like an old skin, shed for her becoming.
The man grunts like a pig. The girl beneath him squeals:
pain, he thinks, revulsion. Is this the first time? In a dank
underground chamber reeking of stagnant water and
mould? In the sweating arms of a middle-aged man who
comes bearing flowers and oblivion in a syringe?

Can you see who she is? Miranda asks.

No, he says, not looking.

You have to know, Nic.

He walks on, knowing she's behind, talking, talking,
and here is another chamber, deeper into the pulsing
vein of rock, the light a little brighter inside. More cries
of pain, a young girl's voice, sobbing.

Look, she says.

Costa leans against the dusty wall. His breath comes
in snatches. His body feels like a lumpen machine beyond
his control. He's stiffening, ashamed of the fact. She sees
this, touches him there.

We're only beasts sometimes.

No, he answers. *Only if we allow it.*

Then the old voice sounds, deeper, impossible to
ignore, chanting, *Look you fucker look and learn.*

The shape in the shadows is pumping from behind at
a girl who straddles the back of a big armchair, face
upturned towards them. His arms hold her legs and the
memory of a childhood game – *wheelbarrow, wheel-*

420

barrow, an act so innocent the memory hurts – races into his head.

There are tears in Eleanor Jamieson's eyes. The girl looks at them from across the years, pleading. Two voices burn in Nic Costa's head, one young and innocent, one old and knowledgeable.

The man cranks up his grinding a gear, forcing himself into her with a brutal, punishing force. She screams from the agony. She begs for his intervention.

This is just a dream, kid, no one gets to change the past, grunts the old voice.

Then he hears her screaming . . . *I'll tell I'll tell I'll tell.*

Nothing changes, not even a break in the rhythm of the panting man behind.

The figure forces himself harder into her. The chair leaps forward propelled by his momentum. A face emerges into the light, distorted, ugly. It wears the mask, grunting, grunting.

He tries not to watch but the mask is staring at him, something alive behind those dead black eyes, the old voice rising, laughing, *Look you fucker look.*

And in the corner, in the darkness, something else. Another pair of bright young eyes, hidden, terrified.

Adele Neri walked out into Cerchi the way she had come, through the main entrance, straight to where Neri had left his men. She blinked at the sunlight then brushed down the cobwebs and crap from her black cashmere coat. Bruno Bucci and his men were standing in the shadows next to a 'Keep Out' sign that lay half askew behind some barbed wire marking the site.

She smiled and walked over to him. Bucci nodded.

'Mrs Neri,' he said carefully. The other men watched him like a hawk. 'Is your husband OK in there? I'm a little concerned if you want to know the truth.'

She put a slim hand on his arm. 'Of course he's OK, Bruno. You know him.' She stared at the men, not letting go until they dropped their eyes to the ground. 'You all know him.'

Bucci was trying to make some private contact with his eyes. She didn't play ball. She just lit a cigarette and stared down the big, busy road, watching the traffic.

'He told you what to do, didn't he?' she asked without looking at him. 'Mickey couldn't hurt his old man.'

A taxi drew up a little way along from them. They watched a tall, dark figure get out. He was carrying a leather bag.

'It's not Mickey I'm worried about,' Bucci grumbled.

They watched Vergil Wallis walk slowly towards them, swinging the bag, whistling some old tune, face expressionless, eyes never leaving the mouth of the cave. He came to stand between them, raised his arms high up in the air and said to Bucci, 'Well—?'

A couple of strong hands undid the leather overcoat and went up and down Wallis's chest, then down to his belt, down his trousers. Bucci swore, put a hand around the man's left ankle and came up with a gleaming silver hunting knife. He held the blade up in front of Wallis's face.

'Forget something?' Bucci asked.

'Guess so,' Wallis replied nonchalantly. 'It's these early mornings. I'm getting too old for them.'

Bucci looked at the knife then passed it to one of his minions. 'This has gone far enough, Mr Wallis. Why don't you just walk away? We can pass on the money. We can pass on any messages too. You can count on me to get what you're buying. This . . . disagreement needs to stop now.'

Wallis laughed in his face. 'Wow. I knew Neri was losing it. But so soon? Are you making the decisions already, Bruno?'

The big Italian hood fought to control his temper. 'I'm just trying to draw a line under all this shit.'

Wallis patted him hard on the shoulder. 'Don't bother. You're still new to all this, man.' He nodded towards the rock. 'You don't want to step out of line now, not with him still around. Mr Neri wants to see me. I want to see him. That's all there is to it.'

Bucci shook his head and reached for the leather bag.

Adele got there first and said, 'I can do this.'

She lifted it up to her chest, ran open the big bronze zip and rummaged thoroughly through the contents with her right hand. It took a good minute or more. Then she smiled at Vergil Wallis.

'You got a lot of money there,' she said. 'I hope you think it's worth it.'

'I hope so too,' he murmured and caught the bag as she flung it at him.

Vergil Wallis walked into the darkness. They listened to him whistling and then the sound died altogether.

Adele leaned close to Bruno Bucci, looked up into his big, impassive face and ran a finger down his arm.

'Bruno?' she asked. 'Do you boys really want to hang around here all day?'

*

By the time Teresa Lupo arrived, the door to Miranda Julius's apartment was down, torn from its hinges by the entry team. Men were swarming everywhere, opening drawers, scattering their contents on the floor, looking for anything.

She walked straight into Suzi's room. They hadn't reached there yet. She was glad. It gave her time to think.

There was a sound from the corridor, a gentle cough. She turned to face it and Falcone stood in the doorway looking as grateful as he could manage.

'Thanks for coming,' he said.

'Why am I here?'

Falcone stroked his angular, silver beard and looked as if he were asking himself the same question. 'For luck I guess. Maybe I'm getting superstitious in my old age. We could use some luck.'

'No sign of Nic or Wallis? I heard when I was leaving.'

He shook his head. 'What made you come to this room first? Do you think there's something we should be looking for?'

'No. Nic and I did look, didn't we? It's just—' The conviction had grown in the speeding police car on the way. 'I should have said something when we were here before. This room doesn't feel lived in. Not at all. People leave their mark. If you go into the mother's room you can still feel her presence. There's mess. Chaos. This—'

She took another look to make sure. 'This is for our benefit. Do we really know for sure that Suzi Julius exists?'

Falcone's eyes didn't leave her. 'We've got video of someone getting on that bike. We've got the photos the mother gave us.'

know. But apart from that?'

'No.' Falcone sat down on a small cheap chair and looked around the bedroom. 'Maybe that was all for our benefit too. Let's face it. If you wanted to stage something for the police there's no better place than the Campo. We're always around. She'd know she wouldn't have to scream for long. You don't need to be a genius to see there's CCTV there either. It's hanging from the lamp posts.'

Teresa could see he was right. 'But *why?*'

Falcone walked silently back into the big living room. She followed, becoming aware of the roar of traffic from outside.

'Look,' he said, and pointed to a pile of old maps. They were detailed drawings of archaeological digs, all over the city out into the suburbs and beyond. She sifted through the top of the pile. There wasn't one she'd heard of. 'The Julius woman was interested in these places too,' he said. 'How many reasons can there be for that?'

Peroni was bent double over the woman's notebook computer, thrashing at the keyboard. Teresa crouched next to him, unthinkingly put her hand on his shoulder and watched, in amazement, as he hammered the keys, working through the machine.

'How the hell do you know about computers?' she asked.

He stopped for a moment, and stared at her, bemused. His right eye was a puffy red mass, almost closed. He looked awful. 'I got kids, Teresa. Who else is suppose to fix their problems?'

It had never occurred to her how family shaped a man

in such small, unpredictable ways. All her preconceptions about Peroni seemed false.

'Gianni,' she said softly. 'What the hell happened to you? Have you seen a doctor about that?'

He laughed. 'It's a punch in the face, for Christ's sake. Ask me something important. Ask me about her reasons.'

'Which are?' she asked and wondered whether she really wanted to know.

'Good ones,' Peroni replied and pulled up some photos on the computer.

Teresa Lupo watched as he flicked through shot after shot and wished she'd stayed where she belonged, safe in the morgue.

Peroni pointed to one of a contemporary Randolph Kirk standing at the dig in Ostia, clearly unaware someone was furtively taking his picture. The expression on his face was one of puzzlement and perhaps a little fear. 'We've still no idea who she is really. According to the British the only woman of that name with a current passport is sixty-seven years old. Also we found these—'

There was a pile of passports on the table. 'Another British one. American. Canadian. New Zealand. She looks different on every one. Different hair colour. Different style. If you'd given me this back when I was on narcotics and asked me her true profession I'd have said she was a mule. But we just don't know. She's into photography though. This . . .' he picked up the picture of Kirk, ' . . . was the inspiration for the photo she gave us to establish a link between Kirk and Suzi. It never existed. She just took his head from that picture and pasted it into the background of one she had of Suzi at the fountain. *Kirk was never there. Kirk never threatened anyone.*'

'Perhaps,' Falcone said, 'it was the other way round. She was blackmailing Kirk.'

Teresa tried hard to think about Miranda Julius. If it was an act, it was a very good one.

Peroni pulled out an envelope, extracted two prints and she believed there was a glimmer of light in the darkness. These were, it seemed, from the series she had been handed by Regina Morrison. They had the same seamy quality, the same backdrop. The time was sixteen years earlier. In one the young Miranda Julius – or whatever she was really called – stood next to Emilio Neri, a big, innocent smile on her face, a glass of something in her hand. Flowers in her younger, brighter blonde hair, the petals falling down onto that stupid ceremonial shift. Teresa Lupo wanted to pick the thing up and tear it into shreds, unwind the years.

He took out the second print and placed it over the first. Miranda was naked now, pale body lolling back drunkenly on what looked like a cheap, fake Roman couch. Her legs were wound round the large, cloaked body of a man who was pumping away for all he was worth and not getting very far either. It was Beniamino Vercillo, already looking old and past it. Teresa stared into the blank eyes of that young face and tried to imagine what it would be like to be in that room. Maybe they thought Miranda was so out of it she didn't understand what was happening. That if they poured enough booze and dope down these dumb kids they'd forget half of what went on, and think the rest was as much their fault as anyone's. You could work that trick on someone like Barbara Martelli, particularly if you threw in a nice job in the police as a reward. It wasn't like that for Miranda. There was physical pain there. There was resentment, hatred too at having this animal steal your innocence on some cheap couch in a stinking damp cave.

'There are more,' Peroni said, reaching for the prints.

Falcone abruptly put his hand on the envelope. 'Not now.' He looked at her a little slyly. 'So what do you think?'

It didn't require a genius. She smoothed back her dark hair, wondering how bad she looked just then. The work clothes were back on. Her mind was in order. But she still felt out of sorts. 'Miranda, or whoever she was, came back for vengeance. But why wait so long?'

'Because this wasn't just about getting raped by these creeps,' Peroni said. 'One of those girls died and Neri told everyone it was a drug overdose. He told Wallis that too. From what we've seen it must have been a pretty plausible story. Until we fished that body out of the bog.'

There was some logic there, she thought. Just not enough. 'So why doesn't she just kill the bastard? Why go to this trouble?'

Peroni took out a handkerchief and dabbed his damaged eye which was surely leaking something and must have hurt like hell. 'Which bastard would that be?' he wondered. 'Mickey? Maybe. Maybe she's not sure. Maybe she knew all along and was just too scared to say. Until she realizes she can finally prove it and, bingo, it's the first plane to Rome. So one day Barbara picks up the phone and it's Miranda saying, "Hi, guess who's in town and you'll never guess what I heard. Our old initiation girlfriend from the fuck club didn't OD. Some bastard cut her throat and got away with it." Can you imagine

Barbara, even the somewhat crooked Barbara we now know existed, enjoying that?'

Teresa Lupo continued to be amazed by the respect they gave their murderous former colleague. She bent down, removed the handkerchief from him, dabbed gently at the wound. Peroni was right. Nothing was cut. It was just swelling, and some weeping from the bruised eye. She touched the corner of his cheek lightly to remove some of the liquid.

'This would explain why the lovely Barbara wanted to put a bullet in my head too, presumably. You can dab away anything wet here, Gianni, but if you touch any place else I'm confiscating the hankie and sending you to hospital. Understood?'

Peroni wriggled in his tight grey suit, took back the hankie and touched it gingerly on the precise spot. 'Thanks. Be honest with yourself, Teresa. In her shoes, in those circumstances, what did you expect her to do? *Explain?* These were women with a mission. God help anyone who got in their way.'

Falcone bent down and peered into Peroni's damaged face. 'Miranda did kill someone. Beniamino Vercillo. We've got the mask. It was dumped in a bin nearby. It's got blonde hairs on it. I'd put money on them being hers. She had the personal motive. We've got the proof here. But she also wanted to expose those papers and bring Neri down for good. It wasn't enough, all this stuff about the missing girl. We'd got distracted then by Barbara killing Kirk.'

'And me . . . nearly,' she interjected.

'And you,' he agreed. 'All the same she had to keep the pressure up. She identified that hair-band from Ostia which could have belonged to anyone. She identified

Mickey when I doubt he's even been near whoever "Suzi" really is. The rest, I don't know. Maybe it would be hard for her to get to Neri and Mickey. Maybe . . . He'll be OK, won't he?'

Falcone was grasping for ideas in the dark and struggling to find them.

'He'll be fine if he can stop poking it,' she replied. Teresa recalled what Regina Morrison had said about the ritual and the roles each participant would play. 'She's what they made her, Neri and the rest. A Maenad. A woman who's all sweetness and light, a warm bed and anything else you want when times are good. And the banshee from hell when she feels she, or one of the sisterhood, has been wronged. Think of it from Miranda's point of view.' She pointed at the picture, with the figure in the mask humping and grunting away. 'Who would you want to kill? Just this sad bastard?'

'The whole damn lot of them,' Peroni said softly. 'As nastily as possible. I'd want to watch them tear each other apart and dance on their graves afterwards.'

They looked at each other, lost for words. Then a woman officer walked through, smiled briefly at Teresa Lupo, and said, 'We've picked up Neri's lieutenant and a couple of sidekicks. In Cerchi. They're not talking.'

Peroni raised a crooked, bloodied eyebrow. 'Is that so?'

Emilio Neri sat at the head of the old table, smoking a Cohiba, ignoring his son, toying with the black gun he'd owned for years, used so many times it was like another limb. Thick grey cigar fumes curled their way up into the darkness, swirling on some unseen current. He watched

Vergil Wallis walk in. The American was carrying a leather bag on one outstretched arm and had the other high up in the air.

Neri looked him up and down and said, 'You met the guys outside?'

'Yeah. What's his name? Bucci?'

Neri hated this man. He had no business knowing the names of his lieutenants. 'He's a good guy. I trust him. All the same—'

He waved the gun at Wallis. 'Put the bag on the table. Take the coat off. Throw it on the floor. Then stand upright, keep your arms out. Fuck around and I just shoot you now.'

Wallis carefully eased the coat off, let it fall, then held his breath as Neri got up and walked round him, patting in all the right places, making sure.

'You can sit,' the old man said finally, indicating a seat at the table with the gun. Then he went back to the other side and resumed his place next to Mickey. 'Show me the cash. Don't reach inside or anything. Just turn it upside down and let me see.'

Wallis took the bottom of the bag and upended the thing. Bank notes, big denominations, tucked into wads straight from the till, fell onto the table.

Neri gave it a derisory stare. 'So this dumb shit of a son of mine's willing to cause all this anguish for this. What an idiot. I'd have given him more as spending money if he'd asked.'

'Perhaps,' Wallis wondered, 'that was the point. He got tired of asking. He wanted a little independence.'

Neri laughed and cast a brief glance at Mickey. 'That worked, huh?' Then he looked at the pictures plastering the room. 'What is it you think this is buying you, Vergil?

That kid Mickey has stashed somewhere? Don't ask me about it. I don't know no details and I don't want to. He was just playing freelance there. That kind of thing's beneath me, but I guess you know that.'

Wallis frowned. 'I got asked to come. I came.'

'You want justice or something?'

'Or something.'

'OK.'

Neri reached into his pocket, took out a knife, flicked open the blade and placed it on the table. He motioned to Mickey with the gun. 'I'm a fair man. I'm going to let you take him. I got to be honest with you, I nearly did the same myself sixteen years ago. I mean, you got a nice party going, you're thinking everyone's having a good time. Then what happens? Your dumb kid comes in all doped up to the eyeballs, hysterical and weeping, saying look, look, look. Here's my girlfriend, dead as they come, throat cut from ear to ear. And I watch him twitching away like that and I think, let's make it two. Because this worthless piece of shit surely deserves it after what he's done. I don't know about you but I was never into beating up women. I'd kill them if it was necessary. But not out of anger or some weird doped-up pleasure. Also . . .' Neri took a last puff of the cigar then threw it on the floor, ' . . . it spoiled a damn good evening. Had to cover up stuff to make sure you wouldn't hear of it for one thing. Not that I remember the details, to be honest with you. Got to admit I was a little out of things myself.'

He looked for some sign of emotion on Wallis's face. The American sat impassive, with his hands palm down on the table.

'We were all out of it,' Neri continued. 'It was a lapse

432

of concentration. Dangerous. But, hell, it was a good party anyway. From what I recall I banged three different girls. Adele being the best, which is why we ended up getting hitched in the end. But three! All in one night. Something else.'

He leaned forward, grinning. 'What about you, Vergil? Tell me. Man to man. How many you'd bang, huh?'

She holds his head. Her tongue, chattering, chattering, soaks his cheek in desperate saliva.

What do you see? she says.

Costa's peering down the blackness, half visible as a corridor in front of him, trying to fight the confusion in his mind, trying to think of some way out.

You know what I see, he says.

Miranda takes his head in her hands, forces him to look into her bright eyes. *No, Nic. Not what you know already. When you look into the corner. What do you see?*

In his imagination, formed by her suggestions, he sees her for sure now. A huddled shape, wretched with fear and shame, hiding in the darkness, thinking itself safe.

What's she thinking, Miranda asks.

Tell me.

Her voice starts to break. *She sees, she knows, she never has the guts to tell.*

In the waking dream the figure sobs, bites her hand, trying to stifle the noise.

Who is she, Nic? Who?

*

'You don't want to say. Well I guess it could be boasting.'

Wallis leaned back in his chair looking bored, saying nothing.

'Maybe you don't remember, huh? It's a long time ago. Which was what puzzled me, you see. When all this shit started happening. When we got to know that body was this stepdaughter of yours. I mean a *stepdaughter*. Not like she's your own flesh and blood, is it? You don't have any of your own flesh and blood, do you? Problems down there or something?'

Wallis nodded at Mickey. 'You think I'm jealous?'

Neri laughed and took the point. 'Over this piece of shit? Nah. Who would be? But I know Mickey. He's just a weak, stupid kid, same as he was then. And all this crap got me wondering. Got me trying to remember, which is hard after all this time. And you know one thing I remember?'

Wallis peered at his nails.

'Vergil, Vergil. This is important. This is the fate of your stepdaughter I'm talking about.'

'What do you remember, Emilio?' Wallis snapped.

'Two things now I come to think about it. Once Mickey started blubbing on about how he'd got the stupid kid pregnant I didn't even *ask* why he'd cut her throat. And one other. She just didn't get the game we were supposed to be playing. You said she'd get turned on by that jerk from the university. That we'd all be having fun. And we did, all except her. She didn't want to fuck with anyone but Mickey. I asked, all nice and polite. Tori Martelli did too. And it was all just those flashing eyelashes, and lemme get you another drink, and then what do you know, she's off with Mickey again. Maybe it wasn't her kind of party. Maybe she was like that because – I got to be blunt here – it wasn't the first time for her, like it was for the rest. And that, if you recall, was one of the rules that university guy you found for us laid down. He said bad things would happen otherwise. Maybe he was right. Where *did* you find him by the way? The cops seem to think he was something to do with me. As if—'

Wallis turned his head, listening, trying to work out if there was anyone else present in the pitch black corridors. 'I move in wider circles, Emilio.'

'Oh yeah. You're *educated*. I forgot. Anyway, what does it matter? I promised you could have Mickey. I don't break promises. You can do what you like. But the knife only.'

He slid the blade across the table. Wallis's hand closed on it in an expert, practised grip. Mickey Neri, blind to the game, hung his head and sobbed behind the gag.

'You can do him like he did the girl, Vergil. Only—'

Neri thought about this. 'Let's give the kid a chance to talk first. Only fair—'

Watching the seated man opposite very carefully he got up and tore the tape from Mickey Neri's eyes in one rough sweep then did the same for his mouth. Mickey screamed from the pain, looked across the table at Vergil Wallis holding the knife and the noise died in his mouth.

'Jesus—' he whispered. 'Dad, don't do this to me.'

'Man's got a right to know what happened to his girl,' Neri said severely. 'Best get it off your chest, son. Best do that now before it's too late.'

She's you, he says in a still, dead voice.

Who?

You.

Miranda takes his pained head, stares at him with two eyes from the present, kisses him, crying, shaking from the release.

He looks at the young Miranda Julius cowering in his imagination. Time has worked such changes on her face, removed so much. No lines. No cares. No jaded acceptance of an imperfect world.

You're beautiful, he says.

A thin, unconvincing laugh now, local, in his own piece of staggering space. Hers.

Only on the outside, Nic. The outside tells you nothing. The outside lies. The only truth lies in your imagination. Forego that and there's nothing but the dark.

Shouts echo through the caverns. Ripples of fear and anxiety – real, not imagined – disturb the wakeful dream inside his head.

He tries to walk and stumbles. The chemical fire is raging unchecked through his head. She holds him. He trembles. He sweats.

There's more, she says.

'I just screwed her,' Mickey bleated. 'That's all. She begged for it. All the time. I got bored if you wanted to know. I wanted to mess around with the others like we were supposed to. She wouldn't let me. It was just, "Mickey, Mickey, Mickey". I said that wasn't the point. She was supposed to mix it. She didn't want to know. She—'

His nervous eyes flickered between the two men.

'She said you was just a bunch of dirty old bastards. She wasn't putting it out for any of you. She just went on about love and stuff. Like the whole world was something special. Even her being knocked up was special and I just wanted her down the clinic, get the thing out. Love? All I did was bang her.'

Wallis watched him, toying with the knife, saying nothing.

'See,' Neri suggested. 'Like I said. The girl just didn't want to play the game. Her choice, I guess. But why come along in the first place?'

Mickey nodded at Wallis ''Cos he made her. It wasn't some birthday present. He thought it'd be good for business. That's what she said.'

Neri cocked his head to one side, thinking about this. 'I find that hard to believe, Mickey. Vergil here is an educated man. He came up with the idea for that party after all. He fixed all that stuff with the robes and the flowers. I just brung the dope and some guys who might be grateful for a chance at some young ass. The girl must have guessed what was coming.'

'*None of them guessed*,' Mickey yelled. 'You were so far out of it you didn't even get that, did you? Him and that professor guy of his just filled them up with so much stuff then put them in a room full of old guys with hard-ons and bolted the doors. They didn't get any choices. They did what you wanted. Then when it turned bad you thought you could shut them all up with a few promises and that was it.'

Neri stared at Wallis. 'Is that right, Vergil? My memory's not so great after all these years.'

The American shot Mickey a hateful glance. 'That fool was shot full of so much dope—'

Neri nodded. 'I agree there, Mickey. You're just trying to avoid the truth. You knocked up this poor girl when

437

you first met her in Sicily. You fucked her rigid that night we came here. Then what? She told you she was coming to me and Vergil to announce a little shotgun wedding? Or did the dope and the festivities just go a little too far and you woke up one moment with a knife in your hand, and her stone dead?'

'*No!*'

Neri grimaced. 'This is going nowhere. We don't have time to piss around forever. Maybe I should just let Vergil do his thing now.'

Mickey Neri turned on his father, pleading. 'Will you listen, for chrissake? I went outside for a smoke. It was driving me crazy in here. All these old guys screwing everywhere, taking junk like they were twenty years younger. And this place. It's like being dead. In the grave. I was out there maybe an hour. I thought I'd go home but I knew you'd be mad with me. Then I came back, into that room you gave us, and *she was there*. Like you saw. *It wasn't me.*'

Neri's mouth hardened into a tight bloodless line. He looked at his watch and said nothing.

'But it's always the same,' Mickey snapped. 'There's shit around and who do you turn to? Me. You never once asked what happened. You just looked at her, looked at me, then shook your head like you always do. You know how many times I've seen that over the years?'

'The girl was dead, Mickey,' Neri said quietly. 'You were the only one who was with her. I was supposed to be doing business with her stepfather who was just a couple of rooms away, out of his head, playing god or something, fucking everything that moved. If I'd hesitated then, if I'd let him know what had really been going on – you screwing the girl, getting her in the way

438

like that – you'd have been dead anyway. Did you ever stop to think of that?'

Mickey was quiet for a moment, a tiny light of clarity sparking in his head.

'No,' he mumbled.

A part of him is almost sleep, hiding behind closed eyes, listening to what she says. Another *sees*. The god is angry. The girl screams. Fists fly, nails tear. Through the dream he feels the pressure of their shrieking rebound off the damp and rocky veins that enclose them. A strong black arm pumps back and forth. She falls, blood pumping from her perfect lips.

He tears off the mask. A black face, rent by fury, demands obeisance, receives only scorn.

I'll tell I'll tell I'll tell, the girl screeches, furious.

The man moves behind her, raises his arm. Silver flashes in the yellow light. Two eyes glitter, terrified, hidden in the shadows, watching, witnessing.

Then the reverie ends. He opens his eyes and walks towards the voices and the light.

Neri glanced towards the shadows, wondering if it were Adele skulking round there now, then nodded towards Mickey.

'So Vergil. What are you waiting for? Are you going to do him?'

Mickey's head fell down on his chest. He began to sob.

'And then what?' the American demanded. 'You shoot me.'

'Nah. What for? You lost a daughter? I lose a son. You probably find this hard to believe but I never killed someone without a reason. Even those cops outside my house had it coming to them. You? Well, you got me in all manner of trouble with them, but you did me a favour too. You reminded me I was ready for retirement. A man should know when to walk off this stage. You did, didn't you?'

Wallis made a lazy wave with the knife point and said nothing.

'Besides,' Neri continued, 'if I just walk away from this mess and leave you sitting in the middle of it, you're going to have so much explaining to do. Reading about all that from somewhere nice and warm and safe could be real amusing. I might just die laughing.'

'You might,' Wallis said, and allowed himself a smile.

'An eye for an eye then,' Neri said, returning the gesture. 'Just as it should be. We agreed? All this non-sense ends here?'

'Yeah,' Wallis said. 'It ends here.'

Neri looked at him approvingly. 'That's good. You don't mind if I ask one more thing though? Just a tiny detail that bothers me.'

The big American had let go of the knife now. His hands were flat on the table, behind the pile of money, unseen.

'It does?'

'One of my cop friends told me the oddest thing. He said that when they found that poor kid she had a coin in her mouth. Some accident, I thought. Then he looks at me the way you look at me. As if I'm dumb or something. Seems this has some *significance*, Vergil. People used to put it there for a reason. You think

Mickey knew that reason? I didn't. We didn't put it there when we got rid of the body out near the airport. See, we're not *educated*.'

Neri picked up the gun in front of him and angled it halfway across the table. 'Oh, but you are. I guess you'd know what that reason is. Kind of a nice reason my cop friend told me. It says farewell, sorry maybe. That professor of yours would know too. But let's face it. He was just some little pervert you picked up along the way to sort things out for you. He didn't have the spunk to kill someone. Besides, why? If you'd gone in there, on the other hand . . . Maybe not taking no for an answer. Maybe finding out about Mickey's little present. Or wondering how the hell you were going to square screwing her with her mother afterwards.'

Wallis's black eyes burned across at him.

'One thing I do remember, Vergil, and it's so clear it's like yesterday.' Neri nodded at the mask at the head of the table. 'You really liked wearing that stupid thing a lot. And when you wore it you know something? I think you thought you really *were* some kind of god. One who was better than the rest of us. One who could do what he liked to just anybody and never feel the consequences. Which is why you came here really. You're scared that little secret might work its way into the light of day, aren't you? You just want to keep it good and buried, preferably with Mickey's name on instead.'

Neri looked at his son then at Wallis, blinking back the fury. 'You're no god. None of us is. You just fuck up the world pretending. Because of that – because I failed to see it – I've been punishing this poor, dumb son of mine for years.'

He waved the gun at the figure across from him.

'Jesus, Vergil. I wish I had more time with you. I wish I could do this some other way and—'

The explosion burst through the gloom. Emilio Neri found himself flying backwards in his chair, clutching his chest, feeling something turn his guts inside out. He landed on the floor, upright enough to see Wallis's hand emerging from the money pile, clutching a small pistol taped beneath one of the bundles.

'Bruno—' he croaked, through a mouth filling with blood, into the reddening darkness.

The uniformed men lined Bucci and three of his sidekicks against the wall just off the main road. Bucci had that punk look on his face, the one Falcone and Peroni knew so well. The one that said, *you can ask and ask and ask but no one's saying.*

'You got any idea what they were doing?' Falcone asked the uniformed sergeant.

Gianni Peroni had recognized Bucci as the leader straight away. Had gone straight up and pushed his face into his, one bull neck against the other.

'No,' the sergeant replied. 'They were walking by the time we stopped them. I guess they saw us first.'

Falcone walked over to Bucci and said, 'I don't have time to waste on you, sonny. I got a man out there somewhere and if he dies I promise you your life won't be worth living. Neri's old goods here. You stick with him you go down with him. Understood?'

Bucci looked at the other three hoods with him and laughed. 'You hear that? What's this town coming to? When a decent Italian man can't walk down the street without some ugly fucking cop coming and staring in his face?'

'Ugly?' Gianni Peroni asked. 'You calling me ugly? No one ever called me ugly before. I take that as an insult.'

Bucci laughed. His shoulders jerked in that punk way the cops all knew. 'Yeah. Ugly. Ugly as—'

It came so quickly even Falcone didn't expect it. Peroni dabbed his big head forward in a single blow, stomped his bone-hard temples straight into Bucci's nose. The big hood fell backwards onto the wall, blood and snot streaming down his face, gasping for air. Then Peroni butted him again, twice, punched a big fist into his guts, got him on the ground and laid in a flurry of stiff kicks. Bucci writhed there, screaming, bleeding, and Peroni took hold of the man next to him, a skinny-looking jerk in his thirties with mud-green eyes now as big as saucers, grabbed his shoulders, pulled back ready to strike.

'Down the road in some fucking cave, man,' the jerk whined. 'Don't hit me. Please.'

Gianni Peroni didn't wait for anyone else. He was first into the dark stinking mouth of the caverns. In seconds he was fighting to find his bearings under the dull yellow lights that ran through the labyrinth, leading into the blackness.

Mickey Neri whimpered. He'd pissed himself. The hot stream felt like acid against his leg.

'Don't do this, mister. P-p-p-please.'

Wallis stalked him with the knife. The big American

couldn't take his eyes off the mask with its dead eyes watching them.

'Got to,' Wallis murmured, coming round to stand behind the figure strapped in the chair. He reached down, grabbed a hunk of Mickey's hair in his fist, jerked back his head, held the silver blade over the pale throat below.

They watch, hidden in the black corner, and two times collide in Nic Costa's head. What he sees before him now is no god, just a man, bright beneath the single yellow bulb, angling himself behind the screaming shape on the chair, pitiless, determined.

Don't fail me, Nic, she says. *Remember what you are. Don't make me the silent witness twice.*

Her hand grips his and passes something over. Its shape slips beneath his fingers, cold metal, the old, familiar dumb machine.

The powerful black arm rose, . . . *rises.*

A figure strides out of the darkness. Vergil Wallis watches and pauses, surprised. A name slips from his lips, hangs in the air between them. He lowers his gaze, nods at the table.

You got your money, the American says, staring at her too-blonde hair, eyes glittering covetously, remembering. *You know the deal. Get gone.*

Her face is more radiant than anything in the room, shining with a living brightness leeched from the vibrant photos pasted everywhere. She shivers, she shakes, rooted to the spot, afraid but not afraid.

Wallis waves the blade at her. *Take it.*

No movement. Fear and resolution.

I know, she says.

He halts, confused. Her golden head shakes. There are tears in her eyes as, stuttering, she says . . .

I saw, I know, I never had the guts to tell.

He looks at the dead mask on the table and laughs, wondering whether to try it on again for size.

So what's one more? he wonders, then laughs, staring avidly at the shining hair. *Afterwards . . .*

The blade rises, then falls. A red line starts on the white, shining skin.

You got a talent for watching, girl . . . he tries to say into the dark air, but finds himself struggling for the words. Wallis looks beyond her, into the shadows, where fire and thunder are shredding the darkness.

He stares at this black shape there and tries to roar, to find the god inside him. Blood rises in his throat. He falls and, in the smoke and powder stink, Nic Costa finds his consciousness fading too. His head spins, his legs become feeble.

On the ground, sight fading. One last memory.

She bends over the fallen man, opening his bloody lips, still mouthing, still trying to say some single word. A coin glitters briefly between her fingers then is gone.

Another room. Smaller. A pool of grubby light pierces the darkness. Her older voice now talks to him and it is calm, unmoved.

Sweet Nic, sweet Nic. You save yourself. You save me.

No, he says, and hears his own voice rumbling around

the inside of this curling, twisting intestine cut into the rock.

He sits on a chair. She crouches above him, holding his cheeks. Her face fills his vision, becomes all there is to the world.

You have to feed the savage sometimes. It's the only way to keep him in his cage.

Fighting to control his hands, his fingers reach her shoulder, push the fabric of her tee-shirt down.

And hears the old voice, laughing, *you should have looked earlier, kid, call yourself a cop.*

Deep in the flesh, dark blue and old the dreadlocked face grins at him, victorious. His mouth closes on the stained skin, swallows its guttural voice. His teeth bite into her, chewing, licking, sucking the vile blue poison from her pores, takes it into himself, feeling the rush.

Voices down the corridor, voices in his head. He snatches a breath and knows: *this is only the beginning.* The dope is moving higher up the ladder, seizing more territory inside his limitless imagination.

Then, like a lifeline from sanity, a familiar voice rings through the guts of the labyrinth, echoing, distant.

Nic! Nic!

A sound from the old world. The real world.

One pill makes you small, Miranda Julius sings.

Nic!

She bends down to kiss him, tongue darting briefly into the corner of his mouth.

'Don't look for me,' she whispers, then vanishes into the shadows, leaving just the aftertouch of her skin, her presence, glowing in his head.

The light dies. It is dark and cold. He shivers alone.

APRILE

It was late afternoon on the first day of April. They sat in the old courtyard garden of the hospital of San Giovanni enjoying the last of the sun. Peroni bolted down the remains of a panino, balled up the bag and despatched it into a nearby rose bed.

'Nice to have you back, Nic,' he said. 'I never had a partner with acid flashbacks before. What's it like?'

Costa gave him a wry look. 'I'll let you know when it happens.'

'Not yet, huh? Did they ever find out what shit that woman pumped into you?'

His partner's eye had mended but still had a rosy bloom above the eyelid. Given the state of the rest of Peroni's face it didn't look particularly out of place. Peroni was unchanged by events. Nic Costa had stared at himself in the mirror that morning and wondered if anyone would say the same about him. He looked older, more marked by the world. He'd even found a couple of grey hairs above one ear. This went with the odd new territory he seemed to have carved out for himself within the Questura. He wasn't a hero, quite. But when he'd walked down the corridors that afternoon, for the first time since the incident, he realized he was now the kind of man who turned heads.

'If they did,' he said, 'they haven't told me.'

'Drop off a bottle of pee with Teresa,' Peroni declared. 'She'll know. I'm serious. That woman's a genius.'

Costa thought of the role the pathologist had played in the Julius case. Maybe she was too. 'So you never found out who Miranda really was?'

Peroni shook his head. 'We got the "daughter" though. Not that it did us much good. She was a teenage model from Prague. Wanted to break into acting. Seems she was picked out of a portfolio for her looks, paid to come here and "audition". Which meant getting her hair dyed a touch more blonde and her picture taken in a few places. You can guess by who. Oh, and doing that stunt on the motorbike for the benefit of the cameras and any cops who happened to be lurking in the Campo at the time.'

Costa thought about this. 'She didn't know anything about Miranda? She was just picked at random because of how she looked?'

'Sure. Miranda claimed to be a big talent scout from America. How many questions do you think would-be actresses ask in those situations? She got her plane ticket. She got put up in a nice hotel. Then, after performing the "action audition" with the bike, she took a taxi for Fiumicino and flew home. You got to admit it, Miranda did a great job. While we were thinking her daughter was lying drugged in a cave somewhere, making out with Mr Beastie and about to get killed, she was actually back at school strutting around in front of her classmates boasting about her new career in Hollywood. She can't give us a clue who Miranda really is. And you want to know something? I doubt we're ever going to find out.'

Costa wondered how he really felt about that. 'Falcone's letting it drop?'

Peroni hesitated, choosing his words carefully. 'I wouldn't put it quite so crudely. You got to remember, Nic. People like him answer to lots of different bosses. Some of them hold the purse strings and ask about the money. Is it really worth it? Ask yourself. Is it?'

'Six people dead. I would have thought so.'

Peroni took a deep breath. 'That's seven actually if you include Eleanor Jamieson. Not counting those poor bastards outside Neri's.'

Costa shook his head. The death toll there had risen to five in the end, some DIA, some cops. It could so easily have been higher. 'We can't just let this drop.'

His partner sighed. 'Nic. Let's have this conversation once and then leave it to one side forever. Most of this is wrapped up already. We got hard evidence that Mickey Neri accounted for that bastard Toni Martelli, for which he will stand trial once we can get him out of the hospital and into a jacket with sleeves. Barbara Martelli, meanwhile, popped Randolph Kirk to stop him talking to us before disappearing down a hole outside Fiumicino. Thanks to you we know most of the rest too. Wallis killed his own stepdaughter and got to Emilio Neri too, before you had the chance to stop him. This . . .' Peroni patted his knee to emphasize the point, ' . . . is all good news for the statistics, and the people who live above Leo *survive* on statistics. Do you think it possible Crazy Teresa has the hots for me by the way? I've been getting some funny looks from that woman lately.'

'No,' Costa objected. 'What about—?'

'Mr Vercillo? Miranda Julius, or whoever she is, did him. There's forensic on that costume we found, and we got some blood stains on a shirt in the apartment too. So you see the dilemma? Do we really waste public money – big public money in all probability – chasing all over the world for a woman who, let's be honest here, probably did the Italian public at large some very big favours?'

Costa scowled and said nothing.

Peroni sniffed a young rose on the bush next to them, just coming into bloom. 'Summer's on the way, Nic. Let's put all this behind us.'

'I'm trying,' he murmured.

Peroni's hand went to Nic's shoulder and that big ugly face now stared up at his. 'OK. I know. I checked the records. It's the first time you shot a man. And it bugs you. I don't blame you. I never shot anyone in my life.'

Costa looked Peroni straight in the eye. 'Did you ever want to?'

A touch of colour rose in Peroni's face. 'Nic. Stop feeling sorry for yourself. As luck would have it I am going to be by your side somewhat longer than I expected. And I do not intend to sit back and watch you choke trying to swallow this. Do you think either of them, Neri or Wallis, was going to let you walk out of there? You're damn lucky the woman did. Still not sure I get that. What I do know is she filled you up with dope before this happened. If you're looking for someone to blame, blame her.'

Costa carefully removed his partner's arm from his shoulder. 'Don't worry. What bothers me is I'm not that bothered. It wasn't the dope, either. Not all of it anyway. I wanted that man dead. He was a monster.'

Gianni Peroni looked at him and Costa was unsure of his expression. It just may have been shock.

'I'm sorry to hear that, Nic,' he said eventually. 'In a way. A part of me wants to say, "Welcome to the real world, Mr Costa. Where most of us go round having some such thoughts on a daily basis." A part of me hopes you don't catch the same bug everyone else gets. Let's not make a habit of it, huh? It's such an easy way out. Is that a deal?'

'Yeah,' Costa replied, feeling a little embarrassed.

'Good.' His partner was grinning now. It made him look younger and a little scary.

'What do you mean you're sticking around with me?' Costa asked. 'I thought you were going back to pushing a desk in vice.'

Peroni took another look at the single rosebud struggling into bloom on the bush next to them then snipped off the stem with his forefinger and thumb and placed the flower in his jacket pocket. 'You wouldn't believe it. That Bucci bastard, the hood I knocked around good in Cerchi, laid in a complaint about me. Amazing. He may even sue too. Police brutality. First time I ever truly hit a man on the job, *and* he's a murdering goon. What with all the hooker stuff that went down before they wanted to kick me out altogether. But old Leo waded in and started screaming at everyone high and low. At least so I gather. He's not even said so much as a word either way to me.'

Costa tried to decode the expression on Peroni's face. 'Is that good or bad? You staying with me?'

'It's good for me,' Peroni yelled. 'I got a job still, and a partner I can live with. How about you?'

Costa shrugged. 'I may need to think about it for a while.'

'Jesus,' Peroni gasped. 'Will you analyse every last fucking event on the face of this planet until it rolls over and dies? *It is how it is*. Nothing I can do will change things. So why sweat over it?'

Costa chuckled.

'Your sense of humour could do with some improving,' Peroni moaned. 'Country boys like me don't get these finer points.'

'I'm sorry, Gianni. Really I am. What about your wife? How are things going there?'

Peroni looked shifty. 'We met at the weekend. I had to go to a funeral back home. She wanted a reconciliation but . . . You know the one thing I have learned from you people? To recognize that dead means dead. And that marriage is dead. I'll see the kids don't get damaged though, as much as I can.'

His battered face was unreadable. 'A funeral?'

'Yeah. That old cop. The Tuscan amateur plastic surgeon.'

Peroni pointed to his scars. Costa was surprised to discover he was now very used to them. This *was* Gianni Peroni. 'The nice guy who did this to me.'

'You went all the way home for that?' Costa asked, astonished.

Peroni laughed and shook his head. 'Christ, Nic. What a pair of lousy detectives we make. You can't see it any better than I could, not that you had as much time of course. He was my old man. He begat me. Half my genes are his. He . . . oh shit, even now I find it hard to use the f-word. *He was my father.* There. I think my mamma must have thought keeping him sweet was part of the terms and conditions of working behind that bar. Who knows?'

Costa looked at his partner. When he was getting to know Gianni Peroni he'd always thought of him as a rock, impervious to the mundane tragedies of the world. It was, he now realized, such a superficial view.

'When did you find out?' he asked, knowing the answer already.

'Just after Christmas. When they worked out his liver was finally throwing up its hands and surrendering. He wanted to see me one last time. So I went and guess what? It was all about him really, not me. He wanted to explain that when he was remaking my face it was nothing personal. It was just himself he was beating up all along because of how guilty he felt about having fathered a bastard at *all*. So we shed a few tears together, me being the utter fool I am, and yes, maybe twenty-four hours later I break the habit of a lifetime and fall into bed with a Czech hooker because, well, *why not, why the fuck not?*'

Peroni put a big hand over his crooked mouth, thinking. 'You're wrong about Teresa, by the way. I just know it.'

'But—' Costa wanted to ask so many questions.

'Ssshhh,' Peroni interrupted, watching a tall figure stride down the arcade opposite. Then he glanced at Costa. 'What I just said is between the two of us, Nic. No one outside my family knows that little secret. No one else will. You share a little of my private burden. I'll share a little of yours if you want me to, before I go back to my true vocation in life and you become my

455

driver. At which point I doubt I'll talk to you at all, the class war being what it is.'

Costa laughed. 'I can't wait for that day.'

'Good. What's more, now we're back on duty, we both get to share a whole load of old Leo's burden. And that is one big load to bear.'

Falcone was beckoning for them to join him. He looked spruced up and dressed in his Sunday best. In his hands was a fine bouquet of roses and carnations.

'Hospital visits,' Peroni said, getting to his feet and patting the tiny rose in his jacket pocket. 'Don't you love 'em?'

Rachele D'Amato sat upright in her bed in a private room. She wore a white silk shirt, torn up to the right elbow to make room for the cast on her arm, with sheets up to her waist. The fading remains of a livid bruise stained her forehead close to the scalp. Leo Falcone, watched by Costa and Peroni from the door, kissed her gently on the left cheek, presented a small golden box of chocolates then removed some old flowers from the vase by her bed and replaced them with his own.

'Here.' He passed the dead lilies and gladioli to Peroni who grimaced at the things then dumped them in a wastebasket in the corner of the room.

'Flowers,' she said, smiling. 'Chocolates. Oh, Leo. How . . . quaint.'

The three men looked at her and understood the position. Nothing had really changed. She wielded the same control over her emotions. Even a bomb couldn't change Rachele D'Amato.

'You're welcome,' Falcone mumbled.

'Sit, if you like. I thought—' She looked at Costa and Peroni. 'I thought you might have come before. I rather expected you on your own when you did find the time.'

Falcone stayed on his feet. 'I'm sorry. They say you're doing well. A couple of days more—'

She played with the flowers, improving the arrangement. 'Can't wait. I'm bored to death. I want to get back to work.' She hesitated. 'I keep hearing all these stories. So tell me. Will you find this woman?'

'We will,' he nodded.

The firmness of his answer surprised her. 'Really? I heard people were starting to consider it was a waste of time. She's out of the country. You don't know where to start. You don't even know her real name.'

'Don't believe everything you hear.'

She stared at the chair next to the bed until he sat down in it. Then he opened the leather document case he'd brought with him. 'When you go back to work you'll have to deal with this one.'

Falcone threw a photo of the young Adele Neri onto the sheets. She picked up the colour print and looked at it.

'Where did you get this?'

Falcone had lost some of his winter holiday tan. He looked tired and troubled. 'The Julius woman was careless. She must have scanned Kirk's photos into the computer to mess with them or maybe just for safe keeping. She thought she'd wiped the ones she didn't want to fool with. She hadn't. Our computer people managed to recover a few. Quite a lot actually. Adele Neri was on several.'

'Oh.' She stared at the photo then gave it back to him. 'Are you telling me Neri's mob is now in the hands

457

of his widow? These *are* changed times. I know that happens in the south. But in Rome—? It seems wrong somehow.'

'It seems wrong,' he agreed.

'And you think she was involved in what happened? With this in mind?'

'Partly with this in mind. I'm certain of it.'

'Can you *prove* anything?'

He said nothing, watching her open the chocolates, put one in her mouth, smile faintly with pleasure then close the lid.

'Life will be interesting when I get out of this bed,' she said, still chewing.

'Quite,' he replied, then very suddenly, too quickly for her to protest, began to extend the tear in the silk shirt, ripping it up her arm with both hands until he reached the shoulder.

'Leo!'

The three men stared at the pale patch there, round, like the mark of a coin. Or a badge. Skin that was unlike the rest of her, bleached, changed.

'I remembered that,' Falcone said.

'I imagine,' she replied, 'you remember most of me. Oh, Leo. You're not that kind, are you? Lying in bed at night, on your own, just thinking of me? Trying to picture what I looked like when I was there under the sheets with you? Really. Aren't you a little old for that kind of thing?'

Falcone couldn't take his eyes off the white patch of skin. 'It never quite works, does it? I imagine they promise no one will ever notice. The tattoo will just go and you get old skin in its place.' He touched her on the shoulder. 'What you really get is new skin that never ages. Not quite right.'

'It's a birthmark,' she said very patiently. 'I told you, surely.'

Falcone wasn't listening. 'Neri worked so hard to clean this up, to keep you all sweet and silent. He married one of you. Barbara he put in the police. He put you through law college, then into the DIA. And another ran away for some reason. She knew all along Eleanor never died from drugs. She just didn't dare say so. Then, when a body turns up, she decides to put matters right. She comes back to make sure you all know the price of what you'd won.'

Rachele D'Amato was into her second chocolate by now. 'These really are delicious, you know. You don't mind my not sharing them. I am still an invalid. Just. And frankly I always feel good chocolate is wasted on men.'

'So she tells Vergil Wallis who goes along with everything,' he continued. 'Perhaps he bankrolls things. This fake abduction. He leans on Randolph Kirk to cooperate. Never understanding that you know already who killed Eleanor. And it's not just him you want. It's all of them, him included. Him especially.'

She closed the box. 'No more. I've put on enough weight in this place already. I must say, Leo. You *are* entertaining today. Is this how the police intend to pursue investigations in the future? Just guess your way through everything until you find an answer that fits?'

Falcone took no notice. 'Someone had to tell her about Vercillo. Kirk wouldn't know him as anything other than a face at the party. There's no reason to think Wallis could have provided his address. But the DIA—'

'*No reason?*' she laughed. 'Have you actually run these fantasies past a lawyer? Is this what constitutes evidence in the police force these days?'

He shook his head. 'And someone had to drive that bike with the bogus Suzi Julius on the back. You have a licence.'

Rachele D'Amato stared coolly at the three of them. 'I have a licence? My. That's incriminating.'

'It bothered me afterwards. I talked to you that day. You were in a hurry to leave for an appointment. I told you, I checked. There's nothing in your DIA diary to account for that.'

'I told you. I met a man. I'm sorry if that hurts your tender ego.'

'Does he have a name?' Falcone asked.

'He's married. I'm not dragging him into this for your sick curiosity.' She nodded at Costa and Peroni. 'Is that why they're here? Is this a formal interview?'

'Just came along to wish you well, ma'am,' Peroni said with a little bow. 'So pleased to see you're recovering your customary composure so quickly.'

'Jesus,' she murmured. 'That man gets uglier by the day, Leo. Did you have to pick him?'

'And your charm too,' Peroni said with a smile. 'Glad that's returning.'

'There was no man,' Falcone said. 'There never has been. Not even me. What was I for, Rachele? Promotion? Or did you just feed back information to Neri even then?'

'This is ridiculous,' she hissed.

'That's what they did to you,' he continued. 'All of you. Barbara. Miranda Julius. They took away any chance you had of a normal relationship. Perhaps that's what you hated most, even more than the thought that they'd tricked you over Eleanor.'

He threw another photo on the bed. She looked at it. 'And what's this supposed to be?'

'You. Dressed up and ready just like all the others. You were there. Which one was it? Do you remember? Toni Martelli? Wallis? Or did they take turns?'

She flung the picture at him. 'Take this away. Go find something better to do, Leo.'

'It's you,' he insisted. 'They even got you to dye your hair blonde back then. Whose idea was that?'

She was laughing at all of them. 'What are you talking about? Look at this girl! It could be anyone!'

'It's you.'

Rachele D'Amato sighed and leaned back into the pillow. 'Do you think you could convince a court of that? And even if you could, *does it matter*? It's just a picture.'

'What about those people outside Neri's house?' Costa asked. 'Don't their relatives deserve some answers?'

'I was one of them,' she snapped. 'In case you forgot. Neri placed that bomb. Neri's dead. How many answers do you need?'

Peroni sniffed and looked at her. 'What about Barbara Martelli? No feeling there?'

She picked at another chocolate then said, 'I never knew the woman.'

'Rachele,' Falcone said, and heard the note of pleading that had crept into his voice. 'You can't just bury this.'

'It's buried already, Leo. You just don't see it. Ask

yourself a question. Are we living in a better world now? Or a worse one?'

'That's not for the likes of us to decide.'

'No!' she yelled. 'Don't take that line with me. You make those decisions just as much as anyone. If you think you have one piece of hard evidence against me then use it. If not I suggest you keep your mouth shut and try catching a few criminals instead of boxing shadows. Now get out of here. And take these with you!'

She picked up the vase of flowers and launched them against the wall next to Peroni and Costa where they shattered noisily, dispensing water, petals and fragments of pottery everywhere.

It was dark by the time they got outside. Falcone clutched his leather case to his chest, looking lost. Costa shuffled on his feet, hunched up inside his jacket, silent, thinking.

'I know—' Peroni said hopefully. 'Let's get a drink. Something to eat. There's a place near here—'

'Is the wine good?' Falcone asked. 'I don't drink any old shit.'

'Me neither,' Costa grumbled. 'And I don't just want salad.'

'Boys, boys,' Peroni sighed. 'Stick with your old uncle, Gianni. He'll see you right.'

Ten minutes later they were in a tiny bar behind the Colosseum. Falcone sniffed approvingly at an expensive glass of Brunello and some prosciutto crudo. Nic Costa was testing a Tuscan chardonnay and some porcini on crostini. Gianni Peroni had one beer under his belt already, along with some translucent slices of expensive pork *lardo* on a slab of country bread.

'I can give everything I've got to the DIA,' Falcone said to no one in particular. 'Let's see what *that* does for her career.'

'You can, Leo,' Peroni said. 'And by the way, thanks for putting in a word for me.'

The tall inspector rolled back on his seat as if affected by some slight. 'I just did my job. They asked my opinion. I gave it to them.'

Peroni ordered another beer and said, 'For which I'm grateful. Let me offer a thought in return. Do you really think the DIA will appreciate if it we keep this thing on life support? I mean, either they know already, in which case it's their problem. Or they don't and frankly I'm not sure they'll be pleased to have it laid on their plate. I mean. She's good at her job, isn't she? She didn't kill anyone. She didn't do anything except ride a motorbike and hand out some information, not that we can prove any of that. Also, maybe they're aware of some of the people who had their photos taken in that place. Maybe some of them *are* those very people.' He paused. 'Have you thought of that?'

Falcone glowered back at him. 'Are you ever going back to vice?'

Another beer landed on the table. Peroni took a deep swig. 'Who knows? Who the hell knows anything these days? How's your drink? How's the food?'

Falcone sniffed at the wine. 'The Brunello is as good as one might expect for the price. I don't mean that as a criticism. The ham is . . . fine.' He took another sip then nodded with a measure of approval before grumbling, 'And we still don't know that damned woman's name.'

Gianni Peroni sighed and stared at his beer glass.

'A good white,' Costa said, holding his glass up to the light. 'Well-balanced. A little under-chilled.'

It was the colour of old straw under the yellowing candle bulbs of the bar. He took a gulp, larger than normal, and paused over the sudden and unexpected kick of the alcohol.

One pill makes you bigger, she sang, and he wondered, once more, why she'd dyed her hair that night.

He recalls a face now, frightened, furious and dying, under the same light, something glittering in its throat, choking as it tries to speak the same word, over and over again into the echoing darkness.

'We do know her name,' Nic Costa says, mind half recoiling from the memory, half flying towards it like a moth dancing for the candle.

'She told us time and time again.'

And no one else was fool enough to listen, says an old, cruel voice, still locked somewhere at the back of his imagination.

'Her name is Suzi.'

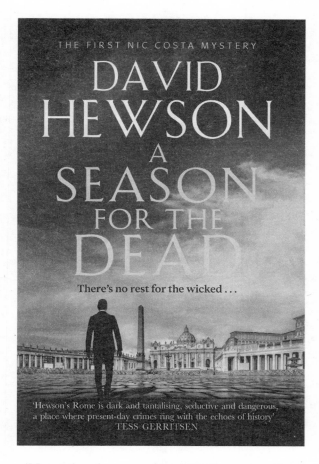

THE FIRST NIC COSTA MYSTERY

DAVID HEWSON
A SEASON
FOR THE
DEAD

There's no rest for the wicked . . .

'Hewson's Rome is dark and tantalising, seductive and dangerous,
a place where present-day crimes ring with the echoes of history'
TESS GERRITSEN

'No author has ever brought Rome so alive
for me'
PETER JAMES

BLACK▼THORN

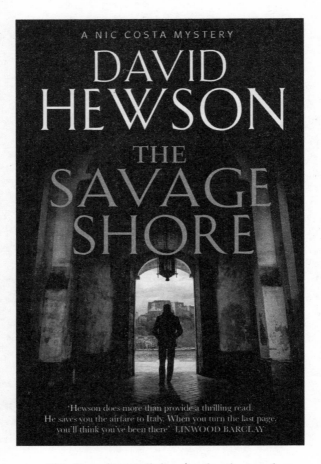

A NIC COSTA MYSTERY

DAVID
HEWSON

THE
SAVAGE
SHORE

'Hewson does more than provide a thrilling read.
He saves you the airfare to Italy. When you turn the last page,
you'll think you've been there' LINWOOD BARCLAY

'Dark and tantalising, seductive and
dangerous'
TESS GERRITSEN

BLACK▼THORN